Holding Their Own IV: The Ascent

By

Joe Nobody

ISBN 978-0615810621

Edited by:
E. T. Ivester

Contributors:

D. A. L. H.
D. Allen

www.HoldingYourGround.com

Published by

www.PrepperPress.com

Other Books by Joe Nobody:

- **Holding Your Ground: Preparing for Defense if it All Falls Apart**

- **The TEOTWAWKI Tuxedo: Formal Survival Attire**

- **Without Rule of Law: Advanced Skill to Help You Survive**

- **Holding Their Own: A Story of Survival**

- **Holding Their Own II: The Independents**

- **Holding Their Own III: Pedestals of Ash**

- **The Home Schooled Shootist: Training to Fight with a Carbine**

- **Apocalypse Drift**

Prologue

10 years before the collapse...

Bishop walked into the gym, his face locked in a grimace that betrayed the foul mood consuming his day. It had taken every reserve of willpower to crawl out of his bed this morning—an epic, internal struggle had raged while the snooze alarm's red digits executed their countdown to the next sounding. This morning's battle was becoming familiar ground to Bishop—a no-man's land between calling in sick and reporting for work. Every day, it grew increasingly difficult to pull back the covers and face life.

Today, a narrow victory had been achieved—a triumph for responsibility. The motivation to get out of bed had nothing to do with honor or professionalism; it was due to a deep-seated, internal terror that forced him to rise and greet yet another day. It wasn't that Bishop feared any man or beast. He was beyond caring about such things as defeat by the hand of another. His nemesis was self-imposed—a pragmatic realization that, if he didn't report for work that morning, he never would again.

This morning's ire had peaked with a cocked .45 caliber pistol aimed at the offending alarm clock, Bishop's finger ready on the trigger. A thread of mercy saved the timepiece—his throbbing head realizing that dropping the hammer would generate an intense wave of sound-induced pain. This was a discomfort that simply couldn't be tolerated so early in the day. His crusade racked up another small win with a successful shower and shave, but the triumph was short-lived. The desperate campaign reemerged as he sat in the truck, attempting to work up the fortitude required to maneuver in Houston's morning traffic. It had been exceedingly difficult not to go back to bed. *You've got to go in*, he thought. *You will end up a reclusive hermit, too paranoid to leave your bedroom and eventually wasting away into lunacy.*

The gym's odors were yet another wave of assault, crashing against the weakened bastions of Bishop's well-being. The mixture of sweat and disinfectant seemed particularly harsh this morning. The echoes of men lifting weights, grunting, and straining gave insult as well. *I'll work out*, he thought. *I need to burn some of this stress.*

Plugging in the appropriate amount of weight, Bishop went horizontal on his back and began to press the bar up and

1

down. His attention was drawn to some activity at the far end of the room; a sparring match between two co-workers distracted him.

Unarmed combat training was a regular activity for the security personnel at HBR. The philosophy was that it was always better to subdue a threat without the use of gunplay or excessive force. Bishop didn't like the training, but he wanted to keep his job, so he attended and did his best.

Today's match involved a co-worker who went by the nickname of Bull. He and a smaller man danced around the mats, throwing punches and kicks. Bishop had never cared much for Bull. As far as Bishop was concerned, the man was large, strong, and stupid. Bull hailed from New Zealand, where he claimed to have been ex-SAS. Bishop thought that was just more Bull-shit. For some reason, the colonel kept the large man around, so Bishop and the other men tolerated the obnoxious fellow—just barely.

Bull was sparring with a quiet, unassuming Korean who everyone called Gangwon. The man had been born in that South Korean province, and the label had just stuck. All of the HBR men knew that Gangwon was hell on wheels when it came to martial arts. This former ROK Marine was strong, fast, and fearless.

There were certain rules regarding hand-to-hand combat at the security center. Pads and gloves were always required, and some types of blows were not kosher. One such outlawed strike was a blow to the back of the head or neck area. As Bishop watched the two skillful men scuffle, Bull essentially cheated by striking a powerful fist to Gangwon's neck. The normally stoic Asian staggered back and raised a hand to halt the match. Bull ignored the signal to stop and landed another kick and punch combination. A loud thump signaled the smaller competitor's violent introduction to the floor.

Bishop became angry. Not only had Bull taken unfair advantage of his opponent, he had engaged in dangerous behavior. Gangwon could have been seriously injured or even killed. Despite a strong urge to become aggressive with Bull, Bishop decided to let the incident go, choosing to leave the area. Some voice of reason had sounded in Bishop's head.

On the way back to his locker, however, the anger continued to well. Bishop sidestepped a construction crew remodeling a section of the facility, and an opportunity to deliver justice presented itself. A large bucket of plaster drew his attention, sparking an idea. Dipping a pair of work gloves into the pudding-like substance might provide an interesting advantage. By the time Bishop got back to the gym, a coating of plaster similar to a cast was hardening inside of his sparring gloves. The sight of Bull leaning against the wall boasting about his victory escalated the fury-driven desire to teach the big buffoon a lesson.

Bishop started taunting Bull. "Why don't you try that shit with someone a little more your size, asshat?" Back and forth, the bravados flew, and eventually the two men squared off in the ring. Normally when sparring, glove-cushioned blows to the head inflict little damage. Bishop, however, was using daddy's little helper that day, and essentially set about tenderizing a little Bull-meat.

The next morning, Bishop found himself at full attention, standing in front of the colonel's desk. Beside him was a rather pitiful looking Bull, both eyes blackened and sporting several dark purple welts around his head. Bishop couldn't be sure, but he thought the man's nose looked a little crooked, too.

The colonel saw little humor in the situation. He peered over the report he was skimming, his voice booming throughout the small office. "I can't believe what I'm reading here. This has to be a mistake. I only hire *professionals*, and every *professional* knows that safety during training is a top priority. Now, let me make myself clear…." The colonel stood and stepped to the front of his desk, hands clasped behind his back. He stopped directly in front of Bishop and Bull, his head snapping back and forth between the two. "If either of you two fucksticks EVER SO MUCH AS COUGH on another HBR employee, I will personally kick your ass up between your shoulders so far you'll have to remove your shirt to shit. I'm officially ordering both of you—this situation between you is to be de-fucked immediately. Furthermore, if there is *even a hint* of another problem, I will terminate your employment at HBR immediately. Do you understand?"

Both men replied with a prompt and clear, "Yes, sir."

The colonel returned to his desk and sat back down. He looked at Bull, saying, "You are dismissed. Bishop, I require a word with you."

Bull pivoted smartly and left. Bishop couldn't be sure, but he thought the man limped just a little.

The colonel waited until Bull had shut the door, and then his entire demeanor changed. "Bishop, we have to fix this problem of yours. Since that incident down at the Tri-Border Area, you haven't been the same. Now, I know how hard that was on you, son. I've been there. But since that episode, you have been quick-tempered, sultry, and extremely aggressive."

Bishop protested, embarrassed that he was receiving a scolding. "Sir, has my work been sub-par in any way?"

The colonel smirked, opened his desk drawer, and

3

removed a sparring glove. He shook the evidence over his desk, and several flakes of dried plaster fell onto the surface. "I found this in your locker, Bishop. Now, I wonder how this interesting substance got inside of your equipment? I also wonder how you managed to pummel a man 30 pounds over your weight, a man known to be an expert striker. I'm curious as to what Bull's reaction would be if he knew you had doctored your gloves."

Bishop started to defend himself. "Sir, he could have killed Gangwon. I was just . . ."

The colonel waved him off, and his voice became soft and friendly—at least as soft and friendly as the colonel could be. "Bishop, I'm not fucking with you. You are one of the best I've ever worked with. We have to fix this issue of yours and move on. I've tried to get you to counseling, and you won't go. I can order you to see the shrink, but I know you would just stonewall him."

It was Bishop's turn to interrupt his boss. "Sir, my apologies. I didn't know my behavior had been so noticeable. It's just . . . just . . . I don't know, sir. Since we lost all those men down in the Tri-Borders, I have been incredibly frustrated. Good people died down there and for no reason. Good didn't triumph over evil, and that is just stuck in my craw."

The colonel nodded. "I understand, son. Believe me, I understand. A lot of people want to lump those feelings of yours into the category of post-traumatic stress syndrome. I don't think that's your problem, Bishop. I think you simply want to reaffirm that good does win most of the time. I also think you'd like a little payback against the dark side."

Bishop shifted his weight and waited for the colonel to continue.

"Bishop, I have a friend who works for the DEA. Every now and then, those Washington brainpans dream up some operation and need help from outside of the normal channels to implement it. He contacted me the other day and is looking for a few highly trained individuals who can keep their mouths shut and well . . . wouldn't have a lot of family members asking questions if said operators didn't return from the 'activities.'"

The colonel swiveled his chair around and looked out the window behind his desk. His voice became distant. "Bishop, you fit the bill perfectly for what my colleague wants. I normally don't become involved in these little mystery missions for a number of different reasons. This time, however, I think it might actually have a purpose. You see, what he has planned will provide ample opportunity to prove what is decent and noble triumphs over wickedness. In your current state of mind, I can't send you on any job for HBR. I also can't afford to keep you on

4

the payroll, if we can't use you. So, I'm going to give you a choice. You can take a few weeks of your vacation and go work with my friend at the DEA, or you can go visit·the company shrink and see if he can get your hostile ass squared away. One way or another, Bishop, I need the man I had before Tri-Borders. It's your call."

Bishop didn't hesitate. "How do I contact your friend?"

The colonel reached in his drawer and pulled out a folder, handing it to Bishop. Inside were plane tickets from Houston to Washington, DC for the following afternoon. The folder also contained Bishop's approved vacation request for four weeks and his next two paychecks. "I'll see you in a month, son. Good luck."

Bishop was feeling a mixture of foreboding and excitement as he flew to Washington. On one hand, his very nature didn't like the mystery of the whole endeavor; while on the other, doing something outside the daily routine at HBR was a welcomed change. During the flight, he mused about being on a super-secret spy mission and was tempted to order a martini shaken, not stirred, from the flight attendant. The mental charade ended when reality overwhelmed his pipedream. After all, Bishop preferred tequila, and 007 had an expense report.

Bishop was greeted at Ronald Regan International Airport by a man who introduced himself as Mr. Smith. After shaking hands, the man looked Bishop up and down and pronounced, "You don't look like a badass." Bishop conducted a visual assessment of his own, deciding that the good Mr. Smith did indeed look like a DEA prick and wanted to inform him of such, but held his tongue.

Mr. Smith had access to a small conference room right on the airport grounds. After punching in a code on the digital lock, Bishop was escorted into an area that contained a conference table, four chairs, and two bottles of lukewarm water. *So much for being treated like a super-spook*, he thought.

His host sat down and began immediately. "Afghanistan produces the majority of the world's opium. The poppy farmers are really nothing more than peasants, cultivating the crop that generates the most cash from their shitty land. As you are no doubt aware, we have hundreds of thousands of men in Afghanistan, but for political reasons, we can't touch the core of the country's opium economy."

Mr. Smith stopped for a moment and waited for Bishop to nod his understanding. Instead, Bishop responded with a question. "Why can't you touch the opium trade?"

The man became annoyed, and responded with a tone similar to a college professor addressing a student's ill-advised

5

question. "The United States is trying to play a specific, narrowly-defined role with our Afghan partners. Many of the regional governors maintain their powerbase using the income derived from the opium trade. The United States needs these men to fight the Taliban. If we turned our Army loose on the trade, we could no longer enjoy the support of the local warlords. Until recently, the prevailing policy was that ignoring the major players was the lesser of two evils."

Bishop digested the answer for a little bit and nodded. Mr. Smith continued, "The situation is further compounded by the fact that the Taliban is also interwoven into the transport and distribution of the opium. The money they make supports *their* war efforts against *our* troops. So, we have a two-headed snake on our hands. Not only does the opium make it to our streets, the money collected from our drug-addicted citizens supports those that are butchering our troops. In effect, American dopers are fueling the conflict that is killing their own friends and neighbors."

Again, Bishop nodded his understanding, wondering what all of this had to do with him and the colonel. Mr. Smith unscrewed the cap of his water bottle and took a small sip. He studied Bishop for a moment and then smiled. "You are no doubt wondering why the DEA or the CIA or some other agency doesn't mount covert operations against these guys, and that's a fair question. Let me just say that the fiasco in Iraq has the press on a rampage. No one at the top, in any organization, is going to risk a black op involving government personnel."

Bishop was beginning to get the picture, but wanted to make sure. "So, you want deniability. You want a bunch of guys to 'disrupt' their drug trade, but if something goes wrong, the DEA can honestly say they didn't do it?"

Mr. Smith smiled, "I see now why the colonel recommended you—not such a clod after all. Yes, you are correct. So here's how all this is going to work. You and a group of other private citizens will be in-country on a United Nations supported, mineral deposit survey. The gentlemen you will be working with all have similar backgrounds as your own. This survey team will receive coordinates indicating where a shipment is going to be. This shipment is to be disrupted by any means."

Bishop smiled at the phrase "by any means." While he had a thousand questions, he decided to wait and see how much Mr. Smith was going to divulge on his own.

"The opium is moved around via caravan. Horses and mules are the most common transport, but some groups have adopted more modern methods, including all-terrain vehicles. The routes snake throughout the deserts and mountains. Some of them have been used for trade going back thousands of years.

The paths are actually two-way streets. Along them, the caravans move bundles of opium into the tribal regions of Pakistan, and return with bundles of cash or weapons. We don't care which direction the convoy is heading, we want the cargo destroyed."

Bishop again nodded his understanding and then muttered a "No problem."

Mr. Smith handed Bishop the key to a nearby airport hotel room. "You'll find all of your travel arrangements, necessary documents and instructions there. The first leg of your trip leaves here at 6 a.m. tomorrow. Good luck."

Two days later, an exhausted Bishop landed at Bagram Airfield, just outside of Kabul, Afghanistan. As he ambled through the main terminal, Bishop was surprised to see American fast food restaurants. Lines of US military personnel were waiting in queue for tacos, pizza, and soft drinks. Bishop's plane had actually landed early, so he asked a passing airman where the PX, or Post Exchange, was located. The aviator corrected him and pointed toward the BX, or Base Exchange. Bishop was surprised to find displays of rifle accessories rivaling any sporting goods store in the States. The size of the facility was evidence of the extensive engagement of Western armies here. Aisle after aisle of shelves was stocked with practically everything one would find in an American grocery store. Another section contained household goods and hardware.

Bishop hadn't been on the ground for more than 30 minutes when he started sneezing. After an hour, his throat hurt, and he was coughing. He was waiting alongside the curb for his ride to show up when he noticed that everyone outside was hacking or sneezing. He overheard one man telling another that Bagram had the worst air pollution problem in the world. Bishop believed it, wondering if his lungs would actually feel better if he smoked a cigar. *A healthy dose of nicotine might just dilute the toxic particles in this atmosphere*, Bishop mused.

About then, a white SUV pulled up with lettering on the door indicating it belonged to the United Nations Reconstruction Council. The blue and white colors of the international organization rounded out its branding. After an exchange verifying who was who, Bishop hopped in the front seat and shook hands with his driver.

Mike Wagner was a Canadian from the Toronto area, and immediately came across as a hard ass. After one of the shortest handshakes Bishop had ever experienced, the man immediately announced he was in charge of the operation and made it absolutely clear that Bishop reported to him. He smugly informed Bishop of his credentials, having been a member of the

Régiment d'Opérations Spéciales du Canada, which was French for the Canadian Special Forces. Bishop had worked with his share of Canadians and respected them. Almost every one of them would use the English name for this, that, or the other, but every now and then, Bishop would come across a guy who wanted to speak French just to be elitist. Bishop started to ask the man if Wagner was a French name, but decided against it.

As they made their way out into the Afghan countryside, Bishop was absorbed in the sights, sounds, and smells of a new place. His fascination with foreign lands had always been a weakness while working at HBR. *A good security man observes and analyzes his surroundings, which is different than gawking around like a tourist,* he reminded himself.

Five mostly silent and extremely bumpy hours later, the SUV stopped at a remote Afghan farmhouse, complete with crude fences fashioned out of local stones and two animals that somewhat resembled cows. Bishop was shown to an outbuilding, which served the dual purpose of being a barn and barracks. Inside he met the rest of the team.

All seven of the gentlemen looked to be hard cases. Most were in their late 30s or early 40s, and all gave the impression of being in excellent physical condition. As Bishop ran the reception line, his handshake was met with single names and single syllable greetings. "Hey. Todd," or "Hi. Jim," filled the air for the next few minutes. *Not a talkative bunch for sure*, thought Bishop, *maybe the food's bad*.

Mike Wagner appeared shortly after Bishop's arrival and called the group together, reminding the team once again that he was formerly of the *Régiment d'Opérations Spéciales du Canada.* Bishop wondered if this pretentious fuck was going to initiate a wine tasting in the middle of the meeting. Additionally, Mr. Wagner left no doubt that he was the man in charge. What followed was basically a military briefing combined with a short lecture on how to interact with any locals who may wander by—the latter consisting solely of instruction to hide and stay out of sight until further notice.

A few minutes later, a man with a dark complexion joined the meeting and was introduced as Mr. Rostenphuse—the team's Pakistani interpreter. The new arrival made the rounds, shaking hands and reintroducing himself in case anybody missed it the first time. The way he pronounced his name sounded like "rotten puss," and Bishop knew immediately that that was what everyone was going to call him.

Weapons were issued next, and Bishop was surprised to find Russian equipment being passed out. AK47s were the norm, with two of the gentlemen being issued Dragunov sniper rifles. This didn't make Bishop happy at all, but it was soon explained that any evidence left behind could not imply Western involvement. Russian weapons, ammunition, and equipment were the norm in the Afghan countryside. Even the load gear and boots were old Soviet surplus.

Next came the clothing, which was described as "Kamiz Shalwar," or coat and trousers. The team members immediately set about changing out of their western duds.

Bishop starting wishing he had passed on this trip and had instead chosen reclining on that couch in the company shrink's office. All of these guys seemed a little odd, and nobody had mentioned using the Russian weapons. When one of the other guys grumbled about his rifle, Mr. Wagner informed everyone that there would be a class in the morning to get everyone familiar with the weapons. *Wow*, Bishop thought sarcastically, *we get a whole day to familiarize ourselves with a completely new blaster? How nice.*

About the time the sun began to set, Rotten-puss brought out food, and the group sat around eating some sort of grilled red meat and rice. Hot, bitter tea was identified as the beverage, and everyone seemed hesitant to inquire about the origination of the entrée that completed the night's menu. After the meal was finished, Wagner got down to operational business, laying out the details for the squad's assignment.

The team would receive the coordinates of any opium caravan that was discovered in the area. They would immediately mount up and navigate to a position in front of the target to stage an ambush. Since roads were very limited and quite dangerous in this part of the country, Wagner stressed that everyone needed to be ready for some serious walking. *Great*, thought Bishop, *give us new, poorly fitting boots, and then tell us we will have to hike halfway across the heart of Asia. I'm going to complain to my travel agent.*

Wagner told everyone that he had an extensive supply of Russian explosives and mines. If things went according to plan, the detonations would eliminate the need for any shooting. Bishop wondered just how much ordnance this guy had, and even more importantly, he questioned the logistics of transporting massive amounts of fireworks to the ambush site. He decided to keep his mouth shut and just listen.

Wagner ended his briefing just as suddenly as he began. Bishop was really puzzled when the man did not ask for questions at the end. Evidently, Canucks had perfect hearing and clarity of mind, so they didn't need to ask questions.

The team slept in the barn on military-issued folding cots adorned with scratchy, wool blankets. As everyone settled in, a few of the men began to talk, and Bishop received a basic understanding of why some of them had volunteered. One guy was a recently retired Army Ranger whose daughter died of a heroin overdose. He volunteered for payback—out of frustration that the government couldn't and wouldn't do much about the opium growing right under the boots of the US Army.

Another gentleman was a retired US Marine whose son, also a Marine, had been captured by the Taliban some months before. The devastated father had been in Afghanistan causing trouble at the US Embassy and gallivanting all over the country raising hell and looking for evidence of his son. For all his trouble, there was little he could do to accelerate the process, and he was looking for a way to gain a little control in his life.

One guy was like Bishop, it seemed. His boss had arranged his adventure based upon work-related issues. The man was a narcotics detective in Washington, DC. Reading between the lines, Bishop guessed he had been instructed to go let off some pressure, or he would be kicked off the force. Maybe he didn't like head doctors either.

Some of the men didn't disclose their background or reasoning, and Bishop decided to join that club.

The following morning was spent on weapons familiarization. The teams were driven to an even more remote area and issued ammunition to zero the Russian firearms. Bishop had fired an AK several times, but that had been some years ago. He didn't care for the weapon for several reasons, but it was an effective battle rifle. His displeasure was mainly due to not having enough time to become "intimate" with a tool he was getting ready to fight with.

The rest of the first full day was spent adjusting load gear and clothing, as well as exchanging boots. A couple of the men needed different sizes in order for the disguises to be complete. Rotten-puss disappeared for a while and then returned with substitutes. That evening, Wagner wheeled in a dilapidated, old blackboard, complete with a single piece of chalk and a rag for an eraser. He began briefing the team on how the ambushes would be conducted.

Wagner claimed that the drug caravans moved in a single file formation due to the narrow mountain trails. He distributed pictures of a few examples, and the team members passed them around. The plan was simple. The team would arrive ahead of time and deploy in an L-shaped ambush, with explosives at the front. When the caravan reached the tripwire, the explosions would kill the personnel. The team would mop up, gather the contraband, and destroy it at another location. The drug lords would think that their convoy had been attacked by rival gangs or pirates.

Bishop sat on the ground, taking it all in. He watched without comment while Wagner drew little diagrams on the chalkboard and explained it all. Again, the man finished without taking questions. Bishop couldn't let it go by a second time.

"Excuse me, Mike, but I have a few questions."

Wagner looked up and seemed a bit annoyed, but nodded his head.

Bishop looked around at the team and then asked, "What kind of detonators do you have for the explosives?"

Wagner curtly responded, "We'll deploy tripwires across the trail."

Bishop was growing very weary of Mike. The man hadn't answered his question. "You don't have any sort of remote detonation? What if the lead elements of the caravan discover the tripwires? What if they have scouts ahead of the main body, and those guys set off the ambush?"

Out of the corner of his eye, Bishop could see several heads nodding in support of his inquiries. Wagner noticed it as well, and changed his tone. "We have to use what I've been issued. I'll try and get some remote units, but this is all surplus Russian stuff, and there are limits as to what is available."

Bishop was at *his* limit of patience and began rapid firing at the team leader. "How much of the explosive do you have? How much is it going to take to establish a kill zone the length of the convoys? How old is the explosive? Does it deteriorate over time like our C4? How are eight guys going to carry enough explosive halfway across this gawd-forsaken real estate? We are going to be hitting these guys on fairly flat land. How do we know they travel single file while on flat terrain?"

The barrage of questions got the others involved as well. Before Wagner could even begin to answer, the rest of the team began voicing their concerns. It was like a dam had burst, and the team leader became very frustrated. "No plan is perfect," he said at one point, "but this is workable."

Bishop didn't think so. By the time the meeting was over, he and a couple of the other men were talking about aborting the effort. Some of the talk was just letting off steam, but Bishop seriously doubted that this operation was going to work. He couldn't fault Wagner. The guy was obviously a professional with a lot of experience. Unlike most US forces, many military organizations didn't have practically unlimited resources and learned to adapt with less than optimum equipment. This methodology, however, often resulted in higher causalities, and Bishop didn't want to be a casualty.

Band-Aids were in short supply by the end of the third

day. Badly fitting boots were mostly to blame. The situation became so bad that Wagner finally capitulated and let all those who had something other than US military issue boots revert back to their original footwear. Bishop wore expensive hiking boots and welcomed discarding the poorly made and designed Soviet models. One man grumbled that the entire restriction was silly, as he had seen hundreds of pairs of US Army boots for sale in a Kabul market. Anyone could buy just about anything in Afghanistan, so footprints meant nothing.

Early on the fourth day, Wagner woke everyone up before dawn and said he had received the team's first assignment. Despite misgivings about the overall tactics, the team hustled and was ready to go in short order. Three white UN marked SUVs left the farmhouse just as the sun was rising in the east. They drove through low foothills and rocky, desert terrain for four hours. Wagner was using a GPS in the lead vehicle, and eventually the small convoy arrived at the jump-off point. Each man had been issued 10 pounds of the oily, Russian explosive plus several magazines for his weapon. Water, a NATO entrenching tool, small medical kit, walkie-talkie with an earpiece, and two protein bars rounded out the kits. Bishop had his knife and survival net along with a few other items packed away in the old, poorly fitting, Soviet load gear.

The team formed up and began trekking across the Afghan countryside. It wasn't incredibly difficult walking, and that was probably a good thing. Most of the team wasn't acclimated to the altitude, and the progress was slow.

They finally reached a crest, and everyone studied the trail below. The ambush site was quickly agreed upon, and the men scrambled down the hillside to set up their individual components of the trap. Bishop was impressed with the other team members and their professionalism. Less than an hour later, everything was in place, and the men took up their positions, ready and waiting for the fly to enter the spider's web.

The fly never showed up.

After waiting almost six hours, water was beginning to run low, aggravation was tracking high, and it was getting dark. Wagner finally relented, and the team meandered back to the waiting SUVs. The drive back to the farmhouse was exceptionally quiet. Bishop was actually glad nothing had happened. The exercise had given the team a little practice, and they would be better the next time. He didn't mind the dry run at all.

On day six, they received the next report of a caravan. The same basic process was repeated, only this time, they couldn't find the trail. After scouring several kilometers of Afghan foothills, Wagner finally agreed to abort. The tired bunch of men headed "over the river and through the woods to the farmhouse"—grumbling the entire way.

On the way back to their wheeled transport, Bishop made a rare, public comment. "I hope we don't walk into a US Army ambush dressed in these clothes and carrying these weapons. I bet they'll shoot first and ask questions later. If there's anyone left to answer those questions, that is."

While the remark generated several chuckles and one "No shit," the concept struck a nerve with the team. While the SUV commandeered the rocky countryside, military fashion and outfitting was the primary topic of conversation. Wagner was asked if there were any way to let the big Army know where the team was operating, as none of the men wanted to make the trip home in a body bag, the victim of fratricide. His curt reply consisted only of "I'll check on it."

The next day, Wagner and Rotten-puss left the team behind at dawn, driving off in one of the vehicles. Bishop was sorely tempted to hotwire one of the other SUVs and head back to the airport to hitch a ride out. He visualized making his report while standing in front of the colonel and quickly decided to stay put.

Wagner returned that night and called everyone together. He said that the team would be provided with more detailed, satellite intelligence and guidance from now on. He claimed that those footing the bill for the operation understood the situation and had pledged to make improvements. Bishop asked about the remote detonators and was given a dirty look followed closely by, "We're working on it."

Early on day eight, the team received another "mount up" order, and again the three SUVs charged through the desert. The location given was far more accurate, and they found the trail after only two hours of walking. The problem this time was the terrain, as there was no good place in sight to set up the ambush. Wagner was becoming impatient and needed results. He ordered the ambush anyway, and the team set about improvising.

Two hours later, Bishop spotted a line of pack animals moving along the trail. He watched with nervous anticipation as the convoy approached the kill zone. By all measures, this was a smallish caravan with only five horses, a short line of pack animals, and approximately 12 armed men.

The ambush had been staged at the bottom of a small dip in the trail. The 10 members of the team were spread along one side of the path, ready to rise up and shoot after the explosives detonated. Bishop was positioned right in the middle of the kill zone, lying prone behind a small pile of loose gravel. It was far from good cover, but this location didn't provide any better options.

There was a single man carrying an AK at the point of the caravan, closely followed by the mule team. All of the men were armed, and they looked like a serious bunch of characters. Their tunics were dusty, as were their lengthy beards. Bishop could hear the escorts talking among themselves, and at one point even caught a short cackle of laughter. His earpiece came to life with Wagner's voice broadcasting the unnecessary reminder, "Everybody wait until they hit the tripwire."

A few moments later, the point man did just that, stepping on a wire that was connected to four clusters of explosives rigged for simultaneous detonation. Bishop realized something had gone wrong before he even looked up. Instead of a roaring blast and shower of rocks, there had only been a meek little boom and unimpressive puff of smoke. When Bishop chanced a glance below, he saw the majority of the Afghans below standing around in shock at the explosion. Only one of the four clusters discharged, killing just the point man and the lead animal.

The men below were recovering quickly. Bishop started shooting.

The sons of Afghanistan had suffered through years of warfare and were known for their bravery. Growing up amidst conflict results in more than just intestinal fortitude, as people develop fast reaction times and recover quickly from explosions, gunshots, and other actions associated with battle. The men guarding the caravan were no exception.

Their first reaction was to hug the earth, followed all too quickly by shooting back. The gunfire spooked the horses, causing the beasts to rear skyward, brandishing flared nostrils and wild eyes. The combination of dust, smoke, panicked animals and a terrible position resulted in Bishop having poor target acquisition while producing ineffective fire. He had to settle for a couple of quick, three-round bursts from the AK, aiming at any movement that caught his attention. Evidently, the return fire from below was louder and more concentrated because the horses ran away from their former masters and up the incline. The charging animals only added to the confusion and multiplied Bishop's problems.

For some reason, Bishop couldn't bring himself to aim at the animals and tried to shoot around them. The Afghans probably knew this would happen because they seized that brief period of Bishop's hesitation to gather their wits, and then began charging up the hill behind the horseflesh line of cannon fodder. It was pure coincidence that the easiest route uphill led directly at

Bishop. All of a sudden, he was dodging sharp hooves as well as a significant volume of incoming lead.

Smoke, screaming animals, gunfire and the shouts of desperate men created mass confusion and the inevitable fog of war. Despite the chorus of bedlam around him, an uneasy feeling rose in the back of Bishop's mind, an eerie sensation that he was the only one shooting. It might have been a trick of sound caused by the bark of the AK rolling off the surrounding hillsides, or perhaps he was in the early stages of panic. Whatever the cause, it sure didn't feel like much lead was being directed at the men charging his position. After the stampeding horses had passed by, Bishop raised up and let loose a long burst of automatic fire. His efforts were repaid by dozens of rounds snapping past his head. The men from the caravan were within 100 feet, shooting from the hip and screaming ferocious cries of battle as they gained ground.

The dire situation worsened when movement caught Bishop's eye. He watched in horror as a grenade arched through the air directly at his position. Managing one and a half steps and then a lunge for the ground, Bishop landed squarely on the AK magazines strapped to his chest. The hard earth, poor angle and badly designed load vest resulted in the impact knocking the air from his lungs. That painful collision was minor compared to the grenade's concussion. A giant hammer slammed into Bishop's left side, picking him up and then flinging him down while vacating what little oxygen remained in his lungs.

Two things happened almost simultaneously. A shadow appeared over Bishop, and the roar of a rifle reverberated off the surrounding stone cliffs. Bishop managed to move his head enough to see the Marine pumping AK rounds into the charging Afghans. Slowly gathering his wits, a stunned Bishop managed to move his body slightly in a vain attempt to use his weapon. He couldn't control his arms.

It was then that the second event occurred. Without warning, the line of men charging up the knoll disappeared in a roaring hailstorm of red rain, flying debris, and dust. The scheme looked as though a curtain of boiling magma had descended of the Afghans. Shocked at the vision, Bishop's attention was then drawn to the sky as a black helicopter roared overhead—a multi-barrel Vulcan mini-gun showering a laser-like beam of tracer rounds and hot lead onto the attackers. Firing over 6,000 rounds a minute, Bishop watched the door gunner walk the stream of lead up and down the group of charging men. The carnage was off the scale.

The Marine yelled, "Oh, yeah! It's the cavalry! Now that's how you take out a convoy!"

Bishop was fascinated as the gunship banked sharply, flared its nose, and quickly lost altitude on the far side of the bloodbath below. Rather than landing, the craft slowly progressed in a straight line, the skids just a few feet from the earth. One by one, five men in full combat load began leaping out and moving toward the site of the ambush. After the last had exited, the pilot landed in a position where the door gunner and his dominate mini-gun could cover his comrade's approach. *Nice*, thought Bishop, *very nice. That's one tricky deployment.*

The haze of smoke and dirt partially obscured the approaching team, but Bishop could see well enough to determine they were skilled. Fanning out from the bird, they spaced perfectly so as to leave a field of fire for the supporting mini-gun.

Two of the men immediately progressed toward the pack animals where they began cutting loose bundles of cash. The other three advanced toward the string of dead Afghans, strewn about in grotesque poses of death. Bishop was shocked when the lead man drew his pistol and fired a round into the first corpse. There was no hesitation. His action was quickly followed by his comrades' systematically depositing a bullet into each body along the line. *What the hell*, thought Bishop, *who are these guys?*

The action of the newcomers tore at Bishop's conscience. Killing wounded men on any battlefield was somehow just wrong. While it was doubtful any of the Afghans had survived the initial attack, that was beside the point. Each summary execution boiled Bishop's anger to a higher temperature. Were it not for being completely outgunned and still recovering, he might have begun firing his own weapon.

Watching as the first bundles of cash were being carried back to the idling copter, Bishop noticed there weren't any markings on the craft. No unit insignia, no numbers—nada.

The Marine next to Bishop was obviously angered as well. In a whispered voice he muttered, "What the fuck? Americans don't do that," and started to rise. Bishop reached for the man's load vest and pulled him down.

"Quiet," Bishop hissed under his breath, "Look at the bird ... these guys *aren't* US military."
He could tell the Marine was furious, but the man held his temper. "CIA?"

Bishop shook his head and whispered, "Who knows? But they aren't searching the bodies. It looks like they just want the cash and don't want to leave any witnesses. You would be a witness."

"No shit."

After verifying they hadn't left any survivors, one of the assault team reached inside his vest and pulled out a stack of papers. While his comrades hauled bundles of money back to their bird, Bishop watched as the man pulled the knife from each corpse and used it to pin a single sheet of paper onto each body's chest.

Ten minutes later, it was all over. The five men humped the remaining bundles of currency back to their craft and were gone. Bishop watched, as the aircraft became a tiny black speck in the sky and then disappeared.

He and the Marine finally rose from their hiding spot, approaching the scene of the crime. They were quickly joined by two other members of their team—the only survivors. Mike and the others had been killed in the initial exchange with the convoy's security force. Everyone milled around, stunned by the surreal chain of events that had just unfolded.

Bishop reached down and picked up one of the papers left by the assaulters. It contained neat, blocked type, both in English and what appeared to be Arabic characters. It read:

TO: General Khumri, Regional Governor, Balkh Province
FROM: Erik King, CEO, Darkwater, Incorporated

General Khumri,

Nine days ago at Firebase Pensive, your men assassinated two of my contractors. Consider this as an act of retribution. The funds confiscated by my team will be used to compensate the families of the men who were murdered in cold blood as a result of your direct orders.

Let me make my position clear, General. Any further acts of aggression against my men, my company, or our associates will be answered with exponentially greater violence.

Erik King

Bishop replaced the paper on the corpse at his feet, minus the dagger-pin. He had read the headlines about the attack at the firebase a few days before. The civilian contractors had been training Afghan policemen when someone tossed a bomb into their barracks. Such atrocities were becoming common.

Darkwater was also a well-known entity. Famous for their security and contract operations in Iraq, the press often referred to Mr. King's contractors as everything from "mercenaries" to "the president's private army."

The rest of the afternoon was spent carrying their fallen teammates back to the SUVs.

Two days of flight time home provided Bishop with opportunity to reflect on the events of the past few months. The colonel was right; Tri-Borders and the loss of life experienced there had eroded a foundational value that he had built his life upon. Perhaps it was being raised in West Texas – maybe all Americans felt the same way. Regardless, some life-experience had instilled the concept that good eventually triumphed over evil.

Bishop wasn't naïve. He didn't view life as if it was a super-hero comic book where all villains eventually met a harsh demise at the hands of those fighting for truth, justice and the American way. Bishop's outlook was rooted in the fact that the species had survived…no, thrived. Evil was destructive, good was constructive. Since society had continued to advance, the constructive side had to be winning – right?

For a while during the flight, Bishop thought time was the component of the equation he was missing. Maybe the destructive energies flowing through mankind won a few battles here and there, but lost the war. Maybe Tri-Borders had simply been the rare example of victory for the dark-side. Even that logic didn't seem to comfort him.

Glancing down at the newspaper sitting on his lap, he re-read the article detailing the attack on the Darkwater personnel. The reporter provided some details about the contractors killed in the incident that had led to Mr. King's revenge. The commentary wasn't in-depth but did include a brief obituary of both employees. They were both family men – decorated veterans with good military records.

Bishop kept circling back to the ambush by the Darkwater team. He had been so furious with the summary execution of the wounded. Watching the act had sickened him, and he had immediately condemned the contractors as war criminals. Reading the names of the deceased changed those feelings. The newspaper's account of the incident somehow managed to inject a human element into Bishop's thought process. *It wasn't what it appeared to be*, thought Bishop. *It wasn't a robbery or act of greed, it was a message intended to stop an escalation of death.*

Folding the paper on his lap, Bishop sighed and looked out the plane's tiny window. *Was anything on this earth what it appeared to be? Was there any way for a man to know?* Bishop leaned his seat back, deciding on a half-hearted attempt at sleep. His racing mind slowed its pace, and exhaustion finally took over.

18

Six days later, Bishop was back in the States, standing in front of the colonel's desk. "I feel 100% fit as a fiddle, sir. I wish to officially report for duty."

The colonel was skeptical, "So you feel like you're squared away, Bishop? No more unresolved issues floating around inside that thick skull of yours?"

"That statement, sir, would be an exaggeration. What I did resolve was that there's no clear line separating good and evil. It's not black and white, it never has been, and it probably never will be. I believe that's about the best I'm going to do with the issue, sir."

The colonel digested Bishop's words, his intense gaze never leaving Bishop's face. Finally, he responded. "Okay, son. So be it. Let's get you back in the saddle and see if your little vacation to the Far East did the trick."

Chapter 1

*The three men were dressed in ninja black, looking
more like choreographed warrior demons than human flesh.
Thick body armor, vests bulging with pouches, and skull-like
helmets added to the sinister effect. Mechanical-looking cylinders
with glowing green pulses provided their vision. They moved with
power and grace, electric pupils scanning right and left, looking
for work.*

*Down the hallway they progressed, silent, synchronized
performers, executing a deadly ballet. Move . . . bound . . . cover
. . . slide— precise motions, accented by sweeping weapons,
ready to destroy any threat. The intent was unquestionable—they
were hunting.*

*Black boots stepped heel to toe, rolling the predators
forward in a well-rehearsed march of coiled violence. Their
advance boiled down the corridor, engulfing the passageway as
dark clouds fill the sky before the thunderstorm unleashes its fury
upon the prairie.*

*Finally, they arrived at a plain, simple-looking door and
stopped. Caution replaced aggression as they were close to their
prey, and the quarry was dangerous. Slowly the leader raised his
hand to the entrance, and then it was open.*

In a single motion, Bishop pushed back the covers and
rolled his legs over the edge of the bed. A second set of neural
commands left him standing upright, the pistol from the
nightstand in his hands. Extended arms moved in blurs as they
followed his eyes, sweeping the room for intruders. If the pistol
could speak, it would protest the pressure exerted by his grip.
Thumb on the safety and index finger on the trigger—both were
ready to engage at the same instant. Bishop's lungs started to
object to their lack of air, the desire for oxygen competing with
the heartbeat pounding in his ears. The impulse to breathe was
pushed back, every fiber of being focused on finding the
invaders. He *had* to protect Terri and the baby. His mind raced
with the taunt, *Where are you—come on out and play.*

Terri rolled over, the movement from the other side of
the bed rousing her from a not-so-deep slumber. Bishop had
been kicking and churning restlessly all night, keeping her on the
edge of a deeper sleep. She blinked the fog from her eyes and
looked up to see her husband standing with his gun pointing
around the room. The light leaking through the window blinds

was just enough to make out the detail of the tightened muscles and straining cords of his body. Had the situation been different, she might have let out a wolf-whistle at the sight. Bishop standing shirtless, glistening with sweat and flexing every muscle on his frame was an image a girl could appreciate. This big pistol in his hand ruined the image though, and her mind immediately shifted to concern for her mate. Her senses expanded for a moment, trying to feel out the room. Her female intuition straightaway determined they were alone. *He's been dreaming again*, she instinctively knew.

Terri waited a few moments and then quietly whispered, "Bishop. Bishop, are you okay?"

Her voice instantly calmed him. The pistol slowly lowered as he relaxed. He turned and faced her, his expression a combination of embarrassment and helplessness. Terri propped up on one elbow and observed as Bishop's shoulders slumped and his head fell forward. The gun was returned to the nightstand, and then he perched on the edge of the bed. His voice was unsteady, "I'm sorry . . . I thought . . . I was sure . . . I just don't know."

Terri scooted across the bed, reaching up to rub the back of her husband's neck. His skin was cold and damp, the sinew around his shoulders taunt. Terri maneuvered beside her mate and simply held his hand. The couple sat motionless for several minutes, Bishop staring down at the floor, and Terri maintaining her warm and reassuring grip. Bishop finally broke the silence. "I hate this world. I'm sick of it. I'm sick of all the killing. I've had enough of all these head cases running around with an attitude of 'every man for himself.'" Bishop rotated his head, trying in vain to release the stress from his shoulders.

Terri leaned up and gently kissed his cheek. "It's okay, my love; you've been through a lot the last few days. I think it's only natural to be a little stressed. Besides, I know you're dreading seeing the colonel today after how things worked out."

Bishop nodded and flashed momentary eye contact. "I did my best, Terri. I don't think I let the colonel down at all. He's going to try and talk me into re-upping with the Army, and I don't want to. I just want us to head back to the ranch and get on with it. I've done my part, and it didn't work out so well."

Terri smiled at the thought of revisiting the now familiar topic. "Like I said, Bishop, I'm good with that. As long as we're together, I'm a happy girl."

Bishop stared deeply into her eyes and pulled her close in a hug, as if offering her one last chance at the security that life on the military base afforded. The strong return of her embrace reassured Bishop of her resolve to stand with him on this decision. The final choice having been made, a moment of inner peace enveloped the young couple. Bishop pushed his wife's hair over her shoulder and kissed her cheek. "The sun will be coming up soon. I'm not going to be able to get back to sleep. I think I'll go for a run. Why don't you try and crash again, and I promise I'll be quiet when I get back."

Terri's yawn was timed perfectly. "Now that sounds like a good idea. The run will work some of that tension out of you. Just don't overdo it—I've got some plans for you a little later on, and I wouldn't want you to be too tired or anything."

Bishop smiled at his wife, raising his eyebrows up and down, "You've got a date, pretty girl. For you . . . I'll even take a shower first."

Terri brought both of her hands to her cheeks in mock surprise. Faking an excited voice, she said, "I get a clean Bishop? Oh-my-goodness! Is it my birthday or something? Christmas isn't for another couple of days."

Bishop moved so quickly Terri didn't have time to protest. He effortlessly lifted, flipped, and gently laid her on her back, his weight coming to rest on top of her, their faces just inches apart. The two lovers stared at each other in the dim light. "I love you," they both declared at the same time.

~  ~

A young man from Iowa, with the rank of specialist, had shown Bishop and Terri to their room soon after delivering a bundle of extra clothing. While the second-hand running shoes weren't a perfect fit, Bishop welcomed the chance to exercise. Life at the ranch since the collapse had been filled with hunting, gathering, and trying to raise a garden. There simply wasn't the time or the calories to run for exercise, and it wasn't as if they were gaining any weight. Thinking about it, Bishop was sure the newly sprouting vegetables in their fledgling garden were all dead now. They had been away for six days, and new growth wouldn't survive long in the West Texas desert without water. *There's another reason to get home as soon as possible*, he thought.

The east was just beginning to glow with the potential for a new sun when Bishop quietly closed the door and exited the visiting officers' quarters building. Terri, from the looks of her, was already off in dreamland, and he hoped she would remain undisturbed for a few hours. *She is sleeping for two*, he mused.

It was a cool, clear morning at Fort Bliss, and for a

moment, Bishop forgot about the chaos that existed beyond the base's secured perimeter. Six short months ago, he and Terri had been living in suburban Houston, suffering through the Second Great Depression like everyone else. Then it had all gone to hell, and they banded together with neighbors to hold back a growing wave of anarchy. When martial law was declared and Uncle Sam's Army rolled in, the young couple had made the most difficult decision of their lives—time to bug out and head west.

Bishop had inherited land when his father passed away. It wasn't a big spread, more like a lowly strip of desert, a leftover from when the ranch had been cut up and sold off years ago. He had spent many years on that ranch as a boy and knew the land well. Over time, he had slowly turned the worthless tract into a weekend hunting retreat with an old camper parked next to the only year-round water supply within 10 miles.

Bishop began stretching his muscles before his jog. He wanted to be careful not to pull or strain anything. While he had been doing plenty of running lately, that had been because people were shooting at him. He wanted a good, long, relaxing run that resulted in that feeling of muscles well used and freely flowing blood. As he was limbering, a white pickup pulled to the nearby curb. The doors, adorned with the military police logo, opened promptly, and two soldiers approached.

Bishop tensed, wishing he had brought his pistol along. There just wasn't any place to carry the heavy piece in sweatpants and t-shirt.

The older one, a sergeant, said, "Good morning, sir. Is everything all right?"

"Yes, sergeant, everything is fine. I was getting ready to take in the air."

The man looked at his watch and commented, "It's still pretty early yet for a run."

Bishop didn't like his tone of voice. Normally, he would have taken the man for what he was—a cop. With the government and the military being divided, and a civil war on, he couldn't help but be wary. "Is this an Army base, sergeant, or did I wake up in the wrong place? I thought pre-dawn runs were the norm for all you warfighters."

The man laughed, defusing the situation, "Sir, nothing is normal these days. We have people trying to sneak in here from El Paso all the time. They're mostly trying to steal food, but after the incidents of the last couple of days, everyone is a little on edge."

Bishop had to hand it to the guy on that point. The president of the United States had been here at the base when several soldiers loyal to the Independents had made an assassination attempt. The base had been in complete turmoil while the rebels had been hunted down.

Bishop replied, "I appreciate your stopping by to check on me, Sergeant. I just want to burn off some stress. Any advice on a good route to jog this morning?"

The MP nodded and asked his partner to retrieve a clipboard from the truck. Bishop continued to stretch while the man returned with the paper. The sergeant flipped a couple of pages, tilting the paper toward the truck's headlights so he could read. After a moment, he looked up and announced, "There's no training scheduled on any of the firing ranges today. I can guide you out that way if you want to run in open country. It'll be about 8K out and back."

Bishop nodded, "Can't hurt to head that way at least. Eight sounds about right this morning, but it's been a while."

The two MPs gave Bishop some general directions and then watched as he began sprinting off into the distance. After the runner was out of earshot, the young private looked at his sergeant and asked, "Did anyone ever figure out for sure whose side that guy is on? I've heard lots of rumors, ya know."

The sergeant turned to his subordinate and smiled. "I know he's been rubbing elbows with the brass since those traitors tried to kill the president. I heard he is the guy who saved the prez and then turned around and got him killed. I also know a lot of guys are pissed off over what he did. That's all above my pay grade and definitely above yours. Let's finish our rounds and get some breakfast."

The ground felt odd at first. It had been so long since he had run for pleasure—strange shoes—new turf, hell, a new world. Bishop took it slow at first, letting his legs get used to the rhythm and his feet get acclimated to the sneakers. Even with the medical facilities at the Army base, blowing a ligament or popping a tendon wouldn't be the highlight of his day. His side ached from the bullet scrape suffered two days ago, but he didn't think his stride would re-open the wound.

After I finish this run, I'm going to go visit the colonel, he thought. Bishop was unsure of how his ex-boss would react to everything that had happened the last few days. As he came to an intersection, his current train of thought was interrupted long enough to recall the directions the MPs had given him. He took a left and accelerated his pace just slightly.

Thinking of the colonel brought on mixed emotions. Bishop respected the man immensely, more so than anyone—other than his father. The colonel had been his boss for almost 10 years while working for HBR. The job involved a lot of travel to remote, dangerous locales, and the man always had Bishop's back.

Bishop's job was to protect HBR assets wherever the international firm decided to explore for gas or oil. Remote jungles, the deserts of Iraq, Pacific Islands, and South American mountains were all on the travel itinerary. If there were someplace dangerous in the world where there might be energy below the earth's crust or ocean's surface, HBR was the company to call. When HBR answered, they protected their people and equipment by hiring guys like Bishop, training the hell out of them, and then sending them along to keep the peace.

Even though he was beginning to breathe hard, Bishop had to laugh at the phrase "keep the peace." He once told Terri his job was like playing outfield on a baseball team. "You go through hour after hour of absolute boredom until some guy gets lucky and hits a screamer your way. For a few short moments, life becomes far too exciting," he had explained.

~  ~

The tiny picture generated by the thermal imager depicted Bishop as a red and yellow blob. The blurred image wasn't due to a lack of capability, but rather the device being a victim of its own advanced technology. As Bishop ran, the passing of his arms and legs heated the surrounding air for just long enough to be detected by the sensitive instrument. The resulting outline was blurred, creating an effect more closely resembling a 70s lava lamp than a state-of-the-art observation scope. The machine was so accurate, even Bishop's footprints showed yellow, the result of his running shoes creating minute amounts of friction-heat on the pavement.

The man holding the FLIR, or *Forward Looking Infrared*, lowered the monocle from his eye and turned to his partner. "Deke, Bishop is going for a run. He just had a quick discussion with two patrolling MPs and then headed into the desert. Make a note in the log for me, would ya?"

Deke pulled a tablet computer from his bag, and soon, the vacant third-story office was filled with the pecking taps of a keyboard. "Done."

The observer stretched high, the sleeves of the Army uniform pulled below his wrists. While the insignia on his shoulders was that of a major, he hadn't been an officer in the United States Army in a long, long time. The rank had been carefully selected. Majors were a dime a dozen on a base of this size and wouldn't be noticed. Yet, they held enough privilege for most activities to go unchallenged.

The man raised the FLIR again, tracking Bishop as he faded into the distance. "I'm off my shift in ten. Anything good for breakfast down at the officers' mess?"

"Same ol', same ol', Moses. You can tell what day it is by the menu, just like when we served Mother Green."

Moses laughed, his eyes never wavering from his vigil. "It's got to be better than that garbage down in Columbia. My gawd—I had the shits for a month of Sundays."

"Nothing was worse than Chechnya. Did anyone ever figure out what that meat really was?"

The observer grunted, "No one wanted to know. That was a good haul though. I'll never forget that Russian's face. You would think a big-time international arms dealer would have a larger pair of nads. I thought he was going to cry like a little girl."

"People tend to react oddly when they realize they've just been had for 1.2 million cash."

"Naw, I think it was your .45 up against his temple, Deke. That's what upset him."

The two men chuckled briefly, enjoying the type of humor shared by long-time comrades who had witnessed much together—sometimes too much. It was an air of confidence with each other, an atmosphere of unspoken respect for the other's capabilities.

As Bishop's image faded smaller and smaller, Moses pulled his eye from the monocle and sighed. "I'm ready to get out of here. If our employer had left any tracks, we would know by now. I think we're wasting someone's money here . . . being a little over-cautious."

Deke chuckled, "I bet no one ever described you as 'subtle' in your status reports, did they? The client says we need to make sure our previous mission goes undiscovered, so that's what we'll do. It's only another day or two, and then we'll be out of here."

The man holding the FLIR set it down, Bishop now out of his line of sight. The lookout glanced over at his relief and flatly stated, "I'm still not for sure why we're here in the first place. We did our job and protected the client. Now we're acting like a bunch of high school kids trying to clean up after a party before mom and dad get home."

Deke smiled. "Money, power, weapons, favors ... it's just a job, dude. It beats the pay grade of an E7 and the eventual half-pay after 20 long, hard years. I don't know about you, but waiting three weeks before landing an appointment with a VA dentist isn't why I humped all those courses and busted my ass through all those schools. I didn't deploy over a hundred times to live out my old age bored to tears and barely able to feed myself."

"Why *did* you do it then? It's not like the Army promised us anything special."

"I did it for God and country, partner—just like you and all the rest of us stupid bastards."

"And when did God and country stop being enough?"

Looking at his watch, the man waiting for his shift sighed. "I don't know. It wasn't like somebody threw a switch, and I suddenly stopped giving a rat's ass. I think it was Mexico that was the final straw. You remember that op—the one where we went in with the DEA teams and snatched Julio Mendez-whatever-his-name-was?"

"Oh, yeah. I remember that one. Gawd, what a palace that guy had. Too bad he didn't spend more on improving his security forces."

"I remember walking around that guy's crib and thinking about my little one-bedroom shithole outside Bragg. I remember all those women and cars and that pool table that cost more than what I made in a year. We found over three million in cash downstairs in the counting room. It took five of us two trips to haul all that money to the trucks. Who would've noticed if a couple hundred grand went missing? I mean, after all, I was the guy who put my ass on the line taking out Mr. Drug Lord's little private army."

Moses shifted his considerable frame, staring away into the distance. "For me, it was when the Secret Service dudes got busted with the hookers down in Colombia. I had just finished 13 months in Kandahar, and my wife's lawyer hit me between the eyes with divorce papers the day after I got back. Those agents and rear echelon pussies were down in Colombia partying their asses off while I was eating dirt and dodging Taliban lead. When the chance came to move on, I didn't even hesitate."

"Maybe when there's a change in leadership, somebody will fix all that. Your shift is up. Why don't you head down and get a bite to eat? Hunger makes you a cynical fuck."

Handing over the FLIR scope, Moses replied, "Look ... dude ... this is just a job. Guys like us, we always do the dirty work and then get thrown under the bus. Bush did it after Iraq; Obama did the same when he came into office. Visions of grandeur are only going to lead to disappointment. My *only* expectation of this job is to get paid."

"You left out living long enough to take the next job."

"Oh, yeah. That, too."

Bishop began to notice more of his surroundings as he progressed further from any sort of man-made structure. He was now running through the open New Mexico desert … or maybe the Texas desert. The base resided partially in both states. The road he was traveling started to weave around low mounds of hard-packed, yellow sandstone streaked with a burnt tint of red. Small bunches of scrub cactus dotted the landscape here and there, accented by varieties of pincushion and ladyfinger.

Every now and then the pavement was crossed by dirt trails, most of which were announced via road signs warning of a "Tank Crossing Ahead." *Gawd that would be fun*, he thought, *busting around in one of those tanks, shooting at targets with that huge gun. What a job.*

It occurred to Bishop that perhaps the tank drivers would think his job was the cat's ass. *I guess the grass is always greener on the other side,* he mused. In truth, Bishop had liked his work for the most part. Like everyone else, he would bitch and grumble about this, that or the other, but he had known a lot of people out of work and suffering badly. The depression had been vicious and long, with the country barely hanging on. This fact wasn't lost on the nation's old enemies, who used sleeper cells and wreaked havoc with strategically planned attacks. The results were horrific, and the country slid over the edge of a deep void. *At least I had a job*, he thought. *So what if people shot at me every now and then—I was getting paid.*

I'll run and then bring Terri breakfast in bed, he thought. *I've been such a pain in the ass lately; it'll be a good make-up gesture.*

Today's visit with the colonel was going to be the first act of what promised to be a very stressful day. After paying his respects to his old boss, there was a second necessary evil—a visit to the general. A few days ago, he and Terri had sat through depositions, recounting their time with the now-deceased leader of the free world. After the legal interviews were over, General Westfield had offered Bishop a commission in the United States Army. The offer was tempting.

He and Terri would be afforded quarters at Bliss. The

base had electrical power, running water, and a goodly supply of food. While no specific duties had been discussed with the general, Bishop imagined he'd still be involved with some sort of security or base operations.

Comparing life on the ranch to the amenities available at Bliss made the decision difficult. Terri's due date in five months compounded the assessment even more. To practically anyone still alive in North America, the base would be an oasis of luxury.

Bishop tried to imagine their lives here. Any duties the general could throw his way weren't the concern. Life after the downfall was a never-ending cycle of hardship that included gathering enough food and providing security. Anything the Army could dream up would probably be like a vacation compared to his workload at the ranch.

Security. Bishop grunted when he thought of the connection between the rule of law and the moral conscious of the human animal—both had evaporated faster than anyone had ever anticipated. Society now required a man to carry a weapon to protect his family and property. It wasn't easy. The necessity of maintaining a constant vigil, of always being on alert, was a distracting, unproductive use of time. Any noise in the middle of the night required effort. Mundane activities, such as walking, gardening, hunting, or gathering were all polluted by a constant shadow of fear—fear of other people. But not here at Fort Bliss.

Observing the awakening base as he ran, Bishop considered the well-manicured streets, immaculate grounds, and general image of an orderly existence that surrounded him. Passing a platoon of soldiers, young men hustling into formation and preparing to exercise, the organization of the place seemed to fill a void inside of Bishop. No, he thought, it wasn't a need—it was a craving, a desire for structure, a hunger for the way things once were.

Despite breathing hard now, the concept brought a smile to Bishop's lips. *You're homesick*, he said to himself. *You're dreaming of a life that will never be again.*

Or would it? It was hard to imagine chaos on the streets he was running through. It was difficult to picture anything but calm here. Maybe he needed to reconsider the general's offer. Maybe this was the closest he could get to what once was.

Stop it! The realization almost caused Bishop to pull up from his stride. *You're fooling yourself—this place isn't any of that.* It dawned on Bishop that he'd experienced more violence in the middle of these supposedly disciplined surroundings than anywhere else. He'd encountered far more treachery, discrimination, and hostility here than out in the world. This place was a façade—a Hollywood movie set with false storefronts and actors parading around in costume. This island of organized society held more danger than the sea of anarchy that existed outside of the base's gates. *You've made the right decision*, he consoled himself. *Go with your gut, and stop second-guessing everything.*

West Virginia, Appalachian Mountains
December 22, 2015

Senator Moreland yawned and stretched, the morning routine seemingly more difficult during the winter months. Finding his eyeglasses on the bedside table, he checked the time and was satisfied with his five hours of sleep. Anything over four was a good night's rest these days.

Leading the council that controlled the Independents was a time-consuming task, often requiring the sacrifice of sleep. The workload had peaked during the military battles that once raged along the Mississippi delta. The resulting clash mauled both sides of the conflict, and a ceasefire had been in effect since the death of the president. No war equaled more sleep.

Moreland rubbed his eyes, thankful for the need to do so. *This stalemate isn't going to last long*, he thought. *Soon you'll need every precious minute of rest to stay sharp and lead our nation out of this mess.*

Slowly meandering to the master suite's bathroom, the West Virginian ran a mental list of his goals for the day while absentmindedly executing the required tasks of hygiene. Teeth, hair, and underarms taken care of, Moreland dressed in casual slacks, a pullover sweater, real wool socks, and penny loafers.

With his assistant out of town, it was going to be a challenge to conjure up a good breakfast. Coffee wouldn't be so difficult, but finding suitable fresh fruit was impossible. *It would be canned oranges and oatmeal,* he decided while descending the stairs.

Approaching the kitchen, he noticed the security man checking the patio doors from the great room. Moreland tossed a cheery, "Good Morning," to the large fellow, only receiving a curt, "Sir," back. *These security types*, thought Moreland, *always so serious. They should learn to relax a little and enjoy the view.*

"Do you work for Erik King?"

"Yes, sir, I'm employed by Darkwater."

Moreland decided to engage the stoic man. "I knew Erik's father when he was in the automotive business. I was on the committee that approved Darkwater's budget during the Iraq war. How's Erik doing these days?"

"I've never met Mr. King, sir."

31

"I see," stated a slightly embarrassed Moreland, and he retreated toward the kitchen.

As he reached to push open the kitchen's swinging door, a wonderful aroma drifted past the senator's nose. "What the heck is that?" he mumbled. Passing through the threshold, Moreland was shocked to find Wayne.

"Well, good morning, Senator."

"Wayne! I am surprised to see you back so soon. When did you arrive?"

"I came in last night, Senator. I didn't want to disturb you."

The older man nodded his appreciation, and then his face became serious. "And how is your family handling the tragedy?"

The assistant lowered his head. "As best as can be expected, sir. My sister's death was unanticipated, of course. The lack of the most basic facilities made the situation even worse. We had to dig the grave ourselves, and there wasn't a proper preparation of her body. I built the casket myself, out of scrap lumber."

Moreland put his hand on Wayne's shoulder and squeezed gently. "I'm so very, very sorry, my friend. You know I wish I could have done more for your family, Wayne."

"Thank you, sir. I do appreciate your condolences. Thank you again for the use of your aircraft. It was more than generous," Wayne replied.

Wayne brightened and changed the subject. "Sir, I have to review the security assignments for the week. Can I set aside some fresh waffles and canned fruit for your breakfast this morning?"

The senator rubbed his stomach and smiled. "Much better than the oatmeal I had planned—much better indeed."

Chapter 2

Meraton, Texas
December 22, 2015

Pete was sweeping the barroom floor while subconsciously running through a to-do list of the day's tasks. Since the marketplace had grown and thrived, it was becoming more and more work to keep his small business up and running.

Whisking the small pile of road dust and sand into the pan, he opened the front door and proceeded to return the collection back to its original location. Pete paused in the threshold, looking at the new sun rising in the east. It was going to be another clear, cool day in Meraton, and the market should see a good number of customers with the fair weather. He smiled and strolled out onto Main Street, heading around the corner of Pete's Place to deposit his dustpan cargo.

After the small pile of sweepings was dumped on the ground, Pete returned to inventory his receipts. *What a funny way of running a business*, he thought. Normally an entrepreneur would count the day's take, but that method didn't apply anymore.

Reaching behind the bar, Pete lifted a cardboard box to the counter and began looking through the miscellaneous items he had bartered in exchange for liquid refreshments.

The first items were bullets. Ammunition was small, easy to carry, and held universal value—or so one would think. Shaking his head, Pete sorted the dozen or so rounds, finding he was the proud owner of several calibers that wouldn't fit any weapon he owned. Those would be traded for something else if he could ever find the time to set up his own table in the marketplace.

The remaining items in the cardboard cash register included sewing supplies, a cigar, three tomatoes, two sets of shoelaces, and a dull pocketknife. Pete thumbed through the hodge-podge, amusing himself as he hummed the seasonal ditty, "Twelve Days of Christmas," with an emphasis on "and a partridge in a pear tree."

It was the stack of handwritten IOUs in the bottom of the box that bothered him the most. Pete read through several of the small notes and grunted. The extension of credit had been a difficult balancing act since mankind's humble beginnings and the establishment of commerce. Pete had happily exchanged a drink for an IOU to help get the town trading again—to help rebuild a society.

At first, he'd had little expectation of ever collecting. Now, he was producing his own libations and had raw material costs. Pete sighed, "I have to eat, too."

Carrying the veggies to the small kitchen in the back of the bar, he couldn't help but analyze Meraton's situation. It wasn't just Pete's Place that suffered from a lack of currency. Betty was managing The Manor, trying to keep the town's centerpiece hotel up and running. Some of the remote ranchers were now coming to town to resupply and trade, and they wanted someplace to spend the night. Establishing fair value for goods and services was often difficult, if not impossible.

Pete smiled, thinking about an argument that had broken out a few days ago. It was a clear example of the problem.

He'd been walking down to visit Betty, when the sounds of a disagreement drifted between the few scattered storefronts in Meraton. Someone was clearly unhappy with someone else, and in these times, that was cause for concern. Mumbling to himself, "What now," Pete set off to find the quarrel's source.

Heading west down Meraton's main drag, Pete could make out more of the angry voices and realized one of them belonged to Betty. Pete picked up his pace, believing something was wrong with his friend. Betty was a strong woman with a frontier attitude, but he always worried about her taking care of that big place all by herself.

The Manor had been known far and wide in West Texas for over 50 years. Famous for being a peaceful retreat with quality service, it had been the primary anchor of Meraton's business district. Now, after the collapse, the one-time vacation destination served as the community's hospital and defensive Alamo. Slowly, it was regaining use as a place for travelers to rest. Almost two full acres of lush gardens were contained inside the fort-like walls of the hotel's grounds. Rare in the barren Chihuahuan Desert surrounding the town, the variety and design of plant life had been a major draw to travelers visiting Big Bend National Park. Many remarked that the stay at the hotel had been the most enjoyable portion of their trip.

Like all destinations in Meraton, The Manor was just a few blocks away from Pete's bar. As he hurried down the street, he soon realized that the argument wasn't coming from the hotel. Two side streets over, he finally found the source of the disturbance in front of Maria Bustou's home.

Betty and Maria were standing in the street, having it out, and Pete could tell neither was backing down. Both women ignored his approach, intent on shouting at each other while fingers were wagged in faces. Pete got close and then joined the fray. "Ladies! Ladies! What is going on here? You two are about to raise the dead."

Both women looked at Pete, but each reacted differently to his attempt to restore balance. Maria crossed her arms over her chest, a look of determination on her face. Betty took a step toward Pete and then pointed her finger back at Maria. "Pete, this . . . this . . . woman bartered four eggs with me yesterday, and two of them are so rotten, my stray cats wouldn't eat them. That's the second time this has happened in the last two weeks. I want half of the beef loin that I traded for them back, but she says her family has already eaten it."

Maria waited for a moment before pleading her case to Pete. "This is so untrue. The eggs were fresh and even if not, senor, I offer Miss Betty replacement eggs tomorrow. My hens didn't produce this morning."

Before Pete could comment, Betty went right back at her, "Maria, I don't want to wait on your hens. I have to feed the people at the hospital and the doctor when he visits. I don't have anything else to barter with today, and the cupboard is bare. I have people I have to feed."

The commotion was attracting other townsfolk. Pete saw three other neighbors approaching, as well as a few faces peering out of nearby windows. Given what he knew about the two women's tempers, he was glad to have the backup in case things got out of hand.

He decided to play peacemaker. "Maria, Betty . . . please . . . let's all settle down and work this out. I'm sure we can come to a reasonable solution that works for everyone. Pete immediately regretted stepping into the middle of the dispute. Both women were now looking at him as if to say, "Well, what's your idea?" He didn't have one.

After an uncomfortable pause, Betty and Maria both started talking at once, now playing to the seven people gathered around. Pete could tell sides were being drawn by the looks of sympathy and nods of agreement being shared with both women.

About then, another man spoke over the top of everyone. "Something similar happened when I bartered with Jose three days ago. I traded a half pound of sugar for an old pistol and a used pair of boots that Jose wanted to get rid of. Problem is, he can't find the boots now and thinks his wife might have thrown them out. That wouldn't be a problem if he could give me part of my sugar back, but unfortunately, his wife made preserves with it already."

Another woman spoke up, "I've had two oil lamps I've been trying to get rid of for three weeks now. I've been waiting to trade them with someone who has something I need, but so far I haven't been able to manage that. Now, I'm not sure I'll ever get rid of them."

On and on the conversation went, with more and more people joining the crowd from surrounding homes. Pete listened, completely sympathetic to the situations. He had a whole boxful of items he had traded for back at the bar, and there had never been time to set up a table at the market and exchange them for his own necessities. It was a growing problem—bartering was becoming a bottleneck.

Pete looked over his shoulder at the sun and realized everyone had been standing around complaining for a long time. "Excuse me! Excuse me! I suggest we have a town hall meeting this afternoon. Let's call the meeting for four o'clock. Let's get everyone together and see if we can come up with an answer to this problem."

Several heads nodded up and down in the crowd. Begrudgingly, Betty and Maria agreed to shelve their problem until cooler heads prevailed.

As Betty and Pete walked back toward Main Street, Pete gently scolded his friend. "Betty, why didn't you tell me you were running low on food? You know I've got plenty and would be happy to share."

Betty didn't hesitate, "Pete, I'm not going to find myself beholding to you or anyone else. It makes me feel good to hear you say that, but I've always managed on my own."

Pete waved her off. "Oh, now, there ya go. You know I worry about you down here all by yourself. You've done a great job keeping the place up without being paid anything. Besides, I think you are the strongest woman I've ever met."

Betty blushed, not sure of how to take Pete's last comment. Thankfully for her, the pair had arrived at the front steps of the hotel, and she didn't have to continue the conversation. She replied, "Why thank you, Pete. That's very kind of you to say so," and rushed for the door. Pete shrugged his shoulders and slowly made his way back to the bar, wondering why he sucked so badly when it came to women.

Bishop ran a slightly different route back to his quarters. He was feeling that tingling rush to the extremities and had finally gotten into what some athletes call "the zone." The sun was fully above the mountains to the east, and the sky was a cheery shade of Colombia blue. Movement up ahead distracted him from the natural warmness of a new day, and he realized something important was going on up ahead.

His route was taking him into Biggs Field, which was basically the base's airport. As he rounded a slight bend in the road, he noticed a flurry of activity around Air Force One. *I wonder if they are going to fly the president's body back to Arlington,* he pondered.

The scene before him elicited a mixture of emotions. He had rescued the Commander in Chief from a certain death. A group of soldiers loyal to the Independents had made a desperate attempt to kill the man, and Bishop had disrupted their plans. Looking back now, it wasn't so much because he was loyal to the old government. He had taken action because he didn't want to see the country fall into a civil war. There had already been one major battle with thousands of men killed, and both sides were gathering enough forces to make that horrific event look like a panty raid at a sorority house.

No, Bishop thought, *I rescued the president because I thought he could stop all this madness.*

The effort was in vain, as the man was shot by a common criminal less than 12 hours later.

Bishop felt a tug of guilt over the incident. While the president had been traveling with him of his own free will, Bishop had made the decision to travel to the small town of Alpha, thinking they would be safe there. It hadn't worked out. *Still,* he thought, *by some thinking, the man was in my charge.*

Another small pickup truck was parked along the road, the logo indicating it belonged to the base's military police. As Bishop jogged past the vehicle, the two soldiers inside watched him without expression. He hadn't run more than 20 steps when he heard the truck's engine start. A quick glance over his shoulder verified the assumption he had already made—the truck had executed a U-turn and was following him.

What now, he thought, just as the vehicle pulled up next to him, and the passenger side window came down. "Excuse me sir, could we have a quick word with you?"

Bishop didn't stop running, but glanced over and replied, "Sure. What's up?"

The specialist seemed annoyed that Bishop wasn't stopping, but didn't voice any protest. After a quick exchange with the driver, he yelled back over, "Sir, there's someone who would like a word with you. I believe he's on his way here right now."

Bishop was confused and stopped running. The MPs braked to a stop, but didn't exit their vehicle. Bishop looked up to see a black SUV rolling across the airport's tarmac. It was one of the Secret Service's escort trucks, and it was heading directly at him.

Agent Powell pulled up next to the MPs and thanked them, making it clear they were no longer needed. After they pulled away, the man in charge of the president's security waved a greeting at Bishop, who nodded back.

"Good morning, Bishop. I hope you don't mind my interrupting your exercise."

"Good morning, Agent Powell. I was getting tired anyway. What can I do for you?"

"Why don't I give you a ride back to the officers' quarters? We can talk on the way."

Bishop considered the offer, but shook his head. "I'd stink up the interior of that expensive government vehicle. I'm good."

Powell laughed, "It's pretty common to sweat in here, Bishop—given the job and all."

It was Bishop's turn to chuckle. He nodded and opened the passenger door, a blast of cool air hitting his body. Agent Powel waited until Bishop was settled and then slowly began driving back to the main cluster of buildings at the base.

"Bishop, I understand we're close to finding the next in line for succession. Before I can make the new president safe, I've got to fill in a lot of the missing pieces to the puzzle of what happened that day. I've read and re-read your deposition, but there are gaps we simply can't fill in right now. Has anything else come to you? Anything popped into your mind?"

Bishop was silent for a bit, eventually clearing his throat and speaking. "No, sir. I've told you everything I can remember. The images I have of the firefight outside the president's office are blurry at best. It was dark, and the air was thick with smoke. Not to mention there was lead flying everywhere. Even the impression I have of the man holding the gun to the president's head isn't really clear. I didn't have a lot of time to take that shot."

Powell thought about his next statement, choosing his words carefully. "Bishop, I believe you, but there is still a mystery here. I don't buy for one second that the Independents could have organized that attempt by themselves. We found only the dead members of the president's team and dead soldiers. No others. I haven't found the head of the snake."

Bishop shook his head at the memory. "Look, I centered

the dot on the guy's ear. I can tell you he was holding a Beretta. The hammer was back. He was saying something to the president. I only saw his profile though. I could help one of those sketch artists like you see on TV draw a picture of the guy's profile, but that's about it."

Powell knew the answer to his next question, but had to ask. "The bodies weren't in the right places. Is there any chance the guy walked out of that room on his own?"

Bishop's head snapped up, his eyes boring into Powell's. "I can assure you he didn't walk out of that room on his own. I had to take a headshot. I didn't miss. I'm 100% sure. I told you where you could find his DNA. I showed you the specific patch of gore on the wall that belonged to the guy. I watched it splash there … I'll be seeing that image for the rest of my life, Agent Powell."

"Bishop, we don't have DNA testing capability, and we definitely don't have DNA matching right now. I'm sorry, but put yourself in my shoes. There was no corpse in that room lying in a position like you described. How did it get out or get moved?"

"Well, sir, I'm no Sherlock Holmes. It was all so fast, Agent Powell. Maybe I'm not describing it well. Maybe my memory is hosed up. It could be that simple."

Powell sighed. "There's no way anyone could have carried that body out or moved the bodies around. Loyal troops were in that room within 20 seconds after you and the president left. Every exit was sealed within one minute. I still can't identity the leaders of the coup, yet no one could have gotten out of that building."

Bishop grunted, "I did."

"Yes, you did. But there was an MP at the exit you used almost immediately after you got out. That was the last of the exits to be covered, at least according to our Army friends."

"That's true. That MP pulled up about 15 seconds after we bolted across the alley. Still, someone might have had time to move the body."

They arrived at the guest quarters, Powell idled with the vehicle in park, a clear sign the conversation wasn't over. "Assuming you're correct, that means there is someone else involved that we don't know about. Someone with internal access . . . hell, it could be another member of my own team."

"I suppose, but wasn't there a lot of fighting going on after I got out with the president? I heard it took the army hours to round up everyone they thought was on the other side. As I understand it, a lot of them decided to shoot it out rather than be arrested. Maybe your missing man was one of those killed in the fighting?"

"Bishop, I can't assume that. You wouldn't if you had my job. My instincts tell me there's more to this than just a bunch of rebel soldiers trying to knock off the chief executive."

The two men sat in silence for a few moments. Bishop understood Agent Powell's dilemma and couldn't blame the man for going with his gut. Such intuition had pulled his butt out of the fire more times than he could remember.

Powell broke the silence, "Could you come over to the HQ building today? We still have the area roped off. I'm hoping it will refresh something in your memory."

Bishop grimaced, not wanting to return. The scene still burning in his mind, the visions extremely unpleasant ... memories of blood and smoke . . . the sounds of dying men . . . it all made Bishop's gut hurt. The carnage had been off the scale horrific. Teams of highly trained professionals going at each other in such close quarters had resulted in a bloody, desperate battle.

I don't need to go back and relive that ... not again, thought Bishop. Looking up at Powell, his tone remained firm. "Man, I've been back there twice already. I think if anything were going to pop into my head, it would've done so by now. Besides, I've got to go see the colonel, deliver an answer to General Westfield's offer, and spend a little one-on-one time with my wife. I'd say I've already got all kinds of opportunity for failure lined up for today, I don't need another task to increase my odds."

Agent Powell grunted, "I've seen your wife pissed. I know where I'd concentrate my energies." Powell cleared his throat, "Speaking of Terri, I've been rolling around an idea and wanted to bounce it off you."

The mention of his wife caused Bishop to stiffen in his seat. "Go on."

"You and Terri were the last two people to be with the president before his death. If the president recognized any of the conspirators, he might have said something to you or your wife."

Bishop shook his head, "How many times are you going to ask me this question, Agent Powell? He didn't say anything to me, and I think Terri would've mentioned something before now. Why don't you stop by and ask her? During the depositions you guys took, I testified to everything I could remember. I'm pretty sure Terri did as well."

Powell chuckled and gave Bishop a mischievous look. "Oh, I believe you. I don't think the prez said a word to either of you. Given what we found at the scene of the assassination attempt, I believe his only thought was about his next breath. The chances of his figuring out one of his protection detail was on the wrong side are slim. No, what I'm thinking is to spread a rumor that Terri saw something. Get the word around, and then see who shows interest in the subject."

"No fucking way!" Bishop tensed, his voice dropping to a steely whisper. "You want to tether a pregnant woman to a stake, out in the open, and see what kind of carnivore comes along to eat her? Are you sick? Over my dead body, *Agent Powell.*"

Powell had anticipated a reaction, but was still amazed. The animalistic ferocity of the man sitting beside him was impressive. The agent had been around his share of well-trained men, professionals who were high-speed couriers of violence. But Bishop was different, and he couldn't quite put his finger on why.

"Now, Bishop. Don't go getting your panties in a testosterone-induced wad. I wouldn't want to put you or your lovely wife in danger. We'd protect you. You know, we're pretty good at that."

Bishop glared, "How's that all-mighty protection been working out lately?"

The remark stung. Powell had lost his President and had been struggling with the emotional ramifications ever since. It was his only professional failure, and it troubled him deeply. The only possible cure was to discover the turncoat on the inside. He could live with himself if that were determined. He could sleep a little better if he caught and punished the traitor.

"Bishop, we have to know if someone on the inside played a role in all this. We can't have a rogue individual threatening our next president. He's going to be busy enough without having to look over his shoulder all the time. I've got to get to the bottom of this. Besides, I would think you, of all people, would grab at the opportunity to clear your name, if not your conscience."

"Look, I understand that your job is to protect the new guy coming in. Believe me, I do. But you're going to have to figure out another way. Terri and I did our part—or at least we tried. It didn't work out so well, did it? Find another way, sir. Leave us out of it. Besides, if Terri found out I agreed to something like that, I'd be the one needing your protection."

Both men laughed and then fell silent. The Secret Service agent pulled the shifter into drive, indicating the conversation was over. "See ya later, Bishop."

"Later."

After exiting the SUV, Bishop strolled through the bleak lobby and down the hall toward room #11. He was a few feet away when the sounds of a commotion coming from the room reached his ears. *Someone is hurting Terri*, rushed through his mind.

On the balls of his feet, Bishop opened the door and

moved inside, crouching in a full combat stance and ready to fight. He was greeted by the sight of Samantha, David *and* Terri bouncing on the bed, hammering each other with government-issued pillows. Bishop exhaled and relaxed his shoulders, almost laughing at his overreaction. The relief was short-lived as Terri squealed and rocketed a pillow toward his head. Bishop ducked the projectile and dove at the three sets of unsteady legs hopping on the mattress. With arms spread wide, he managed to entangle at least one leg each, and the entire heap of pillow fighters collapsed onto each other, laughing.

Samantha landed almost squarely on Bishop's back and immediately protested, "Ewwwwww ... you're all sweaty, Bishop," while madly scrambling to get away.

Bishop rolled over and pinned Terri, privately whispering in her ear, "This wasn't the type of bed action I had in mind." His statement resulted in a sharp elbow to his ribs, quickly followed with a high velocity feather bomb to the ear. It was on!

~  ~

Twenty minutes and two busted pillows later, the warriors had retired, panting to their respective corners, exhausted smiles all around. Bishop was trying to figure out how he was going to explain the damaged room to Mother Green. By his inventory, one lamp had been busted and two large sections of paint were missing from one wall. It had been one heck of a battle.

Samantha, being the smallest, had sided with either Bishop or David, resorting to sneak attacks while one of the bigger combatants was otherwise engaged. She was also the first to recover. "Bishop, are you going to visit Grandpa today?"

Bishop nodded, trying to gather the energy to head for the shower. "Yup, I sure am, Sam. How's the colonel doing this morning anyway?"

David answered for his sister, "He's doing okay, but still can't walk. He was teasing me about my flying skills, which I think is a good sign."

Bishop had to agree. "You'll never live that down, David. For the rest of your life, the colonel is going to repeat stories about how you almost killed him by crashing an airplane." Bishop noticed the boy's serious look, and added, "What you should also know is that as soon as you leave the room, he'll tell the listener what a spectacular job you did landing that aircraft without any fuel on a makeshift landing strip. You don't get to hear that part."

David seemed to get it and smiled at Bishop. "I did okay, ya think?"

His sister joined in, "David, you did great! An airplane that you had never flown before, and we all survived the crash . . . errrrrr . . . I mean landing. If Grandpa gets too mean, you tell him to come talk to Samantha. I'll set the record straight."

To Bishop, that day seemed like a lifetime ago, even though it had been less than two weeks. So much had happened so fast. He glanced at his watch and announced it was time to get going, he had a busy day ahead of him. Samantha and David said their goodbyes and left arguing over who won "The Great Feather War of 2015."

Terri managed a stretch and balanced on the edge of the bed, watching Bishop get ready for his shower. "I can't believe you would attack a pregnant girl, Bishop. I thought you were an honorable man."

"All's fair in love and war, my sweets. Never forget that. As I recall, however, you started it."

Terri winked, and in her most sultry Mae West voice commanded, "Hurry up and get out of that shower big boy, and I'll start something else."

Chapter 3

Fort Meade, Maryland
December 22, 2015

Sophia pushed her chair back from the green metal desk, glanced at the computer screen one last time, and then placed her hands in her lap. *That's it*, she thought, *he's the guy.* Since she had been rescued from her Washington, DC apartment a few days ago, she had worked almost nonstop, trying to ascertain who was next in line of succession for the presidency. The databases available at Fort Meade weren't as detailed as the ones she normally accessed, but they contained enough information to perform the assignment.

Her finger moved to the keyboard, hovering over the button labeled "Print Screen." There wasn't any doubt about the results—Sophia was absolutely certain of her analysis. The cause of her delay was more selfish in nature. She felt safe here. The availability of food and running water was nice too. She hadn't seen the FBI agents who brought her to Fort Meade and wondered if she would be taken back into the city now that her task was complete. She didn't want to go back, and for the first time in her life, she pondered cheating the government she had served loyally for over 20 years. She could stretch this out—pad the payroll—take her time.

Sophia's hands returned to her lap, her distant gaze focused on nothing. She could ask to stay. There didn't seem to be a shortage of space or food, and she could help out around the base. The thought of returning to her apartment made her shiver. What was once a warm, safe place to spend her non-working hours, now seemed so distant and threatening. The drive from Washington had provided Sophia something she specialized in processing—information. Her analysis of that data didn't require a degree in mathematics to postulate; it was going to be months, if not years before life returned to normal in Washington.

Some of the capital's streets had been packed tightly with abandoned cars while others were completely barren. The once proud dome of the capitol building, an icon of freedom for decades, was now scarred and blackened from smoke—the aftermath of a fire that had damaged the building. Fire had definitely been a major issue. When the riots broke out, the firefighters who had remained on the job often couldn't get to the blaze. The streets were either blocked off by abandoned vehicles or occupied by violent throngs numbering in the thousands.

Sophia shuddered at the thought—fire frightened her.

Her escorts had carefully selected side streets for the exodus from Washington. The interstates were blocked by tens of thousands of motorists who tried to escape the inferno. When the electrical grid went down, there was no gas, food, or traffic signals. The FBI agents had told her that most of the stalled cars had simply idled for hours until they ran out of fuel. The frustrated commuters had swelled the ranks of the disenchanted and desperate citizens filling the streets.

According to her escorts, the city had actually been ravaged by three separate waves of violence. The first occurred when the labor riots sacked the White House and other government buildings. The second was initiated by the District of Columbia police trying to restore order. The third rape of the city was by desperate, starving masses—people who were out of food and looting to survive. As they had driven along, Sophia had grown bored with counting the number of smoldering buildings. Without any fire department to fight the blazes, anything could start a fire, and little could control it.

Her escorts had talked extensively about human behavior on the ride to Meade. The men had discussed in great detail that while gang rivalries were to be expected, racial violence, vigilantes and even neighborhood disputes were not. And yet the latter had exploded throughout the area.

Pointing here and there, the FBI agents seemed to have grown numb, unmoved by the rampant destruction passing by the car's windows. Yet, Sophia would never forget the scenes. Staring again at her computer, the analyst decided that such an important decision would require one more pass. She had to be sure, right?

Her little deception manifested itself in a troubled stomach. She would return to her quarters and rest for a bit before beginning the verification of her findings. Sophia sought her supervisor; her guilt required that she at least let someone know she wasn't feeling well.

Two cubicles away, a man stood and scanned the area. Casually strolling to Sophia's computer, he again checked to verify he wasn't being watched. Three clicks on the keyboard later, the small laser printer hummed a signal that it was warming up.

The man stepped to the exit door, carrying the still-warm printout from Sophia's computer. Carefully studying the black and white characters once and then again, he strolled to a nearby dumpster and tore the paper into several small pieces before depositing them into the huge, metal receptacle.

Stealthily, he followed a seldom-used maintenance

walkway behind the HVAC equipment servicing the building. The modified cell phone in his pocket would attract unwanted attention if anyone noticed it. Cell towers weren't functional anymore.

Glancing nervously around one last time, the man hit the send button and waited for the connection.

The call was answered with a question. "Do you have a name?"

"Yes."

The hospital smelled, well, like a hospital. Bishop hated the scent. Despite knowing better, he couldn't help but associate the place with turmoil, pain, and death. *People are healed here too*, he forced himself to admit. *My child might be born in a place like this.*

Each room was marked by a small black placard, advertising its assigned number. Bishop's attention was divided between watching for the colonel's doorway and staying out of the way of the bustling workers who were rushing around to provide care. *Maybe I should come back later when things aren't so busy*, he thought. He quickly dismissed the urge, deciding instead to suck it up and get it over.

The nurses and staff no longer dressed in primary white, despite the place being a military institution, and that seemed to help override the building's sterile, cold personality. Still, to Bishop's eye, it wasn't a place he would describe as warm, bright, or cheerful.

The little black sign beside him indicated the colonel's room was the next threshold. Bishop paused. Like a patrolling soldier who entered a narrow pass, Bishop's eyes scanned forward, wary of the ambush. He listened and watched, secretly hoping some important medical procedure was in progress that would forbid visitors. The area was quiet, no presence of hostiles was detected.

Taking a deep breath, Bishop moved forward and glanced through the door. He could see the foot of a hospital bed and the outline of two legs underneath the covers. No doctor, nurse, or aide was present—the colonel had no other visitors. *Maybe he's sleeping*, thought Bishop. *I wouldn't want to disturb his rest. That's an important part of healing.*

Approaching like a warrior ready to spring on an enemy sentry from behind, Bishop slipped quietly into the room. He found the colonel lying with his head elevated, a magazine unfolded and resting on his chest. His eyes were closed. *I'll come back later after he's rested*, thought Bishop.

Relieved, Bishop exercised extreme stealth while pivoting to exit the room. A voice shredded the calm, "Hi, Bishop! Grandpa will be so glad you came to visit him!"

Behind him in the doorway, Samantha and David carried several books and a tray of food. Grinning ear to ear, Samantha rushed forward, embracing Bishop in a hug. The colonel's sleepy voice sounded out, "Bishop? Is Bishop here?" *Busted.*

"Yes, sir, I'm here," admitted Bishop. Straightening his spine and pushing back his shoulders, he gathered himself and entered the room.

The colonel's genuine smile eased Bishop's apprehension—somewhat. As the two men shook hands, Bishop observed the patient's grip was strong. "You're looking much better than the last time I saw you, sir."

The older man waved off the words. "Thanks in no small part to your efforts, Bishop. I would've surely died in Meraton if you hadn't sent David back with that equipment. The sawbones there said it saved my life."

Samantha regarded her older brother with wide, almost admiring eyes. "Don't forget. David was a hero too, Grandpa. He flew the plane back while people were shooting at him."

The colonel nodded his agreement, focusing his intense stare on the blushing, teenage boy. Bishop decided to bail the kid out. "Everyone did their part, sir. It was a team effort. David and Samantha can work with me anytime."

The colonel was clearly proud of his grandchildren, his gaze approving and sincere. The warm moment didn't last long, however. After a few pleasantries, a quick inquiry about how Terri was doing, and a brief conversation about the weather, the colonel sent the kids away on another errand.

When they were finally alone, Bishop could feel his old boss' eyes boring in. "Did he die well?" The question aired in a low, serious tone.

As simple as the inquiry sounded, the effect on the two men was extraordinarily deep and complex. It was as if a new dimension of time and space appeared, both of them being pulled into a zone of memories and experiences from days past. It was uncomfortable, filled with the faces of colleagues who had died violently and always, always too young. Neither man spoke of the mutual experience, neither having the words to describe memories packed by the sound, smell and fear of death. It was a wet existence—a location soaked in toil, sweat, copper-scented blood, mortal fear, and ultimate desperation. Both of them understood. Both had visited this place far too many times before.

It took Bishop a second to leave that domain behind. The torrent of emotions and recollections created a vortex that was hard to escape. He had to concentrate, forcing the merry-go-round of misery to slow down. Finally, the words came, "The president passed on thinking about someone other than himself, sir. I guess that's as good as it gets. I, for one, am sure glad he did, or I'd still be locked up in the stockade and facing charges."

Bishop couldn't say why, but that last gift by the dying man seemed important now. It felt honorable. It seemed like a worthy legacy. It pulled both men out of the abyss of reminiscence.

The colonel responded, "Yes, I've heard about the pardon. General Westfield stopped by and relayed the story. He even allowed me to read your deposition."

A long pause signaled that the colonel didn't know quite where to go next. "I've been lying here rolling over what I know of the entire episode. I'm not fit to judge—I wasn't there. At least a hundred times I've asked, 'What the hell was he thinking,' as various parts of the story unfolded. I have to go with my trust in you, son. I have to believe you put forth your best."

"If it helps to hear it, sir, I did. We both know how easy it is to second-guess any operation after it's over. I've replayed the entire affair numerous times. I've asked myself a thousand questions. To be blunt, sir, during most of it, there simply wasn't time to think things through. I reacted with pure instinct."

The colonel nodded his understanding. The man's expression seemed to indicate he still had questions, but they never came out. Instead, the colonel met Bishop's gaze square on and said, "I'm not smart enough to play the parallel universe game of 'what if,' Bishop. I've never met anyone who is. I asked you to perform what I thought was a nearly impossible job at the time. Given the president had already made up his mind before you ever left my side, it was all for naught. Still, I hope you realize we had to try."

"It wasn't *all* for naught, sir. We know that the president was killed by a common criminal, probably not the Independents. That little piece of information is critical. If the assassination attempt had been launched as a coup, it might have carved a wound in the nation that would never heal. At least this way the anger can be focused on someone who is already dead."

The colonel thought about Bishop's logic for a moment. "What you're saying is true son, but I'm still concerned. So is General Westfield. He's already been asked why you aren't under arrest. Just because you were pardoned, doesn't mean people are going to assume you were innocent. I'd watch my back if I were you."

The statement caught Bishop by surprise. "Are you saying that people here at the base believe I'm responsible for the president's death?"

"Bishop, listen carefully to me. Most of the officers and enlisted personnel walking around this compound don't have access to the real facts. We both know how quickly rumors and misinformation can spread around an army base. Scuttlebutt seems to have a life of its own. A lot of good men died when the subversives tried to kill the Commander in Chief. A lot more good men died in those battles down in Louisiana. While there's a ceasefire right now, this base is preparing for war. You have an army without a clear chain of command that is getting ready to fight its own countrymen. Emotions are going to run high. I'll repeat, watch your back."

Bishop rolled the colonel's words around for a while, gazing out the window at nothing. Eventually, he came back around to point. "I suppose that shouldn't surprise me any. Hell, there are people who still think the mafia killed Kennedy. I guess there'll always be those that think of me as a modern day Lee Harvey Oswald."

The colonel smiled at Bishop and then became serious again. "By the way, the mafia did kill Kennedy."

Bishop's head snapped up, staring into the stone-like expression of the man lying next to him for several seconds. The colonel couldn't manage a straight face any longer and broke out in a broad grin. The two men were laughing so hard, the nurse came rushing into the room, thinking something was wrong.

~  ~

After leaving the hospital, Bishop headed directly to his quarters, the colonel's warning in the forefront of his mind. Bishop couldn't help but correlate small, hardly noticeable events that had occurred since their return to Fort Bliss. He kept remembering a soldier's odd expression here, an officer's stare there —little things that he normally would've written off as nothing. The MPs' body language this morning, before the run, was another example of odd behavior.

"I'm getting paranoid," he said out loud. "I'm creating bogeymen where there aren't any."

Entering their room, Bishop expected to find Terri inside.

Checking the bathroom, looking under the bed, and opening the small closet, he started to panic. *Something has happened to my wife*, he thought.

Bishop was gathering his rifle and gear when Terri opened the door and entered the room carrying a bag of sandwiches.

"Hi sweeties," she chimed. "How did it go with the colonel?"

Relief delayed his response. Before Bishop could answer, his wife looked at the combat gear heaped on the bed and reached her own conclusion. "Not so well, I take it."

Bishop shook his head, "No, my talk with the colonel was fine. It was easier than I expected—until he got to the part about warning me."

"Warning you?"

"Yeah … he told me I need to watch my back. He told me some people might blame me for the president's demise."

"What? That's ridiculous! Why would anyone put that on you, Bishop?"

When Bishop didn't respond immediately, Terri answered her own question. "They think the president pardoned you because you *did* do something wrong. Why else would you need a pardon?"

Bishop nodded.

Terri was distracted by the concept and absentmindedly went about unwrapping their lunch. After spreading some napkins across the bedspread, she looked up and commented, "When you came back, I wasn't here." She pointed to the pile of gear. "You were coming to look for me."

Again, Bishop nodded.

"Bishop, he scared you that badly? Seriously? What did he say?"

"Really, it was what he didn't say. He didn't even bring up the subject of my rejoining the Army. He just repeated the warning twice—watch my back." Bishop's far off look betrayed his mind's trek. "I mean, think about it, Terri. Fifth graders will hear some version of this story when they study US history. I never was one of those guys who wanted to make a name for myself, and this surely was not how I thought I would make my mark on the world."

Terri gently nibbled at her tuna salad on wheat and changed the subject. "You'd better eat something, Bishop."

"I'm not hungry, but thanks anyway."

Terri set down the sandwich, now upset. "You're not hungry? Really? I don't know if I've ever seen you pass up food, Bishop. What else is going on?"

Bishop pondered his response, seemingly wanting to carefully choose his words. "I can't be sure, Terri, but since the colonel said all that, I keep replaying little encounters with base personnel in my head. I think we should take the warning seriously."

Terri returned to her meal. After a few bites, she responded. "Given our conversation of this morning, I assume you're 100% set on not joining Uncle Sam's Army? I also am guessing that means we need to get out of here?"

"I think that's probably a wise choice. The sooner, the better."

Eyeing the impromptu picnic spread out on the bed, Terri asked, "Can we take one of these cooks with us? The food from the mess hall here is pretty tasty—at least compared to pine nuts and deer jerky."

"Sure, I'll kidnap one of the cooks. We'll hold a hostage until they allow us to leave."

Terri laughed, feeling a sense of stress relief from the gallows humor. It was how they both coped with pressure.

"Can you make sure and snatch that tall blonde with the blue eyes and biceps that just won't quit? I never know when someone's going to beat you to the draw, and I'll need the help around the ranch."

Bishop grinned. "Your wish is my command, my love. Now let me make sure I have this right. Was that particular bicep decorated with an inked rose?"

The first projectile launched at Bishop's head consisted of an empty, wadded-up sandwich wrapper. The missile didn't have enough mass to overcome the air resistance, and Bishop easily ducked the throw. Terri, not to be denied, snatched up a fully wrapped turkey and cheese for her second salvo. She scored a direct hit right below Bishop's ear, despite eyes that were watering from laughter.

Chapter 4

Attendance at the town meetings had outgrown Pete's Place, so the venue was moved to The Manor's garden. As the Meraton market had grown in popularity, the town's informal assemblies had attracted more residents and visitors from the outlying areas. When the change in location had been announced, someone had questioned where the gatherings would be held once the sun became too hot. An optimistic reply had been "In someplace with air conditioning, I hope." Pete appreciated the positive attitude, but had his doubts about ever feeling electrically cooled air again.

The townsfolk drifted into the grounds in pairs and small clusters. Betty had set up three long, folding tables off to one side, ready to accept covered dishes and desserts. Pete noticed there weren't any tablecloths and immediately understood why. Laundry soap was always in short supply.

Still, the air was mostly festive, and the tables gradually began to fill with various delights. Small children fed off the excitement of the social event, running to and fro, playing hide and seek and adding cheer to the chorus of voices filling the air.

The area chosen for the get-together was dominated by a large, circular limestone structure residing in the center. Ten feet in diameter, the fire pit could hold several large logs and had been a popular spot for the hotel guests to enjoy a crackling blaze on cool, desert nights. Surrounded by a limestone retaining wall, the open area was perfect for weddings, class reunions, and now, town meetings.

Stacks of folded chairs leaned against a nearby wall - first come, first serve. Pete had arrived early, only to find Betty unfolding the heavy chairs in an effort to be the polite host. Pete had chided her, "Betty, let these folks set up their own chairs. This is a town meeting, not a shindig being thrown by the hotel."

"I always want everyone to feel welcome here. I think stability is important during these times."

Pete nodded his understanding and gently removed the folded seat from her grasp. "I get it Betty, but it won't help anyone if you wear yourself out or get sick. Everyone can grab a chair, you've done enough already."

Betty reluctantly agreed, choosing instead to greet everyone at the door with a warm welcome and apologizing about not setting up the chairs.

As Pete watched the citizens of Meraton amble into the meeting, the cop inside of him couldn't help but notice most of them carried firearms. It was now such a common sight, he doubted anyone else noticed. *I wonder if the settlers carried their weapons to early town meetings*, he mused.

After a period, Pete determined it was time to start the meeting. He stepped to the center of the group and raised his voice enough to overcome the din. "Everyone! Everyone! I believe we should get started – we have a lot to cover this evening."

The townsfolk eventually settled down and Pete began. "I'm sure most of you have noticed the issues that have cropped up concerning the market and bartering. By any measure, the Meraton market is a success, something we should all be proud of. If we want it to continue as a significant factor in our recovery and raise everyone's standard of living, then we need to make some changes."

Pete's gaze shifted around the gathering, making eye contact with several different citizens before continuing.

"Ladies and gentlemen, we need a currency. Beyond simple trading in the marketplace, the town needs a currency that we can all accept and use as tender. We've all expressed the desire for services. We've all commented on how nice it would be to reopen the school or have dedicated law enforcement. The only way I can figure out how to accomplish all of those things and allow the market to continue to grow is with the implementation of some sort of currency."

Pete noted several heads nodding in agreement. A low murmur coming from the audience carried an approving tone.

"I'm open to suggestions about how we go about doing this. There's probably more than one way. Anyone have any ideas?"

One man from the back spoke up immediately. "Now that the federal government is a bust, we should use gold. It's been used for thousands of years, and the town has all of that loot from those bank robbers stored at Bishop's place. We can ask him to bring it back and divide it up among the townspeople."

Someone else spoke up, "We could print our own. Meraton greenbacks!"

Several people laughed at the comment, and then multiple conversations broke out at once. Pete let the discussions continue for a while, eventually holding up his hands to draw everyone's attention back.

"I think both of those ideas are worthy of consideration. I also have questions about both methods. I don't know of a printing press here in town, and we would need electricity to run it. That might be problematic. As for using the gold, how would we distribute it fairly? And, what would strangers do for currency once they came to town?"

Pete's questions ignited even more breakout conversations among the people. Pete smiled and let the folks go. He drifted over to Betty and whispered in her ear, "This is democracy at work. I love it."

Betty nodded. "It's a difficult problem. I've got an idea though. If I explain it, would you mind telling everyone?"

Pete looked at her and thought for a moment. "Help yourself, Betty. No one appointed me king. I didn't even run for election."

Shyly pressing her skirt to her legs, Betty hesitated. "Oh, I know. But Pete, I'm not a public speaker. Besides, I think you might do a better job presenting my idea."

Pete rolled his eyes and stepped back to the front. "Ladies and gentlemen! Ladies and gentlemen!" Pete commanded in a raised voice. "Betty would like the floor."

Giving Pete a hard look of "I can't believe you just did that," Betty took a few, tenuous steps to the open area in front of the crowd. Her move was so out of character, the group became silent. Betty smiled as she looked around and cleared her throat. "Why don't we just use US currency?" The hotel's manager spread her arms and continued making eye contact with friends and neighbors. Her confidence grew as she continued. "It's already printed and coined. There's enough around town to meet our needs. It would be difficult to counterfeit. I think if everyone agreed to honor the money, it would work just fine."

Pete stepped to her side and spoke, "Now that's a great idea! Anyone have a good reason why we couldn't use the old US tender?"

Someone from the back of the gathering shouted out, "How would we figure out how much stuff was worth? If I bring in a bag of potatoes to sell, how will I know how much to charge?"

The question caused several people to nod their heads, indicating they were curious of how it would all function. Someone else answered, "Same as always, you charge what the market will bear. It may take a bit, but eventually things will establish their own value. For example, I would imagine Pete's liquid goods will fetch quite a price!"

Laughter broke out all around the meeting, causing Pete to look down in embarrassment at the attention. He recovered quickly, raising his hands to settle everyone down. "Even if we decide to go with US currency, we still have the issue of funding projects for the whole town, like the school or a marshal. I hate to use the word, but it seems like we'll need some sort of 'tax.'"

The T-word seemed to generate more side conversations than any other topic so far. Pete had to smile at the reaction, overhearing one man who stated, "Not having to pay taxes was one of the few good things about the breakdown. Guess the party's over."

Another man answered, "Death and taxes buddy ... death and taxes."

Several suggestions came forth from the din, Pete hearing phrases like sales tax, booth fee and monthly dues. It was the foreman from the Beltron ranch that ambled forward and produced a sage piece of cowboy-logic. "It's too much at once, Pete. Decide on some sort of currency first, and then tackle how to fund the town's projects next month. Give everyone a chance to get comfortable with using money again."

Pete nodded at the man. "That's wise advice."

Pete again called for order, and proceeded to float the idea of addressing the issues one at a time. There seemed to be mutual agreement from the folks at the meeting, so he called for a vote on using US currency as the legal tender.

Betty retrieved a piece of paper and made two simple columns: one to vote for the motion, the other against it. The ranch boss monitored the voting as people formed a line to cast their ballots.

The measure passed by unanimous vote.

The significance of the event wasn't lost on the townspeople. They had just held an election of sorts—democracy had been reinstituted in a humble way. Spirits ran high as the group converged around the covered dishes and snacks. Pete couldn't remember the last time everyone was so happy and positive about the future. They had worked as a community on something other than defense. They had pulled together to make things better and taken a step forward.

After the food was consumed and the gardens were cleaned, Pete invited Betty back to the bar for a nightcap. Still excited by the outcome of the gathering, Betty agreed. As the pair strolled down Main Street toward the bar, Betty gazed up at Pete and proclaimed, "I finally feel like I live in a community again, and it's wonderful. For some reason, I don't feel so alone anymore."

Fort Bliss, Texas
December 22, 2015

The major sitting behind the worn, green government desk scowled at Bishop over the pile of paperwork. "Can I help you?"

Bishop waited on the prerequisite "Sir," but the courtesy wasn't extended. "I'd like to speak with General Westfield as soon as possible, please."

Without even a glance at the calendar sitting on the desktop, the man replied curtly. "I'm sorry; the general's unavailable at the moment."

Bishop raised his eyebrows and probed, "And when might the general be available, major? I'll be happy to make an appointment or wait, whichever works best."

After a moment passed, the officer glanced down at the base commander's schedule and flipped a few pages. Looking up at Bishop with a sarcastic grin, he announced, "The general will be available at 14:30 next Friday. Would you like for me to pencil you in for that appointment?"

"Seven days? I hadn't planned on extending my stay here that long, major. I realize the general's a busy man, but that can't be the first opening he has on his schedule."

"That is the first *civilian* opening available. Were this a *military* matter, I could arrange an earlier appointment."

There it is again, thought Bishop. *There's that attitude I keep sensing. This guy has zero reason to be busting my chops.*

Bishop's anger spiked. He inhaled deeply, readying to lambast the officer, but was interrupted by the opening of the door leading to the general's office.

Agent Powell's back appeared in the threshold, closing a conversation with someone inside. The Secret Service agent pivoted and noticed Bishop.

Powell smiled broadly and joked, "Bishop, we've got to stop meeting like this. The troops are beginning to talk."

The joking attitude deflated Bishop's pre-launch tirade, no doubt saving the major from a serious verbal assault. Before he could respond to Powell's humor, General Westfield's voice boomed from within the office. "Did I hear someone say that Bishop's here?" The base commander's face appeared over the agent's shoulder.

The general waved Bishop in. "Well don't just stand out there bullshitting with my staff. They've got work to do. Come on in."

With a clearly satisfied look on his face, Bishop peered down at the major, who obviously wasn't happy with the situation. Passing by the officer's desk, Bishop pretended to scratch his face using only his middle finger, indiscreetly flipping the man an obscene gesture.

General Westfield offered his hand and then motioned for Bishop to take a seat. "How's Terri doing?"

"She's well, sir. She wanted me to express our gratitude for offering the use of the base's medical facilities. The staff is excellent, sir, real professionals."

The general nodded acceptance of the feedback.

Bishop got right to the point. "Sir, I'm here to let you know I've reached a decision regarding your offer to reinstate me as an officer in the US Army. While I sincerely appreciate the opportunity, Terri and I have decided to decline the invitation."

To Bishop's surprise, the commander's face looked like a man just given a reprieve. The general clasped his hands on the desk and responded, "Young man, I fully understand your decision. Quite frankly, given how our situation is evolving, I think it's a wise choice. I won't mince words here; I'm relieved you didn't take me up on the offer."

Bishop tilted his head slightly to the side, experiencing his second surprise of the day. "Sir?"

"I made that offer thinking purely of the country and the hardship we have ahead of us. You must understand, Bishop, it's my job to order people to sacrifice … sometimes sacrifice their lives. Since I made that offer, I've been shocked at the reaction from my command these last few days. My troops aren't responding to the president's death, the coup attempt, and the civil war like my officers predicted they would. That's what Agent Powell and I were just discussing. There needs to be resolution to this situation, and it needs to happen yesterday. The entire thing is teetering on the edge of anarchy."

Bishop could relate to the problem. *I've been in a funk myself, and I know what went down. It's no wonder the average, uniformed soldier is having issues.*

Bishop responded, "Sir, I'm no doubt a distraction here. With your leave, General, I'd like to return home as soon as possible and get on with life."

Westfield smiled, "Of course, son. You're not a prisoner here. I'll arrange transport in the next few days. Have you been by to see the colonel yet?"

"Yes, sir. It was uplifting to see him doing so well."

"I've known that man for over 30 years. He's too stubborn to die because of something as mundane as a plane crash. I believe he'll be joining my command as soon as his health permits. I'm looking forward to his contribution."

Bishop had to agree. "I'm sure he'll make an excellent addition to your staff, sir."

The general stood and offered Bishop his hand. The grasp was genuine and friendly.

Bishop stopped as he reached for the door. He turned and announced, "Sir, if you ever need me . . . I mean *really* need me . . . you know I couldn't deny my country."

The base commander nodded. "I know that, Bishop. Go and take care of your family. I'll keep your offer in mind. Hell, if things keep sliding downhill, I might show up at *your* door asking for shelter."

"You're always welcome, sir."

With that, Bishop opened the office door, only to hear the major say, "He should be leaving here shortly," to someone on the phone. Before Bishop could make it through the threshold, he heard the phone land in the cradle. *That certainly was a noticeably abrupt end to a phone call*, Bishop thought.

Without glancing at his nemesis in the reception area, Bishop made a beeline for the door. Behind him, the general's voice rang out, "Major, a moment please."

Bishop continued moving toward the door, noticing the junior officer jump up from his desk and rush into the general's office. Glancing around, Bishop looked at a pegboard on the wall behind the major's desk. The initials "VOQ," or visiting officers' quarters, were printed across the top of the panel. Below the label were neat rows of small hooks, each numbered, and many with keys.

He and Terri had been assigned #11, and Bishop quickly inventoried the room numbers that were unoccupied. The room across the hall, #12, still had keys dangling on the hook. Without thinking, Bishop threw a fast glance at the general's door, took three quick steps, and dropped those keys in his pocket.

~  ~

Bishop was feeling a little guilty about taking the keys as he maneuvered through the passages of the HQ building. Powell's voice sounding from a darkened doorway made him jump.

"Hey, Bishop, I wanted a quick word."

Bishop threw a puzzled look at the Secret Service agent, exclaiming, "You scared the crap out of me!"

"Sorry, didn't mean to startle you," Powell said, his voice thick with sarcasm.

Bishop didn't buy it for a second, but wanted to get back to Terri. "Go on."

Powell looked down, suddenly finding his feet

interesting. He extended his hand and said, "Bishop, I'm sorry about this morning. I wanted to apologize. I wish you and Terri the very best. After the world gets back to normal, send me a picture of the kid. Would ya? I sure as hell hope that baby looks like its mother."

Bishop shook the man's hand, "Thank you and good luck to you, sir. I've got a feeling you're going to have your hands full for a while."

Powell watched Bishop walk away. Thinking out loud, he whispered under his breath, "You have no idea how busy I'm going to be, Bishop. No idea whatsoever."

As he strode back to the VOQ, Bishop noticed a pickup truck parked nearby. The vehicle was one of the small models used all over the base, not uncommon at all. As he walked down the steps of the base's headquarters, he heard a motor start.

Chancing a glance over his shoulder, he sensed something was different. *The truck had moved - hadn't it?* A vivid imagination might conclude the vehicle was following him.

What is wrong with you, he thought. *You're really getting spooked by all of this.*

Bishop became determined to disprove his suspicions and detoured to a different route. The truck seemed to follow. A burning curiosity began dominating his thoughts. *Who's in the truck? Why are they following me?*

Now determined to confront the situation head on, Bishop executed a couple of quick turns and then hid behind a dumpster. The truck pulled to the curb and idled, still too far away for him to see who was inside.

"To hell with this," Bishop mumbled to himself. He rose up from behind the metal trash container and stepped purposefully toward the pickup.

Whoever was inside evidently didn't want to speak with Bishop. The truck sped away before he had traveled 15 steps, before he could make out any of the occupants' features.

Shreveport, Louisiana
December 22, 2015

Colonel Marcus stood at attention, his shoulders squared and spine taunt. Two lines of soldiers mimicked the colonel's stance while the American flag was raised, the assembly surrounded by scores of well-wishers, friends and the curious. Everyone relaxed a bit as soon as Old Glory reached her home atop the flagpole.

There was a pause while the honor guard marched off, their important function now fulfilled. While he waited, Marcus' gaze scanned the area, a swelling sense of irony filling his thoughts. The flagpole resided in front of a rural Louisiana middle school that had been converted to an armed camp and headquarters for his military operations. The exhausted officer couldn't help but think about the building's original intent. *This place was once used to educate young minds*, he thought. *That was a higher purpose. We need to return it to that function.*

The throng's attention diverted to a makeshift stage adorned with the podium borrowed from the school. Today, his command's new flag would be officially unfurled, and several men who participated in the Battle of Scott's Hill would be awarded honors.

The colonel's overall command had a new designation, bestowed upon it by the ruling council of the Independents. The organizational change was necessitated due to the hodgepodge of assorted units being woven into an entirely new army. Every conceivable size of element imaginable had joined the cause over time. Platoons, rifle squads and even a few full brigades had sworn their allegiance and now needed to be integrated into a functional fighting force. Restructuring and deploying these assets had been a monumental task that had resulted in endless hours of staff meetings, written orders and overall confusion. Marcus hadn't slept more than a few hours per day in over two weeks.

The newly designated ICOMS, or "Independents Command – South," was comprised of over 60,000 men and hundreds of war machines. The original intent had been to occupy the southern section of the Mississippi River Delta and use the region's resources as a base to rebuild society.

A funny thing happened on the way to the recovery, thought Marcus. Both the federal government and the Independents had the same idea. Both had sent sizable military forces to implement said plan, and those armies had collided at a place named Scott's Hill. The carnage had been atrocious, with two full brigade combat teams - over 10,000 men - mauling each other over a worthless piece of rural Louisiana real estate. The butchery had resulted in over 8,000 dead and wounded as well as a tactical stalemate.

A small cluster of VIPs from the Independent's leadership council began their introductions, and a few brief speeches continued the ceremony. With only one exception,

Marcus cared for none of it. *The only worthwhile part of this entire shindig is awarding my men their medals*, he thought. *Medals they earned in battle. The rest of this shit is just pomp and circumstance, and we've got more important things to accomplish.*

The commander was impatient for many reasons, not the least of which was the fact that 70,000 hostile soldiers, still loyal to the old regime, were less than 20 miles from the spot where he stood. Both sides continued to build combat power in the region – both sides expected to receive orders at any moment to reengage.

Slaughter, thought Marcus, *such a defining word*. All up and down the mighty river, similar lines were being drawn between the old government and the new. If another clash ever occurred again, slaughter was the term that would be used to describe the results for the next 200 years.

The combat power of the United States Army had been refined and improved since the beginning of the Cold War with the old Soviet Union. American military planners always assumed that US units would be severely outnumbered in any major conflict. The political environment didn't allow for anything but a volunteer force after Vietnam, so the generals couldn't count on raising an army of equal manpower in a short amount of time. That left one workable alternative – fewer troops capable of projecting more violence per man than any other army on the planet. Technology was the key, and that was a nice fit since America was the global leader in electronics, engineering and software. Defense contractors and politicians were more than happy to get on the bandwagon.

Even the common foot soldier benefited from the resulting investments. A modern infantryman projected more combat power for longer periods of time than his predecessors. A current-day rifle squad, on paper, could easily overwhelm a unit twice its size from WWII. The weapons, gear, body armor, ammunition and optics had all been enhanced. The same could be said of the heavy weapons, such as tanks and artillery.

The Pentagon had never imagined that any force, equal in both size and capability, would tangle with a US unit. The skirmish at Scott's Hill had involved just that scenario, and when it was over, the devastation was shocking. *Now we're getting ready to do it again*, thought Marcus, *only on a scale 50 times larger.*

Marcus heard his name from the podium and refocused his mind back on the speaker. Everyone was looking at him, and he cursed his lack of attention, feeling like a schoolboy who had been caught daydreaming at his desk. Given the expressions of those around him, Marcus realized he'd been called to the front of the formation.

Stepping briskly to the stage, Marcus stopped and saluted the speaker, showing respect to the retired four-star general. The senior officer returned the salute and then offered his hand while whispering, "Sorry to surprise you like this Owen, but the word just came down from the leadership a short time ago."

Colonel Marcus flashed a look of puzzlement at the general and then stood by as the older man returned to speak to the crowd.

"Attention to orders! From Headquarters, the Leadership Council of the Independents has reposed special trust and confidence in the patriotism, valor, fidelity and abilities of Colonel Owen Marcus. In view of these qualities and his demonstrated potential for increased responsibility, Colonel Owen Marcus is hereby promoted to Brigadier General of the Army with a date of rank of December 22, 2015."

Marcus was flabbergasted, forcing himself to keep his expression neutral.

The speaker turned to Marcus and pulled a small box from his pocket. "These were mine, Marcus. President Regan pinned them on me personally. I would be honored if you would wear them."

Marcus was stunned, unsure of what to say. After clearing his throat, he managed a weak, "Of course I would be proud to wear them, General."

Nodding and winking, the older officer removed Marcus's eagles and pinned a solitary star on each shoulder board, and then executed a salute.

Returning to the speaker's podium, the presenter then announced what everyone already knew. "Furthermore, General Marcus is hereby assigned command of the newly formed Army of the Independents – South."

From the side of the stage area, a stern-looking Sergeant Major ordered, "Teeeennnnnnnn hut!"

All of the attending military personnel snapped to attention while General Marcus was presented with the unit's colors, which were promptly uncased and raised beneath the American flag.

It required another hour to award each of the assembled soldiers the various medals they had earned. The ceremony officially ended with the singing of The Star Spangled Banner, the lyrics more poignant than ever. Small clusters of proud men formed, congratulating each other and mingling with friends who had attended the event.

Eventually, Marcus and the other VIPs from the council formed their own small group. "General, I'm sure the council is aware of this," Marcus explained, "but I'm very concerned about how long this ceasefire will hold, sir."

"Owen, let me assure you that everyone on the council is cognizant of how delicate this situation has become. No one wants to see additional bloodshed, but the other side is without leadership at the moment. There's no one to negotiate with."

"Someone's going to make a mistake or get hotheaded, General. It's inevitable. The last battle was started by accident, and it's bound to happen again. There are too many weapons and armed men in too small an area for something not to go wrong."

The older man nodded his understanding, and then added, "Our insiders believe the federal government is close to determining who the next president will be. That individual as well as his political orientation will determine our next course of action."

Marcus nodded, already having realized everything he was being told, but happy to hear it from a trusted source. "Sir, the real issue is the uncertainty. My men don't know what is happening to their families or loved ones back home. On Monday we think we're going to be fighting our cousins and brothers, on Tuesday everyone believes we'll be back to serving as one big, happy family. We saluted an American flag today, sir. We sang the same national anthem. This uncertainty is undermining our morale and making my command less effective."

The general sighed and looked his officer in the eye. "Just continue with what you've been doing, Owen. Prepare your forces for the worst, and hope for the best. There's nothing more anyone can do right now."

West Virginia
December 22, 2015

The view from the floor-to-ceiling windows was something a man never tired of. The rolling West Virginia mountains, trailing off into the distance provided an air of stability, of long-weathered resistance to time and change.

Senator Moreland's thin frame was partially submerged in the cushions of his favorite chair; a steaming cup of afternoon tea sitting nearby was taking second place to the scene he would always cherish. A wonderful aroma drifted past, sure evidence that Wayne was supervising work in the kitchen. The honorable gentleman didn't even have to glance at his watch or the nearby antique grandfather clock to know it was approaching dinnertime.

At the moment, the ridge-top estate was quiet, but these days, that was the exception. Since the location had become the headquarters for the Independents' movement, solitude had been in short supply.

In addition to every spare bedroom and the guesthouse being occupied, several large class-A motor homes resided on the grounds. One member of the management team had commented that Senator Moreland's remote home had been transformed into a state park campground. In addition to the leadership council that included several ex-members of the Joint Chiefs of Staff, Supreme Court and numerous academics, Wayne directed a considerable security force that occupied the area. Moreland shivered, thinking of those hardy souls who spent the majority of their time outside during these winter months. It would take a determined military effort to breach the once private abode.

The long-serving politician hadn't started the Independents as a rebel force. There had been no campaigns of treachery or subversion. His original concept had been to organize an alternative political party and to work within the laws of the land. Then the world had collapsed, terror attacks nudging an already crippled nation over the abyss. Despite martial law and the deployment of military forces, the federal government couldn't control the country.

The Independents had stepped up, more to fill a vacuum of leadership than to seize power. As time went on, the president of the United States had made bad decisions and committed unlawful acts, including launching nuclear weapons against foreign powers without congressional approval. The leaders of the Independents had found themselves with no choice but to try to gain control of the country and initiate change.

Looking back now, Senator Moreland was still unsettled by how quickly lines had been drawn, forces aligned, and a hot civil war had broken out. Thousands of men had died in the initial clashes, and for a while, it appeared as if tens of thousands more would be thrown into the fray.

Someone at Fort Bliss had made an attempt on the president's life. Moreland had been preparing to present the exact same plan to the council - his initial reluctance of considering such a heinous act overridden by the carnage of American soldiers on the battlefield in Louisiana. Before he could convene the small group and put the proposal to a vote, word arrived of an assassination attempt. Someone had beaten him to the punch.

Moreland shook his head, trying to imagine the bedlam at Fort Bliss. Military bases were known for their calm, orderly presence—a strict society of discipline. Bliss would have been chaos.

Whoever had organized the coup attempt had been exceedingly crafty. The few personnel on the base who were loyal to the Independents had been easily recruited—duped by a charlatan into thinking their own organization wanted to eliminate the chief executive. *Such is the weakness of a clandestine union*, thought Moreland. *Imposters are practically impossible to identify.*

The small drips of real information coming out of Bliss that day had been confusing. At first, Moreland believed someone in his chain of command jumped the gun and actually gave the order. It was some time before enough information leaked out to paint a clear picture of what had happened. Even then, the intelligence received indicated that the Commander in Chief had not only survived, but had vanished. Neither side knew where the man was. Some days later, more facts surfaced, and other details slowly drifted in. These included an account of a massive manhunt and a purging of any men at the base suspected of being part of the Independents. The next day, word had arrived that the president had died in some little-known Texas town over 100 miles from Bliss. Little was known of the circumstances that eventually led to his death.

The senator sighed, exasperated by the bloodshed and senseless death. Without anyone in charge, the two armies facing each other would eventually cross swords. His hands were tied—the leadership of the Independents powerless. There wasn't even anyone on the other side to negotiate with—at least, not yet. Even if the two opposing forces held their positions, every moment that passed meant the American people were suffering. That was the worst part—the tens of millions malnourished and ill. They deserved better.

Wayne appeared at his side, clearing his throat to announce his presence. "Senator, my read on your melancholy mood is that a light dinner would best suit your needs. Would some fresh, baked bread and a light soup be agreeable, sir?"

"Wayne, my old friend, yet again, you read me like a book. That would be prefect."

"If you like, Senator, I can set up a table in here. The sun will be setting soon."

"That would be fine, Wayne. And please join me this evening, won't you?"

"Of course, sir, as you wish."

Wayne set up a small dining area for two, including wine, fresh bread, real butter, and an excellent corn chowder. Senator Moreland said grace, and then proceeded to unfold his napkin as his assistant began to cut the bread. The squawk of a walkie-talkie interrupted the meal.

"Wayne."

"Sir, we have an inbound aircraft that is not following procedure."

"A single aircraft?"

"Yes, sir. The bogie is approaching from the southwest on a direct vector. ETA is 12 minutes. Speed indicates it is a rotary unit."

Wayne flashed his boss a look of concern. "Are you expecting anyone this evening, Senator?"

"No, Wayne. I was looking forward to some peace and quiet."

The assistant's vision automatically focused out the large windows, a futile attempt to visualize the oncoming threat. Without his gaze leaving the sky, he held up the radio and instructed, "Scramble five, but do not intercept unless there is a positive identification of a gunship. Let any other type of aircraft land or pass by."

The voice on the other end of the transmission repeated back Wayne's instructions, and then acknowledged the orders.

"Senator," Wayne began, "we should consider moving you to the basement, sir."

"Do you think that necessary?"

"I think it prudent, sir. Necessary is difficult to say." Moreland sipped his soup and then chewed a mouthful of bread. After dabbing his chin with the napkin, he responded. "I'm sure it's nothing, Wayne. While I appreciate your diligence as my head of security, I'm too old to go running to the cellar every time there's a storm cloud in the sky."

"You're probably right, sir. Still, I would appreciate it if you prepared yourself to move that direction quickly."

The senator nodded, enjoying more of the soup.

A few minutes later, Wayne detected armed men taking up positions around the main house. While he couldn't see them, years of military training led him to expect that several more were getting ready in the nearby woods.

A small black speck, complete with blinking lights, appeared in the darkening, gray sky to the southwest. Moving up the valley toward the senator's estate, the single helicopter appeared to be taking the most direct route, the pilot clearly unaware that he was being tracked by two shoulder-fired anti-aircraft missiles of the latest design. Wayne's radio squawked again, "Sir, the aircraft is not, repeat not, a gunship. It appears to be a non-military, government helicopter with 2-4 passengers aboard. From our vantage point, all occupants appear to be wearing civilian clothing."

Wayne looked at his unflappable employer and shrugged. Moreland returned the gesture after his sip of wine.

Almost directly in front of the diners, the craft flared its nose and began a gradual descent onto one of the few flat landing areas available in the hilly terrain.

Before the rotors stopped spinning, two men and a woman, all in business suits and overcoats, departed the craft and began stretching their stiff legs and spines. Their rumpled appearance was what would be expected of tired travelers having just flown quite a distance in the cramped confines of the small helicopter. Wayne looked at his boss and announced, "I'll greet our guests."

Moreland raised his glass of wine in salute.

A few minutes later, Wayne could be heard welcoming the newcomers into the formal living room. Drifts of conversation made it to the senator's ears, but he couldn't discern clearly enough to know what was being said. Before long, Wayne appeared again at his side. "There is a Secret Service agent, a congressman I've never met, and a senior researcher from the Supreme Court. They claim it's urgent and wish to speak with you."

Moreland snickered, "Are they here to arrest me for treason?"

Wayne grunted, "No, as a matter of fact, they act as if they are scared of you."

"Moi?"

"Yes, their behavior was … umm, hard to read. Anyway, I told them you were dining and would join them shortly."

The senator nodded, and after one more bite of bread, he scooted his chair back and longingly threw one last glance at the sunset. *So much for a relaxing evening*, he thought.

On the way to the living room, Moreland noticed five extra security men discreetly entering the residence. He was thankful Wayne wasn't taking any chances with the visitors, but his inner voice told him the concern was unwarranted.

Upon entering the room, all three visitors stood immediately, their demeanor reminding Moreland of how soldiers reacted when a general passed by.

Introductions were made and handshakes exchanged. After everyone was settled, Moreland probed, "You'll forgive my skipping the pleasantries, but I must ask. What could possibly bring all of you on such a long journey to my remote homestead?"

It was the woman from the Supreme Court who responded. "Senator, I'm sure you are aware that the president has fallen. You are no doubt also aware, that several senior members of the executive branch as well as the vice president were killed in the rioting. Others simply resigned their posts. The purpose of our visit is to inform you, sir, that you are next in the line of succession."

Despite his decades of service in the most exclusive governing body in the world, Senator Moreland couldn't keep the look of surprise from crossing his face. Glancing up at Wayne, he managed to muster the words, "Imagine that."

It took over an hour of discussion for the shock to wear off. The West Virginia senator initially thought a mistake had been made, but the visitors were certain of the legal precedents involved. After discussing the constitutional ramifications, the conversation moved on to the process of swearing in a new president.

The visiting congressman said, "Senator … err … Mr. President elect, your predecessor's remains are still at Fort Bliss. There are no surviving family members and very few of the executive staff. A decision needs to be made as to the former chief executive's formal resting place and the necessary arrangements made. Furthermore, there needs to be a proper swearing in by a justice of the Supreme Court. We can arrange to have one flown to wherever the ceremony is to be held."

The Secret Service agent continued, "In addition, sir, I need to provide executive level protection normally afforded to the president of the United States. I will need to deploy my teams as soon as possible."

Moreland held up his hands, a gesture designed to stop the conversation. "Please, everyone, please. I don't mean to seem ungrateful or hesitant, but this is all such an unanticipated surprise. I need some time to digest all of this—to organize my thoughts. Truth be told, Wayne runs the place here, and can easily arrange accommodations. Can we continue this first thing in the morning after I've had some time?"

The three visitors agreed, and after some shuffling of personnel, were shown to rooms in the guesthouse.

Wayne found his employer in the study, sipping a half-full crystal of brandy.

Moreland peered over the edge of the glass and remarked, "Well, this is just a fine how-do-you-do. We accidently start a civil war, thousands of good men die, and all for naught?

In the end, I was going to be the next Commander in Chief anyway."

Wayne smiled at his boss' analysis. "I wish it were that simple, sir. It's regrettable that everyone blames the Independents for the attempt on the president's life. That act has spoiled any possibility of your accepting the presidency."

The senator nodded. "I've been thinking about that. Time has a way of peeling away the layers of deceit from the onion of truth. I didn't order the assassination of the president, and I think time will clear my name."

"Eventually, sir, the truth may come to light. Until then, I can foresee an endless string of legal and political battles raging for years. Even if the culprit who initiated the attempt on the president's life were exposed, your presidency would still be poisoned. Your political opponents would constantly be snapping at your heels and asking difficult questions. Questions like, 'Since you were actively involved in a direct action against the government, did you automatically sacrifice your office as a US senator, and thus, your place in the line of succession?' You must have considered how nagging debates over such formalities could cripple your ability to effectively govern. And in this social and political environment such scrutiny and impending investigations would seriously hamper the recovery of our great nation."

Moreland responded, "You're probably right. There's another issue as well. What about the Independents? Will they view this turn of events as my defecting to the other side? Will the council choose to support my presidency, or would they choose another leader and continue to fight the established government?"

Wayne sighed, "This is a can of worms, sir."

"A barrel full of monkeys, more like."

The assistant retorted, "A minefield, perhaps?"

The senator smiled at his old friend's game of cliché one-upmanship. "All of the above," he closed.

"You're being paranoid, Bishop," was Terri's initial reaction. "We're right here in the middle of an army base. I can't think of anywhere safer."

"Terri, you're probably right, but what will it hurt? I'm sure the general won't notice having to clean another room. We'll spend the night across the hall and leave in the morning. I'll sleep better this way."

Terri shook her head. "Just because some people looked at you funny and the colonel has his conspiracy theories?"

Bishop looked at his wife with a pained expression. "I've got to go with my gut on this one. Again, what will it hurt? It's not like the base has a shortage of rooms right now."

Reluctantly, Terri agreed.

While Terri was preparing for bed, Bishop pulled the multi-tool out of his pack and began working. His first task was to study the doorstop. The spring-like device was screwed into the baseboard, extending just far enough to keep the knob from punching a hole in the wall's plaster.

Terri sauntered out of the bathroom to discover her husband on his hands and knees, grunting and straining. "What are you doing, Bishop?"

"I'm setting up a little alarm system. I'll deactivate it tomorrow before we leave."

Bishop used the pliers on the multi-tool to snip off the end of the doorstop. This provided a tube-like opening where the door would strike when opened. Next, Bishop took a single round from one of his rifle magazines and inserted it in the tube. The snug fit provided would hold the cartridge in place.

Bishop removed a medium-sized wood screw from the back of the nightstand. After verifying the hallway was empty, he carefully marked where the door would meet the base of the cartridge.

The wood screw was torqued into the door precisely on the mark. Finally, using the saw blade, the head of the screw was removed. Bishop filed the metal to a sharp point.

He motioned Terri over to see his handiwork. "If someone busts in through that door, the point of the screw will strike the primer on the cartridge. It will be like a firing pin striking a normally loaded round in any firearm. The entire building will hear the boom."

"What if they don't open the door all the way or gently push it open?"

Bishop shook his head, "The locks on this door will require a fast breach, and that translates into a violent entry. Even if they had a master key for the main lock, there's still the deadbolt and chain to deal with. Defeating those takes time and creates noise – both can be deadly for the intruders. If they're coming in, it will be hard and fast. Besides, if they're breaking in, standard procedure dictates that the door is always pushed open all the way to make sure no one is standing behind it."

Terri, standing with her hands on her hips, still wasn't convinced. "If they're going to be so loud coming in, why do you need the bullet then? Won't we hear them anyway?"

Bishop nodded. "Yes, if we were staying in this room, we'd definitely hear them coming. Since we're going to be across the hall, there's no guarantee. If they have the right equipment, their entry might not be that loud. Besides, the shell exploding will cause them to pause. Not for long, but they will hesitate, thinking someone is shooting at them. That might buy us a little more time."

The couple went about their normal routine for the rest of the evening, finally getting ready for bed around 10 p.m. Terri turned out the lights while Bishop quietly gathered their belongings. After confirming the hall was still clear, they snuck into room #12.

As Bishop secured the door to their new room, Terri started giggling. "What's so funny, Terri?"

"I'm sorry Bishop, but I feel like I'm involved in some sort of college prank here. Switching rooms in the middle of the night, setting up booby traps, and scurrying around like someone is chasing us. It all just seems funny."

After pondering his wife's words for a moment, Bishop had to agree. "Yeah . . . I guess you're right. It probably does seem like getting ready for a snipe hunt or a panty raid."

Terri did her best to sound indignant and whisper at the same time, "And how would you know anything about panty raids, mister?"

Bishop whispered back, "I don't know a damn thing, other than what I've read in books. I was far too studious in college to partake in any such nefarious activities."

"Bullshit."

Terri eventually settled down and went to sleep on the bed. Bishop pulled a chair close to the door and waited, pistol in his hand and rifle leaning against the wall.

Chapter 5

Fort Bliss, Texas
December 23, 2015

It wasn't the booby trap that woke him—something else had disturbed the night. Bishop moved slowly at first, his body complaining about falling asleep in the barely-stuffed, upholstered chair. After cracking a few joints and a good, cat-like stretch, he gingerly shifted toward the peephole and viewed the entrance to their old room. The hallway was empty.

Next, he checked the room's sole window, which provided a wonderful postcard view of the parking lot. Bishop's quick scan through the curtain slit revealed nothing out of the ordinary.

You didn't hear anything. Go back to sleep, he thought.

Bishop stood, vacillating between the torture chair and the inviting soft space next to Terri on the bed. He was scheming about how to get under the covers without waking his wife, when the background hum of the building's furnace suddenly went quiet. Glancing at the alarm clock next to Terri's head, he confirmed the worst case. The big red digital numbers were dark. The building's power was out.

Bishop moved to Terri's side and gently placed his hand on her arm. The drowsy woman jumped just a little and tried to blink the fog out of her eyes. When he was sure she could comprehend, Bishop whispered, "Terri, call the MPs. The electricity just went out—something's going on."

A yawn, followed by a sleepy, "Okay," was her only response.

Bishop whispered, "It could be nothing. Maybe I heard a transformer blow . . . maybe that's what woke me up. I don't like it though." He returned to the peephole, peering out into the hall. The battery-powered emergency lights illuminated the passageway almost as brightly as the normal lighting. The corridor was vacant.

Behind him, Terri set the phone back into its cradle. She whispered, "Bishop, the phone's dead."

"Shit. Not good."

Keeping an eye at the peephole, Bishop could hear Terri rustling around, no doubt getting dressed. He sensed her beside him a few moments later. "What do you see?"

"Nothing—just an empty hall and the door to our old room."

73

"Can I see?"

Bishop started to snap a harsh "No" at his wife, but realized she couldn't help but be curious. He moved away, motioning for her to have a look, knowing it would help them communicate if she could visualize what he was seeing.

Terri let Bishop have his spot back, but remained at his side.

A few moments later, they both heard the sounds of someone sneaking down the corridor. Bishop's eye, glued to the viewer, perceived a dark shadow first, and then two men clearly came into view. He chanced a glance at Terri, held his finger to his lips and then flashed two fingers, pointing at the hallway. *There are two of them outside the door to our old room.*

Both of the men in the hall were dressed in dark clothing and wore masks. *I guess that confirms they're not the cleaning crew*, Bishop thought. One of them kept a vigil, glancing up and down the hall, his pistol pointed in the air. Bishop noted the weapon was equipped with a tube-like device extending from the barrel—a CAN, or noise cancelation device, which would make the small handgun practically silent.

The second man produced a ring of keys and began looking for just the right one.

Clearing the question from his mind, Bishop signaled Terri with two fingers and then pointed to his own pistol. *They both are armed.*

Bishop moved his head to the side for a moment, motioning Terri to have a quick look. When she pulled away from the tiny porthole, her expression flashed a mixture of fear and anger. Quickly returning to watch the men in the hall, Bishop could see a key being inserted into the lock, and then a test of the doorknob—it turned.

The man working on the door shifted to the side, and tapped his partner on the shoulder. Signaling one finger, then two, and finally three, both men bolted into the entrance, flinging the door into Bishop's booby trap. The sharpened screw struck the primer as planned, causing a louder than anticipated discharge. Both attackers froze for just a moment, stared at each other, and then continued their rush into #11.

These guys are pros, thought Bishop. *No one goes into a room like that after hearing a gunshot. That takes balls.*

When the "phfzzt phfzzt phfzzt" sound of gunshots reached Bishop's ears, he reached to open #12's door, and at the same time, he clicked off his pistol's safety. *Those bastards had shot the two lumps of pillows he had left covered in their old bed. Murderers! Cold blooded killers!*

Before he could turn the lock, he felt Terri's grip on his

74

arm. Looking down into his wife's face, he clearly could see her mouth the word, "No."

Bishop ignored her tug, dismissing the protest. Terri held on. She felt his weight shift and sensed the muscles tighten in his arm. She knew Bishop could flick her off without effort, but she held on, determined to stop him from charging into a battle.

Hot, molten rage surged through Bishop's body, his imagination conjuring up images of Terri lying dead in a pool of blood. Those men were trying to kill his wife and unborn child, and he would deal with them. He would put them down—put them down hard.

Terri shifted slightly, trying to wedge herself between Bishop and the door. The move caused Bishop to glance down, and for a moment, Terri didn't recognize the man standing beside her. His eyes were reptilian-like, unblinking, and full of a terrible, cold violence. Bishop wasn't in there anymore—he'd been replaced by something else, something full of fury and death, straining to unleash its wrath.

She tried again, her voice in a hushed, but stern tone, "No, Bishop. Don't go. Stay here with me."

Something about Terri's words cut through the fog of vengeance clouding Bishop's mind. Something about the pleading expression on her face pulled him back, restraining the desire to engage and destroy the evil lurking across the corridor.

Noise from the hallway snapped Bishop's attention back to the peephole. The two assassins were exiting the room now. They paused at the threshold, their body language indicating frustration. One of the men put his hand on his partner's shoulder and pointed at #12.

Terri felt Bishop tense, and then the shadows of the room blurred. Terri sensed weightlessness—her feet dangling in the air—and then the carpet against her cheek. She rolled over, looking up to see Bishop on the balls of his feet, pistol aimed at the door.

They're coming in, thought Bishop. He inhaled, waiting on the sound of a key in the lock, anticipating the door crashing inward. His vision narrowed, finger tightening on the trigger.

The assault never came. After waiting for the breech for what seemed like a lifetime, Bishop cautiously peeked back into the corridor, and found it empty. The partially opened door to #11 was the only visual evidence of the attack.

~  ~

The flashes from the digital camera reminded Bishop of a thunderstorm's lightning as the photographer snapped pictures of the scene in #11. The hallway was filled with military police, nightclothes-clad residents, and soldiers, all milling around and chattering with excitement. Bishop watched absentmindedly as a confused MP struggled to take a statement from a visiting Polish officer, who was staying a few doors down. The detective's frustration with the foreigner's broken English manifested itself when the cop's notepad flipped closed without so much as a single sentence being recorded.

The MP hadn't had much more luck taking Bishop's statement a few minutes prior.

A disturbance appeared at the end of the hall, the sea of onlookers and police officers parting for General Westfield as he barreled his way through. The base commander threw Bishop an annoyed glance and curt nod as he stepped directly into #11 and inquired who was in charge. Bishop couldn't make out any specifics, but the voices drifting across the hall clearly indicated the general was receiving an update.

A few minutes later, Westfield appeared at Bishop's side. "How's your wife, Bishop?"

"She's a little shaken up, but doing fine, sir." Bishop nodded toward the bed in #12, where Terri sat talking in hushed tones to a female MP.

"Bishop, I have a thousand questions for you." The general tilted his head toward the exit, indicating Bishop should follow. The general grunted, when instead of moving immediately, Bishop glanced back at Terri with a concerned look on his face.

"Bishop," the general said softly, "I understand your desire to protect your wife, but I've known that officer sitting with Terri for over two years. Your wife is safe."

Bishop's head snapped toward the general, his voice low and harsh. "You'll pardon me for being a little skeptical of that, *sir*. You'll forgive me for not being 100% convinced that anyone can guarantee her safety right now."

Fire flashed behind the general's eyes, unused to anyone speaking to him with that tone. The anger quickly passed, and the military man's response sounded more fatherly than commanding. "I understand, Bishop, but this will only take a few moments."

With a hesitant shrug of his shoulders, Bishop pivoted to follow the base commander.

Like Moses parting the Red Sea, the crowd in the hallway split for the base commander as he made his way to the front exit. Once outside, he turned to Bishop and questioned,

"Why didn't you tell me you were worried about your safety?"

Bishop stared at his feet. "I don't know, General. I wasn't sure there was anything to investigate, and I didn't want to bother anyone in case my suspicions were unfounded. Even Terri thought I was just being paranoid."

General Westfield didn't buy it. "You weren't sure enough to mention it, yet you steal a key and set up a dangerous booby trap. That doesn't make sense, Bishop."

Bishop began explaining the sequence of events that led to his actions. General Westfield listened intently, interrupting only a few times for clarification. Bishop summed it all up, "So, you see, General, I really didn't have anything to report. I took the precautions mainly because of intuition ... a warning going off inside my head."

Westfield's response surprised Bishop. "I understand. Some of the best men I've ever served with paid attention to that voice inside of their heads. Still, I wish you had come to me. Word of this incident will spread like wildfire across the base. We don't need another distraction right now."

Bishop agreed with the general's assessment.

The sound of more vehicles joining the already crowded parking area drew both men's attention. Out of the sea of headlights and police strobes, Bishop made out two men stepping quickly toward the scene of the crime. It was Agent Powell and one of his men.

The Secret Service man made for Bishop and the general. "What's going on, General? I heard on the radio that there was an attempted ..."

Bishop charged, growling, "You piece of shit! You set us up!"

The attack took Powell by surprise. As Bishop's shoulder slammed into the agent's chest, the angry civilian's palm shot upwards into the shocked man's chin. Powell landed hard and rolled away. Before he could manage to stand, Bishop took one step forward and kicked like a football punter, his boot landing squarely into Powell's midsection. Bishop started circling the panting man like a wolf about to finish the elk.

The other agent drew his pistol, but the action was curtailed by General Westfield. "This isn't a gunfight, young man. I think these two need to work things out."

"You son-of-a-bitch," hissed Bishop. "You don't give a fuck about anything but your precious legacy. You set us up."

"I did no such thing," panted Powell. "You're fucking crazy."

"I'll show ya crazy, federal boy," and Bishop took a step toward his victim.

Powell's leg shot out, catching Bishop above the knee. Before he could recover, the agent swept his leg into Bishop's ankles, causing him to flop and land squarely on his butt.

In less than a second both men were poised in half-bent crouches, slowly circling each other, guardedly watching for an opening. Powell took the offensive, stepping forward and launching three quick rabbit punches at Bishop's face. The blows grazed harmlessly off Bishop's raised forearms, but the action had been a feint. A sweeping roundhouse kick landed squarely in Bishop's stomach, causing the air to whoosh from his lungs and sending him staggering back.

The second agent had seen enough and moved to intercede. Bishop felt what seemed like two steel bands wrap around his chest. Sensing instantly what was happening, Bishop lifted both feet off the ground, the shift in weight causing his captor to lean forward for balance.

When he felt the agent tip forward, Bishop pushed down hard with both legs as if he was trying to jump while tilting his head backwards. The maneuver worked, the back of Bishop's head slamming into the agent's nose and causing him to release the hold.

Powell took advantage of the distraction and was on top of Bishop before the blood had even begun to run out of his partner's broken snout. Powell and Bishop hit the ground rolling, grunting and cursing. Blows sounded from the fray, the dim illumination of the parking lot lights revealing a swirling ball of limbs, fists, and legs.

A gaggle of MPs rushed to the scene and attempted to pull the two men apart. In a few moments, both combatants were on their feet, a military policeman holding each arm and leg. Bishop immediately relaxed, moving his hands into a "don't shoot" position. "I'm done . . . I'm done . . . it's okay guys … really … I'm cool," he announced, smiling.

The two MPs restraining Bishop's arms looked at each other and then loosened their grips, thinking cooler heads were prevailing. Without warning, Bishop's right fist shot out, striking Powell squarely in the jaw and rocking the agent's head backwards. "Bitch," he hissed at Powell as the MPs struggled to control and separate the two surging men.

Westfield stepped between them and shouted, "Enough!"

In a calmer voice, the general continued. "I've let you two blow off some steam, but this ends right now, or I'll have both of you in irons and enjoying a night in my brig."

Powell and Bishop nodded their acceptance of the general's wishes, and with trepidation, the MPs loosened their holds.

Bishop noticed Terri standing nearby, her hands on her hips and a smirk on her face. Glancing over his shoulder to keep an eye on the untrustworthy Powell, Bishop approached his wife.

Terri shook her head, "Assaulted any federal agents lately, my love?"

"He deserved it," Bishop replied, wiping the blood from his lip on a shirtsleeve.

"We can talk about *that* later. Right now, let's get inside so I can look you over."

"I'm fine," Bishop claimed, spitting a mouthful of blood into the grass and eyeing Powell again.

"Uh huh. Come on, Bishop. Let's get in the light."

Hooking her husband by the arm, Terri pulled Bishop back into room #12.

Thirty minutes later, Westfield, a bandaged Powell, and two burly MPs entered #12. They found Bishop perched on the bed, supervising as Terri repacked his blowout bag. Two butterfly bandages and a greasy antibiotic crème accented Bishop's scowl as he looked up.

The base commander wasted no time. "Gentlemen, we need to talk this out. Bishop, you think Powell did something to cause the attempt on your life tonight, but frankly I don't think he had anything to do with it."

"Seems like one hell of a coincidence, sir. Agent Powell approached me about using Terri as bait just this afternoon, and a few hours later, someone busts into our room and starts shooting. One hell of a parallel, if you ask me, sir."

Powell looked at both Bishop and Terri and defended himself. "Yes, I did suggest that in a moment of desperation, but I didn't act upon it. You were right, Bishop. It was a stupid idea."

Bishop shook his head in disgust, "I'm not buying it. No way. You can't really expect me to believe a couple of rogue men loyal to the Independents took it upon themselves to come after us. Why would they do that? The president's dead."

Powell spread his hands in exasperation. "Bishop, there could be a dozen reasons why someone tried to kill you guys. I'm telling you straight up, I didn't do anything after we talked."

Terri interrupted, "Why are you guys saying the Independents tried to kill the president? He told me they had nothing to do with it."

Every head in the room snapped in Terri's direction, Powell and Bishop both uttering "What?" at the same time.

"The president told me while we were walking. He told me he knew who tried to kill him, and that it wasn't the Independents."

Westfield took a step toward Terri, the woman clearly confused over why everyone was staring at her. "Terri," the general said, "this is very important. What exactly did the president say to you?"

The intensity of everyone's reaction made Terri uncomfortable, and she moved to Bishop's side, reaching for his hand. "We were walking . . . the president and I were walking through Alpha right before he was shot. I asked him if there were going to be a civil war, and he said no. He went on to say that he was going to reach out to the Independents like Bishop and the colonel had suggested before things got worse."

Terri glanced around the room, realizing everyone was hanging on her next statement. "I told the president that he was a bigger human being than I was. I said if someone tried to kill me, I wouldn't be so forgiving. He smiled at me and told me the Independents hadn't tried to kill him, but he knew who was behind the attempt. He said he would bring them to justice in due course. Those were his exact words."

"Holy shit," grunted Powell, and turned away.

Terri looked at Bishop with pleading eyes. "I don't understand. Bishop, did I do something wrong?"

Bishop patted Terri's hand. "No, baby. No, you didn't do anything wrong. It's okay."

Westfield's voice became gentle, "Terri, now this next part is critical. Did the president say who had tried to kill him?"

Thinking for a moment, Terri responded shyly. "No, no he didn't. That man popped up right then and began shooting."

"I wish we had known this before now," grumbled Powell. "Why didn't you testify to this in your deposition, Terri?"

Bishop coiled at Powell's tone, his weight shifting to the edge of the bed. The two MPs moved half a step forward, ready to intervene. Westfield raised his hands and his voice, "At *EASE*, gentlemen. You two had better execute a major testosterone dump right-fucking-now, or we'll continue this little powwow down at the brig with both of your combative asses in separate cells."

Bishop relaxed and returned to his original posture, never taking his eyes off Powell.

Terri broke the uneasy silence, "Agent Powell, no one asked me that question in the deposition. I was exhausted, worried about Bishop, and ravenous. How was I supposed to know about the politics of the times? It isn't exactly like we get cable news updates out at the ranch. I didn't think it was important."

"You didn't think it was important," exploded Powell. "The president of the United States was killed, and you didn't think it was important?"

Bishop half stood, clearly his intent to reengage with Powell. Terri hooked his arm and pulled back while Westfield moved between the two men. The general decided to defuse the situation. "Agent Powell, could I have a word with you in the hallway, please?"

Powell, Westfield and the two MPs left the room, closing the door behind them. "Would you cool your jets, Agent Powell?" Westfield began. "That's a pregnant civilian in that room, not a terrorist suspect. I know you need answers and so do I, but we're not going to get anywhere if you keep up with this attitude."

Powell sighed, rubbing his red and swollen jaw. "You're right, General. I'm just so pissed because I knew there had to be someone who knew something more, and Bishop has been uncooperative. I let my friendship with him get in the way of my investigation and my primary duty to protect the president."

The base commander nodded his understanding and responded, "You catch more flies with honey than vinegar, young man. Now, let's go back in there and see if we can calmly get to the bottom of this."

Westfield nodded to the MP, who then opened the door. Westfield barreled in, only to find the room was empty. Bishop, Terri, and their gear had disappeared. A slight disturbance in the air made the curtains move. Westfield rushed to the open window.

Quickly joined by Powell, the two men stood looking at the cluster of vehicles in the otherwise empty parking lot. There was no sign of the escapees.

Powell turned to the general saying, "General, I'll alert my men to help with the search."

Westfield grunted and looked at Powell, "Do you really think we're going to find them? Think about that for a moment, Agent Powell."

Powell started to protest, but the general waved him off. "He'll be in the desert in 15 minutes. That's his turf, if you'll recall. Even if we did find them, what then? Do you really want to risk a firefight with your prime new witness in the middle of the night? Hasn't the Secret Service already taken one black eye today?"

"We can't just let them go, sir."

"Oh yes we can, Agent Powell. We most certainly can. I've used enough body bags this week already, and chasing that man through the desert would only produce the need for more.

Let things cool off for a bit. We will find them later."

Terri glanced out the rear glass of the MP pickup truck. "Are you sure this is a good idea, Bishop?"

Keeping his eyes focused on the road ahead, Bishop shifted gears and responded. "Terri, we had to get out of there. This entire situation is a boiling cauldron of bullshit, and I can't keep the players straight. Someone wants to kill us, and he's still on the loose. I want to believe Powell's innocent in all this, but now I doubt everything and everybody."

Convinced they weren't being pursued, Terri turned to face the front. "I gotta hand it to ya, Bishop; a girl sure doesn't get bored around you. An attempted homicide, assault of a federal officer, and grand theft auto, all in one night. Do you have any more surprises in store for this old, pregnant lady this evening? I'm about at capacity for one day."

Bishop grunted and retorted, "Oh, damn. I forgot our theatre tickets back at the room. My bad, honey."

Terri giggled and then looked around, "Where might we be going?"

"I'm going to drive to the edge of the base, and then we'll be in open desert. I'll leave the truck there."

"Oh, now wait just a minute . . . I'm not walking home through the desert, Bishop. I'm four months pregnant, and my ankles swell really, really easy."

"No worries. I've got a plan . . . I think."

"You *think* you've got a plan? That's not incredibly reassuring right at this moment."

"When I came to the base the first time to deliver the colonel's message to the president, I left some transportation nearby. I'm hoping it's still there."

"And where might you have gotten this *transportation*?"

Bishop glanced over, a sheepish expression on his face. "I borrowed it from a police officer."

"Borrowed?" Terri shook her head in pretend disgust. "Bishop, I had no idea you were a car thief when we met. What else are you hiding from me?"

"Well," Bishop hesitated, "there were those chocolate bars . . . but . . . but that wasn't any big deal."

"Chocolate! You had chocolate, and I didn't get any? Come on young man . . . fess up . . . out with it."

Before Bishop could answer, the pavement ended, and

the truck's headlights showed a sandy path leading off into the darkness of the desert. Stopping, Bishop stared at the compass built into his watch and thought about the direction for a moment.

"We're still headed the right way. I'll keep driving until this lane ends. Hopefully this path will get us close to where I hid our ride home."

The small truck wasn't designed for off-road travel and became stuck less than a mile later. After rocking the pickup back and forth in the loose sand, Bishop determined they were just digging themselves in deeper. "End of the road," he announced.

Switching off the ignition, Bishop looked at Terri and said, "Stay here with your rifle. If you see anyone approaching, head off into the desert that direction and hide. I'm going to go find our transportation and bring it back here. I'll need to transfer gas to our new ride."

"How long will you be gone?"

Bishop took the night vision from his vest and climbed to the top of the cab. Using the mountaintops and the base's lights behind them, it took a few moments to get his bearings. He lowered the device and said, "I think we're about a mile away from where I hid the ATV. It has a single headlight, so if you see one light coming across the desert from that direction, it's me."

"Okay, Bishop. Please hurry. I don't like scorpions."

"Terri, compared to the predators back at the base, I will take my chances with the scorpions."

Bishop put on his pack and double-checked his gear. Leaning to give Terri a kiss, he said, "Be right back," and trotted off into the desert night.

Terri took her rifle and climbed into the bed of the truck, taking a seat on the roof of the cab. The desert night was silent, the star field intense. The environment was peaceful, and she realized that despite being alone, she was more at ease here than back at the base. The M4 rifle across her lap helped, but there was something about the tranquility of the night that made her feel warm inside. She wished it would last, but knew that wasn't their lot in life. "Here we go again," she sighed.

~  ~

Bishop found the overlook where he'd spied on the new subdivision on his way to Fort Bliss. The odor drifting off the piles of trash helped to guide him. While the scenery looked remarkably different at night, it took only 15 minutes to find the

ATV. Judging from the layer of dust on the seat, the machine hadn't been disturbed.

He had hidden the keys on a nearby rock ledge, and they too were right where he'd left them. The machine started immediately, and he began the short trip back to Terri and the truck.

Feeling relief over his luck holding so far, Bishop was back with his wife after only a brief, 40-minute absence. Terri circled the ATV, skepticism creeping into her voice. "We're both going to ride on that with both of our packs, two rifles and a baby?"

"It's going to be comfy close, that's for sure."

"Did you shower today?"

"Funny—I was getting ready to ask you the same thing."

Bishop encountered his first problem with the escape when it became clear that he didn't have a gas can, hose or any other method to transfer gasoline from the truck to the ATV. The issue was made worse by the fact that the truck was stuck in the sand, and he couldn't reach the gas tank. Spiking the tank was out of the question without a few hours of digging.

"Shit. Pop the hood, would you please?"

Terri opened the driver's door and found the handle. Bishop lifted and propped the small truck's hood with the support rod, and then used a flashlight from his vest to look around. Terri joined him, curious as to what he was up to.

Finding a siphoning hose was easy. Bishop chose the one that fed the windshield wiper fluid to the pump because of its small diameter and length. Most newer cars and trucks had anti-siphoning devices in their tanks, and it took a small hose to snake around them. Unhooking the hose gave him another idea, and he used his multi-tool to remove the tank holding the cleaner. He judged it to be about 1.5 gallons—small, but it would have to do.

It took a few tries, and just a bit of gas in his mouth, but the ATV began receiving a transfer of fuel a short time later. After dumping the wiper fluid from the container and plugging the exit port with a stripe of plastic from the front seat, Bishop filled the extra tank to the brim.

It took three attempts at arranging Terri, their gear, and himself onto the ATV. The small storage compartment on the 4-wheeler contained a few bungee cords, and Bishop used these to secure his pack and the extra gas tank.

"Here we go," he turned and said to his wife. "I can't wait to show you my new favorite swimming hole."

"We get to go swimming on this vacation, daddy?"

"Sure we do."

As the ATV slowly rolled away from the pickup, Terri tapped Bishop on the shoulder. "Are we there, yet?"

Bishop laughed at the classic query.

A minute later, Terri tapped him again. "Are we there, yet?"

"Bishop, I'm freezing."

"You're right, it's getting cold. Let's find a place to hole up for the night."

By Bishop's estimate, they had traveled over 30 miles toward home and were making good progress along I-10 heading east. Without the warming rays of the sun, the late-year desert air became cold at night. Traveling via an open vehicle felt like they were riding through a deep freeze. They were cold, hungry, and tired.

Scanning with his night vision, Bishop checked the horizon for some sort of shelter. This stretch of the great interstate was barren of population and exits, the last sign indicating it was 11 miles to the next off-ramp.

That was actually good news, as Bishop was giving any interchange a wide birth to avoid the potential of encountering people. Circumventing these intersections took time, but he felt the extra miles worth the effort, given their experience.

Flat desert appeared in the green and black image of the monocle, featureless earth for as far as the device could ascertain shape and form. Off at a great distance were mountain ranges in practically every direction, but not here.

Bishop had been raised in West Texas, and he knew there was a strong chance that the picture in the scope was misleading. Wind and water erosion were powerful forces of nature, and rarely did any large section of land escape their influence. What appeared to be flat earth most likely hid gullies, streambeds, and other good hiding places. The problem was finding such geography.

"What I wouldn't give for a good outcropping of solid rock," he noted.

Terri glanced up at the clear sky and said, "Are you worried about rain?"

Bishop grunted, "No. I'm worried about helicopters looking for car thieves and people who assault federal officers. Even their most sophisticated equipment can't see through solid rock."

Continuing along I-10, they ate up another mile when Bishop slowed, handing Terri the scope and pointing toward a slight undulation in the desert floor. "That low area you see is drainage for the elevated land to our south. That might be what we're looking for."

"Do you mean a creek?"

"Not really. It does rain here now and then. The soil is packed so hard, the water isn't absorbed like you'd think. A lot of it runs off. If my guess is right, the engineers who built the interstate had to compensate for that. We'll know if I'm right in the next half mile."

"Bishop, I can't see any difference or feature. I'm not sure what you're talking about."

Bishop kept scanning the area, and after telling Terri to "hang on," he steered the ATV off the smooth pavement and out into the open terrain. After a few minutes, he pointed back toward the interstate. "There," he stated, and pointed the ATV back toward the big road.

The gaping mouth of a square concrete drainage pipe came into view as they rolled closer to the highway. The opening appeared to be about four feet wide on each side and was partially obscured by small piles of brush and dried wood that had been deposited by the run-off of the last rain.

Bishop stopped the ATV a short distance from the opening and chanced turning on the headlights. The bright beams illuminated the tunnel running all the way under both the east and west bound lanes of I-10. The concrete floor was remarkably clean and smooth.

"Your luxury suite awaits, my lady."

"Do they leave chocolates on the pillow here?"

Dismounting their gasoline-powered steed, the couple stretched their stiff legs and sore butts. Bishop turned and commented, "We'll have to do this just right. I think we build the fire deeper in the tunnel. Then we set up someplace to sleep, and finally pull the ATV to close off the entrance.

"So we have a fireplace, bedroom and garage all in one? Sounds like a master planned community."

Bishop used his flashlight to gather scraps of dried wood and other burnable debris from the entrance. There wasn't enough fuel for a big fire, but Bishop didn't want a roaring blaze inside the small area anyway because there wasn't a chimney, and the smoke might be an issue.

The shelter was a little difficult to navigate because of its height. Bending at the waist and carrying bundles of wood worked well, but twice he stood without thinking, and cracked his head on the roof.

Before long, a small fire was burning, its warm glow coloring the walls of the structure a calming yellow and red hue. The extremely dry wood didn't make much smoke but also burned quickly. Bishop estimated they had perhaps an hour's worth of fuel.

Terri was spreading the survival nets on the floor to provide some insulation from the cold cement beneath when she noticed Bishop carrying in a handful of rocks and creating a border around the fire. Puzzled, she asked, "Are you worried the flames are going to spread?"

"No. I want to heat these rocks. It's going to get cold in here tonight, and the fire won't last long. The rocks will retain heat and we can move them closer to our bed."

Terri unpacked some of the food, and began to think about what she wanted to eat while Bishop filled the ATV's tank from their makeshift fuel can. He appeared with his rifle at her side and announced, "I'm going to go walk around a little bit and make sure we aren't overly visible. I'll sleep better tonight knowing we're not broadcasting our whereabouts."

"Okay. I'll have something for us to eat by the time you get back."

Bishop propped Terri's rifle against the side of the tunnel and made sure she had her pistol—just in case. He moved off into the desert using the night vision and began to scout the area. His primary concern wasn't other humans in close proximity, but rather how visible their campsite was to anyone who may pass by in the night. Moving off at right angles to the opening of the artificial cavern, he found the glow of the fire almost undetectable after a few hundred meters.

Satisfied with the light discipline and the lack of inhabitants nearby, Bishop's only real security concern was the smell of smoke drifting over the area. Anyone walking or driving down I-10 in the night would probably detect their fire immediately. There really wasn't much he could do about that and decided it was an acceptable risk for Terri to have a good night's rest.

While Bishop walked through the desert, Terri set about preparing their meal. The army surplus pan and aluminum utensils were perfect to sit over the fire supported by two rocks. Before long, the aroma of MRE meatloaf and gravy replaced the smell of moist concrete that dominated the tunnel.

Bishop returned and announced his satisfaction with their location. The couple sat and consumed their dinner in silence, both enjoying the crackle of the fire and the absence of the ATV's constantly droning motor.

Terri took the soiled pan and utensils outside to clean

while Bishop rearranged the hot rocks around their bedroll. Terri used handfuls of fine sand to scrub the food from the pan before applying a little water and rinsing off the remaining grains. In the morning, she would boil Bishop some coffee water, completing the sanitization.

Bishop joined her outside, and they both brushed their teeth - the lack of toothpaste hardly noticed, the ritual important for both physical and mental well-being. After they were done, he pushed the ATV into the entrance of the cave and climbed over the cooling machine.

Watching Terri brush her hair in the fading light of the fire warmed Bishop's soul. Despite being covered in road dust and lacking any makeup or other frills, Terri had never appeared more beautiful to him than at that moment.

"What are you staring at, young man?"

Bishop smiled and said, "Darling, despite all we've been through, you could still stop a clock. It never ceases to amaze me how I ended up with such a pretty girl."

Terri swatted playfully at her mate, embarrassed at the attention. "You're just hoping to get into my pants. I'm too tired and feeling grungy, so save your energy, stud."

Bishop pulled her close, gently kissing her forehead and caressing her hair. "Good night, beautiful lady."

Chapter 6

West Virginia
December 23, 2015

The following morning, as Wayne consumed his breakfast, the senator joined him in the kitchen. "Good morning, Mr. President."

"Now don't you start."

Wayne handed his boss a steaming cup of coffee, complete with fresh milk bartered from a farmer down the road. "I kind of like the sound of it . . . Mr. President."

"I'm glad you do, but I'm not so sure about the committee. We started the Independents for a lot of good reasons. A lot of people took extreme risks for our movement; some even gave their lives. I'm afraid my joining the other side might cause trouble."

Wayne seemed relieved. "Yes, sir. You're probably right to be concerned. There's only one way to know how everyone is going to react—tell them."

Moreland considered Wayne's logic for a moment while sipping his java. "I need to stall our visitors for a bit. Play along, would you?"

The longtime assistant and friend grunted, "Of course I will. Did you really feel like you had to say that?"

The ever-present radio on Wayne's belt squawked, "The visitors are on their way from the guesthouse."

"I need to finish supervising security, sir. As usual, I'll leave the politics up to you."

The legislator from West Virginia, the President pro tempore of the United States Senate, sat at the head of the large dining room table. Small talk had dominated the conversation to this point—concerns about the recovery of the country, the civil war, and the future of mankind in general.

As the group pushed their plates away, Moreland cleared his throat and announced, "I need some time to make a decision regarding accepting such an important position. I hardly slept last night, excited at the prospect of taking the reins and leading our great country out of this mess. On the other hand, I'm not a young man anymore, and the job is daunting. I may not be

89

the best candidate. I will give my decision in 48 hours."

The guests began to protest, clearly confused by the senator's words. Moreland held up his hands to restore calm. "Please, you landed on my front lawn just a few hours ago and dropped the biggest bombshell anyone could ever imagine. I need just a few hours to gather my wits and make the proper decision."

Moreland's tone indicated he wasn't going to be persuaded otherwise, so the conversation moved on to how the senator could contact Washington with his verdict. A satellite phone was left with Wayne, the only reliable form of communication known to the visitors.

The Secret Service agent presented the next challenge. He desperately wanted to provide the president pro tem with protection. It took Wayne several minutes to convince the man that Senator Moreland couldn't be any safer. Wayne's radio call, summoning several heavily armed men, did the trick.

After handshakes were exchanged, the trio boarded their aircraft and proceeded back to Washington.

Moreland looked at the satellite phone left behind and grunted. The device was so primitive compared to the system used by the Independents. That thought quickly led to a mental comparison between the antiquated government and the goals his movement wanted to accomplish. It was the old versus the new at more levels than he wanted to comprehend at the moment. He forced himself to focus on how he could best help the American people. If he didn't accept the presidency, the Independents would most likely carry the day. The other side would be leaderless for some period, and his cause could move quickly to assume control.

An opposite reaction could occur as well. If he didn't accept the position, Washington would find someone else, and who knew what their philosophy would be?

Moreland looked at Wayne, "If I become the Commander in Chief, I have to find a way to bridge the two sides. I'll have to do a lot of fence mending on both fronts."

Wayne stared at the wall, clearly trying to see several steps ahead. "Sir, I'm going to solicit that you not accept the position. I see your path as leading the Independents to victory—a second revolution of sorts. I've been thinking this over as well, and my humble advice is to stay the course you've charted and fulfill your destiny via the Independents."

The senator seemed surprised by his friend's comment. "Wayne, I'm a little taken aback. It's not like you to take such a position so quickly."

"Sir, many of us feel very strongly about what the Independents stand for. As you noted, many men have given their lives for the cause. While I'm sure your leadership would enable the old government to succeed in healing the nation, I also believe that eventually things would return to business as usual in Washington. That's not why you started the movement; that's not the goal of the council."

Moreland nodded his agreement. "This is far too important a decision to make quickly, Wayne. I formed the committee because they are all good, wise men. I will seek their counsel before making any final decision. I must tell you though, my gut tells me to accept and become the chief executive. I have faith that the truth will prevail, and the American people can embrace my presidency."

Wayne responded, "The committee will begin arriving tomorrow afternoon. I suggest we have a good, solid presentation ready for them."

Moreland's head snapped up, "Don't we always make a professional presentation, Wayne?"

The other man met the senator's gaze. "Yes, sir, we do. Do you know why? Because your heart is always aligned with your presentation. We have to get you squared away with this decision before we present to the council. If we do that, I'm sure the best decision will be reached."

The West Virginian smiled at his old friend. "You always seem to boil it down, don't you?"

"I stay with you, Senator, because you're one of the truest, clearest thinking men I've ever encountered. I believe you'll be an excellent leader for our people. While I feel a strong loyalty to you, my cause is the Independents and what they represent.

Moreland looked down. "Why thank you for that, Wayne. Thank you most sincerely."

"One additional observation, sir, there are still two armies facing each other in Louisiana. Every second that goes by increases the odds something will go wrong down there. I think everyone would be wise to keep that fact in mind."

Moreland sipped his coffee, his gaze focusing on nothing. *That's it*, he thought. *I've got to take the job. If I don't, those two military titans could clash, and the country would never recover intact after that.*

Bishop woke just before full light, his first instinct to check on their surroundings. The desert was just how they had left it before bed, calm, quiet, and seemingly devoid of life. Pushing the ATV from the entrance disturbed Terri, who rolled over and looked up with sleepy eyes.

The couple went about their morning routine quickly. Bishop rekindled the fire with the few remaining scraps of wood. Terri made him some coffee and mixed up some powdered eggs she had acquired from Bliss.

Forty minutes later the couple was on the road again, Bishop using the flat terrain to avoid driving on I-10. They hadn't traveled far when something caught his eye, and he cut north of the big road apparently heading off into nothing.

"Where are you going?"

"I remember something I saw as a kid, and I think it's right up here."

Terri couldn't see anything but flat, featureless sand but didn't comment further. They rolled along for another few minutes when she noticed the soil changed color, progressing gradually from the common yellow-red to a bleached white. Bishop stopped the ATV and half-turned to Terri. "Time to stretch our legs for a bit."

"Cool."

They dismounted the 4-wheeler. Bishop immediately bent and pinched a bit of the white soil. Gingerly tasting the sample, he nodded at Terri and announced, "That's what I thought. It's salt ... salt for as far as the eye can see."

Terri tasted her own sample and then gazed across the landscape. Stretching to the horizon, the desert floor was completely devoid of vegetation and colored the same bright white. "Is this a dried up salt lake or something?"

"Yeah, I think so. I remember my dad stopping here when I was a kid on a trip to El Paso. It looks strange, doesn't it?"

"I thought that place where they raced cars was in California?"

"The Bonneville Salt Flats is what you're thinking of, and it *is* in California. This is a smaller example, but there's more salt here than we'll ever need. I'm going to mark it on the map in case Meraton or Alpha ever runs out. This could be an important resource." Bishop bent and began scooping several handfuls of the crystalline substance, eventually filling one of the ATV's storage bins.

The couple continued driving across the salt flats for several more miles before the formation ended, gradually transforming back to the more common sandstone hardpan. Bishop steered them toward the southeast and home to Meraton.

The unused third-story office had an occupant again. Deke sat on the corner of the dusty desk, his mind needing isolation to play out the next moves of their strategy. Undercover work was always exhausting. It didn't matter if the role was of a drug runner, currency trader, arms dealer or army officer, every movement and action had to be perfect. The stage wasn't important either. Be it Arab sand, elite tropical resort, or army base, any failure to play the part perfectly could result in a critical review delivered by high velocity death. Like the thespian before an audience, his men donned costumes, makeup, accents, and backgrounds. They rehearsed lines and stories, often portraying both the living and the dead. But that's where the similarities ended. Unlike Broadway or Hollywood, a bad day on their stage could lead to pain, death, and bodies that were never recovered. In their world, the props were real weapons, and the filming never stopped. It fatigued the mind and body, and weary men made mistakes.

That was really the difference, he smirked. The ability to act—immersion into the depth of a role and pulling off the character—that's really what the managers looked for in a recruit. That was the true barrier to entry—the pinnacle that separated his firm from everyone else.

Yes, he thought, *you had to have proven yourself with special skills. You had to have achieved the status of elite in your specialty.* But there were lots of *those* men and women walking the earth. Warriors and doctorates were a dime a dozen, as were great actors. People who achieved all of the above were asked to join the firm.

It had been eight years since he had been recruited. His world back then had forced his mind to store memories by numerical context. It was a survival mechanism conjured up by gray matter that was being pulverized by practically constant violence. The location, date, or mission didn't register anymore—everything was recalled by the number. Even today, so many years later, those numbers came floating back into his mind.

The heat index in the jungle was 130.
Two was the number of men they lost that morning.
The cost of the lead that had killed his friends was a number as well, $1.03.

When his unit finally caught up with the hunter-killer team it was chasing, it had ended quickly. He remembered

93

standing over the enemy's fallen and evaluating their equipment. State of the art holographic optics adorned weapons bristling with infrared scopes and laser range finders. Practically every rifle was new—sporting accurate barrels and quality triggers.

A comparison to his team's equipment was inevitable. Despite working for the richest country in the world, his men carried worn out rifles that never hit the same spot twice. They were forced to use iron sights, poor triggers, and scratched up, old binoculars that had probably first seen service in the Korean conflict. The body armor worn by the corpses at his feet weighed a third as much as the unit strapped to his chest, yet protected twice as well.

There wasn't any mystery why so many body bags were being shipped home to the States. They were fighting a foe that outstripped their technology by 30 years. They had lost Mark today; his three kids would never see their father again. Danny had fallen as well—his disabled mother wouldn't be receiving any more of her son's pay.

The irony was persistent that day. Normally his feelings of injustice would fade quickly, overridden by the responsibilities of command and a certain satisfaction with victory. But not that day. The dead men scattered around his feet weren't elite warriors—most probably weren't even military. They hadn't attended the backbreaking schools of war located at Fort Bragg, Quantico, or San Diego. The corpses littering the small patch of unnamed jungle that day weren't even that well led or organized.

Yet, despite the sweat, strain, and sacrifice of the world's finest training, these ragtag bands of men were holding their own. They did so because of money, or more specifically, the advantages technology could provide on the battlefield.

Another defining number was 52. He had tried every requisition, purchase request, and avenue possible to get his men better equipment. The responses, 52 of them, were always the same—no. No budget. No appropriation. No need.

Looking down at the enemy gear, he felt more frustration. They weren't even allowed to utilize captured equipment as a spoil of war. It too had to be inventoried and shipped back to the States.

As his team searched the dead, they separated what they found into various piles. Weapons here, personal effects there, and money and valuables in the middle. All of the men they had killed that day carried wads of cash, gold watches, and bracelets—rings with jewels that cost more than his annual salary. Every piece was inventoried, photographed, and packed for shipment back to Miami.

The four-hour hump back to their camp had mellowed

his mood somewhat. Their weekly resupply had arrived via Blackhawk while they were out on the op. The always-uplifting event dulled the edge of his anger even more.

One of the men subscribed to a hometown newspaper, the airmail delivering a three-week-old copy. As he passed out the bundles of envelopes and small packages, something on the front page caught his eye. The paper's headline story was a piece on how welfare benefits for the people of Pennsylvania exceeded $50,000 per year.

There was another number for his mind to index—50K. Standing there in that South American jungle - filthy, hot, and suffering from crotch-rot, foot fungus, and diarrhea, he experienced an epiphany. He could resign, move to Pittsburgh and double his standard of living without working. No one would be shooting at him, and his body would no doubt last twice as long without the abuse. Best yet, he wouldn't be required to write letters explaining to grieving family members why their son wouldn't be coming home.

The next morning, there were visitors. Some prick from the State Department and his entourage added to the burden by flying in and demanding attention. The man had three bodyguards who stayed with him as he toured the forward operations center. Each of them carried state of the art weapons, load gear, and optics. Better yet, they were shaven, didn't smell to high heaven, and not a single one of them had scratched his balls during the entire visit. Nope, not a single case of jungle-sack among them.

"How do I get a gig like yours?" he had asked one of the security men.

"When's your commitment up?"

"Next month."

The man produced a business card. "Call this number before you re-up. The food's better, the pay is great, and we get to play with all the new toys."

Five weeks later, he accepted the offer letter from Darkwater, Incorporated, and never looked back.

A light tap on the door signaled his men had returned. The brief radio transmission had forewarned him that something important had occurred on the base. Now it was time to debrief and determine next steps.

Moses opened the door and peered inside before maneuvering his huge frame through the opening. He was quickly followed by Grim, the team's best shooter.

The two men were dressed in the uniforms of military police, complete with proper insignias and name badges. *Again*, thought Deke, *the actors on the stage were in appropriate costume, given the base was silly-thick with Army cops at the moment.*

Moses was excited. "Somebody tried to kill that dude and his wife. They weren't in the room, and now they've bugged out. Nobody knows where they're at. It was a professional hit job. The power was cut to the building. They used silenced weapons, and nobody got a good look at the shooters."

Grim chimed in, "Something spooked the husband. He freaked, and they moved out of their room. Here's the interesting part; Westfield and his boys are all a twitter over something the wife said. Rumor has it that our deceased Commander in Chief told her the Independents weren't responsible for the attempt on his life."

Deke was puzzled by the report. "I read their depositions, and there wasn't anything in there about that."

Deke paced the office floor for a few seconds before continuing. "This is the sort of information the client wants to know. I'll fill him in immediately. Good job, guys."

~  ~

The enhanced cell phone buzzed in Deke's pocket. He set down the duffle bag he was packing to answer the voice on the other end of the line.

"You called?"

"Yes, sir. There has been an event here at Bliss that I thought you should be aware of." Deke went on to explain what his men had uncovered.

The odd hum of static, generated by the satellite relay, was his only response.

"Are you there, sir?"

"Yes . . . yes . . . I'm processing this new information."

Almost a minute went by while Deke stood quietly, waiting on instructions.

"There's been a change in plans," the warbled voice announced.

"Yes, sir."

"The woman who claims to have new knowledge about the assassination attempt on our former president—we need to interview her in private."

"I beg your pardon, sir, but I don't follow."

"We need to interview this woman alone, without the act being common knowledge. I want you to detain her and find someplace where she can be debriefed in private."

Deke scratched his head, the whole thing not making any sense. "The husband's not going to just let us waltz off with her into the sunset. What are we supposed to do about him?"

The response sounded especially cold over the connection. "He has a warrant out for his arrest, a known fugitive. Don't let him become a factor in all this. Don't let him get in the way."

"So let me clarify—you want us to eliminate this Bishop character and grab his wife? I'm going to need a little more justification and a lot more manpower and assets."

The voiced boomed through the small speaker. "You don't need shit! This is a matter of national security, and directly related to the security of your contracted protectorate."

Deke pulled the phone away from his ear, sorely tempted to disconnect the call. Thoughts of going back to his North Carolina home and scavenging for food entered his mind. He fully understood that if he didn't accept the job, someone else would. Besides, the client had a point.

After another pause, the voice continued. "Moreland is the new president."

Deke was stunned, the news causing his mind to race in an effort to analyze what it all entailed.

"I understand," he answered meekly. "We'll get on it right away. I'm still going to need more personnel and equipment."

"Send me the list of what you need."

The connection went dead.

~  ~

Once again, everyone's attention in Meraton was drawn to the sky. Main Street was bustling with preparations for the day's opening of the market. Stalls were being set up, and the air was filled with the aroma of baking bread, cooking meat, and the promise of commerce. Everyone was in a cheery mood because it was Christmas Eve. Several shoppers were waiting, last minute gifts on their minds.

Overriding the din, a distant whining noise soon morphed into a constant thumping of the air. Pete was talking with Betty when the sound interrupted their conversation. Pete looked to the northwest with a scowl, "Tell me that's not Santa and the reindeers—he's early."

The small speck gradually grew larger as the Blackhawk helicopter zoomed overhead. Two black stars were painted on the fuselage directly above the stenciled "US Army." The craft buzzed low over Main Street and then made a slight banking turn above the open desert to the south.

Betty shielded her eyes from the sun and watched. "News of the market must be spreading, Pete. We've got customers flying in from all over."

Her remark drew a chuckle from the town's bartender, who winked and then strode off to see what all the fuss was about.

The large chopper approached Main on the outer edge of town, slowly losing altitude and lifting its nose. A billowing veil of desert sand rose into the air, surrounding the craft with a thick brown and yellow haze.

The helicopter landed gently on the ground, its powerful motor slowing to a redundant idle. As Pete and several other onlookers gathered at the end of the market, three dark images emerged from the cloud.

"I guess word of my new distillery has spread all over—even the army has dropped in to sample a shot," commented Pete as he watched the soldiers come closer.

The young officer approached the growing throng of Meraton residents, two armed enlisted men at his side. "We're looking for a couple who go by the names of Bishop and Terri," he announced. "I've got a warrant for their arrest."

Pete glanced at Betty, a look of concern on his face.

Being an ex-cop, Pete couldn't help himself and said, "My name's Pete, and I'm the mayor and law enforcement in this town. Could I see this warrant, young man?"

Annoyed, the officer reached into his pocket and produced several sheets of official looking papers. Pete began reading, the military men looking impatient and slightly concerned about the ever-increasing number of onlookers surrounding them.

Pete whistled and scanned the crowd, a huge smile on his face. "Hey everybody, this piece of paper says here that Bishop and Terri are wanted for two counts of assaulting a federal officer, material damage to facilities at Fort Bliss, and theft of a military vehicle. Sounds like our Bishop, doesn't it?"

The air was filled with several chuckles and gaffes, one man raising his voice and asking, "Whose ass did Terri kick?" The question was almost immediately followed by someone else commenting, "I don't know who it was, but they're damned lucky she didn't shoot 'em." The crowd erupted in loud laughter.

The army officer found no humor in the situation and became unfriendly. "This is a federal law enforcement matter. Has anyone seen these two suspects?"

Pete folded the papers, and handed them back to the military policeman. "Son, Bishop and Terri haven't been here in a long time. Even if they were here right now, you won't find anyone in this town who would help you arrest them."

The officer looked at one of his men and then back at Pete. "Harboring a criminal is a serious offense, sir."

Pete grinned and shook his head. "There is no federal government here, young man. We've been on our own for so long I don't think anyone recognizes your authority. That piece of paper you just showed me might be valuable as toilet paper, but other than that, it means nothing here."

The officer noticed several heads nodding in agreement with Pete's statement. Betty stepped forward and pointed her finger at the soldiers. "You all come dropping in here and stirring up a ton of dust like you're God or something. Where were you when we needed medicine, or when bank robbers almost took over the town, or when we needed food?"

"This is still the sovereign territory of the United States of America. The US Army has authority under declared martial law to enforce rule over this land."

Another man stepped forward and spit on the ground. His voice was stern. "There ain't no USA anymore, sonny. There ain't no taxes, no elections, and no government. The only thing that holds us together is the people you see around you. I, for one, like it better now that Washington isn't screwing everything up."

Deciding to ignore the remarks, the officer stood on his toes and addressed the crowd in general. "All of you folks, please listen to me. I have a lawful warrant to arrest these two people. If anyone has any information that would assist in the apprehension of these two fugitives, please step forward."

One man pushed his way through the throng and stood in front of the officer. "I've got some information for you. I've seen Bishop in action. The next time you come looking for him, I'd bring a few more men . . . maybe even one of them big tanks of yours."

Comments like "That's no shit," and "They'll need more than that if they're after Terri," floated above the laughter. The army officer became frustrated and looked at Pete, "We'll be back. These two individuals will be brought to justice." The man motioned to his two comrades, turned, and purposefully strode back toward the helicopter.

Betty looked up at Pete and smiled, "Well, at least we know they're still alive."

Pete nodded, adding, "It's always good to hear when a hometown boy does well."

The crowd began disbursing, random mumblings and murmurs drifting through the air. "They could've at least stayed and bought some stuff at the market."

Bishop sat on the ATV while Terri used the ladies room behind a nearby outcropping. He estimated they were at least 2,000 feet above Meraton, their roost providing a grand view of the small town. The businesses lining Main Street looked like small specks; the single highway, a dark thread winding its way through the valley. What made the vista even more impressive were the flat, open spaces beyond the town that ended in black, angry looking mountains in the distance. Bishop knew he was probably looking at Santiago Peak, the northernmost point in the Christmas Mountains.

The peaks' name reminded him of the quickly approaching holiday, and the need to shop for a gift for Terri. *Just like the typical male*, he thought, *waiting until the last minute to do your Christmas shopping.*

Bishop raised his rifle, the 4-x optic doing little to enhance the details of Meraton. Movement did, however, catch his eye, and he watched, fascinated as a helicopter lifted into the sky and began flying northwest. After a few minutes, he could make out enough detail to realize it was a military bird, and then it dawned on him what the purpose of the Army's visit might have been.

Terri's voice sounded behind him, "What are you looking at, Bishop?"

"I think I might have underestimated how pissed Agent Powell is. I think they've sent people to Meraton to hunt us down."

Bishop pointed to the flying helo, now fading into a tiny dot in the western sky. "That copter just took off from Meraton, and I'm sure they weren't there to enjoy The Manor's gardens."

"Do you think they left people behind to wait on us?"

"No way to tell, but we should sneak into town. Betty will tell us if we're stepping into a trap."

A few minutes later, Bishop was negotiating the ATV through the foothills of the Glass Mountains, snaking between sheer cliffs and impassable stone formations.

They decided to hide their transportation on the outskirts of town, leaving the ATV behind Betty's old bed and breakfast. It was a half-mile walk to Main Street where they found the market in full swing.

Sneaking in the back gate of The Manor's gardens, Bishop stored their gear while Terri went to look for Betty. A short time later, Terri returned with Pete, who immediately grasped Bishop's hand in a robust handshake while proclaiming he was happy the couple had made it back in one piece.

"I hear you've been a busy young man, Bishop." Pete began. "I hear half of the US Army is out looking for you and this pretty lady. You are officially on the Most Wanted List."

Bishop looked around the town, "Pete, I don't want to bring any more trouble to Meraton. I think we should probably load up the truck and get out before bad things happen."

Pete waved him off. "Trouble? Bishop, you and Terri are now officially heroes to most of the townsfolk. It's not every day we have bona fide outlaws roll into town . . . our very own Bonnie and Clyde."

Terri shook her head, "Very funny, Pete. But seriously, we don't want to be a bother."

Pete smiled, "You two stay as long as you want. Just be prepared to be treated like rock stars if you wander out into the market."

Bishop looked at Terri, thinking of Christmas. "There are some things I need. Want to go shopping for a bit before everything closes down?"

Terri pretended to be insulted, "Since you've known me, when have I ever turned down a shopping trip, mister?"

Pete started to turn, but remembered something else. "Oh, and by the way, the market is accepting US currency now. I just thought I'd warn you."

Bishop started to ask Pete what that was all about, but he had already turned and walked away. Terri was concerned. "Bishop, do we have any money-money?"

Digging in his pack, Bishop produced the truck keys. "I think my wallet is in the truck. I know there's some spare change in the console."

Terri clapped her hands in mock joy. "Oh, boy! I get to raid your wallet again! It's like civilization has returned while we were gone."

Two hours later, the happy shoppers returned with a few bundles and sacks of goods. After saying their farewells to their friends, the couple started Bishop's pickup, and drove west toward the ranch.

Chapter 7

Bishop's Ranch
December 24, 2015

Bishop waited until Terri announced she was taking her usual mid-afternoon nap, and then made a beeline for the Bat Cave. It took him a few moments inside to gather his gear, and then his head showed around the corner, peeking out the entrance, making sure the coast was clear. After verifying that Terri was nowhere to be seen, he exited, carrying his loot. He taped a note to the camper door that read, "I need to check the tripwires. Be back soon."

Slinking off like a thief, Bishop hastily beat a noiseless path toward the front of the canyon, a bag and length of rope on his shoulder.

Returning just before dusk, he quickly hid his tools and then checked on Terri, who was just waking up. Hiding the note in his pocket, he bent at the waist, kissed his wife and smiled.

"Do you know what today is?"

Terri blinked twice, clearly trying to figure it out. "No, should I?"

Bishop smiled, obviously pleased with himself—almost gloating. For once, he had been the one to remember a special day. Normally, it was Terri who reminded *him* of birthdays, holidays, and other special occasions. Not today.

Brushing back Terri's hair, he declared, "Well, I'll tell you later. Right now, I need a favor. I want you to stay in the camper for another 30 minutes or so. I'll come get you when I'm ready. Deal?"

Terri's expression betrayed her curiosity, wondering what Bishop was scheming. She smiled and agreed. "I've got to get washed up anyway. I'll sew that tear in your pants while I'm waiting."

"No peeking now," Bishop said, wagging a finger at his wife.

After giving Terri a peck on the cheek, Bishop hurried to a boulder up the canyon from the camper and began carrying armloads of firewood toward the spring. He retrieved a five-gallon metal bucket from the Bat Cave and began to heat water on the fire.

Terri rolled her eyes as Bishop left the camper, almost laughing out loud at his lovable, child-like demeanor. She knew very well it was Christmas Eve, but didn't have the heart to let him know she was in on the secret. *Besides*, she thought, *it will make my surprise for him even more special.*

She had mended his pants days ago, but kept them hidden. Her current project, hiding in plain sight in the sewing basket, was his main present. She had picked up a few other goodies at the market as well.

The last light of day was fading quickly when Bishop finished his chore and returned to the camper. Scanning the area one last time, he nodded and smiled. It was perfect. He approached their abode and yelled out, "Terri, can you come help me for a second? It won't take long."

Bishop heard muffled footfalls inside the camper. A few seconds later, the door opened, and Terri's head popped out. "Can it wait just a second, babe, I'm ..." Terri froze mid-sentence, her open mouth slowly turning into one of the biggest smiles Bishop had ever seen. Her eyes sparkled as she gazed around the canyon. "Oh my goodness, Bishop! It's beautiful!"

"Merry Christmas, Terri. Do you really like it?"
Terri didn't answer at first. She stepped down from the camper, one hand covering her heart. All around the canyon walls, luminaries generated a glow of soft light that warmed the red rock. Bishop had set out dozens of individual candles in nooks and crannies all over the rock formations. The flickering lights cast the stone formations in a gentle radiance that produced a magic atmosphere around their home.

Terri was simply stunned. "How did . . . when did . . . Oh, Bishop. I've never seen anything so wonderful."

Bishop smiled, "Welcome to Enchanted Canyon Spa, Madame. The lights should set the mood for your bath. Special water has been drawn for you."

Terri's head pivoted toward the hot tub. What she saw there brought both of her hands to her cheeks, her mouth opening in surprise. All around the pool of water, dozens of candles projected their light onto the canyon wall above. Floating on the surface were several more, gently drifting on small disks made of reflective paper.

The lights, combined with the reflection from the water's surface, turned the smooth granite face above the pool into a mural of multi-colored, gently shifting patterns of illumination. "It's the closest I could get to a big screen TV," whispered Bishop.

Terri embraced Bishop but never took her eyes from the display. "It's almost hypnotic," she said in an amazed tone. "I've never seen anything like it."

Bishop kissed his wife on the top of her head. "You should hurry with your bath, ma'am—before the water gets cold. I've got one more surprise."

The couple strolled to the small pool, Terri's gaze moving between the surface and the light show above. When they were standing on the edge of the tub, Bishop said, "Stick your toe in and make sure it's not too hot."

Looking up at Bishop with a questioning expression, Terri kicked off her sandal and dipped her toe into the heated water. After a moment, she began smiling again. "It's perfect!"

"Good. Now here's your final Christmas present. Bishop bent over and retrieved a small bottle, pouring the thick liquid into the pool. After the container was empty, he began stirring the water gently so as not to capsize the candles.

Terri stared in amazement as bubbles began appearing on the surface, and the gentle fragrance of flowers and mint filled the air. Her expression was completely child-like now. "Where did you get bubble bath?"

"I'll tell you later. Now hurry up and get in before the water gets cold."

In less than three minutes, two piles of clothing rested on the rocks beside the spring.

On Christmas morning, Terri snuck out of bed early, determined to deliver her own version of post-collapse holiday cheer. Quietly pulling shut the thin folding door that separated their sleeping quarters from the main area of the camper, she checked one last time that Bishop was still asleep.

All of the couple's cooking was performed outside since the LP gas had run out a few months before. Bishop maintained a large pile of wood by the entrance to the Bat Cave, and Terri had become an expert in preparing meals over an open flame.

She had put in a special order with the butcher at the Meraton market some weeks before, and yesterday the man had delivered. Unwrapping the plain brown paper, Terri's nose detected the unmistakable aroma of bacon. Not just any bacon, but peppered, thick-sliced slabs of mesquite smoked, salt cured wonderment. It had cost her 20 rounds of Bishop's ammo, five pounds of venison and half a bottle of Pete's best.

The iron skillet was crackling with the meat, four brown eggs ready to fry after the bacon was crisp. Bishop would be ecstatic, as the man simply loved bacon.

While she waited on the food to cook, Terri realized how simple it had all become. *Here I am, barefoot, pregnant, and cooking outside over an open fire. Six months ago, the same characterization would have raised my dander.* The expectant elf was as excited about giving this gift as any in memory. A humble meal, something that would have cost less than $10 only months before, was now as important as any set of golf clubs or hunk of gold jewelry. She believed with all her heart that Bishop would appreciate it more than any of those vastly more expensive items.

Watching the bacon closely so as not to let her super-expensive investment go up in smoke, Terri gently turned each slice like it was a rare antique, worthy of extra-gentle handling. When the meat was perfectly done, she dried the grease on a clean towel and arranged the strips on a plate in neat lines. *I had better taste just one piece*, she kidded herself, *just to make sure it's okay to serve to Bishop.*

While she chewed the small slice of pure heaven, four large eggs joined the bacon grease that coated the skillet. Terri's mind drifted back to previous holidays, and she began to wonder why things had become so shallow and artificial. She remembered a time when money was tight and they had set their gift budget at a mere $100. Both of them had been upset over the small sum—Bishop had cursed the economy and inflation, and Terri had worried that their Christmas would be ruined because of the cash crunch.

"How stupid we all were," she mumbled aloud as she flipped the eggs. "We were senseless to feel that way and idiots to let the world transition to that point."

Terri suddenly realized this was her first Christmas without her mother, and the thought put a momentary damper on her spirit. She remembered how her mother would complain about the crowds at the malls and how outrageous prices were. Terri could still hear her mother's words. "This entire Christmas thing has gotten completely out of control. When I was a small girl, we were happy to get a single orange for a gift. Homemade dolls, secondhand clothing, and cards created with coloring crayons were the norm for our celebrations. We got along just fine. Who needs all of these expensive gifts and artificial crap?"

Terri had politely nodded at the time, secretly hoping she would never become an old fuddy-duddy like her mom. With her eyes watering at the memory, Terri gazed to the heavens and whispered, "You were so wise, mom. I love you. I miss you. Merry Christmas."

The eggs were perfect, and Terri refocused her attention on the preparations. Drying the grease from the eggs, she slid two of them onto Bishop's plate and the others on her own. Making sure the fire was burning down and under control, Terri almost skipped, heading back to the camper, eager for

Bishop to see what she had made.

"Bishop, guess what? Santa's been here to see you. I guess you weren't on the naughty list after all," she announced while carrying the plates back to the bedroom. Bishop rolled over and opened one eye. He took a single pre-yawn breath, and sat straight up in bed. "Bacon? Where on earth did you get bacon?"

Terri sat the plate down in front of her husband and then stood back to watch his reaction. She wasn't disappointed. Bishop picked up a single slice and looked at it like a jeweler would peer at a perfect diamond. He inhaled deeply, enjoying the aroma. "Terri, my love . . . I don't know what to say."

Terri smiled, "Well, why don't you try eating a piece before you tell me this is your best Christmas ever?"

Bishop agreed and bit off a large portion of the slice. He chewed slowly, savoring every sensation of his taste buds, and actually moaning once. "I've never tasted anything so good in my life," was his eventual assessment.

After they had finished the meal, Terri produced a small package. "I made this myself, Bishop. I hope it's the right size."

Wasting no time, Bishop ripped open the parcel and pulled out a rifle sling made of Paracord. "Oh, Terri! It's perfect. You know I always like having lots of cord around. This will be a real space saver."

"I tried to model it after your favorite one. There's a full 100 feet of cord in it. It's all one piece."

"Honey, this . . . this is just the best Christmas I've ever had."

"Really, Bishop? It just seems like so little compared to what we used to buy each other."

Bishop thought about his wife's statement and nodded. "I was worrying about that when I was setting up the candles. I was scared you wouldn't have a good Christmas. But you know, I enjoyed doing that as much as anything I ever bought you at a store . . . maybe more so."

Terri agreed. "I understand that feeling. While I was weaving the cord, I kept thinking about how you would always have something from me with you, no matter where you were."

Bishop pulled his wife close in a warm embrace. "This is the best Christmas I've ever had, Terri. Thank you for making it so special."

Terri squeezed her mate tightly. "Me too, Bishop. This is truly a special day."

"Hey, I just had an idea of how we can make it even better. How about we drive up to Alpha? We'll splurge on the gas just to celebrate. I bet Deacon Brown's church is having some sort of service today, and it'll be good to see Nick and Kevin."

"Bishop, that's a great idea. Are you sure we can use the gas?"

"It's Christmas! We'll figure out how to get more gasoline later."

An hour later, after all the tripwires had been reset, Bishop pulled out onto the highway and surprised Terri yet again. Putting a CD into the truck's stereo, Bishop turned up the volume, and the cab was immediately filled with Mannheim Steamroller's *Carol of the Bells*.

The first thing Bishop noticed as they entered Alpha was a change in the people. While the outskirts of the small West Texas burb still looked like a ghost town, the closer they drew to the church compound, the more citizens were seen out and about.

The people walked with purpose, often carrying boxes, bags, or even pushing a wheelbarrow with shovel handles sticking over the side. Bishop was so enthralled with the activities going on that he almost became involved in the village's first post-collapse traffic incident. He was gawking at a group of children playing in a neighboring park when he nearly sideswiped an electric golf cart as it went speeding through the intersection. Both drivers stopped to apologize and verify everyone was fine after the near collision.

The couple continued to the church without further incident and found Deacon Brown preparing for her Christmas morning service. After an exchange of hugs and warm greetings, Terri decided to stay and help Diana get ready and made it clear that Bishop should find company elsewhere.

Bishop meandered through the main hall of the church, impressed by the bustle of activity and the attitude of the people. The choir was in full regalia, sporting royal blue robes with white collars and gold buttons. Candles adorned the sanctuary, accenting the beautiful colors generated by the building's large stained-glass windows and the early morning Texas sun. Every pew was shined, and the carpet looked freshly swept. It was an entirely different atmosphere than when this same building had been a fortress of last resort just a few short weeks ago.

Bishop found Nick loitering in the lobby of Deacon Brown's office, the big man going through a box of secondhand clothing, trying to find a jacket that would accommodate his massive shoulders.

"It's not going to do you any good, pal. I don't care how pretty of a jacket you find, it's not going to make you the best looking guy at the service, now that I'm here."

Nick, already frustrated by the hunt for clothing, pivoted to address his antagonist. When he saw Bishop, his grimace turned into a huge smile. "Bishop! What a surprise. How are you?"

The two men traded greetings and hugs. Nick remarked, "I've worried about you a dozen times since the president was killed and those army dudes hauled you back to Bliss. Diana asks me every day if I've heard anything."

"I've got hours of boring stories to tell you, my old friend. We'll have to catch up. Hey, I really noticed a difference here in Alpha as we drove through."

Nick nodded, "We've been working hard, but I'm still concerned. It seems like every single day more new problems arise than we can solve."

"How's Diana holding up?"

"Oh, she's a trooper, Bishop. That's one strong woman there—but then, you already knew that."

Bishop nodded and smiled in agreement. "You'd better mind your Ps and Qs, brother, or she'll kick your sorry ass."

Nick smirked, "A truer statement has never been made. But then again, that makes two of us."

Piano music drifted from below, a sure signal that the services were about to begin. Nick gave up on a jacket, hoping his plain white dress shirt wouldn't get him in hot water with the preacher.

The service was beautiful, and the choir exceeded expectations. With every seat full, Diana delivered a heartwarming sermon on the true meaning of Christmas, during which Bishop and Terri exchanged knowing glances.

A potluck brunch was announced, and the worshipers ambled toward the main dining area to feast on tables full of covered dishes. Bishop bragged to Nick about Terri's breakfast while Nick boasted about the battery-powered helicopter he had secured for Kevin.

After filling themselves on potato salad, beef brisket, and freshly sliced apples, Nick wanted to walk off his meal, and get some fresh air. Bishop decided it was an excellent idea and tagged along.

After catching up on the all the latest events in Alpha and Meraton, Bishop paused for a second and looked at Nick. "Hey, I know this isn't the best time to ask, but I can't figure out any other way. I need some hardware and there's nothing at the market in Meraton like what I'm looking for. I was thinking Alpha might be a better place to scavenge."

"Hardware?" Nick chuckled, "With all those soldiers after you, what you need is a mini-gun, land mines, a couple of battle tanks, and artillery support. Sorry, pal, but I've not seen that sort of hardware lying around in Alpha."

Bishop grinned. "Yeah … a couple of tanks would be nice, but I can't afford the insurance or the gas. No, what I'm thinking about could probably be found in the average pre-collapse hardware store."

"Oh, you mean regular hardware, hardware."

Bishop nodded. "I've got an idea for an irrigation system that I can install at the ranch. I think over time Terri and the kid are going to need more greens. I'm sick of pine nuts myself and want to expand the garden at the hacienda."

Nick tilted his head and grinned at Bishop, "I can't wait to hear this one."

Footfalls from behind the two men drew their attention, a happy Deacon Brown approaching across the lawn. "What are you two boys up to?"

"Plotting to rule the world," Nick replied.

"That wouldn't surprise me at all," she grinned.

Nick gave Diana a warm hug, "Bishop has a plan that I actually think might work. He needs some supplies though, and we were just talking about where he could find them. We both think he might be able to scavenge what he needs from Alpha."

Diana's face showed a scowl. "What kind of supplies?"

Bishop said, "I need some hose, a garden sprayer and a few fittings. Stuff a garden supply place or a hardware store would carry."

Diana thought about Bishop's list for a moment. "I suppose no one in Alpha would have a problem with it. Ownership of any sort of property is a touchy subject. You'll forgive me Bishop, but as time goes on, any little thing might become critical to our recovery."

Bishop nodded his understanding. "I could barter, I suppose."

Diana shook her head, "We are weeks, if not months behind Meraton when it comes to trade. Right now, our biggest task is just to make the place secure and feed everyone. I wouldn't know what to trade, how to value it, or even who to trade with. You helped us secure the town and beat those criminals, so I don't think it's a stretch to pay you back with some pipefittings or whatever you need. We'll call it even for your help."

Bishop smiled and bowed, "Glad to be of service, ma'am."

Diana swatted him playfully on the shoulder, and then became serious. "I can't spare any men to go with you, and there's still a lot of this town we don't control. You'll be on your own."

Terri's voice sounded from the front steps of the church. "What's my husband up to now?"

Bishop winked at Diana, "Don't worry honey, Diana and I were just planning a shopping trip for you in Alpha."

"Shopping?" Terri's voice sounded as she stepped toward the gathering. "I'm always up for shopping. Let's go!"

A short time later, Diana motioned for two passing men to join their little group. After explaining what he was looking for, Bishop watched the two men think over his request.

"The Home Mart store out on the edge of town was where most folks shopped for home improvement stuff," replied one of the men.

The other agreed. "No one's been out there as far as I know. We've still got our hands full around here. If you want to take the chance, that's probably about the best place if it didn't burn down or get looted to the floor tiles."

After thanking the men for their advice, Bishop asked Terri if she were up for a little adventure.

"What adventure?" she replied. "Either the stuff you want is there or it's not, right?"

Diana spoke up, "Well, maybe. Don't forget this place was ruled by rogue criminals just a few days ago. There are still plenty of desperate people around."

Terri shrugged. "I've got my rifle; I'm not worried about it. Oh, and Bishop's along—he can help take care of any light work, if need be."

Diana picked up on the girl-power direction the conversation was steered, and before Bishop could protest, agreed. "That's a good point Terri, but you need to keep an eye on him. He hasn't been watching his diet lately, or so I hear."

Bishop rolled his eyes. "Well, Miss Bodyguard. If you're ready, we should get moving."

Chapter 8

Alpha, Texas
December 25, 2015

Like many small towns, Alpha had experienced growth on the fringe of the city limits. Cheaper real estate and less congestion lead to strip malls, box stores, and fast food restaurants built away from the city center. Showing almost a herd mentality, these businesses tended to cluster together in order to take advantage of each other's customer traffic.

Alpha's Home Mart was no exception. Located on the outskirts of town, Route 67 experienced a burst of growth a few years before the economy had tanked. Rows of department stores, restaurants, car repair shops, and dry cleaners had initially hurt the downtown area. Shoppers, lured by the newer, larger facilities, began spending less and less time in the core of the city. Mom and pop hardware stores had suffered badly, unable to compete with the volume purchasing power of the big, national chains.

The free enterprise system was dynamic though. Downtown changed, adapting to take advantage of its strengths—quaint shops, sidewalk cafes, and theme restaurants began reversing the trend. The citizens of Alpha benefited from both areas, a quick need being satisfied by the big stores, a day of more pleasurable shopping available in the downtown district.

The new area of development had begun after Bishop had moved away from the town years ago. As he and Terri slowly maneuvered the truck away from the city center, he commented, "When I was a kid, this was all barren land out here. I can't believe how much it's been built up."

The view out the truck's windows was engrossing. Highway 67 was four lanes here, the expansion being required with all of the new construction. Each side of the roadway was lined with businesses ranging from dentist offices to gas stations. For the most part, the buildings, signs, and parking areas were intact. Bishop noted that every single door appeared to have been vandalized, no doubt by looters foraging for a meal.

The parking lots were empty for the most part. Unlike most municipalities across the country, Alpha's death knell hadn't been due to riots, starvation, or fires. When the power grid had failed, a tremendous explosion at the town's chemical plant had covered much of the area in a poisonous cloud of lethal gas. The deadly vapors had been released early on a Sunday morning, descending on thousands while they prepared for church or slept in.

Those who survived had waited for days, hoping for rescue from the outside. Little did they know that the entire country had slid off the edge of the abyss. Eventually desperation had set in, and hunger caused the remaining populace to begin scrounging for food. Bishop imagined it had been the same almost everywhere, the primary difference here being that much of the population had died immediately rather than over time.

Terri remained silent, her head pivoting left and right, taking it all in. It took Bishop a moment to realize that with the exception of Meraton, his wife hadn't been in any sort of town during the daytime since the downfall. They had left Houston at night and avoided civilization as much as possible the entire trip west. He almost chuckled at her girlish amazement at the sights passing by.

She finally commented on her surroundings. "Bishop, this is so weird. It's like all the people just disappeared into thin air and left everything right where it was."

"Appearances can be deceiving. Look closely at the doors. They are all busted open. This area has been looted, at least for food."

The statement caused his wife to pay a little more attention to their environment. A tone of concern crept into her voice, "Do you think there still might be people around?"

"Hard to tell, babe. My guess would be this area was picked clean pretty quickly, but we need to stay frosty."

"Frosty?"

"Calm, cool, and alert."

"Oh."

Up ahead, Bishop could see a huge sign advertising Home Mart. The lofty logo brought back memories of dozens of trips made to the Houston version of the same franchise. He and Terri had scraped, struggled, and done without to purchase their home - no easy feat in the middle of the Second Great Depression. The real estate brochure had been absolutely accurate in its claim that the place required a little "tender loving care." The home's condition had resulted in a seemingly infinite number of improvement projects and repairs. Bishop felt like he had beaten a path to Home Mart.

"In a way I feel like I'm entering familiar territory, Terri. I know the layout of these stores like the back of my hand."

Terri smirked, her recall of Bishop's frustration with being a handyman still fresh in her mind. "If you had spent a little more time learning some basic carpentry skills and less time shooting, you could have cut the number of trips in half."

Bishop grinned and threw a glance at his mate. "Well, given that we had to abandon the house, I guess you're just lucky that I spent so much time at the shooting range, huh?"

Pulling into the empty parking lot, Bishop's state of readiness elevated. His eyes darted from the weeds growing through cracks in the pavement to the shattered glass surrounding the front door. As expected, someone had been here as well. He asked Terri to drive completely around the building once. It took a bit to circle the property. The complex included an office supply store adjacent to the Home Mart. It appeared to have been ransacked as well.

Bishop asked Terri to leave the truck close to the Home Mart's main entrance. He had to laugh when she started to pull into the first row of painted spaces. "Terri, seriously, move up next to the building—a few feet away. We don't have to use the parking spaces anymore."

"Sorry. Habit."

Bishop ducked down from his defensive position sticking out of the truck's sunroof. Before exiting the back seat, he explained, "Terri, I'm not sure what we're going to find inside. I know you can handle yourself, but I want you to safety that rifle and stay behind me until we're sure the entire place is unoccupied. Please keep your flashlight off and stay at most three steps behind me."

Reaching toward the floorboard, he retrieved Terri's body armor and handed it to her. "Please put this on, too."

"Are you really expecting that much trouble? I hate this thing. It cramps my fashion style."

"I know, but better safe than sorry. Please just wear it until we're sure no one is inside."

Terri agreed, mumbling under her breath while putting the heavy vest over her blouse. "Does this body armor make my ass look fat?"

"Makes you look hot as hell, darling. Do you think they sell mattresses in here?"

The come-on earned Bishop a swat on the shoulder.

Moving toward the door, the first thing that struck Bishop was how dark the interior was. The sun's illumination brightened the first 10-15 feet of the entrance, after which, a wall of blackness met the couple's gaze.

"It will take a bit for our eyes to get used to the darkness. Until then, I'm going to use the night vision. Try squinting really hard for 10 seconds after we get inside. I've heard it helps."

"Seriously?"

"Yup. Some Special Forces guys told me that once, and

it seems to work. Otherwise, it'll take your eyes about 30 minutes to adjust."

Bishop mounted his night vision onto his rifle, pushed the power button for the light amplifying device, and began scanning the interior of the cavernous space. The first thing that caught his attention was the long row of cash registers lining the front of the store. Each drawer had been pried loose and flung to the floor. Given the store was closed when the failure occurred, Bishop thought the whole endeavor was just plain stupid. There wouldn't have been any cash in the drawers, and you can't eat money. Why bother wasting the energy?

Moving a few steps further inside, Bishop started scanning the aisles. Double decker, heavy metal shelving was used to display most of the store's wares. It looked to Bishop as though the pilfering had been random, with some passages almost completely blocked where scavengers had pulled items from their storage areas. Other sections seemed untouched, ready for the next day's shoppers to browse.

Hanging from the ceiling were directional signs advertising the general category of goods located on each row. It didn't take long for Bishop to figure out what people had found valuable during their rampage, and what they had ignored.

The section with pesticides and gardening tools appeared untouched while the display of electric home generators was completely bare. *Damn*, thought Bishop, *Alpha could use all the generators they can get their hands on.*

As the couple walked down the main path behind the cash registers, Terri whispered, "Look at the candy displays, Bishop. Picked clean to the bone."

Bishop pretended disgust. "You mean they're out of beef jerky? Dag nab it."

After passing the length of the store, Bishop turned to Terri and said, "Okay, I don't see or hear anybody. Let's check out the back of the store and all of the offices. If those are clear, I'll get to work on my list."

"What about *my* list?"

"If the place is empty, you're welcome to shop all you want. Just don't go over your VISA limit."

"Funny."

The couple walked down the corridor containing lighting displays, light bulbs, and ceiling fans. This area was undisturbed; apparently, no one needed a new chandelier. At the end of the aisle, they came to the appliance department where rows of washers, dryers, and refrigerators sat on display.

"Oh, Bishop, they're having a sale on those new high capacity washers. Do we have time to take a look?"

116

Bishop was about to retort when a noise echoed through the store. He immediately crouched and began scanning with the night vision. Terri moved a little closer to his side.

It was impossible to tell where the sound had originated, but Bishop's instincts told him it came from the back of the store. After listening for a while, he began moving toward the rear of the retail area, passing displays of tile, wood flooring, and carpeting. It took a bit of searching before they found an entrance to the non-public portion of the building.

Bishop quietly opened a steel door labeled, "Loading Dock," and scanned the area with his optic.

Not seeing any threat, the couple cautiously entered the warehouse and dock area. Several concrete truck ramps lined the rear wall of the building, complete with huge garage doors. Three yellow forklifts sat parked, their electric recharging plugs secured to the wall.

Looters had visited this area more so than the main retail section of the store. Practically every box had at least been opened, many having their contents dumped on the floor. The large expanse of concrete was littered with paper, plastic wrap, and scraps of garbage.

From the far end of the warehouse, a scraping noise broke the silence, quickly followed by a sound that resembled a door slamming. Bishop motioned for Terri to stay close and began stalking the source of the disturbance.

Halfway there, the scrape … bang echoed through the space again.

Cautiously, Bishop peered around a stack of boxes and spied a pool of light on one of the loading ramps created by an open emergency exit door. He could make out two people on the ramp.

Scrape … scrape … bang!

Bishop figured it out on the second glance and exhaled. He reached behind him and motioned Terri to come up and have a look.

Scrape . . . scrape . . . scrape . . . bang!

Terri moved beside Bishop, and peeked over his shoulder. When she finally discerned the source of the noise, she grinned and rested her head on his shoulder in relief.

Two young kids had a skateboard and were trying to ride it down the ramp. From what Bishop could see, they weren't very good and kept falling off. Each time they lost their footing on the toy, it would flip over and slam into the wall, producing the bang.

"What do you want to do?" Terri whispered to Bishop.

"I think you should leave your rifle here with me, and go

talk to them. A woman probably won't freak them out as much as a man."

"Little do they know at such a young age, eh?"

Terri handed Bishop her weapon and slowly ventured closer to the children. She cleared her throat to get their attention.

The two boys froze immediately, their eyes growing wide. Without a word, both of them bolted for the exit door, all trace of them evaporating into thin air. Bishop could hear their running footsteps fade into the distance.

Terri turned around and looked at her husband, making a motion of "What the heck?"

Bishop whispered, "Maybe your reputation preceded you."

"Bishop, did you see them? They were filthy little ragamuffins. Their clothes were torn and covered in dirt. I think they live here."

Bishop handed Terri back the rifle and then moved to the door. Peeking through the small glass window, he couldn't see anything but the empty back lot of the loading dock. He started to turn away when the distant sound of a slamming door sounded from outside.

"I don't think they live here, but I bet I know where they do live. Come on."

Bishop headed outside, Terri close on his heels. He made for the loading dock of the adjacent office supply store. "This sunlight will ruin our vision again. Let me go in first with the NVD."

When Bishop opened the door, a chorus of sounds escaped from inside. Rushed footfalls, brushes of cloth, and a chorus of "shsssssssssssss" filled the air. He turned to Terri and said, "There's a bunch of them in there. Maybe a whole family. We need to be careful of protective parents."

Terri nodded and stepped closer. She poked her head around the corner and spoke in a friendly voice. "Hey, you guys. My name's Terri, and I don't want to hurt anyone. Why don't you guys come outside here so I can meet you? I promise I won't hurt you."

Terri's greeting was met with more scrambling, followed by a few whispered "Be quiets."

Bishop moved into the opening to scan with the night vision and promptly jumped back. Several pairs of scissors, a handful of exacto knives, and an assortment of other heavy objects bounced off his chest and legs. A few pieces of the barrage missed, rattling across the pavement. If one of them hadn't bounced off of Bishop's sore head, the attack would have been comical.

"So much for the friendly approach. Why did they throw scissors?"

"Probably because they were taught not to run with them—that sharp objects are dangerous. Probably the only thing they could find in an office supply store. What are you going to do, Bishop? Start shooting?"

Bishop tilted his head, pretending to take the comment seriously. "Well, that's an idea. I'm out of hand grenades."

Terri shook her head and then moved closer to the door, yelling inside. "Now stop throwing stuff at us. My husband's here with me, and we don't want to hurt you guys. Please don't throw anything else."

Bishop popped his head around the corner again, ducking back quickly in case another barrage of sharp office supplies came flying. None did.

"Terri, there's a bunch of them in there. The place is full of boxes, nooks and crannies. We'd never find them all. We need a different approach."

Terri rubbed her chin, and then her eyes brightened. "How about the pied piper routine?"

"Do you have a flute in your load gear?"

"Funny, Bishop. No, we need something to lure them out, or at least a couple of them. I wish we had some chocolate—that might do it."

"If we had chocolate, you would've eaten it all by now."

"You're right about that. What I would give for a chocolate Easter bunny right now."

Bishop laughed, and then pondered Terri's idea, a thought suddenly occurring to him. "How about soft drinks?"

"Sure, that might work. Are you going to run to the corner Stop 'n Pick, and grab a case of sodas?"

"Nope. I do have a secret supplier though. Come on."

Trotting back to the Home Mart, Bishop made a beeline for the employee break area. The glass front of the candy machine had been broken out, all of the snacks long gone. The soft drink machine next to it appeared unharmed, however. Bishop found the padlock on the side and noted someone had tried to pry it off but apparently had failed.

"Stay here for a minute, I need a tool."

"Why don't you just shoot it off?"

"Because we would both be deaf from the blast in this small of a room, and the potential for a ricochet is high. Beside, padlocks only succumb to bullets on TV shows, not in real life. Not only that, shots being fired might drive our little friends next door even deeper into hiding."

Jogging out to the main retail area, Bishop found the tool section. He hefted a few pry bars until he found one sure to do the job. Rushing back to the lounge, he showed Terri his find.

"I love a man with a long, hard tool," she joked.

Rolling his eyes, Bishop inserted the tip behind the lock. Using the machine as a fulcrum, he applied considerable force in a single jerk. The lock didn't break, but its bracket did. The machine was full of soda pops.

The couple filled a cardboard box with a few handfuls, hoping it would be something to attract the children next door. Heading back to the neighboring building, they felt a little like Hansel and Gretel as they began laying a trail of soft drink-breadcrumbs from the doorway out into the open lot beyond. Bishop stacked several of the shiny cans where they could be seen from the inside.

Terri returned to the entrance and yelled, "Hey, kids. Just to show you we are your friends, we've left some cans of soda out here. There's grape and orange. They are a present, so come on out and help yourself."

Motioning Bishop to move away, the couple hid behind a stack of pallets piled nearby.

A few minutes went by without anyone taking the bait.

Terri looked at Bishop and shrugged her shoulders. Bishop returned the gesture, saying, "Well, it works for child molesters. Maybe they think you look like a pervert."

Again, Bishop's shoulder received a swat.

"This isn't working," Terri stated. Handing Bishop her rifle, she slowly walked to the mound of soda cans and sat down on the pavement. Choosing a grape, she popped open the can and took a small sip. She sensed eyes watching her every movement, so she began a routine of sipping the soda and then smiling at the door.

Bishop was on edge, extremely unhappy with Terri's maneuver. If someone came out of that doorway shooting, he wouldn't be able to protect her. He was just about to stop the whole affair when rustling could be heard from inside the building.

After Terri's third drink, there was a commotion inside the doorway. Bishop heard a child's voice whisper, "Mindy! Mindy! Don't do it."

A mess of curly blond hair emerged from the entrance, barely visible from Bishop's vantage. It disappeared quickly, more hushed warnings coming from inside. Terri stayed put, smiling at the empty door.

The little head appeared again, this time staying longer. Terri waved for the child to join her, "Come on, baby, come on out and have a drink. You're okay."

The little girl hesitated, taking a single step outside and then glancing nervously left and right. Terri played it well, acting like she was distracted by reading something on the soda can. More voices came from the inside, warning Mindy of a trap and begging her to come back and hide.

Mindy wasn't interested in the liquid treats. Her gaze fixed on Terri. "You look like my mommy," the little voice squeaked. "I miss my mommy. You're pretty like she is. Do you know where she is?"

"I might know where she is, Mindy. I can take you to where there are lots of nice people. Why don't you come sit down and tell me about your mom? You can have a drink while we're talking."

Out into the daylight the child strode. Bishop was shocked at the youngster's appearance. Her hair was hopelessly ratted and tangled, the back full of dried leaves and other bits of debris. Bishop guessed the girl was about 6 or 7 years old. She wore what was once a red and white checkered dress. The clothing was now a filthy brown color, several tears in the material showing here and there. The inner elbows and wrists of the girl's arms were caked with dirt, her hands almost black. The tiny little legs below her skirt looked just as soiled and were rail thin all the way down to what were once white socks with a frilly lace trim. Her face was creased with a coating of dark smudges and sleeve-wiped dirt. Bishop's chest hurt, the pitiful vision in front of him welling up emotions like he'd never felt before. *That could be my child*, he thought. *It's always the worst when the innocent suffer.*

Terri maintained her smile and patted the pavement, signaling Mindy to join her and have a seat. The girl was mesmerized by Terri, never taking her eyes off of the woman's face. Slowly, step by step, the child inched closer and finally sat down.

"What flavor do you want, Mindy?"

"I don't want anything to drink. I just want to go home. You're not going to eat me, are you?"

Terri recovered quickly from the shock of the question. "Of course not, Mindy. Why would you think I was going to eat you? I don't eat people."

"Billy said all of the grown-ups wanted to eat us. They came here a long time ago with guns. They walked around the buildings and took stuff away."

"No, baby, we're not going to eat anybody. We're here to help you guys."

"Mr. Wilson made us hide when people came around. He said they were dangerous."

"Who's Mr. Wilson, Mindy? Where is he?"

"Mr. Wilson was our Sunday School bus driver. We were on the bus when all the people started falling over. The other kids said they were dying, and I hid under my seat. Mr. Wilson drove the bus way out here . . . he was scared."

It was all coming together for Terri now. She chanced a glance at Bishop, and then asked, "Where's Mr. Wilson now, Mindy?"

"He died after we found this place. One of the other kids said he needed pills for his heart." Mindy pointed to the empty desert behind Terri. "The boys dragged his body out to that field because it didn't smell very good. We watched the dogs eat him."

Terri was stunned. She wanted to scream at the injustice, cry over what this little girl had been through. Taking a deep breath, she said, "So how many kids are inside the store, Mindy?"

"There are a lot . . . Billy, Cindy, Marty, Trevor . . . a lot."

"Mindy, do you think I'm going to hurt you?"

"No, I guess not. But I'm scared of those bad people with guns." Mindy seemed to remember that Terri wasn't alone. She began nervously looking around, acting as though she was going to stand up and run. "Where's the man that was with you? He had a gun, too."

"It's okay, Mindy, that's my husband. His name's Bishop, and he won't hurt anyone."

The girl settled down, returning her stare at Terri. "We shouldn't stay out here very long. Sometimes people walk by here, and they look mean. Sometimes they have guns, too."

Terri patted the girl on the arm. "Don't worry; Bishop will protect us. He's a nice man and very protective of me. He won't let anyone hurt us."

"My daddy was like that with my mom and me. He went away to the army a long time ago and didn't come back. He died in some place called Aff...Afgan... I can't say it. I don't remember him, but my mom used to show me pictures and tell me stories."

Bishop looked at the ground, the moisture from his eyes streaming down his cheeks. *When will all this end? When will we quit doing this to each other?* He thought. *When does the suffering stop?*

Terri soothed the girl's tattered hair, "I'm sorry, baby. We need to get the other kids to go with us and see if we can find their parents, too. Do you think they would like to go for a ride in my truck?"

Mindy ignored Terri's question, something reminding the child of her friend inside. "Do you have any medicine? My friend Trish can hardly walk. She skinned her knee real bad and now it has yellow junk coming out. She says it hurts a lot, and she shivers all the time."

Terri nodded, "Yes, we have medicine, and I even know where there's a nice doctor. Can you show me where Trish is?"

"Yeah. She's lying in her box. She hasn't come out for two whole days! I think she's very sick."

Mindy stood, motioning for Terri to come with her. Terri reached out for Mindy's hand, gently stopping the girl. "Mindy, I need for Bishop to come with us. He has the medicine in his pocket. Would you like to meet him?"

The little girl nodded. Terri waved for Bishop to join them, ready to grab Mindy if she spooked and ran. Bishop rose from behind the pallets and slowly sauntered over, trying his best to smile and look friendly. "Hi, Mindy, my name's Bishop." The child backed against Terri's leg at first, ignoring Bishop's extended hand. "It's okay, Mindy. I promise," Terri consoled.

Ignoring Bishop, the girl tightly grasped Terri's hand. "Come on, I'll show you Trish's box."

Following the girl to the entrance, Bishop heard more scrambling inside as they approached. He snapped the night vision off of his rifle and held it to his eye as they entered the darker area. The inside of the place astounded him.

Piles of garbage were everywhere. There was a packed carpet of empty wrappers, papers, and trash, evidence that the kids hadn't been real tidy while eating. Discarded plastic bins of pretzels, trail mix, and other bulk snacks were strewn throughout the area. Bishop motioned to Terri and said, "I would've never thought of that. These office supply stores sold large containers of finger foods and other stuff to their customers. Mr. Wilson was pretty smart bringing them here."

There were also toys, drawings, and every type of writing instrument imaginable scattered around. Evidently, the drawing supplies had been a big hit with the children, a virtually unlimited number of pens, pencils, and crayons they used to occupy their time. Like their refrigerators at home, it looked as if several of the children had found scotch tape and tacked their artwork to the walls and boxes that filled the space.

Mindy led them around a corner of the warehouse. Bishop could hear small scratches of movement all around them and assumed the other children were curious about what was going on, but still trying to remain out of sight.

Mindy stopped, pointing down at an empty box about four feet high and lying on its side. Terri bent to the opening, the odor from the inside surprising her for a moment. She flicked on her flashlight and found another small girl inside.

"Trish, Trish, I found some people with medicine for your leg. They're nice, Trish."

The girl didn't respond, and Terri could see why. Right below the child's knee was a swollen, red area that was clearly infected. The dirt and grime soiling the child's skin made it difficult to judge how bad the injury was, but Terri could see enough to sense it was very serious.

"Trish, my name's Terri, and I'm going to help you out of the box. I won't hurt you Trish; I just want to see your leg."

The small body inside moved a little, more of a moan than any acknowledgement of Terri's words. Gently grasping the ankle of the uninjured leg, Terri pulled Trish out of the box.

Movement from behind drew Bishop's attention, causing him to spin around. Standing behind them was a handful of children, the oldest of which was a boy of about 11 or 12 years. The skinny pre-teen held a claw hammer in his hand, a Home Mart price sticker still visible on the handle.

"Stay away from her," he hissed.

Bishop decided to intimidate the lad, "Chill out, young man. We're not going to hurt anyone. We're here to help you guys, so put down that hammer right now."

It didn't work. The boy charged Bishop, wildly swinging his weapon at Bishop's head. Bishop easily sidestepped the attack, catching the boy's arm mid-swing at the wrist. The hammer was twisted away without issue, and then Bishop gently shoved the surprised kid backwards into his peers. Bishop tossed the hammer aside.

"Do something stupid like that again, and somebody will get hurt. Now cool your jets. We are here to help you."

The gang of adolescents backed away from Bishop, not sure how to react.

Bishop stayed where he was and calmed his voice. "Look, you guys, I don't know what you've been through, but I have a truck out front. The people back in town have food, shelter, and medicine. I want to take all of you back with us so you can find your parents and families."

Terri interrupted Bishop, concern in her voice. "Bishop, this little girl is in really bad shape. We have to get her back right away to see the doc. She's not breathing very well."

Bishop said, "Okay," and then turned back to the group of kids. "Look, all of you had better come with us. We'll take you back to town in the truck. Go gather everyone up and meet us by the back door."

The kids started mumbling among themselves, not sure

whether to trust the couple or not.

Mindy's small voice sounded out. "They didn't eat me. They are nice. I'm going with them."

Her endorsement seemed to make it through to most of the kids and several left, walking toward the exit. Sure the confrontation was over, Bishop turned to the injured girl and scooped her into his arms. Looking around, he yelled out, "Come on, hurry up. Follow me to the truck."

Terri and Mindy lagged a little behind, both trying to convince any stragglers.

A few minutes later, the couple led a virtual parade of ragtag, filthy children through the Home Mart and out to the pickup. Bishop opened the camper top and sat Trish inside. He then began lifting the smaller kids up into the bed while Terri climbed up, making it clear she was riding in the back.

A short time later, Bishop drove off, 11 kids crowded into the bed of his truck.

As they approached the church's compound, Bishop honked the horn a few times to draw attention. Several people were outside on the grounds and began walking toward the entrance as Bishop pulled up. Deacon Brown appeared at the top of the steps, a questioning look on her face. "Bishop, what's all the commotion about?"

"Hi, Diana. I've got a surprise for you. Look what we found at the store."

Bishop opened the camper shell and then the tailgate.

"Oh my goodness!" Diana exclaimed! "Where did you find them?"

The kids started piling out of the back, several of the church's patrons now gathered around. One reunion was almost instantaneous. "Billy! Billy! Is that you? Oh, thank the Lord! I thought you were . . . I thought you had . . . I had given up hope, Billy!"

"Grandma?" Billy rushed to the older lady, wrapping his arms tightly around the sobbing woman.

Two of the men immediately rushed Trish to the community's makeshift infirmary, the rest of the children were greeted with a crush of concerned adults.

Terri began filling Diana in on the story while Bishop made sure the last of the children were receiving proper attention.

Relief came flooding over them, washing away the stress and emotion. Bishop embraced Terri, the couple sharing a moment. "We did a good thing today," Bishop whispered.

"I wish the world didn't need deeds like that."

Chapter 9

The children rescued by Bishop and Terri accented a growing problem that had already manifested during Alpha's short recovery—quality medical care. Despite better nutrition, security, and support, people, who had been barely surviving on their own, needed more skilled assistance than what the well-intended good Samaritans of the church could provide. The limited medical supplies available to the townsfolk didn't enhance the situation at all.

Smokey and the other prisoners had raided the town's pharmacies early on, carrying load after load of prescription drugs back to the county jail for safekeeping. Any medications known to give the criminals a buzz had been used quickly, leaving a hodgepodge of other pills, syrups and crèmes. After the fall of the criminal element, most of the church's caregivers didn't know how to use, or even how to identify the remaining piles of medications.

The children recovered from the outskirts of town just added to the mounting problem. They suffered from scurvy, malnutrition, and various other conditions including head lice, ringworm, digestive problems, and topical infections. Everyone's instinct was to immediately feed the little ones, but this quickly proved to be a mistake. Abused digestive systems reacted poorly to proper food, and some of the children didn't respond as anticipated.

Dental care was quickly becoming a nightmare in its own right.

Alpha was particularly hard hit. The berg's hospital, really more of a large clinic, was located in the epicenter of the poisonous gas cloud. According to the few survivors, there had been a fire at the chemical plant prior to the explosion. Several first responders, including most of the town's trained emergency medical technicians, had rushed to the scene and were killed instantly when the deadly vapors escaped.

In anticipation of numerous causalities from the fire, all of the local doctors and nurses had been paged that fateful morning; the hospital's administrators issued an "All hands on deck" request. All had been lost.

The child with the gangrenous leg forced the situation into the limelight—her treatment requiring a decision. Half of the caregivers believed the leg should be amputated, the other half wanted to begin a regimen of antibiotics.

"I'm not God!" Diana said in frustration to the gathered parishioners. "I won't make life and death decisions. There has to be another way."

The church elders didn't respond, all of them staring at the carpet.

Deacon Brown sighed, "I'm sorry … I shouldn't raise my voice like that. I know this is difficult on all of us, but I'm not qualified to determine who receives care and who doesn't. You're coming to me and asking that I triage life and death. I simply can't do that."

"Deacon Brown," offered one woman, "if you can't, then who can?"

For what seemed like the hundredth time since this had all begun, Diana found herself wanting a doctor, or nurse, or someone with formal medical training. The limited resources available to them just weren't enough.

"The only doctor we know of is in Meraton. He's got his hands full already. There has to be another way."

"Maybe he could visit us one or two days a week. Even that would be a big help. We could provide care if we just knew what to do or which medications to provide," offered another.

Several heads nodded in agreement. One gentleman added, "If we only had some idea how to use those pills were that we found at the jail . . . that could make a tremendous difference."

Diana looked around and sighed. "How would we get the doctor here and back? I'm sure he would agree to help us, but fuel is a big issue right now. We are using more and more each day, and the supply is not being replenished."

Like so many of the problems facing the people of Alpha, no one could propose any viable solution. Diana turned and looked at the image of Jesus Christ, portrayed in the church's beautiful stained glass windows. "I could use some answers here, Lord," she whispered under her breath.

"Let's all think about this problem. Please let me know any ideas," Diana sighed, the familiar closure to the conversation becoming worn and tired.

The group began to disperse, most of them feeling the same frustration as their leader. Diana proceeded back to her office, weary of always having to put off critical issues. The medical treatment of Alpha's citizens was one of the worst dilemmas because more and more people were going to suffer and die until they decided on a plan of action.

Nick was behind the Deacon's desk, working on his own set of quandaries. He looked up and could see the frustration on Diana's face. "Another bad day at the office?"

His attempt at humor was met with a frown. "We're losing here. I was just asked to make a decision about amputating a little girl's leg. The people caring for her think they have identified strong enough antibiotics to fight her infection, but if they're wrong, we won't know until it's too late. On the other hand, if they cut off her leg, she may die of infection afterwards, regardless. How am I supposed to make those decisions, Nick?"

"Should we load her up and rush her to Meraton?"

"We should, but I've got half a dozen people in dire straits right now. So we load them all in a truck and rush them there? Who makes the decision on which people get to see the doctor? We can't run everyone back and forth to Meraton all the time. We don't have the gasoline, and pretty soon Meraton's people will begin to question their resources being used for strangers."

Alpha, Texas
December 27, 2015

Kevin was still asleep, performing that miracle of teenage years that allowed adolescents to snooze for seemingly endless periods of time. *He's growing again*, thought Nick, *and growing is hard work*.

Making his way up the church stairs, Nick wandered to the kitchen area, but it was too early for breakfast. One of the kind women did manage a cup of instant coffee, complete with a dash of fresh cow's milk. He checked the time again and wondered if Diana had risen yet. Begging a second cup for the deacon, Nick made his way to the boss' office. He found Diana asleep on her office couch as usual, a stack of papers and notes resting on her chest. Shaking his head, he longed for the day when she could work and sleep like a normal person.

Careful to be quiet and let the woman rest, Nick wandered into the reception area outside Diana's office/bedroom as of late. He was setting her coffee on an end table when an old magazine cover caught his attention.

During the Second Great Depression, the church had evidently been required to tighten its belt like everyone else. Picking up the slightly crumpled publication, he noted the issue was almost three years old. Still, the picture on the cover intrigued him.

The magazine was titled *West Texas Lifestyles*, and the copy Nick held with such fascination was from May of 2013. On the cover was a picture of a barren, desert landscape with a mesa in the background. Sitting atop the flat half-mountain was a farm of giant windmills.

Nick flipped the dusty pages back to the cover story and anxiously began reading. Three pages later, he lowered the journal and proclaimed, "That's it! Why didn't I think of that?"

"Why didn't you think of what? Do I smell coffee?" A sleepy looking Diana questioned from her doorway.

"Diana, where's that engineer guy? You know, the one who retired from the electric company."

"What? You mean Chancy? Why do you want to talk to him? What's going on, Nick?"

Nick unrolled the magazine and shoved the cover in Diana's sleepy face. "This could be the answer to our problems, Diana. This could be what we've been looking for. It could change everything."

Her vision still groggy and unable to focus quickly, Diana gave Nick an annoyed look and took the pages from his hand. She rubbed her eyes and then scanned the cover. It took her only a moment to connect the dots. She glanced up, now wide awake, and responded, "You don't think . . . it couldn't be that easy?"

"Oh, I'm sure it won't be easy, but it's the best solution I've seen or heard so far."

Nick idled by, pacing only a little, as Diana read the article. Now and then she paused and commented, making statements like, "So, this windmill farm went live in 2013," and "It can produce enough electricity to power 5,000 average homes."

Finishing the article, Diana was excited, but more reserved than Nick. "Nick, nothing is that easy. Having electrical power would make such a difference, but I can't get my hopes up just yet."

"I know, I know. I probably shouldn't get so excited either, but it gives us hope. We need to talk to Chancy."

"Let me get cleaned up and sip some of that coffee. We'll go talk to Chancy first thing."

~  ~

130

An hour later, Nick and Diana walked up the front steps at 204 Elm Street, the long-time residence of Mr. and Mrs. Chancy Morse. No one seemed to refer to Mr. Morse by his last name, and Diana had always followed the lead and referred to him as Mr. Chancy. The two-story clapboard home resembled dozens of others that lined Elm. A brick porch, complete with swing, fronted the dwelling. Other than an off-shade of pale yellow paint, there were few other defining features.

Diana rapped loudly on the screen door's garden-green frame.

Alpha still wasn't a completely docile community, and a challenge sounded from inside. "Who is it?"

Nick could envision the older gentleman standing away from the door, shotgun in hand.

"Chancy, it's Diana and Nick. We need to speak with you."

The door opened a crack, and the visiting couple could see a swath of gray hair behind the opening. After confirming their identities, the noisy rattle of a chain sounded inside, and then Mr. Morse appeared in the threshold. "Well, good morning, Miss Brown, Nick. What brings you two over to Elm Street so early in the morning?"

"We want to talk to you about electrical power, Chancy. I hope we've not come at a bad time."

Opening the screen door and waving the visitors inside, the old man didn't wait to hear his guests out. "Now, Miss Brown, we've already been over this a dozen times. I'm sorry, but there's just no way we can fire up that power plant over at Fort Stockdale by ourselves. Please believe me, ma'am, I would if I could."

Diana smiled at Chancy's legendary grumpiness. "We're not here to talk about that gas-fired plant, Chancy. We're here to talk about this," and she handed over the magazine.

Glancing around the living room until he found his reading glasses, Mr. Morse began analyzing Diana's offering.

"I remember reading about this. They started building these generators after I retired, but I was still very interested in them. Very complex engineering involved."

Chancy continued reading, at last finishing the article and looking up. "So you're wondering if these windmills can power our town?"

"Yes," both Nick and Diana said at the same time.

"Technically, yes. According to this article, there's more than enough power being generated to run Alpha, as well as three or four more cities of equal size. The problem would be routing the electricity to our regional grid. Most of the output from these wind farms was directed to the big metropolitan areas in

East Texas, like Houston, Austin, and San Antonio."

"Can we hijack the juice?" Nick asked.

"I'm not sure," replied Clancy while shaking his head. "These were installed after I was out of the business. This article says this Sandy Hill facility was integrated into the West Texas regional distribution system, but I've no idea how that entire complex worked."

"What would you need to know or see? Is there a control station or something that you could look at to determine how it's all wired?"

The retired engineer thought about the question for a few moments before answering. "Yes, I suppose there would be . . . would have to be. I can't tell you where it's located though. With all of the terrorist threats against our infrastructure in those days, the power companies didn't make a lot of things known to the public."

Nick thought about that answer for a bit. "If I were to take you to those windmills, could you tell from there?"

"Oh, no, no. The only thing at that location would be rectifying and control equipment. They would need to control the current before it went to the transmission lines."

"Where would the transmission lines lead?"

"To a controlling substation, in all likelihood. That's what I would need to see in order to answer your questions."

Nick looked at Diana, both of them a little disappointed. Still, Nick was determined to see his idea through. "If I were to take you to the wind farm, could we trace the lines to the control station?"

The retired engineer answered almost immediately. "Yes, these pictures show above ground high tension lines. They would be easy to trace, but those lines could run for a considerable distance. There's no way to tell how far—could be over a hundred miles or more."

"So you're saying at the end of those high tension lines will be a control station? If I find the control station and take you there, what do you think the chances are that we can divert the energy to Alpha?"

"Oh, Nick, there's no way I can hazard a guess. The technology was changing so rapidly when I left the industry. If you get me to that control station, I'll be able to tell you pretty quickly though."

~  ~

132

Nick and Diana paced back to the church compound in silence, each trying to determine whether to be disappointed or not. As they reached the building's steps, Nick was the first to speak. "Diana, we've got to try. I know the effort will use valuable resources, but we've got to try."

Diana sighed. "Nick, it's not the resources I'm worried about. It's you off on some wild goose chase, traveling through a very dangerous countryside. Who knows where those lines will lead and what condition the territory will be in? I've listened closely to what you told me about your experiences along I-10. We both know what was going on here in Alpha. It's a crazy world out there, and I can't stand to lose anyone else I care about right now."

Her statement caused Nick to think of his son. Still, electrical power could save a lot of lives.

Nick finally decided he needed more information. "I need to talk to someone who knows that area. I need someone with local knowledge."

Diana smiled, "How about Bishop? Didn't he grow up around here?"

"Now that's a good idea. I wonder if his lazy butt is up yet."

"Terri said he's been running a lot lately. They're sleeping at the Higgins place. Go find out."

"You want me to do what?" Bishop asked, not quite understanding Nick's request.

"I want you to help me trace some power lines. We have to find this power control station thing . . . and the only way is to track these lines from their source."

Bishop scratched his head, "My friend, I'll help you with anything you need, but I still don't get it."

Nick showed Bishop the magazine containing the information on the windmills. Bishop read the article without comment, eventually handing back the journal. "That's some rough territory down that way. I used to hunt around Sandy Hill as a teenager. I find it a little difficult to believe they did a major construction project in that area."

"Can you drive your truck around there?"

"No way," Bishop answered, shaking his head. "That whole region is full of cliffs, steep-sided gullies, and hills. There's not much vegetation. You couldn't even get around with a dirt

133

bike or a horse. Unless they've built roads, that's some serious hiking, climbing and humping."

Nick sighed. "They had to have gotten heavy equipment in there somehow. They didn't airlift in those huge blades—some of them are over 100 feet long."

"Access to Sandy Hill proper wouldn't be that difficult with some large earth movers and plenty of money. They probably built a road to the top of the mesa and hauled the blades and generators up via trucks. It's the area all around the actual mesa that is so nasty. I don't know how they would have set up towers or laid the cables to carry the electricity."

"Well, there's only one way to find out. You up for a field trip?"

"Sure enough, Nick. You want to leave in the morning?"

"What about Terri? You think she'll be okay staying here in town?"

Bishop rubbed his chin for a minute, and then responded, "I don't think anyone knows we're here. She and Diana can take care of themselves pretty well. Kevin is pretty tough, too."

"Let's do it."

"Let's do what?" sounded Terri's voice from down the hall. She approached the two men with her arms crossed and a look of skepticism covering her face. "I get really, really nervous when I see you two plotting quietly in the shadows. This can't be good."

"Nick wants to see me do my world famous Don Quixote imitation, honey. He wants to see me chase windmills."

West Texas
December 28, 2015

The drive from Alpha was uneventful, but Bishop hadn't really expected any trouble. After leaving the confines of the small town, he and Nick had journeyed through one of the least populated regions in North America, a constant eye-diet of desolate West Texas desert passing by the truck's windows. The route passed by Bishop's ranch, and the duo decided it best if they upgraded their firepower in the unlikely event there was any trouble. "We're going to be in some pretty wide open spaces," Bishop had informed his friend. "I'd like to change out to the .308 so I can do some long distance dialing, if need be."

Nick grunted, recalling the old television commercial. "Reach out and touch someone, eh?"

Bishop pulled off the two-lane highway into what appeared to be random, open desert and stopped. "Hang on a sec; I've got to tie on the drag."

Nick watched fascinated as Bishop walked over to what appeared to be a random pile of dead branches and vegetation. Pulling a short rope from the bed of the truck, Bishop attached the brush heap to the trailer hitch and then drove slowly across the hardpan desert floor.

After a few hundred yards, well out of sight from the road behind, Bishop stopped again and unhooked the load. Nick got out and investigated their trail, amazed to find no evidence of their passing.

"I had to play with the weight for a while to get it right. It doesn't work if it has rained and the soil is moist, but as you can see, we don't have a lot of wet days around here."

Scanning the surrounding terrain, Nick had to agree.

Smiling at his friend, Bishop reiterated, "Always cover your tracks."

Nick just shook his head, "Always."

They continued driving through a seemingly featureless landscape of short ridges, erosion-walled valleys, and massive rock fields accented with the occasional small boulder. There was very little vegetation; a few variety of cactus and patches of chest-high scrub oak dotted the earth. Mostly it was barren, hard-packed sand.

"How often do you have to mow the grass out here?" Nick asked.

"Oh, I don't worry about that—I hired a yard crew for the landscaping duties."

Bishop maneuvered the truck into what appeared to be a slot canyon, the floor of its valley littered with larger random rock formations. There didn't look to be any path wide enough for the truck to pass through. Bishop stopped and said, "I've got to get out and disable the tripwires. Given I've had visitors lately, I think it wise to scout ahead—just in case someone is waiting for me to come home."

"Home?" Nick questioned, looking from one side of the canyon to the other. "This is home? Do you live under a rock?"

Bishop laughed, "In a way, yes. Why don't you drive while I scout ahead on foot? Just follow me, and you'll be fine."

Bishop climbed out of the cab and proceeded to make safe the multiple tripwires lining the canyon. Nick followed, nervous as he crept through gaps of sharp granite that missed the truck's side mirrors by inches.

After a hundred yards of weaving between slabs of sandstone and bus-sized boulders, the obstacles began to thin out, and driving became easier in the open floor of the canyon. Nick looked up the gradual incline and noticed the camper for the first time.

Walking in front, Bishop indicated Nick should park and join him. The two men worked together in an effort to verify no one was lurking in ambush around Bishop's place. After clearing the area, Bishop motioned Nick to the Bat Cave and unlocked the heavy steel door.

Nick stood in the entrance of the rock room, scanning both the natural formations and Bishop's collection of hardware. "Well, the name is appropriate, Caped Crusader. Can I be Robin?"

Bishop laughed and moved to his rifle rack. It took a few minutes to switch weapons, ammo pouches and magazines. Nick walked around the room, taking it all in and displaying just a tinge of envy.

"How did you come across this place?"

"My father worked on this ranch when I was growing up. There wasn't a lot to do around here as a kid, so I hunted this entire area. I came across the spring when I was about 11 years old and found this room the same day. This little canyon became my favorite place when I was growing up, mainly because the room was always so much cooler than the open air outside."

"So you bought the ranch?"

"No. The original owner died, and his kids didn't like the West Texas lifestyle. They decided to split up large tracts of the land and sell them off. My father had been a foreman, and it's kind of tradition to pass along a little land to key employees. Basically, I inherited the place. Over the years, I would come out here a few weeks at a time and make improvements. I had visions of a nice hunting lodge, not a home."

Bishop handed Nick a two-way radio. The big man looked at the device and asked, "You don't have cell service out here?"

Bishop laughed, "No, I couldn't afford Terri's extra minutes."

He locked up the Bat Cave, and the duo reversed their earlier procedure, resetting the tripwires as they exited the ranch. On the open road again, Bishop commented, "Sandy Hill is neither sandy, nor a hill. It's a gray rock mesa about eight miles off this highway. You can barely see it from the road on a clear day."

Nick looked out the window at the desolate Chihuahuan desert scrolling by. "We've got to walk eight miles through this stuff?"

"I hope not. I'm counting on someone having built a road during the construction. I can't imagine machinery like those windmills being maintenance free, so the power company would need a service road too."

A few minutes later, Bishop slowed as they approached the crumpled wreckage of the small Cessna that had delivered the colonel and his grandchildren a few weeks ago. "I need to stop here for a minute."

Leaving the truck idling in the road, the two men exited and examined the wreckage. To Bishop's eye, the scene appeared undisturbed. He walked a few yards away and found what he was looking for—a small mound of rocks covering the shallow grave of Mrs. Porter.

Bishop lowered his head for a few moments, a show respect for the dead.

Looking back up at Nick, he explained, "Here lies Mrs. Porter. She was the colonel's friend, and those druggies executed her right in front of the colonel and his grandkids." Bishop then pointed to a high ridge in the distance. "I was up there watching the whole thing, but I couldn't stop them."

Nick, returning his gaze to his friend, could see the pain on Bishop's face. "I'm sorry, Bishop. It's always worse when you're watching and can't do anything. I've emptied many a bottle after losing friends. I was always trying to convince myself I wasn't the one who fucked up."

Bishop nodded, taking a few steps across the road and checking the remains of the two executioners. The desert scavengers had picked the corpses clean of any flesh, leaving the scattered bones of the two Colombian enforcers to bleach in the sun. Nick noticed a large bullet hole in the skull of one of the bodies, but didn't comment.

After a moment, Bishop turned away, his voice low. "Those hombres paid for their crimes. I didn't bury the bodies . . . there was little time and a lot of spite."

It was a few seconds before Bishop's mind returned to the present. "We had best get moving. The days are short this time of year. I really just wanted to make sure Mrs. Porter's grave was still intact. It was a hasty effort."

After the two men returned to the cab and began navigating toward Sandy Hill, Nick could sense his partner was in a funk. He decided to try and distract his comrade. "I noticed your CD collection. I was kind of surprised to see so much stadium rock from the 80s. I figured you for a 'second British wave' type of guy."

Bishop took the bait, "Hard to beat Page as a musician; he broke a lot of ground. I still think that overall, the quality was about the same—foreign or domestic."

And so, it was on. Nick pretended shock at Bishop's position on the subject and quickly countered. As the miles sped by, the cab of Bishop's truck raged with friendly debate. Topics ranged from the greatest rock guitarist of all time, to who was the best tank general in history.

They sped south for another 15 miles before Bishop slowed. Pointing to the southeast, he handed Nick the binoculars and announced, "Sandy Hill is over that direction. You might be able to see the windmills from here."

Nick raised the optic to his eyes and scanned the horizon, finally centering on a distant point. "Found them," he declared.

"Cool. So if I were the boss of the construction company, I would build the access road the shortest distance possible. This highway runs straight north and south, so we should find the path when the windmills are directly to our east."

"That makes sense."

Nick watched their position, and before long Bishop slowed the truck so as not to miss any turnoff. On both sides of the highway, the desert began right as the pavement ended. There weren't any utility poles, fences or mailboxes. Nick noticed the lack of civilization. "What's the speed limit on this road? I've not seen a single highway sign since we've been driving."

"There is no speed limit. The road dead ends at Big Bend National Park, another 40 miles further south. There's a border patrol inspection station on down, but other than that, there's nothing out here. You can drive as fast as you want."

"Damn, I knew I should have taken the Porsche today."

Off in the distance, Nick noticed the parallel lines of a lane snaking through the desert. "Got it. I can see the path leading up to the summit. We're getting close."

A few miles further south, Bishop braked hard, bringing the truck to a sudden stop. "Almost missed it," he declared. After backing up a few hundred feet, Bishop pointed out the window.

Nick identified two worn paths winding across the terrain, eventually merging into a single line in the distance. There wasn't any road sign warning against trespass, or other indication of what lay beyond. Bishop turned the truck onto the lane and slowly began maneuvering toward Sandy Hill.

~  ~

Pete closed the door and locked up the bar. Reaching up, he hung a small chalkboard sign on a nail, the scrawled message indicating the bar would open at 3 p.m.

The decision to close Pete's Place and set up a table in

the market had been driven more by curiosity than any financial consideration. Switching from pure barter to currency-based transactions was exciting—a sign of progress that he wanted to witness and be a part of.

For the first time in months, he was carrying actual money in his pocket, including coins. The bulk of the money clip felt odd against his thigh, the weight of a few coins noticeable in the opposite pocket. *Still*, he thought, *carrying a bit of cash around was much lighter than a box of goods to barter with.* It was an inconvenience he would gladly embrace.

He paused before beginning the stroll down Main Street, taking a moment to absorb the sights and sounds. As usual, the marketplace was bustling with pre-opening activity. Citizens of Meraton were setting up tables, unwrapping boxes of goods, and gossiping with their neighbors.

The outlying ranches and homesteads contributed as well. Horse-drawn wagons were common sights, hauling items that ranged from live animals to the crops from vegetable gardens. Some of the bigger outfits still had fuel, and they used pickup trucks to deliver everything from goat milk to freshly butchered sides of beef.

Sewing supplies were becoming a popular trade, months of wear and tear taking its toll on everyone's wardrobe. The market now boasted two cobblers - both offering not only repairs, but also leather moccasins, slippers, and even fancy boots as part of their storefronts.

Pete stood and took it all in, taking a moment to reflect on how special it all was. There hadn't been any radio or television advertisements to draw the crowds. No newspaper ads had touted any specials, and coupons weren't even a consideration. The market was a spontaneous result of society— of humankind. Pete wondered how many of the transactions were born of necessity versus those being conducted simply as an excuse for social interaction.

Continuing his tour, the barkeep passed tables offering a wide variety of goods. Books were a very popular item these days, both as entertainment and education. One crafty woman had set up an exchange of sorts —offering to accept trade-ins, sell on commission, and loan out for a fee. It was one of the most popular booths in the market. Pete's mind immediately traveled to the motley assortment of items he had accumulated in trade during the last few months. *I might need to take advantage of this*, he considered.

The segment of Meraton's population boasting a Latino heritage dominated a large percentage of the stalls. Before the collapse, a combination of financial status and tradition had often led to a do-it-yourself mentality rather than relying on store-bought goods or services within their culture. Everything from small engine repair to sewing, canning, leather working, and traditional food preparation was part of their daily lives. Now, that knowledge was even more valuable, and the community was thriving because of it.

As he toured the street, Pete began to watch for price tags. He had more than a few boxes of unused goods he wanted to sell today, and was hoping to get an idea of how much to charge based on what others were asking for their wares. There weren't any prices displayed.

Stopping to chat with a few of the vendors, he realized the town's decision to go with currency wasn't being implemented yet. "Pete, I don't know how much to charge. I'm afraid to go first. I'm going to stick with barter right now until I get a feel for how much to ask for my candles," commented one lady.

Another booth owner, displaying a fresh crop of cherry tomatoes testified to a similar fear. "Pete, I only get a crop every few weeks. If I don't trade for everything I need, I'll be doing without until the next harvest. I have no idea how much to charge my customers."

The conversation was interrupted by one of the Beltron ranch hands strolling up, a heavy looking burlap sack carried at his side. "Heya, Miss Sylvia, I've got a nice fresh batch of fertilizer for you. You okay with our normal trade?"

The woman nodded, scooping up a quart-sized box of bright, red vegetables and offering them to the cowboy. He smiled and set the bag next to her stall, the aroma of cow dung drifting past Pete's nose. After shaking hands with the man, Sylvia continued, "Pete, how much do I charge him for those tomatoes? How much should he charge me for the manure? We all went to the town meeting full of vim and vigor, but implementing the decision isn't so easy."

Betty's voice sounded from up the street. "Pete, now don't you go getting the ripe ones before I have my pick!"

Pete and Sylvia greeted Betty, the two women exchanging a hug. "Oh, these look good, Sylvia. Nice and plump. Will you take our usual three eggs for a quart?"

"That depends on their size, Betty. How big are the eggs?"

"Oh, these are nice ones. Anita started feeding her chickens more corn, and it seems to be working." Betty produced three brown eggs from her apron pocket, gently setting the valuable commodity item on the table.

Sylvia nodded, apparently happy with the rate of exchange and scooped up another box of tomatoes.

Pete shook his head, understanding the complexity of the problem. *You can lead a horse to water*, he thought, *but you can't make him pay with the coin of the realm*.

Strolling back with Betty, his voice was full of frustration over the situation. "Betty, I was so excited by the town's decision to start using money. I even closed up the bar today in order to get rid of some of my prior trades. Now, I'm not sure we solved anything."

Betty stopped for a moment, browsing a table full of secondhand clothing. After smiling at the couple manning the stall, she continued walking with her friend. "Pete, someone needs to prime the pump. Someone needs to go first and establish a value. I'm not sure how to go about it, but that's what everyone is waiting for."

It was Pete's turn to pause their discussion, stopping to check a booth displaying several dressed quail. The smiling man behind the table started his pitch, "I just shot them yesterday evening, and they've been sitting in salt water ever since. They're very tasty this time of year."

"What are you looking for in trade, friend?"

"Well, sir, I'm running low on shotgun shells for one. I'd make a fair exchange if you've got any 12 or 20- gauge buckshot."

Pete smiled at the man, "I've got four 20-gauge shells of #7 shot someone traded me a while back. My shotgun is a 12, so I'd be willing to offer all four shells in exchange for two birds."

The hunter thought for a moment and then shook his head, "No, sir. I wouldn't feel right about that barter. How about a single bird for all four shells?"

Pete pretended insult, faked turning away from the booth—all part of his negotiation strategy. "There isn't that much meat on those skinny frames, friend. Shotgun shells are few and far between. Before I walk away, let me ask you this. What caliber is your sidearm?"

The man nodded, patting his holster. "Yes, sir, I've a .38 special."

"Well, now, that's good news. I just so happen to have six unused .38 cartridges as well. Let me propose this, I'll trade the four 20s and the six .38s for three birds."

After a moment of consideration, a hand was offered. "You've got a deal, sir."

Pete smiled and accepted the handshake. "I'll bring the ammo back in just a few minutes. Please keep three of those fine birds aside for me."

Betty waited until they were out of earshot and smirked at Pete. "You paid too much for those quail, Pete. He would've given four birds for that much ammo."

Pete stopped and grinned at Betty, "Maybe, maybe not. That's the problem isn't it? Let me ask you something, Betty. How many eggs did Anita have this morning?"

"Oh, Lordie. . . . I think she had a couple dozen or so. She keeps her inventory secret, always mumbling something about supply and demand. When you're negotiating with that woman, it's like pulling hen's teeth."

Pete chuckled at the analogy. "I understand. I'm going back to the bar and pick up those cartridges. I'll see you later, okay?"

After swapping for the game fowl, Betty's words prompted an idea. *Someone needs to go first and prime the pump*, he thought. *Might as well be me*.

Approaching Anita's booth, Pete asked how many eggs she would trade for two of the quail.

After inspecting the goods, Anita's voice was firm. "Four."

Pete protested, his indignation partially genuine. "Four! Why you shyster. Those two birds are worth eight eggs as sure as I'm standing here in West Texas."

A few minutes later, Pete walked away with six large brown eggs. Storing the remaining bird and two of the eggs in his kitchen, he then retrieved a piece of cardboard and a pencil.

Not long afterward, Pete opened his table at the edge of the market. A small sign hung from the front, advertising eggs for $1.00 each – cash only, no barter.

As the hours went by, Pete's sign drew a lot of attention and quickly became the talk of the market. The bartender had to laugh at the constant stream of onlookers gawking at his little homemade billboard. It was the biggest news to hit Meraton since everything had gone to hell.

Pete had just about given up hope of selling any of his eggs when a man shyly approached and pointed to the sign. "Pete, I've been a loyal customer since you opened the bar. I need some eggs, but I've got to be honest with you." The man pointed over his shoulder and continued, "There's a woman over there, goes by the name of Anita. She's got eggs that look just as good as yours and is selling them two for a dollar. I'll make you the same offer."

Pete couldn't suppress his grin. The Meraton Market was indeed a place where cash could be used.

Chapter 10

West Texas
December 26, 2015

The dirt path leading to Sandy Hill was a washboard of a ride. After crossing several miles of flat desert, the road eventually began a gradual climb before quickly turning into a series of switchbacks. At the top of the mesa, a chain-link fence surrounded the broad, flat summit of the formation. Bishop stopped the truck, both men alternating their gaze between the padlocked gate blocking their progress and the enormous windmills scattered across the flat surface.

Bishop was amazed at the scale of the machines. Each unit was mounted on a tower that was over 20 feet in diameter at the bottom and soared hundreds of feet into the air. Concrete bases, large enough to support a good-sized home had been poured beneath each of the mills. At the base of each tower was a metal door, no doubt leading to a staircase used to access the machinery at the top.

The huge blades rotated slowly, their appearance reminding Bishop of giant propellers for a mountain-sized airplane.

"I knew they would be big," commented Nick, "but this is amazing. Have you ever seen anything like this?"

"No. I've seen fields of these things while driving across I-10 north of here, but you can't tell the scale from the interstate. Up close and personal, they look like the propellers for God's Cessna."

Nick looked at his watch, "We need to get moving. Are you going to push through the gate?"

"Nope. I'll just pop the lock. I don't want to ruin my paint job."

Nick looked at the bullet hole in the back window and the bloodstained back seat, evidence that Bishop's truck had seen some rough times. "I don't blame ya one bit," was his only comment.

Bishop retrieved a crowbar from the bed and began twisting the gate's chain. The small lock gave up without much grunting or sweat. No foul language was required. A few minutes later, Bishop parked the truck next to a small building at the edge of the complex.

Nick began investigating the grounds, still gawking in awe at the scale of the project. Bishop made for the edge of the mesa; his focus was on a utility tower containing six wrist-sized

143

cables leading off into the distance.

From their elevation on the hilltop, both men could see the high capacity power lines stretching down the side of the mesa toward the northeast. The thick cables were easy to track, gradually sloping down to sag in the middle before beginning their rise to the next tower. From their perch, Bishop estimated they could see well over ten miles before the atmosphere began blurring the view. He counted 21 of the steel framed supports, each supporting approximately a half mile of cable.

"This is going to take a while," observed Nick.

"No shit."

Nick studied the terrain sloping away from the mesa. Sharp ridges and raw rock dominated the view, gradually flattening out to a smooth looking desert floor of a pale yellow color. It didn't look like a friendly environment.

"Well, there's good news. We don't have to worry about rock climbing today. The lines clearly stretch beyond the high ground and out into the flat desert."

"You don't sound real happy about that."

"I'm not. That's all private ranch land for at least 100 miles. There aren't any public roads. Most of the ranchers aren't just exactly embracing strangers these days, and many of them have their own private armies of some pretty rough characters. Trespassers will be prosecuted to the full extent of a large caliber deer rifle."

"Ahhhhh, good point."

Bishop looked around, trying to ascertain the next step. The small building next to the truck grabbed his attention. Motioning to the structure with a nod of his head, Bishop suggested, "Let's take a look inside, maybe there's something useful in there."

The door was locked, but not overly sturdy, and succumbed to one kick from Nick. Bishop mumbled, "We missed our calling—we should've been burglars."

Nick grinned, adding, "How do you know I wasn't?"

The building appeared to be a control center and office of sorts. The interior was filled with a few desks, dark computer screens, and a room full of electronic gear that neither Bishop nor Nick understood. As the two men moved toward the exit, Nick looked at the wall and asked, "Would that help?"

Bishop followed his gaze and recognized a large map with several multi-colored lines overlaid on the surface. Stepping closer, it took him a minute to orientate himself to the area depicted and the scale of the drawing. Finally, Bishop turned to Nick with a big smile. "I think you just saved us a lot of time and trouble."

Tracing with his finger, Bishop pointed to the map. "We're right here. These lines look like the high voltage power leads outside. They end here at this blue square that's labeled 'Pecos River Control Station.' I think that's where your engineer needs to be."

Nick whistled, looking for the map's scale. Using his fingers, he estimated the cables outside ended just over 90 miles away. Pointing to a series of lines and squares in close proximity to the control station, Nick asked, "What's this place?"

Bishop double-checked before answering, but was sure. "That, good sir, is Fort Stockdale."

"Well, that's good news, right? I mean, we don't have to go trespassing across 50 miles of ranch land, dodging bullets or anything."

Bishop sighed. "I'm not sure if that's good news or not. There have been some rumors . . . a long time ago . . . about Fort Stockdale. A few people claim that some county official took control of the town after the collapse. Some folks say he fancies himself as emperor. It's all just rumors I heard some months back."

"Where did you hear this?"

"At Pete's, when we first arrived in Meraton. There's probably some people around that know more than what I remember hearing. Maybe some of the Beltron Ranch hands have ventured up that way."

Bishop reached up and pulled the map free from the wall. Rolling it up, he winked at Nick and grinned. "A life of crime."

"We can return it later and pay for the lock."

"Let's hope it comes to that, my friend. I would welcome the chance to do so and relieve my conscience. Let's head back to town. I'm anxious to see if we'll end up with electricity and cable TV. It's almost time for the Super Bowl."

~  ~

Bishop scanned the town with his optic, occasionally making a note on the small pad of paper lying beside him. A gas station owner in Alpha had provided a detailed street map of Fort Stockdale, about the only thing left on the premises that hadn't been looted.

While it was good to know the street names and intersections, what really mattered was the buildings and activity surrounding the substation. There was also a strong curiosity regarding the accuracy of the rumors about the brutality of the people who controlled the West Texas berg.

Lying on the top of a 20-foot high desert knoll, Bishop was trying to find a route into the southwest section of the city. They needed a path that would avoid people - their intent being to sneak in, route the wind farm's power west, and sneak back out undetected. Behind him and out of sight sat Nick, Diana, and Mr. Chancy on the open tailgate of Bishop's truck.

The tales concerning the harsh rulers of Fort Stockdale had been substantiated. One of the first images through the riflescope had been of human skeletons nailed to telephone poles along the main highway into town. Cross members had been added to the utility poles to support the weight of the bleached bones, each of the remains adorned with a hand-painted sign indicating the offense of the deceased. Single word declarations such as "looter," and "thief" hung above the skulls of the crucified bodies, their public positioning clearly intended to send a message to anyone approaching the town via the main road.

It had required all of Bishop's concentration to complete his task, his mind forging images of men with torches and pitchforks nailing the pleading victim to raw lumber and hoisting the accused to the delight of gathered onlookers. *I wonder if they had witch trials too*, he thought.

There was also a homemade sign sitting right in the middle of the highway. The faded lettering was difficult to read at first, but eventually Bishop obtained a focus tight enough to make out the general meaning of the notice—visitors were not welcome in Fort Stockdale. Some lines of text were still quite readable, phrases such as "No water, No food and NOT WELCOME HERE" could be plainly identified from his vantage.

Continuing to study the town, Bishop concluded that Fort Stockdale wasn't suffering from an overpopulation problem. The homes and businesses within his view appeared to be abandoned and other than two scrawny dogs and one man on a bicycle, he hadn't seen a single living entity.

Backing slowly off the ridge, Bishop made his way to the truck and the anxious faces of the team. "So, here's the good news, it's not like Times Square around the town. I saw one guy riding a bike and two sick-looking dogs. Other than that, there's no obvious movement."

Diana said, "So we can just drive in and get this over with? Sounds easy to me."

Bishop shook his head, "I wouldn't advise that." He then went on to recount the crucifixions and signage. "I think if they caught us, we would face a similar fate. The whole place has this

146

macabre feel to it. No children laughing or playing, no engine noise—nothing."

Nick wanted to take a peek, and Bishop welcomed the second opinion. The two men scooted up the slope and slowly breached the crest so as not to profile themselves to anyone looking just the right direction from below. After ten minutes of observation through the scope, Nick nodded, and the two men cautiously returned to the truck.

"He's right," started Nick. "Even though we can't see a lot of activity down there, I think it wise to sneak in and out. Doing this right won't take more effort anyway."

"The substation is on the outskirts of town. I could see the high tension wires sloping downward, but the actual building was blocked from my view," Bishop added.

Mr. Chancy was clearly keyed up. "Oh, this is exciting. At my age, not many adventures come along. Do I need a rifle?"

After reassuring Mr. Chancy that he didn't need a weapon, the group studied the street map and Bishop's notes. They quickly determined that Bishop should go in alone and set up an over watch position with his longer-range rifle. After he was in position, he would radio Nick to bring Mr. Chancy up to the substation.

Diana had one final question, "Should we wait and do this at night?"

Bishop nodded, "I thought about that, but I'm the only one with night vision, and the moon's not full tonight. Besides, fumbling around inside of that building with flashlights would probably draw attention. Let me get in closer and gather some Intel."

After pulling on his pack and checking his gear, Bishop saluted and made off along the edge of the rise. He knew it likely that any elevated section of desert would have a low spot where the seasonal rains would run off. If the higher ground covered enough area, dry creek beds would be nearby. His luck was good today, as he quickly found a wash running through the desert floor that was about waist deep and wide enough to drive a car through. The small gully ran directly toward the edge of Fort Stockdale.

Keeping bent low and moving quickly, Bishop made his way to the edge of town. When he could finally recognize the rooflines of buildings over the bank of the wash, he slowed his progress and moved with more caution.

Rounding a small bend in the creek, Bishop spied the first bridge spanning one of the town's streets. He scurried to hide under the structure, taking a moment to catch his breath and adjust his load. His hiding spot was one street over from where the substation was located and about four blocks west. While he still couldn't see the building, the thick electrical wires were like a beacon to their target's location.

The closest building to Bishop's bridge was a mobile home. The beige and white metal-skinned house sat in a weed-filled lot along with two abandoned vehicles whose layers of rust indicated they had been parked at the residence for years. The window nearest Bishop was broken out, shreds of screen wire flopping loosely in the slight breeze. The metal skirting that had once surrounded the bottom of the trailer was torn loose here and there, its sharp edges poking out at odd angles. There weren't any signs of occupation.

Bishop judged the mobile home as a good spot to oversee the entire area. While he couldn't be 100% positive it was unoccupied, the roof of the structure should provide enough height and angle to observe the substation and its surroundings. If trouble did come along, Bishop was only 200 feet from the gully and the cover it provided.

Crawling from one patch of weeds to the next, Bishop slowly approached his destination. It took several minutes before he reached the edge of the lot, a boundary marked only by a slightly lower height of weeds and other native flora.

Close enough now to make out more detail, Bishop could see the remains of a clothesline strung between two posts in the backyard, the drooping wire still containing the remnants of two wooden clothespins and their rusty hinges. The high vegetation also had concealed a faded blue kiddie pool, complete with garden hose leading back to a faucet rising from the ground next to the back door. Several broken children's toys littered the area along with a chain stake next to a small doghouse adjacent to the driveway. *So depressing*, thought Bishop. *Looks like even the dog moved on*.

Bishop scurried through the backyard and scampered next to the skin of the home. He put his ear to the metal siding and listened for over a minute. No noise came from within the building's shell. Moving to the back door, Bishop reached up and slowly twisted the knob, the bolt opening without any resistance.

The back door led into a small area that had once been the laundry room. Shattered wood paneling and pink insulation laid everywhere, the residence smelling of mold and stale air. It took Bishop only a few seconds to determine the structure was unoccupied and decaying. Whoever had lived here must have intentionally moved away because the home was completely void of any personal effects. No pictures, clothing, or appliances were present, the only life being a nest of sparrows who didn't welcome Bishop's visitation and the droppings of what appeared

148

to be a large colony of field mice.

Returning to the backyard, Bishop stepped to a loose section of skirting and pulled an eight-foot length of it free. His knife made short work of the clothesline. He used the plastic coated wire to secure one end of the skirting while tying the other to his belt.

The railing bordering the back stoop made a perfect stepladder to the broken window, which gave Bishop enough height to pull himself up on the flat roof of the structure. Before climbing to the top, Bishop pulled the color-matched skirting up, hoisting it to the roof with one hand. One good pull-up later, and Bishop was lying on the trailer's roof underneath the sheet of metal, observing his surroundings.

Anyone who looked closely would wonder how the sheet of metal had ended up on the mobile home's roof, but Bishop knew the color match and the breakup of his outline would fool all but the most careful observer. The camouflage also allowed him to use his riflescope without fear of reflecting the sun's rays.

Using a slow belly crawl and pulling along his cover like a stiff blanket, Bishop made his way to the end of the roof, closest to the substation. As he neared the end of his approach, the sound of singing drifted by, causing him to freeze. The musical voices passed quickly, and for a moment, he wondered if he had really heard anything at all.

Once in position, he began to study the area beneath his perch. There were a few other homes on the street, one building that appeared to be a business and a church steeple several blocks away. Not a single human appeared to be in the area.

The substation was finally in clear view, and Bishop recognized immediately they had a problem. Surrounding the small, brick building was a sturdy looking, chain-link fence, no doubt intended to keep people away from the massive green and black transformers, isolators, and other heavy duty electrical equipment installed next to the control house.

Using his scope, Bishop could clearly make out a heavy-duty padlock and chain securing the gate. Defeating the lock would take time and create noise, neither of which was going to be a valid option. Scouting the fence line, Bishop looked for a tear or breach in the wire but didn't see any such easy option. He did detect a low area where it appeared some animal had dug out a small portion of earth trying to enter the property. Bishop judged it wasn't nearly a large enough opening for a man to crawl through, but it could be widened.

One last visual tour around the target made up Bishop's

mind—his co-conspirators would be required to excavate their way into the compound.

The front door to the control station appeared to be rather sturdy as well. Painted a government-green color of metal, the threshold was windowless, and two large bolts appeared to secure the entrance. The words, "Danger – High Voltage Electricity" were stenciled right above the knob.

Bishop pulled the radio from his vest and made sure the volume was low. He keyed the device and asked, "Nick, you there?"

"You're clear."

"You're going to need a shovel, my friend. There's a good fence surrounding the place, so you'll have to dig under it. Go to the northwest corner. It looks like some groundhog started your work for you."

"Great. I just love to dig. One problem though, I don't have a shovel."

Shit, thought Bishop. *I've got the entrenching tool in my pack. Reaching the damn thing is going to be next to impossible under this metal blanket.*

"Let me think about that for a bit. The door is pretty heavy duty, but there's a window along the west side of the building. It's out of sight from the town, so that might be your best bet."

"Gotcha. What about a shovel?"

"Did you see me climb on top of the trailer?"

"Yes."

"Approach the same way I did. By the time you get here, I'll figure it out."

"On the way."

Bishop had attached his pack to his ankle to drag it across the roof, the technique useful in keeping a stalker's profile low. Trying desperately not to move his covering of skirting, he hooked his boot on the pack strap and lifted his leg. It was a struggle, but eventually the pack was accessible.

The entrenching tool was at the bottom of his rucksack. Cursing Murphy's timing, Bishop slowly dug through the contents while trying to remain as motionless as possible. By the time his hand reached the tool's handle, he heard Nick key the radio and whisper, "Coming into the yard."

Bishop took a big risk and moved his arm from under the cover. After warning Nick with a quick "heads up," over the radio, Bishop flung the small shovel over the edge of the trailer.

"Got it," sounded the radio a few moments later.

Shoving everything back in his pack, Bishop anxiously returned to his scouting, worried that their unwise movements had alerted some passerby. It seemed like no one had noticed their comical hijinks. While he watched his partners scamper across the road and move toward the substation, the hum of music and singing drifted past Bishop's position again. Like before, it passed quickly, but Bishop was certain he had heard it this time.

From his vantage, Bishop spied his three comrades approach the substation. Like any good over watch, he tried to focus on potential threats in or approaching their path. Nick began digging under the fence, the short handled entrenching tool making the excavation difficult at best. Bishop chuckled out loud when his friend took a short breather and flipped a middle finger in Bishop's direction.

"I saw that," Bishop whispered in the radio.

Nick's response was to raise both hands and flash a double obscene gesture.

Five long minutes later, the raiding party was crawling under the fence, the excited look on Mr. Chancy's face betraying the man's obvious lack of a criminal background. Nick moved immediately to the western-facing window and using the butt of his knife, smashed through the glass panes.

Bishop grunted when Nick turned and picked up Diana as if she was a small child and effortlessly lifted her through the opening. A protesting Mr. Chancy quickly followed.

~  ~

Diana watched Chancy as he examined one panel and then moved to a different piece of equipment. Nick patrolled the exterior of the small building, ready to give the alarm if anyone approached.

After 20 minutes of notes, diagrams, and fiddling with various pieces of hardware, Mr. Chancy finally signaled he was through.

"Okay," sounded the retired engineer. "I understand how this substation functions, and I believe we have a solution." Diana's voice was eager. "You can send the windmill power to Alpha?"

"Not specifically, but I can re-route the output west. Right now, it's going nowhere. When the grid failed, safety systems kicked in and disconnected the generators from everything. I believe this control here will channel the electricity in our direction."

"Well, sir, what are you waiting on?"

Mr. Chancy shrugged his shoulders and ambled over to a bank of large handles. Looking more like a man about to execute a convict sitting in a nearby electric chair than someone about to improve the quality of thousands of lives, he threw the switch.

Nothing happened.

"That's it," replied the engineer. "It won't be steady electricity unless the wind is moving the blades. I would guess Alpha, Meraton, and several of the local ranches will have power 70% of the time. More, if people conserve."

"Let's get out of here."

Bishop heard the music again, and this time it was steady and louder. The volume was such that he quickly zeroed in on the source—the small church directly up the road. He sucked in his breath when the front doors swung open, and six men carried out a plain looking, pine box . . . clearly a casket. Bishop's heart began to race when a horse-drawn wagon pulled up in front of the church and received its cargo from the pallbearers. Bishop scanned the terrain from the church to the cemetery just south of the substation and realized they had a big, big problem.

Keying the mic, Bishop declared, "Nick, we've got trouble. There's a funeral going on right down the street from your locale. Dozens of people are about ready to start walking your direction. I don't think you've got time to get out of there."

Bishop watched as Nick rushed to the corner of the building and peered up the street at the church. "Shit," was his only reply.

The big man moved to the busted window and said something to the pair inside. His voiced sounded in Bishop's ear, "Do you think we can just hide here until the funeral is over?"

Bishop scanned the fresh, dark pile of dirt left behind by Nick's digging and thought it would be obvious to anyone who passed by. "I don't think that's a good idea, buddy. I think the broken window and the fresh dirt are noticeable."

"Any other suggestions?"

Bishop scanned the procession already forming in back of the hearse, and the image appearing in his riflescope wasn't reassuring. Each of the pallbearers wore a gold badge on his belt, and each was armed. Behind the formation of lawmen stood another five men with long guns and cowboy hats marked with a star on the front of each. "Nick, this just keeps getting worse. The deceased was evidently a police officer, and his mourners are all cops. It looks like they're going to even give a 21-gun salute; there are so many firearms around."

"Shit."

Bishop judged the distance, angle, and options. While the procession might pass by the substation without noticing anything amiss, it wasn't an acceptable risk. Nick and his party would be trapped like rats in a cage behind the fence.

Exhaling loudly, Bishop made his decision. "Nick, I'm going to distract them and pull them to the south. You guys get the hell out of there and pick me up on the highway around five miles outside of town. I don't know how long it will take me to get there, but Terri will kick your ass if you leave me stranded out in the desert."

"You sure, man? That's a tall order even for you, Bishop."

"It's the only way. Now get your asses out of there and pick me up later."

"You got it, buddy. We'll be there."

Bishop reached into his vest and pulled out an extra magazine and his earplugs. He used the scope's rangefinder to gauge the distance. The horses were a mere 250 meters away, so close the .308 bullets he was about to unleash wouldn't even drop more than an inch or so. Lifting his metal cover just slightly, Bishop plotted his escape route. He wasn't sure how fast or intense the pursuit would be, but he figured on a hot and heavy chase.

He waited until Nick was helping Mr. Chancy out of the window. As his three teammates began running for the fence, he switched his focus back to the church. Centering the crosshairs six inches in front of the lead horse's hoof, Bishop flicked off the safety and whispered, "Send it."

The rifle's report, combined with the impacting round, startled the horse and Bishop. The animal surged backwards, the wagon's driver barely maintaining control of the panicked beast. Before anyone could react, Bishop started pulling the trigger, sending round after round into the ground surrounding the line of cops. The reaction was bedlam.

Bodies were flying everywhere in a desperate attempt to seek cover. The wagon's master gave up trying controlling the team, instead choosing to dive for cover behind a wheel. Shouts and screams sounded from the gathered throng, and men shoved women to the ground while others ran for the cover of the church.

Bishop used all 20 shots in the rifle's magazine, ejected

the empty and slammed home a full box of pills. After shoving the spent mag into his dump pouch, Bishop began crawling backwards under the cover. Swinging his legs over the edge of the trailer and then hanging by his hands for a moment, Bishop dropped to the ground and began running away to the south.

Distance was life now. Bishop had picked his next spot, a small adobe home surrounding by a waist-high rock wall. Covering the ground at a full sprint, Bishop hurdled the wall and then cut hard right, intent on using the structure as cover.

Peeking over the top, he could see heads and arms waving back at the church. It appeared as though his targets were still a little confused and disorganized, but Bishop knew it wouldn't last. As he watched through the optic, one woman appeared to be rallying the men, her arms pointing in Bishop's general direction. It was less than a minute before a small gaggle of the lawmen formed behind the wagon and then began to charge across the road in Bishop's direction.

Again aiming low, Bishop flipped off the safety and sent five more rounds screaming through the air. The effect was as anticipated, the formation of men scattering for cover, no longer interested in pursuit.

Bishop was just about to rise from his cover when chips of stone and masonry stung the side of his face, quickly followed by the report of a distant rifle. One of the lawmen had found Bishop's position and sent a well-aimed round his direction.

Bishop ducked behind the wall and rolled twice to the right. He backed away from the barrier about the same distance and length of his barrel, the maneuver allowing him to rise above the partition with his weapon already in position. He had a pretty good idea where the shooter was, and intended on discouraging the man from hindering any further retreat.

Taking a deep breath, Bishop rose from behind the wall and centered his sights on the only tree in the church's grounds. He saw the man try to move his barrel toward Bishop's new position, but the guy was too slow.

Bishop's round slammed into the old pine right next to the fellow's head, spraying bark and resin into the shooter's eyes while knocking the rifle loose in his grip. Convinced he had bought some time, Bishop began zigzagging across the yard and heading south.

The pattern was repeated twice. Bishop would gain a little distance and then hole-up and send a few rounds back to scatter his pursuers. Despite the inaccuracy of his fire, the men chasing him didn't seem all that eager to close ranks. On the second cycle, he actually had to wait a minute before his targets came into sight.

They're not very good, he thought. *I would have split my group up and tried to flank me before now.*

The fourth time Bishop stopped for a breather, the flanking maneuver was executed, but not by the original funeral goers. Bishop saw two men with rifles strapped across their backs riding bicycles down a parallel street, obviously attempting to get in front and hem him in.

Bishop changed direction, heading directly toward the two cyclists. When he reached the corner of the street they were using, he hurried to follow behind them, having to pace himself to keep them in sight. A few blocks ahead, the two men jumped off their two wheel rides and moved to a position designed to intercept Bishop if he was still on his original path. He wasn't.

Sneaking up from behind the two, Bishop paused and then fired a quick shot at each, intentionally missing high. After their recovery, Bishop waited to make sure they saw him, and then he cut right down a small side alley. Pulling off a bundle of Paracord, Bishop strung a length across the narrow passage, securing one end to a gas meter and wrapping the other once around a drainage pipe. Bishop ducked behind two garbage cans and waited.

The sounds of the peddling and panting preceded the two men, and they flew around the corner and entered the alley. Bishop pulled the Paracord tight and braced for impact.

The first cyclist actually avoided being clotheslined. Slamming on the brakes while pulling the bike into a sideways skid didn't really help the rider. Bishop winced as he visualized the guy's skin peeling away when his grinding slide continued along the gravel surface. The second man caught the cord chest high and was immediately unseated. In slow motion, the cyclist landed on his backside, bounced once, and then bled off momentum with several tumbles. The two riders actually ended up almost on top of each other in a tangled mass of bruised and bleeding flesh.

Bishop stepped from behind the garbage cans and quickly shoved his rifle into the face of the closest man while putting his boot on the barrel of the other's weapon. The guy's eyes grew wide at what must have been an unusual sight. Bishop was dressed in a full combat load, baklava mask, shooting goggles and bush hat. The .308 AR10 was a large weapon, the 24-x scope extending almost the entire length of the barrel. Bishop was sure the muzzle, just a few inches from the gentleman's nose, must have appeared from his vantage to have been the size of a small cave.

"Be stupid and die. Be smart and live. It's really that simple," Bishop growled.

The guy nodded, his eyes never leaving the barrel of Bishop's weapon.

"You head on back and tell your friends that I've been shooting high and low on purpose, but I'm tiring of the game. I'm heading out of town and won't come back. If they keep coming, people are going to die."

Again, the guy nodded.

Bishop pushed the muzzle a bit closer and sighed, his voice going cold. "Forget that. I'm thinking you assholes are too stupid to understand the message."

Bishop flicked off his safety and moved his finger to the trigger. The man beneath him closed his eyes in anticipation of dying. By the time he opened them, Bishop was gone.

Evidently, the message was delivered because the chase ended. Careful he wasn't being followed, Bishop eventually found Nick and the others parked about five miles south of Fort Stockdale. The team happily headed for home, not sure they had accomplished anything other than scaring a horse and rattling a few lawmen.

Pete was talking with two customers at the bar, both men complaining about how bad the homemade bathtub gin tasted before ordering a refill. A humming noise caused all three gents to stare at the ceiling and then the walls. "What the heck is that?"

A few moments later, the forgotten jukebox in the corner began blaring out a melody. Smiling, Pete reached for a nearby wall receptacle and plugged in the neon sign mounted on the wall behind the cash register. They all watched in fascination as the name of a popular beer blinked once, twice, and then showed brilliant red, white, and blue neon.

All three of them stood in awe, staring at the light for several moments. Pete finally broke the silence, "Isn't that the prettiest thing you've ever seen in your life?" Both customers nodded, completely unable to move, mesmerized by the glowing sign. "The next one's on the house, boys."

Betty was carrying water into The Manor's kitchen, the bucket's wire handles burning into her hand. An odd shadow of flickering light caught her eye, and she panicked a bit, at first thinking something was on fire. Tiptoeing slowly into the main lobby, she glanced up at the humming fluorescent lights hanging from the ceiling. "We'll, I'll be," she mumbled. Immediately she hurried to the poolroom and tested the wall switch. The stained glass light, hanging over the table, illuminated immediately, showering the green felt surface with a brilliant glow. The hotel's manager stood fixated at the miracle, her mind racing with how easy life was going to be with running water, washing machines and electric ovens.

The women working the infirmary in Alpha were cleaning up after splinting a nasty compound fracture suffered by a member of the cleanup crew. The bloody wound had taken all of their skill to repair. The numerous candles spread around the basement room generated heat and smoke, transforming the makeshift clinic into a hot and sweaty place to work.

As they were mopping up the blood and cleaning the area, one of the good Samaritans thought she felt a breeze. The sensation passed as she gathered the red-soaked bandages used in the procedure. Stepping toward the door, she felt cool air again and stopped, trying to determine the source. Looking up, she noticed the air-conditioning vent above her head and raised a hand to feel. "Praise God," she whispered. Turning to her co-workers, her excited voice rang out, "Ladies! Ladies! Look!" Rushing to the nearby wall switch, she paused, and said, "Let there be light," and flipped the switches.

All over Alpha, people stopped what they were doing and stared at various sources of electrical wonderment. Flashing neon in the long unused café declared the establishment was open. Despite being looted to the bare shelves, the sign at the corner gas station began revolving high on its pole, while flashing numerals atop a nearby pile of rubble declared that the Texas lottery was at 12 million dollars. Music drifted down one street, a home stereo having been left on when the grid went down. Six months ago, the loud rock n' roll might have drawn a neighbor's complaint, but today, it made everyone smile.

~  ~

The team returning from Fort Stockdale saw the first hint of their success as they approached the outskirts of Alpha. Cresting a small rise on the highway, Bishop's initial reaction was to slow the truck down. The town was aglow, and no one believed the setting sun to the west was the source.

Diana commented first. "Is Alpha on fire?"

"It's not the right color," answered Nick.

"I think we're seeing streetlights. Oh, my gosh! Our little scheme worked!"

As the team progressed closer to town, it was confirmed their mission had succeeded. Windows glowed from electric beams, the bright white illumination completely different from the candlelight everyone had become accustomed to. "I'm gonna miss candlelight," Diana confessed. "It took 10 years off my profile!" The group chuckled at the idea of such a striking woman needing the advantage of soft lighting.

Pulling into the church, the team was met with a hero's welcome, big smiles and happy faces all about. Terri embraced Bishop, a look of wonderment on her face. "This is so fantastic!" she declared. "It's like Disneyworld all over again!"

Kevin approached Nick and Mr. Chancy, his hands filled with two cups. "Let me be the first to offer you a *cold* drink of water." Nick was pretty sure it was the first chilled thing to hit his pallet in six months.

The rest of the night was occupied by people strolling the streets and admiring the lights. The display wasn't anything special or noteworthy. Before the world had gone to hell, no one would have even noticed the common streetlamps, business signs, or household illuminations.

To the people of Alpha, it was a spectacle worthy of awe. Bishop and Terri walked hand-in-hand with the small groups of citizens, sauntering through the cool night air, gawking and pointing like everyone else.

Terri gazed up at Bishop and said, "I'm getting tired, would you like to turn in?"

"And miss all the excitement? Are you sure, Terri?"

Terri winked at her husband, "I figure since everyone is out looking at the show, we might find some alone time and won't be missed. The lights are progress, Bishop. They make me happy and hopeful, and I thought we might celebrate in private."

Bishop smiled and looked around to make sure no one was watching.

Moving so quickly Terri didn't even have time to flinch, Bishop scooped her up in his arms and held his wife like a baby. "You don't have to ask me twice."

It was several hours later when the lights began to dim, the event causing people to question what was going on. Mr. Chancy explained the cause, the cooling of the atmosphere no longer generating enough wind to spin the giant turbines to the south. Word spread quickly and while disappointed by the fading lights, most of Alpha's residents retired that evening with an improved optimism. Bishop and Terri never noticed.

Chapter 11

The time has come for all young men
To bow their heads and say amen.
The time has come to take a stand;
To voice beliefs across the land.
The time has come to raise up arms;
To make aware and set off alarms.
The time has come to make repairs;
To fix what's wrong when no one dares.
The time has come to set things straight;
To change our ways 'fore it's too late.
The time has come to hold our ground;
To circumvent without a sound.
The time is now.

DALH November, 2012

Alpha, Texas
December 27, 2015

Early the next morning, Bishop and Terri set about saying their goodbyes and best wishes. Reestablishing electrical power hadn't been a completely positive experience for the town as reports of two abandoned homes burning to the ground had filtered in.

Nick was busy organizing a team to go house to house and turn off breakers where there were abandoned homesteads. They were also going to warn property owners that electrical appliances left unused for months posed a fire hazard.

There were a hundred new tasks to be assigned and managed, but the entire population showed a vigorous attitude, anxious to get on with rebuilding their little corner of the world.

As Bishop negotiated the ever more crowded streets on the way out of town, he noticed Terri was as happy as any of Alpha's residents.

"Why are you all shits and giggles this morning, young lady?"

Terri reached across and brushed his hair. "Because of last night. Last night was extra special."

Bishop grinned, his chest slightly expanding. "I was on my game, wasn't I?"

Terri playfully swatted her husband. "No, that's not what I meant, and you know it. I meant the huge step forward we took as a society last night."

Bishop played hurt, his bottom lip slightly protruding in a pout.

Terri spotted the reaction and smiled, touching Bishop's cheek. "You're always on your game, my love. I'm a very lucky girl."

As they drove, Bishop couldn't remember a time when such optimism dominated Terri's conversation. "This is a pivotal moment," she declared. "This is everyone's big chance. I just hope we do the right thing this time."

"What do you mean?"

Terri rubbed her chin. "I can't help but feel like this is our second chance. I just hope we're good enough not to mess it up this go around."

Alpha, Texas
December 31, 2015

Nick was laughing at how sleepy Kevin was. Reminiscing about his own teenage years, the big ex-Green Beret still couldn't resist teasing his son about the need to sleep in until noon. "Kevin, wake up son. You're missing the best part of the day. The sun will be up in an hour; snap out of it, boy."

The younger man's response was a half-hearted attempt to stifle a yawn. It only gave his father more ammunition. "All week long, all I've heard was your begging me to take you deer hunting up in the mountains. 'I'm bored, Dad. There's nothing to do, Dad. Please, Dad, please.'"

Kevin decided to push back, "I didn't know deer hunters had to be in the woods before dawn. Nobody gets up this early to hunt. I don't even think the deer are awake yet. Are you sure you know what you're doing?"

Nick laughed, draping his arm around the boy's shoulders. "Yes, son, I know what I'm doing. I took my first buck when I was 17. Your grandpa rousted me out of bed extra early, and I managed to bag a 12- pointer. I'll never forget that glorious morning, that day, or that shot."

The duo continued down the main drag of Alpha, Texas, strolling toward the courthouse where the electric golf carts were charging. As they passed the spot where the president had been killed, Nick wondered if the town shouldn't construct some sort of monument. He quickly dismissed the thought—there were simply higher priorities right now.

After the collapse, Alpha had initially been overtaken by the prisoners from the city and county jails. No one really knew how they had deposed what little was left of the local government. Only the barricaded compound of a local church

160

escaped their harsh rule, and that had started what amounted to a range war.

Nick and Kevin helped defeat the criminals and reestablish legitimate rule. Now the town was recovering, making its way down the bumpy road on its journey to normalcy—at least as normal as things could be without any sort of state or federal government. The restoration of electricity had really made a difference. Things had been going well enough for Nick to take a break from rebuilding. It was a good time to take Kevin hunting in the nearby mountains, famous for their trophy white-tail deer population.

They had asked permission to borrow a golf cart, the preferred method of cross-town transportation. Generators were no longer needed to recharge the fleet of electric powered cars every night. Now they were plugged in to the charging equipment salvaged from the local golf course, making them ready to conduct the town's business the following day. Gasoline was always in short supply, and the electric transportation had been a godsend.

While he and Kevin could've walked, Nick wanted to save the boy's strength to climb to a good altitude for the hunt. If they did harvest an animal, the golf cart would come in handy to bring the meat back into town. Meat was in short supply as well, so the semi-personal usage of the cart had been a no-brainer.

Less than a block away from the courthouse, movement along the row of basement windows caught Nick's attention. It was just a flicker of a shadow, a hint of light. "Kevin, did you see that?"

"What?"

"I saw something along the windows over there."

"What?"

"I don't know what—something moved. Can't you say anything but 'What?'"

If nothing else, Nick now had his son awake. "I don't see anything, Dad."

Again, one of the basement windows flashed bright for just a moment, and then the illumination was gone. Nick looked at his son, who nodded—he'd seen it too. "What would anyone be doing in the basement of the courthouse this time of night?" Nick didn't have the answer for that. "That's a very good question. It might be another one of the leftover prisoners. Let's go check it out."

Since the congregation of the church had taken over the town, they still encountered the occasional stray convict now and then. When the prisoner army had scattered, some fled to the desert, a few had surrendered, and many had died from wounds suffered during the battle. A handful of others had fled to the outskirts of town and gone underground. The church people still encountered the occasional vagabond—normally hungry and ready to surrender. A few decided to shoot it out rather than return to captivity.

Nick and his son moved up the courthouse steps with caution, approaching the doublewide glass doors. Sure enough, the chain securing the entrance had been cut. Nick glanced at Kevin who nodded his agreement—they had to go see who it was.

Before the collapse, Kevin had been the stereotypical army brat. Girls, basketball, video games, and cars had consumed the lad's interest, often to the chagrin of his father. Nick found himself constantly pressuring for better academic results—pushing desperately for his son to prepare for college.

Being in Special Forces meant a lot of time away from home, a career choice Nick could have never accepted if not for his own father's help. Kevin often lived with his grandpa, and the two became close during the long periods when Nick was gallivanting around the globe and combatting terrorism.

The last few years of his distinguished military career allowed Nick to accept domestic training assignments at various US bases, and he utilized his free time to reestablish a strong bond with his son. The master sergeant's retirement papers had been submitted just a few months before the crash. Fate was with him once again when the world fell apart. Finishing out his tenure in the military by taking months of accumulated leave, Nick and his father had been on a fishing trip when everything fell apart.

Since then, Nick had utilized his skills more than ever, life being a constant struggle merely to survive. Kevin had been right there with him . . . video game controller replaced with a rifle, hard fought basketball games replaced with tense gun battles.

Nick's father had been killed by the Rovers just a few months after anarchy broke out, something both son and grandson thought about every day. There hadn't even been time to give the retired Marine a proper burial.

There were also positive aspects to this new life. When lives are on the line, the bonds of friendship and personal relationships grow strong. Bishop and his wife, Terri, had entered Nick's world by accident, and the couple had fought side-by-side with his family. Nick's relationship with his son was stronger than before—the distractions of civilization no longer between them.

Nick had met Deacon Diana Brown via random circumstance. Now he was in love with the de facto mayor of the small town. Life was looking up, and for the first time in years, Nick felt like he had a future right here in Alpha, Texas.

The light in the courthouse basement was possibly an intruder, intent on harming Nick's new home. He and Kevin moved into the building with caution, each man naturally falling into his role. Nick led, sweeping the hallways and doors with his weapon, with Kevin behind, covering his father's back.

They encountered nothing unusual en route to the basement steps. The lower floor of the courthouse contained records storage, a fact announced by the sign hanging on the wall next to the door leading down into the darkness below.

As far as Nick knew, there was one way in and one way out of the basement – the doorway he and Kevin now flanked. Nick racked his brain, trying to remember the contents below. As far as he could recall, there wasn't anything down there but boxes of old documents and archives stacked on the top of rows of file cabinets. *Why would anyone be down here at this early hour? It's not as if the office is open to apply for a deer-hunting license,* he thought.

Nick's thought was interrupted by another flash of light illuminating the staircase. He glanced at Kevin, a look of puzzlement on both their faces. "I'm going to check it out. You stay up here in case he gets behind me."
Kevin nodded.

Nick started down the stairs, staying close to the edge to minimize any creaking from the old wooden steps. The smell of old paper, floor wax, and stale air drifted up from below. Absolute darkness at the bottom of his descent gave him pause, making him unsure of his bearings. From a far corner, the light flashed again.

The brief spot of brightness etched in his mind, Nick began moving, his rifle up and ready. Reaching the long row of storage containers, he paused again—waiting for the intruders to show themselves.

Despite being ready this time, he was still shocked when the temporary beam of a flashlight illuminated two men standing in the aisle. He could clearly observe the outline of rifles slung on their shoulders.

"Can I help you gentlemen?"

Out of habit, Nick moved back two steps after his challenge. It was a fortunate move. Two shots roared through the pre-dawn calm of the musty smelling basement, the flash of the weapons like a strobe on a dance floor. Nick felt the bullets slam into the wall right where he'd been standing.

Undaunted, he flipped off the safety of his M4 and returned a couple of shots himself—still sure it was nothing more than two escaped criminals loose in the basement. He fully expected their surrender after being fired upon.

"I've got men at the top of the stairs," he warned. "Give it up, and no one will get hurt."

There wasn't any response. Brief whispers of sound came floating across the basement. Odd little scrapes, brushes, and movement of cloth. *They're moving*, he thought. *They're trying to get out.*

Nick turned to intercept his quarry at the bottom of the stairs, but was too slow. A violent storm of gunfire erupted as he detected shadows skirting toward the opening. Before he could shoulder and fire, the movement was past, and then the basement was calm again.

Rushing in pursuit, Nick yelled, "Kevin, I'm coming up!"

Taking the stairs two at a time, Nick burst out onto the main floor of the courthouse, his weapon swinging back and forth, searching out the threat. The hallway was empty.

He sensed, more than saw, Kevin leaning against the wall. "Did you see them, son? Which way did they go?"

"Dad, I . . . I . . . I don't feel so good."

Something in his son's voice struck that dreaded cord embedded in all parents—a tone recognized from an early age—the sound of a child who is really hurt. Taking his eyes from the hall, Nick glanced over and realized a parent's worst nightmare. His son was propped against the wall, staring at his hand, which was covered in blood. Kevin flashed his father the most hopeless look the veteran warrior had ever seen, and then slowly slid to the industrial tile floor, his son's body coming to rest sitting upright. Kevin's arm flopped lifelessly to his side, revealing the bullet hole.

"Nooooooo!"

~  ~

Nick quickly moved to his son and laid him gently on the floor. Tearing open the boy's shirt, he measured the wound with experienced eyes. Nick had seen more than his share of human flesh damaged by piercing lead. He knew immediately his son was in trouble—serious trouble.

The bullet had entered Kevin's chest two inches right and one inch above his sternum. There was no exit wound. Reaching for his blow out bag, he was momentarily surprised by its absence, quickly recalling they had prepared this morning for a hunting trip, not a combat mission. The medical kit was back at the church, hanging uselessly on his load vest.

The bullet's entry had left a small blackish-colored hole, about the size of a pencil eraser. A steady stream of blood drained from the wound, but that wasn't what sent a chill through Nick's soul. Small pinkish bubbles appeared every time his son took a breath. The lung had been pierced and would soon collapse if Kevin didn't get some medical care quickly. The other lung would follow shortly after, and his son would basically drown in his own blood.

Nick used the palm of his hand to apply pressure, an automatic reaction drilled into every soldier's head over and over again to stop the bleeding. As a Special Forcers operator, Nick had received more medical training than the average trooper. He desperately tried to remember the lessons taught so long ago in the humid forests of Fort Bragg and reinforced too many times on the battlefield.

Instead of the cool, business-like demeanor typical of such an elite warrior, Nick struggled to think clearly. The fact that it was his own flesh and blood lying on the floor unhinged him. Instead of a meticulous sorting of medical procedures stored in his mental inventory, a whirling carousel of visions invaded his mind. Images of Kevin's first steps, a wobbly bicycle ride, and that first jump shot quickly led to remorse. *I missed so much more*, he thought. *I wasn't there.*

Squinting hard from the effort to force the images of fatherhood out and allowing the trained professional back in, it all came flooding back into his conscious. *Seal the wound.*

Without his medical kit, he didn't have the right tools for the job. Nick stood, head pivoting desperately, trying to recall the courthouse's layout. He couldn't remember seeing any first aid kits or other medical supplies anywhere. His instructor's voice echoed in his head, "Use a rubber glove, plastic wrap, a condom – anything that will cover the wound with an airtight seal."

Nick rushed to the closest doorway leading off the hall. It was an office, but a quick search produced nothing useful. As he returned to check on Kevin, something caught his eye. Inside the doorway, leading downstairs, was a roll of packing tape hanging on a nail. Fifteen seconds later, Nick wiped the blood clear, pinched the opening closed as best he could, and applied a long strip of the tape across the opening. He watched anxiously, sighing with relief when no more bubbles appeared. He'd bought his child some time.

Scooping up the unconscious young man, Nick turned and made for the front door. He glided down three steps, looking up to see several people approaching, concern displayed in their expressions.

The first woman to arrive gushed, "I heard the gunshots, how bad is he?"

"I'll get a cart," yelled another man.

"I'll run ahead and warn Deacon Brown you're coming," offered another.

Nick didn't hear any of it. He paced quickly toward the church, his entire focus on getting help for his son. The desperate father was only a block closer to the sanctuary, when a man pulled up in the golf cart. Somehow, Nick acknowledged the motorized vehicle was faster than walking, and sat on the back of the small transport, holding Kevin like a baby in his massive arms.

By the time they arrived at the compound, word had already spread. Diana met the electric ambulance at the front steps, several of the church's women standing by to assist. The congregation had been at war with the criminal gang for months, and several of the members had seen their share of gunshot wounds as well. All of them were eager to help the quiet, polite young man.

Nick carried his son into the main building, guided by Diana through a few twists and turns, eventually arriving at the makeshift infirmary. Someone had spread a clean, white sheet over what was probably a cafeteria table, and Nick gently laid his son's motionless body on the surface.

The still air meant that the advantage of electrical power had dissipated with the quiet evening. Bright flashlights turned on, all focusing their white beams of light on the wound. Several pairs of experienced eyes scanned the damaged flesh while other hands checked the patient's pulse, took a blood pressure reading and laid a damp towel on Kevin's forehead.

One of the older ladies looked up at Nick and remarked, "Chest wounds are bad, young man. No one here has the skill to remove the bullet that's still lodged in there. I hate to say it, but we didn't save very many who were shot in the chest."
Two of the helpers looked down at the floor, slightly nodding their heads in agreement.

Nick wasn't ready to accept the death sentence. "Surely there's something we can do. My training is limited, but enough to keep someone alive until they can be treated by a doctor."

Diana rested her hand on Nick's shoulder. "This is the same dilemma we've faced so many times. We don't have any doctors in Alpha."

I'm going to save my son, thought Nick.

Suddenly Nick's face brightened, a decision having been made. He turned and looked at Diana, hope in his eyes. "I'm taking him to Meraton. I don't care if I have to carry him there. Is there any gasoline?"

Diana nodded, "Yes." She then turned to the caregivers. "Do you think he can survive the trip?"

One of the ladies looked at Kevin, "He's young and strong. He's not bleeding much externally. He might survive the trip if you hurry."

Nick said, "Let's do it. I can't let him just lay there and die without trying."

Diana nodded, asking one of the women rushing out to make preparations. Taking Nick by the arm, Diana led him aside. "What happened?"

Nick relayed the story of seeing the light in the courthouse basement and all that followed. After he had finished, the town's leader frowned. "There's nothing down in that basement but old annals. It's full of property deeds, tax records and notes of town council meetings – that sort of thing. Why would anyone shoot a child over that?"

Nick couldn't answer the question. "Whatever it was they were after, it was worth killing over. They knew what they were doing—it wasn't just a couple of bumbling thieves. They blew past Kevin and me like we weren't even there."

Diana's gaze drifted off, thinking of the recent loss of her own son. She placed a hand on each of Nick's shoulders, embraced him warmly, and peered into his eyes. "We'll do everything we can for Kevin. After we get back, we can worry about what those men were after."

Five minutes later, Diana was driving a pickup truck, speeding through the deserted streets of Alpha. In the bed of the truck, Nick was keeping a watchful eye on his son, lying comfortably on a soft mattress of hastily gathered quilts and blankets.

Bishop's Ranch
January 1, 2016

Early New Year's morning, Bishop set about policing up his decorations from the canyon. While he was sure most of the candles had burned themselves out on Christmas Eve, he wanted to gather up any remaining scraps of wax. Such things still held value at the market.

Halfway through the task, he rounded a large rock formation on the western rim, and stopped cold. Disturbing a loose swath of sand, the clear outline of a boot print stood out like a neon sign on a dark night. Bishop immediately swung the M4 around from his back and moved to the nearest cover. He was positive he hadn't walked that way—at least not in recent memory. The wind and rain would cover a print like that in a matter of days; it had to be fresh.

Peering from behind his cover, Bishop meticulously scanned the surrounding rocks and desert. There were a million places someone could be hiding, and he'd never find them. His next step was to mentally retrace his last few movements. Glancing back over his shoulder, Bishop admitted he'd been exposed for more than long enough for someone to have taken a shot and picked him off. *Either they're gone, or they don't want to shoot me just this minute,* he thought.

Uneasy with coming out of his hiding place, Bishop's thoughts were troubling. He knew he wouldn't hear the gunshot if a sniper was waiting for him. Any rifle used for such activity would fire a supersonic bullet—lead that would slam into his body before the sound waves caught up with the flying death. On the other hand, he couldn't stay up here until it became dark. He had to expose himself . . . he had to take the chance.

Cursing his lackadaisical attitude and short-sided holiday spirit, Bishop regretted not donning his body armor that morning. He needed to check the canyon perimeter, but didn't want to do so unprotected. As he debated the merits of wandering around exposed, one overriding thought caused his head to spin back toward the ranch—Terri.

His wife was asleep down in the camper. He needed to get down there, wake her up, gather up some gear, and then go scout the area. Holding his breath, Bishop moved from behind the rock. Despite his determination to hurry back to Terri, he couldn't help himself and avoided the direct route, stalking in non-linear lines, and taking advantage of as much cover as he could. It was silly, really. Even a novice-level sniper could pick him off with ease.

After making some progress toward the camper without a bullet tearing into his body, his attitude began to improve. Perhaps the footprint belonged to a wandering passerby. Still, how did any drifter get around his multiple layers of tripwires? Maybe it was from his boot, and he just didn't remember walking through that area. But he just couldn't shake the idea that this wasn't going to be such a Happy New Year, after all.

~  ~

Verifying the sun's position wouldn't reflect off his binoculars, Deke raised the glass to his eye and focused in on Bishop. "He's found something. He's hiding behind some rocks, peeking out like a school kid hiding from the neighborhood bully."

His two partners looked at each other and shrugged, really more interested in the MRE (meal ready to eat) they were consuming than the activities of the target below.

"He's come out of hiding now. For sure, he's onto something. He's worming his way back to the camper like he's scared to death. One of you two clowns must have dropped something."

"Bullshit," responded Moses. "He probably heard the wind whistle through the canyon and freaked out. Nobody dropped anything."

"He's an amateur," announced Grim. "Those tripwires were so-so, but anybody with any sense wouldn't hole up in a dead-end box canyon."

"He sure as shit wasn't an amateur the other night, was he? Made a fool out of those two at the VOQ."

Grim chuckled, "Even a blind squirrel gets a nut every now and then, bro. He got lucky. We'll snatch the woman in a bit and head back."

"Happy fucking New Year."

~  ~

Rushing to the camper, Bishop was relieved to find Terri deep in la-la land and undisturbed. Her reaction to being rousted so early in the morning wasn't positive.

"Bishop," she yawned, "Why are you waking me up at the crack of dawn on New Year's Day? Don't you know by now people have hangovers? There's no football on today either. Go back to sleep, anxious boy."

"I found a footprint up on the canyon wall, and I don't think it was Kris Kringle. I also don't believe it's one of ours. I need you to wake up, be alert, and carry your pistol. I'm going to check it out."

"What? You found a footprint? How is there a footprint on the canyon wall? Isn't that solid rock?" Terri, convinced her slumber-logic had solved the mystery, rolled over, and pulled the covers over her head.

"Terri, I'm serious."

"Bishop, you're paranoid," sounded the muffled voice from under the bedroll.

"I seem to recall your saying that exact same thing a few nights ago at Fort Bliss. You remember, the night someone broke into our room and shot at our bed?"

He had a point. Terri sighed loudly, throwing back the warm blankets and rubbing her eyes. She grumbled, "My pistol is over there in the top drawer. I have to visit the powder room."

Bishop retrieved her 9mm as Terri padded by. While he waited on his wife, Bishop checked the weapon's condition. There was a round in the chamber, and the weapon was well oiled and spotless.

Upon returning, Terri stretched and conceded, "Okay, Bishop. What do you want me to do, and more importantly, what are you going to do?"

"I'm going to load up and go search for other signs. Maybe I'll run into our new stalker . . . maybe I'll figure out it *was me* after all. Until I get back, I need you to be vigilant and armed."

"Okay, Bishop. Be careful. I'll stay in here or in the cave. Signal me when you're coming back in."

~  ~

Bishop strode to the Bat Cave casually—just in case there was a stalker nearby. The stone walled room wasn't really a cave at all, merely a deep recession in the canyon face created by years of erosion. Before society had taken a nosedive off the edge, he'd mounted a heavy steel door into the bedrock to create a secured space about the size of a two-car garage.

The Bat Cave was their storage room and Fort Knox. Heavy locks and thick, stone walls made the perfect place for Bishop to store his weapons, ammunition, and other equipment carried with them on the bug out from Houston. When the ranch had been used merely for a hunting retreat, he'd still kept spare tools and other assorted items locked away inside the rock room. Those supplies had been a godsend now that the ranch was their full-time residence.

Along one wall rested several metal lockboxes full of gold, property of the town of Meraton. After the harrowing journey across a Texas landscape ruled by anarchy, Bishop and Terri had arrived in the tiny West Texas town to find it occupied by a gang of bank robbers. Eventually, the couple had helped the townsfolk overcome the thieves. Now the gold was hidden here in the cave so as not to draw every desperado for 100 miles into Meraton.

Entering the cavity, Bishop closed the door behind him and secured the heavy latch. This wasn't his usual routine. Normally, he appreciated the airflow allowed by the open entrance. Today was different—today, he didn't want anyone sneaking up on him. He immediately set about putting together his gear. Load vest, ammunition pouches, magazines, night vision, body armor, and an assortment of other equipment were assembled on the smooth, stone floor.

As he worked, Bishop glanced over at the gold, its presence reopening a quandary that had been bothering him since he'd seen the footprint. How did anyone find the ranch? Only five people knew where his spread was located, and he doubted two of those could find it again. The colonel had been here, along with his grandson, but that had been after a dramatic plane crash, and he doubted that they had noted landmarks on the way in.

Pete, the sort-of mayor of Meraton, had a map in his safe, emergency instructions in case the town needed help. Bishop grunted, sure his friend would die before giving up the location. In reality, he could say the same for the colonel.

So how had anyone found my ranch?

Bishop resigned to having to wait for an answer, so he pushed the mystery to the back of his mind and finished loading for the scouting expedition. With 40 pounds of ammo, weapons, body armor, and gear on his back, Bishop exited the Bat Cave on the sly. Instead of walking out into the open area of the canyon as usual, he skulked off the opposite direction.

The steep, igneous walls rose over 20 feet vertically at this end of the canyon. The floor narrowed here, almost at the dead end of the box. Bishop hugged the rock face, knowing this route would obscure all but a few points where anyone hiding above could observe his movements. It wasn't foolproof, as anyone on the east rim could detect him, but the path did reduce some risk. The footprint, however, had been on the west rim, and he hoped if any stalker was out there, he had stayed on that side.

Behind a sheet of reddish-gray granite, Bishop moved into what was essentially a deluxe-sized crack in the wall. It wasn't easy, but he knew from his boyhood days it was just wide enough to climb to the plateau above. This had always been part of the plan for an emergency escape route.

With the heavy load, climbing through the narrow gap proved to be more difficult than he remembered. Foot and handholds were sharp cuts in the stone or the edge of fallen rock. If the ascent had been any more than 20 feet, he wouldn't have attempted it with the weight and bulk of all of this gear.

After 15 minutes of grunting and cursing, Bishop's head appeared at the top, slowly peeking out like a prairie dog popping out of his burrow. The exit point wasn't visible from most angles, large boulders and mounds of sandstone blocking it from observation.

Staying low as he crawled out of the crevice, Bishop slinked to a nearby outcropping and peered over the top. *If I had the ranch under surveillance, where would I hide?*

The terrain to the west rose into a staircase of rolling, barren foothills, eventually cresting at Crosby's Peak some five miles away. The vista from Bishop's position was misleading, the land appearing gradual in its climb, almost featureless. Bishop knew that wasn't the case. Sheer drops, boulder fields, sharply defined valleys, and finger canyons existed between his position and the 6,000-foot high mountain in the distance. Practically void of vegetation or discernible feature, the great distances involved were deceiving, painting a picture of calm, gently undulating landscape. In truth, it concealed some of the harshest hiking trials in the state.

If I were trying to scout the ranch, where would I be?

There was one foothill, higher than the rest and slightly south, that Bishop thought would provide the best angle. He had brought along his big rifle, an AR10 with a 24-x scope. The .308 was heavy, longer, and more cumbersome than his M4, but in the desert, he felt like the extra range it provided was well worth it. He slowly raised the weapon and braced it on the rock he was hiding behind. Focusing the optic, he began a slow, detailed search of the area.

While it was nearly impossible to judge the angle, Bishop believed anyone spying on the ranch would have to mount the crest of the distant hill to obtain the best vantage. He concentrated his visual along the very top of the knoll, slowly moving from rock to cactus to mound, looking for anything out of the ordinary. It was a slow process examining every detail, trying desperately to keep his imagination from seeing things that weren't there.

The three men finished up the last of their box-feast and began readying equipment. The plan was simple enough, they would surprise and overwhelm Bishop and take Terri back with them. If she resisted, each man carried a Taser in his kit that would subdue even the most voracious wildcat.

While reports of Bishop's escapades during the coup attempt hadn't escaped their attention, there was little concern among the team. After the crew had reviewed Bishop's military records, they were all convinced he was hardly at their level of combat skill or training. The rancher below was deserving of caution perhaps, but no more of an obstacle than what they routinely overcame. Their prey was also well beyond his prime - a serious consideration by men who believed peak physical conditioning was a critical element in this sort of operation. Confidence was high that their superior numbers, training, and conditioning would crush any resistance in short order.

Deke whipped his hand in a tight, circular revving motion, a signal it was time to mount up and get moving.

Grim was ready. "'Bout time we got out of this shithole landscape. I like trees and water. This place is as bad as Iraq, maybe worse."

Moses concurred, "Yeah, let's go get this over with. I've got better things to do."

Moving out at an aggressive pace, the team proceeded down the slope toward Bishop's ranch.

Bishop was thinking the search was a waste of time. There was too much territory to cover, and what he was looking for might not even exist. He persuaded himself that checking out the footprint was the smart thing to do. There was a chance it was his, maybe even Terri's.

He was picking up the rifle when movement on the downslope of the hill caught his eye. He immediately returned to the scope's eyepiece, scanning for a moment until he found them.

Three men came into view, all dressed in neutral browns and tan. They wore bush hats, load vests, and packs, and carried what appeared to be three different models of battle rifles. Bishop watched with keen interest as the men progressed, their confidence and economy of movement were obvious even through the tiny glass portal of the riflescope. These weren't drifters or random hunters—the men in his sights were professionals, and they were headed directly toward Terri and the ranch.

A million questions flooded Bishop's thoughts. The approaching team was well over 1,000 yards away, out of range. Should he move to intercept them? Who and why would anyone dedicate such a highly trained resource to his ranch? Should he beat it back to the camper and warn Terri, or should he engage them as far away as possible? Should he and Terri just hide in the hills?

The rifle he carried was a tool for long-range

engagement, not "close in" fighting. Its magazines didn't hold as many rounds, and the optics weren't right for close-in battle. He monitored their progress for a little longer, trying to judge how long he had before they reached his property. He determined he didn't have time to change equipment; he'd have to "run with what he brung."

The predators were on a track that was practically a straight west to east line. Bishop's position was slightly to their north. Determined to keep them away from Terri, he moved to engage them before they reached the vicinity of the camper. *Maybe I can scare them off or delay their approach*, he thought. *Maybe I can buy some time to think of a way out of this mess.*

Bishop began scrambling from the outcropping to the mound, heading south on an intercept vector. The weapon he carried had an effective killing range of 1,000 yards in the right hands. Bishop thought his skills with the current calm conditions were more in the range of 700-800 yards. Another factor that crossed his mind was the body armor being worn by the intruders—the further away he engaged, the less likely he would be able to penetrate that layer of protection.

Trying to calm the fear building inside of his gut, Bishop began assessing the promised encounter. The advantages in his column included knowing the terrain, having the element of surprise, and having a longer-range weapon. His foe possessed greater numbers, more combat power, and the ability to maneuver. The analysis didn't prove promising.

Taking the best cover he could find on the run, Bishop went prone behind a steep ledge of rock a little over a foot high. He could fight from here, and there was a reasonable path of egress if he couldn't hold the position. It was over 400 yards back to the camper, with good cover along the way. This is where he'd make a stand.

He steadied the rifle, lowering the magnification to expand his field of view. It took almost a minute to find the approaching threat, but there they were, maintaining the same course as predicted.

Using the hash marks on the scope's crosshairs, Bishop estimated the distance to the men. They were just over 900 yards and closing in. He proceeded through the mental checklist required for a long-range shot. Achieving a natural point-of-aim was first, which required him to shift his body just slightly while arranging two small stones under the rifle's fulcrum. The goal was to avoid having any part of his body touch the weapon, to let it rest naturally while on target. Human frames breathe, shake, and move, the effect of which would result in missed shots.

Next was the calculation of the bullet drop. Bishop carried a small notepad containing all of his DOPE, or data on previous engagements, in his kit. He knew from practice and experience that at 800 yards, his bullet would drop over 80 inches. There wasn't any wind, but at that range, the twist imparted by the grooves inside the barrel would cause the round to fly a few inches to the right. Bishop removed his hat and rolled it into a tube. Inserting the wad of material between his shoulder and the rifle butt provided an extra cushion to isolate the weapon from his pulse or other movement.

Finally, he forced himself to relax. Starting at his toes, he mentally commanded every muscle to go limp. This was extremely difficult to do when facing a potential gunfight.

His breathing under control and timed, Bishop nudged the rifle ever so slightly to bring the crosshairs onto the guy walking point. He nudged the rocks under the pistol grip to allow for the drop and disengaged the safety. No part of his body was touching the rifle except his cheek welded to the stock, and a finger barely touching the trigger. The aim was perfect.

Bishop stopped, pulling his head back from the weapon's stock. What if these guys are just passing through? What if they're just here to deliver a message from Fort Bliss? What if they're just three guys from Meraton, trying to find the ranch from the hand-drawn map he'd left with Pete?

Bishop couldn't do it. Despite the state of society, regardless of the attempt on their lives just a few short days ago, he couldn't send death screaming out of his rifle barrel. It didn't matter what the odds were, the suspicions and circumstantial evidence didn't mean a hill of beans. He didn't *know* for certain these men were a threat; there was no proof. He just couldn't do it. *Not everything is as it appears*, he thought.

By the time Bishop gathered himself, the approaching team was within 800 yards. Bishop held the crosshairs off aim and squeezed the trigger, the roar of the powerful rifle split the desert calm like a clap of thunder rolling across the plains.

The bullet landed slightly right and 10 feet in front of the lead man. As expected, Bishop watched his adversaries scatter to cover. Their movements revealed excellent discipline and quick reactions.

Most people, when shot at, stayed put. Even experienced infantrymen would show respect for a sniper, no matter how far off the first shot had been. Bishop's mouth fell open as he watched the three men through his optic. After an all too brief, momentary pause, the team in front of him resumed their approach—this time moving with haste and caution.

His warning shot had backfired, the justification now clearly flawed. The element of surprise evaporated—his single most important advantage no longer playing a role. Now the approaching gunmen knew he was alert. Dodging, ducking, and rushing from cover-to-cover, Bishop watched, horrified at the efficiency of their movements. *These guys are pros—these guys have skills.*

Now convinced of their objective, Bishop had no reservations about shooting anyone. The problem was he couldn't get a clear shot. No two of the men exposed themselves at any one time. There wasn't a single instance where any of them were out in the open long enough to take aim. They alternated movements, going in random order, and always hustling from one spot of cover to the next.

Bishop tried to focus on one assaulter, waiting for the man to raise his head. They were just too fast and too disciplined. At 700 yards, Bishop was becoming worried. At 600 yards, the sweat was pouring down his brow and into his eyes.

Think, damnit! screamed inside his head. *You've got to hold this ground, and your advantages are disappearing quickly.* In another few minutes, they would be so close his longer-range weapon wouldn't matter. Another advantage would vanish.

Instead of trying to fix on the moving men, Bishop forced himself to study the terrain in their path. At about 450 yards was an open area with little or no cover. Scanning their general path, Bishop desperately tried to put himself in the foe's position. *I'd gather up at the edge of that open area, and I'd rush my team across all at once. The first guy to raise his head will be to draw my fire; he'll be a feint. He won't expose himself until the others are moving.*

Bishop calculated the drop of his rounds while he waited. Sure enough, the team went to cover at the edge of the open ground.

It took them longer than he expected to initiate their next move. Time was no longer flowing at normal speeds, perhaps it was just his imagination. He knew exactly where all three had hit the ground, and he watched, promising to ignore the first man who showed himself.

There he was, the one in the center—the diversion. Bishop watched as he rose from behind a mound, moving slower than normal. Adjusting the crosshairs away from the bait, Bishop spotted the body of a second man rise from behind a boulder. He whispered, "Send it," and pulled the trigger.

Not waiting to see the results, Bishop managed a second shot as another intruder ran bent at the waist across the opening. That fast, the three men had cleared the open ground and were again advancing with good cover. Or were they?

Bishop twisted the rifle back to the first target and saw a man rolling on the ground. A hit! He couldn't believe it when the guy rolled twice, and then suddenly rose up and ran back to the rocks. *Damn it! I must have hit his armor.*

Before he could ponder a next step, bullets started impacting around Bishop's position. It took him a second to realize his shots must have given away the hiding spot—probably the dust kicked up from the muzzle blast. Staying low, Bishop retreated to a spot he'd identified before, disgusted and worried by the results of the first encounter.

Deke was hurting. That fucking shot had entered one of the spare magazines strapped across his abdomen, goring through to the Kevlar vest beneath. While the bullet hadn't penetrated his body, the kinetic energy had knocked the air from his lungs, and he was sure at least two ribs were broken.

Pushing back the pain, he gritted his teeth and used hand signals to let his teammates know he was okay.

The ambush was a minor annoyance. Their target had shown his inferior tactics with the warning shot, an important indicator of his mindset. It was unlikely they would receive another warning, but that was acceptable. They knew where he was.

The round that found its mark on his chest was probably luck. There was no foolproof way to cross an open area, and the shooter had just been aiming at the right place at the right time. They would have this operation wrapped up by lunch. Deke hoped the kill shot would come from his weapon, payback for the sore ribs.

When the first shot had echoed down the canyon, Terri had been folding laundry while wondering if Bishop were using the Christmas gift she had made for him.

"He was right about the footprint," she said out loud. Her hand drifted to the pistol on the counter as she peered warily outside. She couldn't see anything from the tiny camper window, its view restricted to a small portion of the canyon's opening.

"God, please keep my husband safe."

When the next volley of gunfire bounced along the rock walls, Terri made up her mind to move. Bishop had always warned her that the camper was a bad place to be if anyone ever attacked the ranch. As she put on her shoes, she remembered his words. "Terri, if someone starts shooting, the skin of the camper is like cardboard. The bullets will go through like a hot knife through butter. Don't stay in here—go to the Bat Cave if you can make it safely."

Terri intended to do just that.

Wishing she'd paid more attention when Bishop had tried to teach her about self-defense, Terri pushed open the camper's door and paused. After hundreds of bullets didn't come screaming through the opening, she popped her head around the corner once, twice, and then sprang from the doorway.

Running as if she was being chased by wild demons, Terri made for the Bat Cave. Breathless, she pulled the heavy steel door closed behind her and dropped the latch. Terri leaned against the cool, stone walls, drinking in the air and plotting her next action. She looked down at the small pistol in her hand, and then at the rack of rifles hanging along the opposite wall. "I need a bigger gun," she announced.

~  ~

Bishop sprinted for the boulder, the crack of passing bullets snapping at his back like the jaws of a ferocious dog. Cutting behind the large hunk of granite, he circled the stone and came out firing on the other side. Instead of surprising the pursuing attackers and catching them out in the open, Bishop was knocked flat to the ground. Lying stunned, he couldn't comprehend what had just happened. His vision was blurred, and he felt like someone had just hit him in the forehead with a baseball bat.

More bullets reached for his body, the puffs of stinging sand scratching at his face. Only extreme force of will pulled him out of the daze, giving him the wherewithal to roll hard and get behind the boulder. He managed one knee and leaned out; sending two quick rounds back, a desperate act designed to inform the stalkers they had missed. He had no idea where the bullets went.

Bishop lowered the weapon, noticing something different. He was shocked after looking down and finding the rifle stock covered in blood – his blood.

Removing his glove and gingerly feeling his scalp, he discovered a long gash on his head. His ear was too painful to touch. *That was close*, he thought. *Terri's going to start calling me numbskull.*

Despite the throbbing, burning pain building inside his head, Bishop knew he would live—at least for a few more minutes.

Several hostile bullets plastered the rocks he was using for cover, their angle advising Bishop his adversaries had advanced, signaling it was time to move again.

Bishop's legs pushed hard, thrusting with every ounce of power as his body launched over the waist high pile of rocks. Twisting in mid-air, he landed with a rolling motion to dissipate the force of the impact. The heavy barrel of the AR10 came up quickly, three shots barking where he anticipated the closest predator would appear. All three rounds pinged off the rock face, harmlessly flying off into the desert without touching human flesh.

Kicking with his legs while using his elbows, Bishop scooted on his belly to the stone barricade he had just hurdled. Geysers of desert sand erupted where an elbow or leg had been just a moment before, chasing him like a cloud of stinging bees until he was tight against the rock. This was his fourth egress since firing that first shot at the attackers.

Fear was now a second adversary, a foe as dangerous as the men trying to kill him. He fought hard to push down the determined uneasiness, a sensation trying its best to build into full-blown panic. Bishop was scared because he'd never encountered anyone quite like the team pursuing him. They moved as if controlled by a single mind. Their lines of advance were always perfect, their timing impeccable. No patterns were repeated, no mistakes made.

One shooter would cover two with withering fire, soon followed by two covering one in the advance. They didn't spray or rush their shots, their rhythm like a metronome of hot lead and crackling death. Regardless of the movement or cover, they always projected more fire at Bishop than he could return. As individuals, they rarely offered a target, forcing Bishop to expose himself at great risk. Exploding shards of rocks burning into his cheeks dissuaded Bishop from using that tactic more than once. Screaming ricochets from near misses were always pushing him down and back, herding him into the dead-end canyon for the eventual kill.

Two of them would spread left and right, bounding from boulder to the outcropping, never moving at the same time, never in the open, unless one of their own was pouring round after round at Bishop's head. It was a small miracle he hadn't been flanked yet. Twice they had been within a few steps of that goal. It would all end quickly if they achieved that advantage.

Back, ever back they had pushed him, herding his retreat into the canyon he called home. Now, the camper was in clear view over his shoulder. *This is it*, he thought, looking at the open spaces behind him. *I can't go backward any further – there's no cover – no place left to hide.*

Trying to anticipate their next move, Bishop popped up and snap-fired three rounds, but only insulted the desert air with the attempt. The rifle locked back empty. He ejected the spent magazine and slammed home another—his last one. His hands a blur, Bishop punched the bolt release and slapped the forward assist. This was his last 20 rounds. After this, it was his pistol, and that might as well be a squirt gun against the body armor worn by his attackers.

Terri had her rifle loaded and a spare magazine lying on her lap. She was sitting in the old lawn chair, rocking nervously back and forth, listening to the sounds of the battle outside. It hadn't escaped her attention that the gunfire crept closer and closer.

After securing her rifle, she had occupied herself scooting the heavy metal boxes of gold away from the wall, the effort taking all of her strength. She figured to hide and fight from behind them, if and when the bad men tried to enter the cave.

Three times the gunfire had subsided long enough for her to think Bishop had either won or been killed. Despite knowing he would be furious with her for leaving the safety of the Bat Cave, she had risen with the thought of going outside and checking on her husband. The sounds of more shooting rolling down the canyon walls always made her return to her perch.

Now, the gunfire was close, very close. She could discern at least two different types of rifles by the sound of their discharge. Bishop was up against more than one person, and she concluded he was losing. There was no other explanation for the movement and pattern of the fighting.

Thoughts of the child growing inside of her faded, replaced with love and concern for her husband. *I'm still pretty lithe*, she told herself. *I'm going to at least stick my head out and see what's going on. Bishop might need me—it's happened before.*

Deke wasn't pleased. This entire operation was taking longer than anyone had anticipated, and his ribs were aching to high heaven. The man they were engaged with was the luckiest fuck he'd ever encountered—always moving just in the nick of time, foiling the kill.

In the grand scheme of the universe, it didn't matter. They had him pinned now, no place to run, no escape. The boulder field he had been using to cover his retreat had thinned out to a flat, barren surface. If their target made a mad dash for the camper beyond, they'd cut him to shreds within 10 steps. If the fool decided to make that last little mound of rocks his Alamo, so be it. He would die just as badly there as anywhere else.

He decided to give his men one more minute of breathing before he would signal the final advance. He slowly scouted the area in front of his team, mentally planning the final push. This job was nothing different, just another snatch and grab after removing the protection.

Glaring at the rock Bishop was hiding behind, he snorted. "I am Godzilla; you are Tokyo."

Bishop used the pause to draw air, not inspiration. He guessed his antagonists were plotting their final rush, no doubt exchanging hand signals while out of sight. *They'll throw a head-fake at me again*, he thought. The first guy I see won't be the real attack.

The problem was he didn't know if it would be the left or the right side that charged his position. He guessed it would the left. There was slightly better cover, and the guy on that side had seemed the most aggressive of the three.

Bishop was wrong.

Without warning, all three attackers popped up at once, rifles firing where Bishop's head was peeking over the top of the rocks. Ducking and rolling once to his left, Bishop fired two shots, adjusted, and fired two more. The incoming lead followed to his new position, so he rolled right, and again, sent more rounds down range.

Back and forth the exchange went, Bishop counting down the rounds remaining in his weapon. When he got to five rounds left, he was going to have to risk exposing himself for a better shot. He pulled the pistol from its holster, sitting it beside him just in case.

He was down to eight rounds when he changed his mind. *Fuck it*, he thought. *They're going to get me anyway. At least I can make the odds a little better for Terri if I can take one of them out.*

Boldly, he rose from behind his cover and remained exposed, almost daring one of the assaulters to take a shot. The man flanking right obliged, spinning out from behind his shelter and firing. Before Bishop could adjust for a shot, a new weapon joined the fray, sending the man shooting at Bishop scrambling for cover. Confused, thinking someone had gotten around him, Bishop pivoted to address the new threat and stopped cold when he saw Terri firing at the bad guys. She had snuck into a small notch in the rock wall and appeared to be well protected.

Terri's fire surprised the attackers, breaking their momentum and leveling the balance of combat power. With her covering one side of the canyon, Bishop could focus on the other. He was in position and waiting when the two men rushed around a truck-sized boulder, charging Bishop's position.

Bishop almost smiled as his weapon's recoil pushed into his shoulder. The closest man went down, his forward progress causing him to hit the earth hard and tumble. The second dude cut right just in time, Bishop's rounds chasing him back into the boulder field.

Terri kept up a steady stream of bullets, suppressing any forward movement from the right side of the canyon. More than just covering an angle, her presence broke the rhythm of their attack…made the musicians in their band play off tempo. Popping three shots here, three there, she was keeping the bad guys from storming Bishop's position and giving him the opening he needed.

Movement caught Bishop's eye, and for a moment, his heart froze. An arm arched over the top of a nearby boulder, a small metal object flying through the air directly at Bishop's position. Grenade!

Bishop buried his face in the hard dirt and steeled himself for the blast. He heard the metal canister strike stone and bounce once—it sounded very close.

Rather than an ear-shattering explosion, Bishop heard a wimpy little "pop" followed by a hissing sound. Exhaling, he realized his foes hadn't thrown a hand grenade, they had popped smoke. This was probably a tactic to break contact and rescue the downed man.

In the next few seconds, Bishop had to decide between

shooting through the gathering cloud, per chance hitting someone trying to rescue the wounded man, or using the drifting white wall of smoke to make for Terri's position. *An injured man will slow them down*, he thought. *I'm about out of ammo – it's time to get out.*

A minute later, Terri and Bishop were in the Bat Cave, breathing hard from the sprint. Bishop immediately moved to switch rifles and began loading magazines for the new weapon into the pouches on his vest. Terri covered the door until he was ready. Bishop turned to his wife as he made for the opening, "Stay here."

"Hold on just a second there, mister, you're hurt. There's blood everywhere."

Terri moved to check Bishop's wound, but he waved her off.

"Stay here, Terri, *please*. These guys aren't some amateur bunch of bank robbers, or thug criminals. These guys are pros. I've got to get back out there."

"I know, and I'm going with you. But if that wound gets infected, you're in a lot of trouble. We can take three minutes to clean and bandage it."

Bishop exhaled, exasperated. "Terri, I think they're falling back to regroup, and then they'll be back. If I don't get out there, we'll be trapped inside this cave until who knows when. I can move faster without you."

With her hands on her hips, Terri made it clear she wasn't letting Bishop out of her sight.

The pounding in his head was becoming worse, and the blood was beginning to dry, adding to the discomfort. Pulling the chair around so he could watch the door, Bishop sat with the rifle across his lap.

Terri took a clean cloth and dipped it in the bucket of water they kept in the cave. She gingerly dabbed the head wound, trying not to hurt her husband. Bishop sat stoically, eyes never leaving the entrance. "Hurry," he said.

Giving up on gentle cleaning, Terri picked up the bucket and warned, "There's too much blood to clean the wound that way. Tilt your head and close your eyes."

Terri poured a steady stream of water over Bishop's injury. She had to repeat the pour, wipe, pour process until the bucket was empty. Sitting the bucket on the floor, she stood up to check the wound and gasped.

"What?"

"Bishop, the top half of your ear is gone, baby. I'm sorry … but it's just gone."

Bishop's hand immediately went to his head, feeling his

ear. His touch caused a painful wince, and he gave up trying to assess the damage.

"Just pour some of the powdered antibiotic on it—I've got to get moving."

Terri dug in the kit and found the small packets of medicine. She poured as much of the brownish granules as possible into the gash created by the bullet, a shot that had missed killing her husband by less than half an inch. Next was a bandage, which she wrapped around and around his head, taping off the loose end. Finally, she found the bottle of painkillers and made him swallow a full dose.

Bishop stood, stepping immediately for the door. His second stride was stopped by Terri moving in front of him and putting both of her hands on his chest. "Bishop, please wait. Let's take just a minute to talk this over."

"I'm all ear."

Terri snickered, more from relief that her husband was back to his normal cornball humor, than the play on words.

"Bishop, I'm going with you. If I stay here, they could get behind you and kill me anyway. If I'm with you, I might be able to help. I should mention that I just bailed your ass out, in case that thump on the head has damaged your memory."

He had to admit, she had a point. If she came along, he'd be worried. If she stayed here, he'd be worried. His head was pounding so badly now, he didn't have the mental energy to argue with her.

"Okay, you're with me. But, please do what I ask you to do—nothing more and nothing less."

Terri picked up her rifle and stuck two full mags in the back pockets of her jeans. Despite the blood and sweat, Terri reached up and brushed Bishop's hair. "I love you, and don't worry about that wound. I still think you're *ear*-resistible."

184

Chapter 12

Bishop's Ranch
January 1, 2016

Hugging the canyon walls, Bishop moved to the point of last contact with the intruders. It didn't take him long to find their trail. The blood spots, boot prints, and other disturbances to the earth were easy to follow. Bishop turned to Terri, and warned, "We need to be extra, extra careful here. They don't seem to be concerned about anybody following them. It's almost as if they want us to find them. That's a sure sign someone is setting an ambush."

When they reached the area where Bishop had been shot, he paused and bent to pick up a spent cartridge. Examining the brass, he announced, "This is a 5.56 NATO round, the same caliber issued to the military. I can't be for sure, but I don't think this is a military round."

"How can you tell?"

"Most military ammunition is made in only a few different plants. Each manufacturing facility places its own unique stamp on the base of each round. Lake City, Radford . . . they all have a distinctive mark. This case is different. The other thing odd about it is that military grade ammo uses a box primer. This is more like a civilian primer. I've never seen anything quite like it."

"So you don't think they were military?"

"It's hard to tell. I've heard stories about the different Special Forces units making their own rounds. I've also heard of their evaluating small lots of ammo, so these might be test rounds. Two of their weapons were not military issue."

Bishop moved from one disturbed area to another, checking the ground and picking up spent brass. As Terri watched, Bishop leaned against a rock, apparently dizzy. "You okay, Bishop?"

"Yeah, I'm cool. My head is thumping like a brass band is all. Let's keep moving."

The couple resumed following the trail, slowly picking their way through the boulder field, heading toward the edge of the canyon.

Something didn't feel right about the desert. Bishop couldn't quite put his finger on it . . . was it a sound . . . a vibration?

Out of nowhere, three ATVs zoomed across the open terrain in front of the couple, each machine carrying one of the attackers. Bishop raised his rifle to fire, but the speeding vehicles never provided a clear shot. One of the men slowed his ride and looked over his shoulder directly at the astounded couple. The man flipped Bishop a middle finger, and then gassed his unit, heading into the desert.

Bishop glanced at Terri, "Gee, I hope that bumpy ride doesn't hurt the guy with the wounded leg."

Terri chuckled at Bishop's remark. "Those things scared the beejeebers out of me, Bishop."

Since there was no need to track down the intruders, the couple casually headed back to the Bat Cave. After unloading their gear, Terri wanted to look at Bishop's wound again.

"We need to go to Meraton, Bishop. This needs stitches and probably a stronger antibiotic than what we have here. Let's go to town and let the doc look you over."

"You just want to go shopping."

Terri rolled her eyes at Bishop's logic. She went to the stack of stainless steel lockboxes and lifted one, testing its weight. Hefting it to eye level, she held it so her husband could see his reflection.

Bishop winched, wondering if the slight distortion in the metal made things worse. He looked like hell warmed over. Small abrasions covered his face, each about the size and shape of a fingernail clipping, many of them surrounded by the discoloration of a newly forming bruise. *Rock chips*, he thought. *One shouldn't partake in gunfights around solid rock.*

Terri adjusted her stance and Bishop's view. The new image made Bishop inhale sharply. There was a two-inch gash cutting through his scalp, starting just above his forehead and ending at his ear. With the chunks of dried blood and mangled flesh, it was difficult to tell how much of his ear was left. Terri was right, the wound needed sewing up. It was bleeding again already.

"Okay, you win. We'll go shopping."

Terri just tilted her head and smiled at Bishop's stubbornness. "I know you'll want to take some stuff to the market, so don't blame everything on me. Can you get ready while I go to the camper and pack up some things in there?"

"Yeah, it will take me a few minutes to gather everything. Can you get me a change of clothes while you're packing?"

"No problem." She paused before going to the camper. With a twinkle in her eye, Terri added, "You won't mind if I take along a few extra things, will you?"

Bishop had his back turned and didn't read her expression. "What kind of things?"

Terri replied, "Oh, nothing major, just some odds and ends I've had *ear*marked to trade."

Before he could turn, Terri was scampering out of the Bat Cave, giggling like a schoolgirl all the way to the camper.

West Virginia
January 1, 2016

The leadership committee of the Independents projected an assortment of facial expressions ranging from patient to apathetic. Moreland stood from his seat at the head of the conference table and concluded his presentation. "Ladies and gentlemen, in summary, this is why I've called this emergency meeting. We have a decision to make. It's quite simple really. Should I accept the presidency or continue to lead our movement? I want to hear your thoughts."

The first person to Moreland's right was a retired four-star general, former chair of the Joint Chiefs of Staff. Clearing his throat, the military man began to voice his position. "Sir, my belief is that you should become the president and immediately defuse the situation in Louisiana. While I fully understand that you will have to compromise the Independents' core beliefs in order to effectively rule, the country needs leadership right now, not political positioning."

Moreland nodded, "Thank you, General."

The next was a retired Supreme Court justice. "Senator, I'm afraid I have to take the opposite position. I don't believe you will be given the chance to govern. As soon as the establishment realizes you were the leader of our movement, they will fight you every step of the way. You may be effective while martial law is in effect, but after that you will be stonewalled time and time again."

Moreland rubbed his chin, "Do you believe this would be due to my being the leader of the Independents, or because of the assassination of the president?"

The retired justice responded, "The attempt on the former president's life would be a difficult hurdle to overcome. Political spin, proper management of the press, and good public relations could smooth over the actions of the Independents up until that point. Ordering the death of any world leader, ours or anyone else's, is unforgivable."

Moreland scanned the room, noting the heads nodding in agreement. "But you all know I didn't order any such attempt on the president. I want to believe the truth will eventually win out."

The wise man from the Supreme Court smiled at

Moreland. "Just a few years ago some newly uncovered facts came to light about the assassination of President Lincoln. Consider. . . a modern day controversy erupted due to a book that claimed new information about a slaying that occurred 150 years ago. Over 40 years after the assassination of President Kennedy, a vast majority of Americans believe they still don't know the whole story. There is less information available about what happened at Fort Bliss a few days ago than either of those events. What makes you believe a simple claim by this council would have any political impact? Why should this situation be any different than previous assassinations?"

Moreland sighed, "You have a point, sir. Perhaps I'm being too naïve."

"Senator, I've spent over 50 years deciding legal cases. Over 2,000 times I've sat while the two sides presented their evidence, and then I've made a judgment based on what was presented. In this case . . . the case of who ordered the attempt on the Commander in Chief's life, I would have to find the Independents guilty based on what I've heard so far. I have a feeling the American people will come to the same conclusion."

Again, several of the council members agreed.

Moreland returned to his chair. "If our innocence can be proven, if an investigation uncovers additional facts that point to another culprit, would this sway the council's opinion?"

Several side conversations broke out, mumbling and whispering around the group. Moreland let it go, remaining quiet at the head of the table.

The justice spoke again, "Senator, I believe it would. If we could remove the stigma of ordering that attempt on the president's life, then any other objection to your presidency could be overcome."

Another hour of discussions flowed around the table. It took a few heated debates and creative solutions, but a consensus was finally reached. If the Independents could clear the movement's name of any assassination attempt, then Moreland should accept the presidency.

After a few rounds of handshakes, the meeting adjourned, and Moreland headed directly for his study for a sniffer of brandy. Wayne joined him after making sure the council members were all safely on their way.

Moreland's aide started the conversation. "Announcing that most of the council members would have cabinet positions in your administration was a stroke of brilliance, sir. You would have a ready-made executive branch that was politically aligned to our movement. Very wise."

Moreland nodded, "Thank you, Wayne. I hope this entire

exercise isn't for naught. Tell me more about this woman who was with the president before his death."

"We know very little about her, sir. As of the latest information available to me, no one is even sure of her whereabouts."

Moreland's face twisted into a frown. "As I understand it, she told General Westfield and a Secret Service agent her story, correct?"

"Yes, sir. That is what I understand as well."

Setting the brandy down on his desk, Moreland rose and looked Wayne square in the eye. "We have the opportunity to make a difference here. We can change the destiny of the entire country. I want you to verify what that witness heard. I want General Westfield to find this woman."

Wayne nodded his understanding.

Moreland continued, "Let our friends from Washington know I've decided to accept the presidency. I want the four senior senators from the other party to arrange transportation to Fort Bliss. We will fly there ourselves in a few days. If we find the woman, she can testify and clear our name. If we don't, then we'll have to pray that General Westfield's recounting will be good enough for the opposition."

Wayne shook his head. "Sir, I don't think this is a wise course of action. It's not in the spirit of what the council agreed on."

Moreland waved off Wayne's protest, his voice firm. "This country can't wait any longer, Wayne. We've got to move - and move right now. Perhaps I'm crossing the line with this gamble, but I feel strongly that it's necessary. What do we lose if those senators don't buy Westfield's story? Then the Independents will continue, and we will have civil war. I will sleep better at night knowing we tried."

Wayne's expression showed he wasn't convinced, but he didn't protest any further. "Yes, sir . . . I'll get things moving in the direction of Fort Bliss and let the base commander know to expect a lot of visitors."

Meraton, Texas
January 1, 2016

The trip to Meraton was uneventful, the couple arriving as the market was in full swing. Circumventing Main Street and its myriad of stalls, tables, shoppers, and vendors, Bishop maneuvered the pickup through the side streets and parked behind The Manor.

Betty was nowhere to be found, but that wasn't unusual

this time of day. Terri suggested they use the back street and visit Pete while they waited to be checked into a room.

"Are you ashamed to be seen in the market with me?" Bishop teased.

"Well, honey, you are covered in blood, sweat, and grime. You look like death warmed over. I think it would be *ear-responsible* to risk frightening small children in the market."

Bishop grunted, "Ear we go again."

Pete's Place was only a block away. The couple arrived to find the local watering hole's door locked and posted with a sign, "Be Back in 30 minutes."

Bishop read the sign and furrowed his brow, "Terri, you don't think Pete and Betty are . . . well . . . you know . . . an item?"

Terri smiled at her husband's phrasing, "Could be, Bishop. They're both consenting adults. Maybe they are off enjoying a little midday romance. More power to 'em."

"Midday romance? You mean a nooner?"

"Bishop! Not everyone's a perv like you. They might simply be enjoying a walk in the park."

Bishop had to laugh, the effort causing his scalp discomfort. The pain was quickly followed by a warm liquid feeling running down his neck. Terri saw it too. "Bishop, let's go find the doctor—you're bleeding through the bandages."

Backtracking to The Manor, the couple entered the famous gardens of the remote retreat. Betty, through methods unknown, somehow managed to keep the renowned landscaping perfect. This was no small feat, given the general lack of civilization and its associated fertilizers and pesticides.

The pool was also pristine, but that wasn't such a mystery. The pumps and filters were solar powered, and the hotel had a significant supply of chemicals on hand when the world had gone to hell. As they walked by, Bishop had to wonder how long those pre-collapse supplies would last.

The town now used one wing of the hotel's rooms as a makeshift hospital. It seemed logical to Terri that they would find the doctor here. No such luck. All of the doors were closed, the garden absolutely quiet with the exception of the singing birds enjoying the variety of plant life.

"There's nobody around, Bishop. Let's go back to the truck, and I'll change the bandage myself."

"Do you promise not to crack anymore ear jokes if I agree to submit?"

"No."

Bishop did his best to act hurt; the faked pout on his face only served to make Terri laugh. "Poor, poor, Bishop. He has a booboo, and it's ouchie. Come on young man, I'll put a Band-Aid on your skinned knee."

"Terri, you can try to mother me all you want, but it's going to take more than a lollipop to reward *me* for good behavior."

Bishop made a half-hearted attempt to grab Terri's backside, but she was too nimble and escaped, scampering a few steps ahead of him and staying out of reach as they made their way to the parking lot. At the back of the pickup, she suddenly turned and tried her best to be serious. Poking her finger in Bishop's chest, she commanded, "Now you behave yourself, young man. If you make me jump while I'm dressing your wound, I might slip and cause you additional pain or injury."

"Okay."

Bishop removed his hat and sat on the tailgate while Terri worked on his wound. She was about halfway through the procedure when Betty's voice sounded from the gate.

"What's going on out here? Terri, is that you?"

Terri leaned around the cab and waved at Betty. "Hey there. Have you seen the doctor?"

Betty didn't answer the question directly. "What's the matter, Terri? Is something wrong with the baby?"

"Oh, no . . . well . . . not *this* baby," replied Terri, while rubbing her tummy. "It's my larger baby that needs medical attention."

It took Betty a second to figure out whom Terri was talking about, the realization causing concern. "Bishop?"

Rather than trying to explain, Terri waved her friend over to see for herself. Betty rounded the pickup's bed and saw Bishop sitting there, her view restricted to the uninjured side of his head. "Terri, thank God the baby's okay. You had me worried there for a second."

Again, Bishop faked hurt feelings. "I'm not hurt too badly, Betty. Thank you for the concern."

The remark drew a stern look from the hotel's manager. "You look fine to me, Bishop. What's wrong with. . . ." Bishop turned his head slightly so she could see the damage.

"Ouch! Let me take a look at that."

Bishop turned his head so Betty could see the full extent of his cranial damage, half-expecting sympathy.

Betty responded to the carnage. "So, Bishop, you finally drove poor Terri over the edge, and she took a shot at ya, didn't she?"

Terri struggled to keep a straight face, finally snorting loudly as she tried to turn away. Betty wasn't done yet. "I see that super thick skull saved you again. Good thing she didn't borrow my 12-gauge, or you'd be done for. As it is, you need to see the doctor."

"We've been looking for the doc," Bishop commented.

"He's taking care of that kid that got shot this morning from Alpha." Betty hesitated, trying to recall the name. "You know the one. His father is a friend of yours—the big guy and his son that showed up at Pete's last week."

Bishop hopped off the pickup's tailgate, "Kevin! Someone shot Kevin?"

Terri was in shock as well. "Oh my God, Betty. Is he going to be okay?"

"He was hit in the chest is all I know. They sped into town just after first light this morning, horn blaring, and raising a fuss. Pete and I helped them get the boy into a room where the doc's been working on him ever since."

"Betty, we walked by there, and everything looked closed up and quiet. I don't understand."

"Doc felt like he needed more light to treat the patient. We moved them to one of the rooms in the main building, it has a lot bigger windows and not as much shade. The boy's father and that woman from the church in Alpha are both in there; Pete just took them some food."

Betty read the horrified look on both faces. "Come 'on, I'll take you over there. The doctor is going to do surgery soon, but I don't think he's started yet."

Terri finished wrapping Bishop's head, and then everyone rushed back into the gardens. A short time later, they entered The Manor's main building, and Betty knocked gently on the doorframe.

Diana answered, her eyes showing surprise at seeing Terri. While the girls were hugging, Diana acknowledged Bishop standing nearby. "Well hello, stranger. I've not seen you in a long time."

"Hello there, Ms. Brown. It's good to see you too. What's it been, two days? How's Kevin?"

Nick, curious about the commotion outside, stuck his head out into the hall. When he saw Bishop and Terri, he stepped into the hall, closing the door behind him. Terri embraced him while gushing, "Oh, Nick. I'm so sorry. How is Kevin? How are you?"

Nick flashed Bishop a look of, "Am I glad to see you," while the two men pumped hands. Facing both of his friends, Nick began. "Kevin and I were going hunting this morning. I rousted him before dawn, and we were heading into the mountains. As we were walking past the county courthouse, I saw a light flash in the basement. We went to investigate, and two guys shot Kevin on the way out."

Terri raised her hands to her cheeks, "How bad is it?"

"He took a rifle round to the lung. The bullet shattered his shoulder blade and fragmented there. The doc is trying to figure out how to drain his lung and then operate, but the lack of equipment is holding him back. It's 50/50 right now."

Bishop had to ask, "What happened to the two guys who shot him? Who were they?"

"They got away clean. I have no idea who they were or what they were after. Kevin stayed back while I went into the basement to see what was going on. They got around me somehow and shot Kevin at the top of the stairs."

Bishop was puzzled. "No idea who they were or what they were after? Is there food or fuel stored in that area?"

Deacon Brown cut in, "No, it doesn't make any sense. There's nothing down in that basement but old tax records, marriage certificates, birth records, that sort of thing. There is nothing of value down there, nothing worth killing a boy over."

Something in Diana's explanation connected with Bishop. He hesitated for a moment and then asked, "Did you say old tax records?"
"Yes, why?"

Bishop's felt weak, and it showed. Terri went to his side, taking an arm. "Bishop, what's the matter? You don't look so good."

Nick cut in, "That was *my* next question. Bishop, you look like you've taken an ass kicking."

Bishop looked at Terri, his expression pained. "I paid the ranch's property taxes at that courthouse every year. That's how they knew where the ranch was."

Nick and Diana didn't get it and started peppering questions. "What? What do you mean, Bishop? Who knew what?"

Bishop held up his hand to stop the barrage. "I've got to sit down, I don't feel so good."

Betty opened the door to another room, escorting Bishop to a chair. After he was seated, she smiled lovingly and said, "You need to have your head examined," which everyone thought was very funny.

193

The doctor looked over the top of his glasses. "Bishop, I don't have any local anesthetic to give you. Maybe we should ask Pete if he'd donate some of his bathtub gin to take the edge off. It worked in the old Western movies."

Bishop waved him off. "It's okay, Doc. I can stand a few staples."

"I don't have any staples, only an old fashioned needle and thread. That ear is going to take a lot of sewing, Bishop. I found a considerable amount of tissue still there, hanging loose. I can reattach it, or I can amputate it. It's up to you."

Bishop sighed, "That's Terri's call. She's the one who has to look at me. We don't have many mirrors around the ranch."

Terri, resting in a nearby chair, rose to get a closer look at what the doctor meant. Bishop could feel the probing as the doctor indicated his plans to Terri.

"You see this section here . . . and here. I can sew those back on. It won't look like his other ear, but it will help even things out a little."

Terri moved to face Bishop, her expression deadpan serious as she held her husband's hand. "Bishop, how is your eyesight?"

Puzzled, Bishop frowned, but answered. "Okay, I guess. I've not noticed any issues so far. Why?"

Terri looked down at her feet before responding, a prediction of bad news. "Because if we don't sew on those ear-scraps, I don't think you'll ever be able to wear glasses."

The doctor chuckled out loud, quickly trying to recover from the indiscretion. "Sorry."

Bishop just rolled his eyes at Terri's joke. "How many stitches, Doc?"

"I would estimate about 80 or so. You've got a two-inch long gash that's down to the bone. The ear will take the majority of the work. I suggest you sample some of Pete's latest concoction before I take a needle to your head."

"I'm not much for drinking, Doc, but it sounds like Pete's wares might help a little. Putting 160 more holes in my head doesn't sound like much of a party."

The sawbones nodded his understanding, "If the situation were reversed, I think a few nips would be in order. It's the best we can do. I'll send someone down to Pete's to retrieve a bottle. Meanwhile, I want to clean all those little lacerations on your face and apply some antibiotic crème."

Looking up at Terri, the doctor winked and added, "Oh, and Bishop . . . I'm going to *eari*gate that wound."

Bishop mumbled, thinking of drinking for the first time in years. "For medicinal purposes only."

Pete knocked on the doorframe, holding a bottle of some yellowish liquid and a paper bag. "What's this I hear of Bishop getting into a fight with Mike Tyson?"

Bishop looked at his wife smiling. "Now *that's* funny."
"I think Mike Tyson was before my time," she needled. "Perhaps you *old* timers could explain it to me?"

Nick, hearing the voices from across the hall, decided he would take a break from his bedside vigil and joined the group.

Pete poured a small shot of the beverage, pulled a homemade tortilla out of the bag and handed it to Bishop. "I don't know if you've had anything to eat, but you don't want to drink this stuff on an empty stomach."

Bishop nodded his thanks and chewed a mouthful of the wonderful, fresh flatbread. Nick sauntered over and picked up Bishop's rifle. Stopping at the bed, Nick snapped his fingers and demanded, "Hand it over, buddy."

"What?"

"Your pistol," he demanded. "No mixing firearms and alcohol in polite company."

Bishop unsnapped his holster and handed the weapon to his friend, who then asked for the patient's knife. Bishop, after a long hesitation, surrendered that as well.

Nick disappeared from the room, returning a short time later. "Betty put them in a safe place. I'll get them back for you later."

Bishop nodded and raised the glass to his lips. Pete warned, "Go easy now—that stuff has aged a grand total of about two hours. It can hardly be called mellow."

Bishop took a small sip and grimaced. "Hell's demons and rabid bats, Pete. What *is* this stuff? Napalm and phosphorus mixed with kerosene?"

Pete snorted, "Pretty good stuff, wouldn't you say? That's a five dollar bottle of my best right there."

Bishop smiled at his friend. "If you were an undertaker, I'd say that stuff is a great marketing tool for drumming up business. And what do you mean 'five dollars?'"

Pete replied, "Since we're using real money now in the market, I had to put a price on my goods."

Bishop grunted, "Someone would actually buy a whole bottle of that stuff?"

"Well, no one has yet, but there's always hope," the bartender said laughing.

Terri chimed in. "I don't think we brought any cash, Pete. We took off in such a hurry."

Pete pointed at the bottle, "Well, your credit's good today."

Nick's thoughts drifted across the hall to Kevin and his condition. *Nothing is going to happen soon*, he thought. *One will be okay.* Nick reached for the liquor, deciding to join in. "I'll have a sample myself. Besides, it would be rude to let a wounded friend drink alone." Nick took a healthy mouthful of the liquor and swallowed. "Oh. . . . Wow. . . ."

Pete pulled a third glass from the table, not wanting to be left out. As he proceeded to pour a few fingers in the glass, he said, "I'd better sample this, make sure it's a quality product. Either you two are pantywaists, or this batch didn't turn out so well."

Pete threw back the entire pour, smacking his lips and looking into the empty glass. "Oh, that's good. Can you guys taste the apple?"

"Apple?" both men replied.

"Since I can't age it properly, I'm trying some flavors to make it interesting. I can taste the apple I used in this batch."

Bishop held up his glass for a toast, "Salud."

The room was filled with clinks. Bishop downed a little more, refusing to admit it didn't burn as much as the first gulp. "Pete, if you ever decided to get out of the bartending business, you could always use this stuff to clean fuel injectors."

Nick laughed and nodded in agreement. "Diesel fuel injectors." Holding up his glass for another toast, the big man announced, "To clean injectors!"

Pete, loving the attention, poured himself another.

It didn't take long before Bishop was feeling in a lighter mood. Nick, true to his word, refrained after one. Pete, obviously with a higher tolerance, kept up with Bishop but showed no sign of consumption. Terri sat in her chair, watching the proceedings, interested in how three of the men she adored most in the world would interact when inebriated—or at least, with a good buzz on.

Nick, politely ignoring Bishop's slurred words, wanted to talk. "Bishop, who did this? Who's after you and Terri?"

"I don't know, Nick. I've been asking that very question since this whole thing got started. It could be the group that tried to kill the president. They might be pissed because I thwarted their efforts. But that's not logical either—the president ended up

196

dead anyway."

Pete offered, "Do you think it's the gold?"

"No, these guys made a try for us at the base. Unless they thought we would tell them where it was, I don't think the gold has anything to do with it."

Terri added, "None of this makes any sense. Who has resources like that? Why would anyone waste the time to come after us?"

Nick thought about Terri's comment for a bit. He sighed and said, "There are lots of non-military teams with that level of training. ATF, FBI, State . . . all of them have specialized teams for various purposes."

Bishop took another sip. "The Secret Service has something to do with this. Powell wouldn't have wanted to use Terri for bait if he didn't know something was going on. I think our answers are only going to come from Agent Powell."

Nick's gaze traveled across the hall where his son was fighting for his life. His voice became very low, almost a growl. "I'd like to have a few moments alone with this Agent Powell. Do you think he's still at Bliss?"

Bishop shook his head, "No way to tell. When we left, there was talk of burying the president at Bliss and building a monument there. I would guess they won't do that until the new guy is sworn in. I would like to be in on any conversation you have with Agent Powell—I have a few questions for him myself."

Pete glanced from Nick to Bishop, feeling the fury resonating from both men. "I don't think I would like to be this Agent Powell when you two catch up with him."

The doctor interrupted the discussion, sticking his head inside of the room. "Bishop, you ready?"

Throwing back the last of his glass, Bishop thumped his sternum with his fist. "Let's get this over with."

Deke closed the door, assured his man was receiving proper medical attention. Bishop's .308 bullet had destroyed quite a bit of thigh flesh, but the wounded man was expected to recover. It was a shame, really. After all of the years of training, hard work, and hundreds of missions, Grim's career was over. It was doubtful anyone could meet the team's strenuous physical qualifications after such an injury.

The gentle vibration of Deke's cell phone broke his concentration. Out of habit, he looked at the screen before answering, but it was a wasted effort. The caller-ID feature didn't work with the satellite modifications installed in the device. Besides, there was only one person it could be.

"Happy New Year."

"Will he keep the leg?"

"Yes, but I'm not sure that's much solace right now. What does a man like that do with the rest of his life?" Deke prompted.

"That risk is part of the job."

Deke leaned against the wall and sighed. "I'm not so sure about that anymore. I think the scope of our agreement is expanding, and I don't like where it's headed."

"Is there a problem?"

"When I start losing men, I always have a problem."

There was a pause of static on the line. The eventual response had an edge. "If your firm can't handle the contract, I can make other arrangements. Should I contact your supervisor?"

"That is up to you. This has gone well beyond mere asset protection."

A grunt sounded through the tiny speaker. "We have an agreement, and nothing has changed. We purchased services that, according to our contract, are proactive and preventative."

"I could justify our actions a few weeks ago. It all made sense—I could reconcile things then. Now, I'm not so sure."

Slightly distorted by the earth-space-earth connection of the satellite phone, the chuckle sounded almost cartoonish. "I can't imagine someone in your line of work having a conscience. I thought men such as you followed orders as long as you were paid. We're still the highest bidder, aren't we? The only bidder, I'm sure."

The team leader didn't hesitate. "Doing a snatch and grab on some terrorist financier is easy to justify. Blackmailing the occasional arms dealer was morally rewarding in a way. Hell, I've even enjoyed a kidnapping game we played with a cartel down in Bogota. But this . . . it all seems . . . seems so macabre."

The caller's voice became soft. "Those missions served a dual purpose. You put money in your pockets and delivered a strong message—'Don't fuck with America.' Now, it's all about power, not drugs or weapons. There's a vacuum, and someone is going to fill it. It's going to be a mad, desperate scramble to get to the top of the heap. That's why your firm was employed, to protect our man until things settle down and enable a smoother transition to the top. It serves a dual purpose, just like your previous engagements."

Deke had expected that response. "I hope you're right

about that."

The voice on the other end spoke again. "I need to talk to that woman. I don't care if you can comprehend all of the moving pieces or not, do your job. It boggles the mind how your firm can boast of taking out some of the biggest, most well protected men in the world, and yet you can't deliver some cowboy's wife. I wonder if I'm not a victim of false advertising."

"We'll get the woman. You can rest assured of that."

The phone's tiny speaker didn't do justice to the grunt issued by the caller. "Both rest *and* assurances are in short supply these days. I'll expect a call soon. Very soon."

Chapter 13

Meraton, Texas
January 2, 2016

Bishop slept most of the next day, a combination of pain, exhaustion from the firefight, and the aftermath of Pete's product. It was mid-afternoon before he managed to rise, his scalp sore and head throbbing. After a quick check-over by the doctor, Bishop was given permission to take a dip in The Manor's pool. The water was cold, but the shock of submersion took his mind off of the pain being generated by his injury.

The quick swim refreshed his spirits somewhat, and he decided to dry off and warm in the sun. A squeak from the pool's gate announced his wife had joined him. Terri pulled up a deckchair and handed Bishop a plate of food. "You'd better eat something. It will help."

Nibbling on a ham sandwich made with pita bread, Bishop asked Terri how Kevin was doing.

"The surgery to repair the lung went well. He's out of immediate danger. The doc is still worried about the shoulder though . . . that and the risk of infection."

"How are Nick and Diana handling it?"

"They're doing as well as can be expected. Just losing her own son not long ago makes it a little tough for Diana to cope. Nick just sits beside Kevin's bed all day. I don't think he's moved."

Bishop continued eating his meal, the food energy making him feel slightly better. "Terri, I'm worried about going back to the ranch. The location being a secret was our best security, and now that's no longer the case. We got very, very lucky holding out against that last attempt. The next time they will come back with more men and maybe even belt-fed, automatic weapons and hand grenades. We wouldn't last three minutes."

Terri nodded, the situation being on her mind as well. "We could run . . . find someplace else to hide, but I don't know where that would be."

Bishop shook his head, the pulling of his stitches causing him to wince. "I don't want to be a refugee. Seeing those crucifixions at Fort Stockdale deters my wanderlust. Besides, we barely get by now, even with all of the supplies and amenities at the ranch. Going on the dodge with only what we can carry in the truck . . . no known supply of gasoline . . . I don't think it's a wise path."

"I know, Bishop. I thought about moving to Alpha or

Meraton until this all blew over, but if those men find us here, a lot of people could get hurt. They didn't strike me as the types that would hesitate to shoot up an entire town."

Bishop grunted, "You're absolutely right about that."

Finishing the last bit of food, Bishop continued. "So we can't run, and we can't move to town. That leaves us only one option that I can think of—we need to fortify the ranch."

Terri looked at her husband with questioning eyes. "How would you do that, Bishop? The place already makes me nervous with all of the tripwires and traps. Would we live inside the Bat Cave and never come out?"

Bishop stared into the distance. "I've got some ideas. Part of the supplies we picked up at Home Mart in Alpha could serve that purpose. Still, I'm not sure it will be enough. If we only knew what they would come after us with, it would help me devise a defense."

"Don't you always tell me to never underestimate the violence that people are capable of?

"Yes, but there are limits. If the Army is after us, then nothing I can do will keep them at bay. We can't stop tanks, attack helicopters, or airborne assault teams dropping in on ropes. If this is some isolated group that is hunting us, then I can definitely discourage them."

Terri pondered Bishop's statement for a bit and then stood, preparing to take his empty plate back to the kitchen. "Bishop, you know a million times more about all this security stuff than I do. It's your call, babe. If you think the ranch is the best, then I'm in. If you think hiding is best, I'm with you. As long as we're together, I'm good."

Two days later the doctor delivered good news to both Bishop and Nick. Kevin was showing no signs of infection and was out of the woods. Bishop was healing nicely as well, and the sawbones released Bishop from his care.

During his recovery, Bishop had tried to think up every possible defensive modification for the ranch. The exercise had been frustrating because there simply wasn't the equipment or raw materials available to enhance the security of the place.

Most of his existing precautions had relied on early warning devices. Bishop's mindset had been focused on the rogue criminal or wanderer happening upon the place and felt confident in his ability to overcome any such accidental discovery, if he had warning. The tripwires had satisfied that need, until just a few days ago.

Other than the geography and small arms, there really weren't any other defensive measures in place. He also was faced with a manpower issue. Terri was a good fighter, but she was becoming less and less mobile. That left a single man to defend the property, and the task would be impossible against a determined assault. That fact had just been substantiated.

One man with enough ammo and firepower could withstand a considerable force if he could channel the opposition into a small enough area. This was often called a fatal funnel. The problem with the ranch was the open terrain surrounding the homestead. The box canyon provided some measure of protection, but even that could be overcome by an attacker with the proper skills and equipment. There was simply no way to corral any attacking force into a specific avenue of approach, let alone a funnel.

Bishop struggled to keep emotion out of the equation. It was easy to become angry or to let ego influence his thinking. In order to stay grounded, he forced himself to relive the firefight of just a few, short days ago. If Terri hadn't taken the chance to come help him, both of them would have surely perished. *No*, he kept telling himself, *this is pure, simple mathematics. Keep it there.*

All of this analysis led Bishop to a single conclusion—he needed what the military guys referred to as "area denial," a term used to describe methods or equipment implemented to deny access to a specific avenue of approach. Minefields were one of the most common examples of area denial. Barbwire was another. Throughout history, military forces had spent considerable sums developing such technologies because there was often a legitimate need.

It wasn't always a matter of money or resources. The Viet Cong were famous for their punji stakes, tension-powered booby traps, and other clever devices. Most of these area denial systems were extremely effective and required little more than a shovel and bamboo. Ingenuity was still an effective weapon on the modern battlefield.

In Iraq, improvised explosive devices were another form of homemade area denial systems. Often used more for harassment of US troops, some gorilla encampments were known to have been ringed with such deterrents. They were effective.

Bishop eventually came around to the main element that limited his defensive capabilities—BTUs.

British Thermal Units, or BTUs, are a generally accepted measurement of how much energy a substance contains. A gallon of regular gasoline, for example, contained 112,000 BTUs. Explosives were also measured in BTUs, everything from dynamite to TNT having a specific rating.

Bishop didn't have any TNT. The IEDs in Iraq had been powered mostly by the explosives found in artillery shells, or plastic explosives available to military units. Bishop didn't have any of these either. About the only items available to him were gasoline and his gunpowder used for reloading.

In addition to BTUs, there was one other important factor involved in explosives - the burn rate, sometimes called the rate of expansion. Military grade explosives contained a very low ratio of BTU per pound, but they released their energy at an extreme speed. This was why hand grenades "pushed" their shrapnel at several thousand feet per second.

Bishop's smokeless reloading powder didn't burn all that fast, and thus, wouldn't make an effective bomb or mine. Besides, he didn't have all that much.

On the other hand, gasoline had both an exceptional burn rate as well as a good BTU per pound energy density. Its major drawback was that oxygen was required for the burn.

Gasoline had a mixed reputation from past conflicts where anti-armor munitions were in short supply. While it had proven effective against early tanks, as an anti-personnel weapon, it wasn't overly useful. During the Spanish Civil War, the use of the petrol bomb was well documented. Even Britain, anticipating invasion by hordes of German armor during WWII, had manufactured millions of "Molotov Cocktails." Throwing a Molotov Cocktail wasn't effective against foot soldiers. The puddle of burning gas could easily be jumped or run through without injury. Bishop didn't expect battle tanks to attack his ranch. Nor did he anticipate artillery or air strikes. What he did feel was a reasonable threat was a good-sized assault by infantry, military or non-military.

One idea that he kept rolling around in his head involved "misting" a thin spray of gasoline over a broad area of terrain and then igniting it when needed. A fuel-air mixture of the right proportions would generate a powerful explosion and heat wave. Over a broad enough region, it could serve as an area denial system against infantry.

Performing a mental inventory of his supplies and equipment back at the ranch, the only thing Bishop had on hand that might work was the hose and fixtures he had recently scavenged from the Home Mart in Alpha. Sitting with a pencil and paper, Bishop began to sketch out a diagram of a series of nozzles and hoses that just might work. It wouldn't be easy to build, but in theory, it would add another defensive layer to his property.

The sun was beginning to set, and Bishop wanted a cup of coffee. As he meandered into The Manor's kitchen, he found Betty preparing the evening meal for her guests.

"How are you feeling, Bishop?"

"My head's doing better. I think a good cup of your world famous coffee would set things right."

"There's a fresh pot sitting right over there. I'm peeling potatoes, so it's self-serve right now."

"Anything new on Kevin?"

"No. Last I heard, he's going to be fine. I'm more worried about his father right now than the wounded boy. I don't think he's been out of that room at all today."

Betty's comment gave Bishop an idea. Nick was ex-Special Forces, and those guys had a reputation regarding improvised weapons. Maybe Nick could help Bishop with his defensive plans.

Pouring a second cup of java, Bishop headed up the stairs.

When he arrived at Kevin's room, Bishop didn't knock or announce himself. The door was already slightly ajar, and Bishop gently nudged it just wide enough to fit the cup of steaming joe through the opening. He held the cup there for about 15 seconds and then withdrew the bait.

A few moments later, the door swung wide open, and a stiff, tired looking Nick appeared in the doorway, smiling when Bishop handed him the coffee.

"How's he doing?"

"He's a lot better, and the doc is pretty sure he'll be fine."

"Why don't you let Diana or Terri have a turn sitting with him? I need your help, and you need some fresh air."

Nick stretched his large frame and nodded, "Getting out of this room does sound like a good idea. What do you need my help with?"

"Improvised defenses and area denial systems."

Nick grinned, "For your ranch?"

Bishop nodded.

Nick looked back in on Kevin and found the lad sleeping soundly. "I've got time for a walk. Let's go drink this down in the garden and chat. This sounds like fun."

The two men exited the hotel and found a quiet spot to discuss their ideas. Nick began, "I'm especially interested in your little project because I think there's a good chance the guy who shot my son might encounter some of my toys the next time the bastard visits your place."

"The problem is my lack of resources. I don't have any explosives, and the desert isn't like the jungle where you have all kinds of vegetation to conceal booby traps."

Nick reassured Bishop that he had learned some neat "tricks" in Iraq as well as other deployments. Assuming Diana and Terri could watch Kevin tomorrow, Nick agreed to ride with Bishop out to the ranch and study the problem in detail.

"Besides," noted Nick, "the sooner you get out of this town, the less likely it is those guys are going to come here looking for you. I've got an *earie* feeling they'll be back."

~  ~

The next morning Nick and Bishop were up early. Bishop was anxious to get back home, and Nick was suffering from cabin fever. Diana and Terri had agreed to take turns sitting with Kevin and assured his worried father that the boy would be pampered.

The drive to the ranch was uneventful. Upon their arrival, Bishop and Nick scouted the general vicinity, making sure they were alone. Both men had commented that they hoped the bad guys had returned and were waiting on them, but the duo experienced no such luck.

Bishop pulled the irrigation equipment from the Bat Cave, and they proceeded to walk the canyon to see if Bishop's concept would be effective and logistically feasible.

"Nick, if I run that hose along this wall, about 12 feet off the ground, I think the mist will fall to the earth before anyone could get out of there."

"Gasoline vapor is heavier than air, so I think it would work. How are you going to pump the gas?"

Bishop pointed to the garden sprayer he had picked up at the Home Mart. "You pump that can up with the handle on top. It will handle about 45 pounds per square inch. People use those to spray insecticides on their veggies."

Nick looked at the device with skepticism, "Do you think 45 P.S.I. is enough pressure?"

"Not sure," admitted Bishop. "The only way to tell is to test it."

Using the reel, Bishop unwound 150 feet of high-pressure hose while Nick filled the garden sprayer with water from the spring. Walking off the first 90 feet, Bishop sliced the black tubing and spliced in a brass pressure washer nozzle. He repeated the process every 15 feet until four of the devices were installed in the last 60 feet of the hose.

Attaching the open end of the hose to the garden sprayer took a bit of plumbing work, but two pipefittings later, the men had the contraption ready for testing.

Bishop pumped the small black handle several times, watching the pressure gauge approach its maximum rated value. "Here goes," he warned Nick and released the valve.

As the water was pumped from the pressurized container into the black hose, the tubing jerked once and then rested. Both men smiled as they approached the nozzles, each emitting a fine mist of water vapor into the air. Nick stuck his hand in the closest one and then his face. "Feels nice. You should install these around your patio like folks used to do back in the day. Terri would love you for that."

"I should probably build a patio first, huh?"

After less than a minute, the spray lessened and then stopped. "It doesn't last long, but I would say ten seconds would be more than enough gasoline to cause a real nice explosion and fire. At minimum, you'll scare the hell out of anyone in the area. How are you going to light the gas vapor from a safe distance?"

Bishop shook his head, "I was hoping you could help me with that one. I don't have any tracer rounds."

"We need to make a spark. Do you have any iron? If you shoot iron it sparks . . . sometimes."

"I've got to be a safe distance away before igniting that cloud, or I'm going to lose my eyebrows. It needs to be something I can shoot and hit under duress from a distance."

Nick looked around the desert. "Are any of these rocks flint?"

Bishop laughed, "No, I don't think so. Besides, I don't have any steel-headed bullets."

Nick's face brightened. "Do you have a 12-gauge?"

"Yes, of course I have a couple of shotguns."

"I've got some flares in the glove box of my truck. They're left over from the boat. I bet if you fire one of those into that gas cloud, she'll light up like the Fourth of July." Nick announced proudly.

With that problem solved, the next step was for Nick to tour the area and help Bishop design some booby traps.

"Bishop, the booby traps don't have to be overly effective, they just have to convince anyone who is around that they'll work. Nobody wants to travel through an area known to be full of snares. Most guys will pick another way in."

The two men began walking around the perimeter of the canyon, Nick pointing to this or that and occasionally drawing a diagram in the sand. Bishop was amazed at the man's knowledge and training and started feeling better about his chances of defending the ranch once he had set everything up.

~  ~

Terri was trying to figure out how to play checkers with Kevin without making the lad sit upright. She had exhausted all conversation in less than an hour and could tell the teenager was bored, neighboring on cabin fever. His eyes brightened when she proposed a contest, Betty providing the board and pieces from The Manor's lobby below.

The boy's wound simply didn't allow for a good place to set up the game. Terri remembered a taller nightstand in an adjoining room, and told Kevin she'd be right back. The young man didn't respond, and Terri glanced to see an expression of sheer terror on his face, his eyes fixated over her shoulder.

Spinning to see what had elicited such a fearful expression, Terri found herself staring into the barrel of a rifle, the doorway of Kevin's room crowded with men in full combat gear. After inhaling sharply, Terri took a step back and reached for her pistol. The man with the rifle snapped, "Don't!"

Before she could react, the room was filled with three men. The first barked, "What is your name?"

Terri started to answer, but Kevin's voice interrupted with, "You're the man who shot me."

Terri's hand was already on the butt of her pistol. Kevin's warning told her she was in trouble, and her survival instincts kicked in. As fast as a striking snake, Terri pulled her 9mm and fired; the weapon's roar filling the small room.

Her first shot struck the closest man in the chest, pushing him backwards against the wall. Her barrel was moving to cover the second man when she felt a small pinprick on her shoulder and then her legs and arms would no longer answer her commands. As the floor of the room came rushing toward her face, her last conscious thought was of the light reflecting off the two thin wires leading back to a pretty yellow plastic pistol in one of the attackers' hands. She knew she had been tased.

Kevin tried to sit up, the boy ignoring the pain in his chest and shoulder. A rifle barrel pressed hard against his head—stopping the effort cold.

Without any words, one of the men pulled the pitchfork-shaped prong from Terri's torso and then rolled the semi-conscious woman over. In seconds, her hands and feet were bound. Then she was hoisted over a shoulder, and the men were gone.

Betty heard the shot and was approaching the stairs with her shotgun. She saw the legs of the first attacker coming down the steps and yelled, "Who is that? Stop right there!"

A stranger's head showed over the railing and then ducked back quickly. Betty shouldered the shotgun and flicked off the safety. "Stop, or I'll shoot!"

Betty heard a fizzing sound and then watched as a small canister came bouncing down the steps. At first, she thought it was a can of hairspray, but the size wasn't right. White smoke began spraying out of the device, quickly filling the room and blinding the hotel manager. The thick fog burned Betty's eyes and throat, making her retreat toward the kitchen.

Pete was opening the bar and also heard Terri's pistol. "Probably Anita scaring off a coyote from her hen house," he mumbled to himself. After a moment's thought, he pulled a rifle from behind the bar and strolled off in the general direction of the disturbance.

The smoke rolling out of the open front door of The Manor doubled Pete's pace, with thoughts of a fire without a fire department driving his legs faster. Betty appeared out of the cloud, waving her hands in front of her face to clear the air. She saw Pete and shouted, "They took Terri! They took her out the back!"

Momentarily puzzled by Betty's words, Pete paused for a second before the message sunk in. Another citizen was walking by, curious what all the commotion was about. Pete yelled for the man to follow him and made for the back of The Manor.

Rounding the corner, Pete saw the three men hustling away, a limp Terri draped over one of the fellow's shoulders. Pete turned to his comrade and instructed, "Go and get help. I'm going to follow them." The man nodded with big eyes and hurried away.

Pete's age and knees didn't leave him with the option of running after the kidnappers, but he did the best he could and managed to gain a little ground. Six blocks later, on the outskirts of town, the three men cut into the yard of an abandoned home, scurried behind the structure and out of sight.

Looking over his shoulder, Pete could see four men with rifles running to catch up—the reinforcements boosting his confidence. As he approached the edge of the property where the men went to ground, he heard the rumbling of motors, quickly followed by three ATVs roaring down the driveway, directly at him. Pete raised his weapon to fire when he saw Terri sitting in front of the lead vehicle's driver, her head bobbing weakly from side-to-side with eyes closed. Pete lowered his rifle, unable to shoot for fear of hitting the hostage. He watched helplessly as the three men sped past, the last kidnapper flipping Pete a bird and laughing as he went by.

Standing helpless on the street, Pete watched the off-road machines grow smaller and smaller in the distance. "Why didn't you shoot, Pete?" asked one of the first helpers to arrive.

"They had Terri, and I might have hit her by accident. I never had a clear angle."

"Do you know who those guys were? Why would they want to take Terri?"

Pete didn't answer, instead lowering his head, and then slowly walking over to perch on the guardrail bordering the street.

One of the men stepped over, concern showing on the gent's face. "Hey, Pete, you okay?"

Pete looked up with sad eyes and mumbled, "I'm not looking forward to telling my friend we let someone kidnap his wife."

~  ~

Pete rushed about inside the bar, trying to organize a posse. Motor vehicles were in short supply in Meraton, anything capable of off-road travel rarer still. Someone had recommended horses, and messengers had been sent to several outlying homes and ranches, soliciting help.

Being a retired cop, Pete had questioned Betty and Kevin, the wounded boy still in a partial state of shock. He had also walked the crime scene, noticing Terri's spent shell casing, the wires from the Taser, and the lack of blood anywhere in the area. He surmised that Terri had hit her target, but the assailant had no doubt been wearing body armor.

Terri's 9mm pistol was left behind, further evidence that the men who abducted her weren't common criminals. These days, any firearm was valuable, and everyone knew it.

A hundred things were happening at once, including speculation on the range of the getaway ATVs, where they would take Terri and even one person suggesting a courier be sent to Fort Bliss to ask for a search via helicopter.

Frustrated by a lack of resources, it soon dawned on Pete that any effort to rescue Terri was hopeless. Every minute that went by gave the kidnappers more of a head start, and the trail would quickly grow cold. There simply wasn't any way to organize enough men and transportation to be effective.

Pete considered opening the bar's floor safe and retrieving the directions to Bishop's ranch. He could send some men to fetch Bishop and Nick, but no one knew for sure where the two men were headed. Besides, Bishop was already furious over the place's whereabouts being known by whoever attacked yesterday. Increasing the number of people who knew the secret location would make things worse. Even if he did risk sending someone, by the time they made the round trip, the kidnappers' trail would be cold.

The only positive aspect of the morning was the arrival of two Beltron ranch hands, the men taking the day off to shop in the market and refresh themselves at the bar. Excited by the furlough, they had left the distant spread before sunrise, riding their horses into town less than an hour after the crime.

Pete knew both of the men were expert hunters and experienced with the surrounding terrain. Both had eagerly agreed to follow Terri's abductors as best they could. Watching the two horsemen ride off, Pete was somewhat relieved to at least being doing *something*, even though he doubted the horseflesh could catch up with the motorized kidnappers.

Before their departure, Pete had issued a serious warning to the two cowpokes while holding his hands a few inches apart from each other. "These guys came *that* close to killing Bishop at his ranch. They shot Kevin. They carried smoke grenades, Tasers, and assault weapons. Don't try to be heroes— you'll end up dead. Just trail them, find out where they went, and get back here. We'll decide what to do then."

~  ~

It was late afternoon before Bishop pulled the truck into the parking lot behind The Manor.

"Hey," Bishop teased, "do you think my head wound qualifies me to park in the handicapped spot?"

"I don't know if I would be *earitating* Betty if I were you."

Tired from the long trip and anxious to see Kevin and Terri, the two travelers stepped down from the cab and stretched their stiff arms and legs.

As they made their way to the front entrance of The Manor,

Bishop noticed that the few men who were around avoided eye contact with him, prompting a comment to Nick that he'd better take a shower as soon as possible.

"What's going on?" Nick noticed as well. "I thought these people liked you."

A small crowd of locals was gathered around the front steps of The Manor. Nick noticed several people looking down and avoiding eye contact with the approaching duo. "Something's wrong."

Pete separated himself from the group, walking briskly to intercept the two men. Focusing on Bishop, Pete said, "Bishop, I'm sorry to tell you this, but. . . ."

"Terri?"

Pete looked down and spread his arms in frustration. "Bishop, we tried to stop them. They took her from Kevin's room and . . . ."

"Terri!"

Bishop meant to shove past Pete, but the stout bartender put his hand on Bishop's chest and stopped him. "Bishop, they grabbed her about an hour after sunrise and headed northeast. I've got men out ..."

Bishop's head started swimming, the result of a massive adrenaline surge and the shock of the news. Staggering a half step, Nick and Pete quickly moved to stabilize their friend.

While Bishop began mumbling half-formed questions, Nick and Pete bracketed him and made for the hotel's lobby. Pete told Nick, "Kevin's okay, but still a little shocked. He can't hear real well because Terri got off a shot in that little room, but the doc says he'll be okay."

The two men managed to get Bishop into a chair, and one of the women fetched some water from the kitchen. After he was sure his friend was stable, Nick headed for the stairs. Pete warned, "Nick, Betty is standing guard with her shotgun in Kevin's room. Give her some warning."

Nick nodded and proceeded to take the stairs two at a time.

"Betty," he shouted from the top of the steps, "it's Nick. I'm coming in."

"Dad!" Kevin looked up, flashes of relief crossing his face. "Oh, God, dad! They took Terri!"

Nick moved immediately to embrace his son. "I know son, I heard. How are you? You doing okay?"

Kevin started weeping in his father's arms. Between the sobs he managed to blurt out, "I tried to stop them, Dad . . . I couldn't move . . . it was the same man who shot me in Alpha."

Nick soothed his son's hair, answering each statement

with, "I know, son . . . It's okay . . . I know. . . ."

Bishop recovered quickly, becoming ultra-cold and logical. "Pete, tell me what you know so far, please."

During Pete's retelling of the morning's events, Bishop didn't stir or blink, his breathing remained even. The only sign of the fury surging through the man's veins was the white-knuckled grip being applied to his chair. When Pete finished, Bishop had questions.

"Pete, did one of the men carry a SCAR rifle?"

"I don't know, Bishop, what's a SCAR?"

Bishop went to the hotel's front desk and retrieved a piece of paper and pencil. He quickly made a rough sketch, showing Pete a drawing of a modern looking battle rifle with a folding stock.

"Yes . . . yes, one of them did have a rifle that looked like that."

Bishop nodded, now sure it was the same men who had attacked the ranch, 99% sure it was the same men who broke into their room at Fort Bliss.

"Pete, how long have the cowboys been tracking them?"

"They left about an hour after the kidnapping, so roughly eight hours."

Bishop paced back and forth across the lobby floor, his path taking him from the front window and back to his chair. "Pete, I know you and Betty did your best. I'm not upset with you. I just can't figure out what to do. I've never felt so helpless."

"Bishop, the good news is the doc doesn't think the shock from the Taser would harm Terri or the baby."

Bishop nodded, thankful for the small bit of positive thinking. "I'm trying to figure out where they would take her. They clearly have access to equipment like ATVs. They must have a pretty good supply of fuel as well."

Terri remained conscious throughout most of the affair, but without the use of her limbs, she couldn't fight back. She slowly regained the control of her body during the ATV trip, but having her hands bound during the unstable ride didn't afford much opportunity to resist, let alone any attempt at escape.

Halfway through the journey, she decided to make her captor's life miserable using the only weapon she had at her disposal—vocal cords.

"What kind of cowardly man uses a Taser on a pregnant woman? Can you just tell me that? Do you have any idea of what my husband will do to you once he finds you? He'll skin you and your friends alive and boil your bones in his piss …"

The driver of the ATV listened in silence for the first four or five minutes, never acknowledging a word she said. She was about to give up, when the man took a hand off the handlebars and reached to his side. Producing a large knife, the thug held it in front of Terri's face, and said, "I'll cut your cheek meat into thin slices if you don't shut up. You won't be so pretty once I'm done. It's *your* call."

Something in the man's voice convinced Terri that he'd actually do it, so she decided to be quiet. Besides, she had practically exhausted her extensive repertoire of insults anyway.

For what seemed like hours, the three ATVs roared across open desert, climbed foothills, and skirted around deep canyons. The constant bouncing, jarring ride, combined with her physical condition, caused Terri's bladder to work overtime. She half turned to the rider and announced, "I'm a pregnant lady, and I've got to use the bathroom." Her request was ignored by her chauffer. Less than a minute later, she tried again. "I can pee all over both of us, or you can stop and let me go behind the bushes. It's *your* call."

After a few moments, the driver zoomed to the front and held up his hand, signaling a stop.

Terri was roughly lifted off the ATV and practically carried a few feet off the path. The man unbuttoned the top of her jeans and despite her protests, yanked her pants below her knees. He grabbed Terri's jaw with an extremely strong grip and hissed, "Shut up and piss."

Terri glanced at the two other riders, the smirks on their faces indicating they weren't going to be gentlemen and look away.

"I can't go with someone watching me. It's called bashful kidneys," she announced with a defiant tone.

"Whatever. You're not going to run far with your pants around your knees."

And with that, her captor turned away and walked toward the other two riders. "Give her a break," he growled.

A few minutes later, they were bouncing across the desert again.

214

With her hands behind her back, Terri tried to think of anything she could do to facilitate her escape or rescue. She recalled writing down a shopping list of items she could use at the camper, her intent being to visit Meraton's market before the day's end. Slowly, as the ATV jolted from side to side, she managed to feel inside her back pocket, and tear off a small scrap of the paper. When she was sure the trail diverted the driver's attention from her actions, she let a small piece blow free in the wind. It was probably useless, but she had to try.

As often as possible, Terri dropped a paper-breadcrumb, her hopes being that anyone trying to follow the kidnappers would come across her litter.

Doing something to resist helped her fight the despair that was welling up inside of her. As the hours passed, and they traveled further and further away from Meraton, Terri realized her chances of rescue were dwindling. Anguish soon gave way to desperation, which was quickly followed by an overriding sense of gloom.

Eventually the three vehicles pulled into what appeared to be a warehouse, the building accessible via a little-used exit off of a major interstate. Given the direction and distance of their travel, Terri assumed the big highway was I-10. The large metal building didn't have any signage or distinguishing marks, apparently having gone out of business some time ago. Her captors had evidently been using the abandoned facility for some time as someone lifted a loading dock door upon their approach.

Terri noted all of the windows had been covered with tin foil, probably to block any light leaking out after dark. Once the three ATVs were inside, the door was pulled down; the silence seemed odd after so many hours of listening to the roar of engines.

Again, her dignity was insulted as her captor lifted her off the seat with little effort. Making sure she was standing, the brut spun her around and got up close to her face.

"I'm going to explain this to you one time, and one time only. You are going to be questioned by the boss. He'll be here soon. Until then, if you try and escape or cause me one iota of bullshit, I'll bleed you. I'll do it slow and make you wish you were dead. After the boss is done, it's his call what happens to you. Do you understand?"

Terri shook her hair away from her eyes, and looked up

at the man with a harsh expression. "And who's this boss of yours? What does he want to know?"

With a movement so fast, Terri didn't have time to flinch; the knife was on her cheek. "No questions. Keep your mouth shut."

Terri nodded her head in agreement; the cold steel against her face was very pervasive.

"Good," the man said, and then nodded at one of his comrades.

Terri was taken to a dark doorway, the entrance to what was a completely empty room except for a five-gallon bucket and a gallon milk jug full of water. Her escort cut the nylon tie restraining her hands and then shoved her inside.

"The bucket is the head, the water is to drink." Then the man closed and locked the door behind her.

Terri paced around the room a few times, the damp, dark cell having no windows or other features of note. Despite a comfortable temperature outside, she felt cold—the foreboding situation and dark quarters causing her to wrap her arms tightly around herself as she paced.

After a few trips around the clammy concrete floor, Terri took the potty-bucket, flipped it upside down, and made a stool. Her dire predicament beginning to crush any sense of well-being, Terri's primary concern was for her unborn child. She really didn't feel any fear over what these evil men had in store for her, and honestly told herself that she would sacrifice her life right now if it would guarantee the child's survival.

Terri's eyes grew wet as she thought about the future and wondered if Bishop would be able to find her. "You can't count on that," she mumbled quietly. "You can only count on yourself."

There was also a bit of anger in her soul. She hadn't done anything to anyone as far as she knew. She was completely unworthy of kidnapping. Fear of not being able to provide whatever these men wanted began to creep in. Would they kill her and the baby after convincing themselves she didn't know or have anything of value?

Terri had never felt so alone before. The walls of the room seemed to draw closer and closer. All she could do was pray.

Meraton, Texas
January 6, 2016

The sun had set over an hour ago, and Bishop was about at the end of his rope. Pete had been convincing, using the logic that everyone should just wait until the trackers returned. As dusk had passed to night, Pete's argument had made even more sense, given the chances of a misidentification leading to an accidental shooting were higher at night.

Betty and Nick had done their best to sooth Bishop's nerves, the former pouring an endless supply of coffee while the latter repeating, "We'll get them brother . . . if there's a God in heaven, we will find them . . . and when we do. . . ."

The sound of hooves galloping down Main Street drew everyone to The Manor's front windows. Over a dozen men had gathered, many riding in on horseback and prepared to give chase. Each time another had arrived, Bishop rushed to the glass, hoping it was the trackers returning with news. This time, it was.

Bishop was outside before the men could even dismount, his face eager for news of his missing wife. The older cowboy spoke up first. "We found a trail; we're pretty sure your wife left us clues."

"Did you find them?"

"No, sir. But we've got a good idea of where they're at." Reaching in his pocket, the younger cowboy pulled out three small scraps of paper.

"We found these little pieces of paper spread along the trail. They kept us on track over solid rock until we could pick up their tire tracks in the sand again. We ran out of daylight, but I'm sure they were headed for the old Robinson garage up by I-10."

Bishop wasn't familiar with the place, and his expression indicated as much. He started to ask more questions, but the old tracker said he could explain better with a cup of coffee and a map. Seeing that the men and horses were exhausted, Bishop held his tongue until the trackers could get some caffeine.

Pete unfolded a map on The Manor's pool table and everyone gathered around while Betty filled two cups. After a few sips of coffee, the older man continued. "Those machines they were riding have limits on what terrain they can cover. We use 'em out at the ranch all the time. Sometimes, in rugged country, ya just can't beat a horse."

Pointing toward the map, the man continued. "That ruled out this whole section of the Glass Mountains—there's just no place to go, even with a horse. So, we picked up the first tire tracks about here."

The younger man joined in. "Over here is where I found the first piece of paper. I thought at first it was just random trash, but a half mile further north, I found a second one. It was right beside a tire track and the same type of paper."

"We found the third scrap all the way up here, and if you

connect the three dots, they make a straight line."

After another sip of coffee, the man continued. "We rode until it got to dark and found the last tire track five miles south of Robinson's old place. That's the only shelter for several miles either direction and would be a good place to hide out. Pete told us not to be heroes, so we turned around and came back."

Bishop glanced at the map, "So, can you describe Robinson's garage? What type of building is it?"

"It's one of those inexpensive metal buildings, nothing fancy at all. Old man Robinson did more welding and equipment repair than anything else. He closed it up about six years ago when the economy got real bad. He died a few years later, and I think the county owns the place now since no one paid the taxes."

The younger cowboy jumped in, "It sits all by itself off of the exit. Country Road 413 runs through here," and the man pointed at the map. "It's very isolated out there. If I were of a criminal mind and needed a hideout, I couldn't think of a better place."

Bishop studied the map again, memorizing as much as he could. He glanced up at Nick and asked, "What do you think?"

"I think you and I are going to walk I-10 again, my friend. It wouldn't be the first time."

Bishop nodded. "I think the first step is to verify they're actually there. Once I get a look at the place, we can decide what to do."

"Sounds like a plan."

Bishop turned and looked at the gathered men. "I want to thank each and every one of you for volunteering to help. I won't forget it. I think for tonight, Nick and I should go scout the place out. If we all go charging in there, they might hurt Terri. Nick and I'll be back by sunrise, and we'll determine the best plan of action then. You all go home and get some sleep—we may need you in the morning."

Several of the men approached Bishop and patted him on the back or shook his hand. Every one of the men pledged to do anything Bishop needed to get his wife back.

After the meeting had broken up, Bishop turned to Pete and said, "I've got another issue. Nick and I used a lot of gas in the truck today. I'm not sure I've got enough left to make two round trips. Any ideas?"

Nick chimed in, "You could use some of Pete's bathtub gin—that shit would power the space shuttle."

Pete thought for a moment and replied, "No problem— just go down to the gas station and inquire about bartering for some fuel."

"I'm not sure I've got anything with me of value, Pete. Roberto is a tough customer."

"You've done business with him before. I'm sure your credit's good."

Bishop and Nick loaded up their gear in the back of the truck and drove the few blocks to Meraton's only gas station. The place had been turned into what could only be described as a fort. Old cars and trucks ringed the facility, creating a wall. Barbwire, bartered from local ranchers, was woven throughout the barricade making access to the liquid gold stored in Roberto's belowground tanks very difficult. Bishop pointed to the ever-present sniper on the roof and commented, "Roberto has a lot of kids. They sleep up there during good weather."

A new protocol for requesting service had been established, thanks in no small part to the numerous attempts by various passersby to rob the place. Bishop stopped the truck in the middle of Main and honked twice.

A flashlight beam could be seen swinging back and forth behind the car-fence, evidence that someone was responding to the greeting. Before long, a voice called out, "Senor Bishop? Is that you?"

"Yes, it's me, Roberto. Sorry to bother you so late."

Shadows played through a small gap in the barrier, and then an armed man approached the truck. "Senor Bishop, what can Roberto do for you?"

"Roberto, I need gasoline. My wife, Terri, has been kidnapped, and we think we know where she's being held. I've been driving too much lately and am running low."

The thick-build Latino nodded his head, "Yes, senor, I heard about Miss Terri. I'm so sorry. I would be happy to give you some gas as she was always so kind to my children."

"Roberto, I don't have anything with me to barter with. I promise I'll make it up to you later if we can come to an agreement."

The station owner got an odd look on his face, apparently having trouble understanding Bishop's intent. Finally, the translation registered and he began shaking his head. "Mister Bishop, Roberto will give you gasoline to contribute to the rescue. I'm only sorry my age and family do not allow me to accompany you to get Miss Terri."

Without waiting on Bishop to answer, Roberto turned and yelled a few short bursts of Spanish toward the station. More flashlight beams began sweeping the area, and in a few minutes, two teenage boys slid through the opening, each carrying a five-gallon, red plastic can.

Roberto turned to Bishop and said, "Senor, if I may ask

you to turn off the truck please. Sometimes a little fuel spills when using the cans. A fire would not be good."

Bishop did as he was asked, the irony of it all making him smile. Here he was, parked in the middle of the street, the truck loaded with weapons of war, begging for a few gallons of gas to rescue his wife from kidnappers. He had an ex-Green Beret sitting next to him, and the visit to the gas-fortress was no doubt being covered by at least one sniper rifle. All of this, and Roberto wanted him to turn off the truck for safety sake. *What a world we live in*, he thought.

Bishop exited the cab and helped the two lads pour the fuel into the truck while Nick and Roberto talked about the latest Ford V-8 and how Caddy's just weren't what they used to be.

When the cans were empty, Bishop thanked the boys and turned to Roberto. The two men shook hands while Roberto said, "Senor, if that isn't enough, please come back. We like Miss Terri mucho and want to help if we can."

As he and Nick got back in the cab, the big man turned to Bishop and commented, "You should be nicer to people, Bishop. Terri's probably getting tired of carrying your unsocial ass all of the time."

Bishop responded with a grunt and put the truck in gear.

The men sat in silence eating the MREs. There wasn't any problem between them, no ill feelings or issues unresolved. They had simply sat together and performed the same ritual so many times there wasn't anything that needed to be said.

Deke finally rose from his perch and walked to a nearby drum to toss in his empty paper. Strolling to a cardboard carton, he looked at his watch and stated, "It's time to feed the woman. Do you think she would like the meat loaf or the beef stew?"

"Why don't you drape a napkin over your arm and go take her order. You might need the practice being a waiter before this is all over."

Grunting, Deke bent and dug around in the box, eventually settling on the meat loaf because it was the most edible served cold. After making his selection, he looked up and commanded, "Well, come on."

Moses sighed and lifted his rifle. It was a rule that no one had contact with a prisoner alone. As the two men walked to the makeshift cell, the escort noted Deke's selection. "You're going to give that to her cold?"

"Oh, now who's the old softie? What? We should heat it for her?"

Stopping, Moses reached into his pocket and produced a chunk of C4 explosive. Unwrapping the soap-like substance, the guard took his knife and sliced off a small portion. "We're not animals," he commented.

At the door, the Deke yelled inside, "Move to the far corner if you want to eat."

Removing the steel crossbar and opening the door, both men stayed back until it was verified Terri had complied and moved to the far corner. Stepping inside, Deke dropped the MRE on the floor and then lit the C4 with a metal lighter. The dangerous plastic flared, burning steadily with a yellow hue. "Use this to heat this meal. It will burn long enough if you hurry."

He then checked the water in the milk jug, noting the woman had consumed a few inches of the liquid.

Backing out, the men replaced the bar and returned to the main area of the garage.

"Any word on when the client is going to be here?" One of the others asked.

"In the next few days is all I know. Our instructions are to keep the girl here until he arrives."

A grimace crossed the face of the man, an unusual display of emotion that didn't pass unnoticed by the leader. "What's up, Chief? Why the sour puss?"

"I don't know, Deke. This job just feels wrong. I'm up for a snatch and grab as much as the next operator, but this one ain't sitting well with me. That lady in there ain't no drug dealer … or terrorist mastermind. Hell, she reminds me of my sister."

"You know the rules, Chief. We do what we're hired to do—it's just a job."

One of the other men chimed in, "He's just pissy because he took one in the chest from her pistol. That bullet bouncing off his armor must have stirred up some pussification inside. Next thing ya know, he'll be looking at all our asses and wanting to decorate the place."

Chief turned to his antagonist and grabbed his crotch, "I got your decorations . . . right here, bitch."

Muffled chuckles sounded around the group. Deke, always observing his command, couldn't let it go. "Chief, ignore that fuckstick—that's an order. Now explain to me what's rolling around inside that overprotected cranial cavity of yours."

"Oh, come on, Deke. You know exactly what I'm talking about. This isn't our typical gig."

"Chief's right," added another, "It's like we're playing some sort of high school social game here. I think this job smells more of someone's personal vendetta than protection."

Deke thought about the team's growing sentiment. If he were to be honest with the men, he would have to admit to having similar feelings. This entire contract was way, way out of their normal line of business. But, then again, their normal line of business didn't exist anymore.

"Look, guys," Deke began. "I hear you, and have to agree. One thing we've got to keep in perspective is that the world has changed. Most of the rules have evaporated. How we used to make a living doesn't exist anymore."

~  ~

Bishop and Nick had a much longer drive than the horseman had ridden. Going cross-country as the crow flies with off-road vehicles and horses was a much shorter distance than taking the rare highway in this part of the world.

Bishop removed the fuses from the pickup's electrical system so they could drive without brake, interior or dash lights and accidently giving away their position. Using his night vision monocle to steer while Nick rode ready to rise out of the sunroof with his rifle, the truck became as stealthy and protected as was reasonable.

Traveling down the highway at night without headlights took a little getting used to, and Bishop could sense the nervousness in Nick's voice. "So if you're not using headlights, how do bears and moose and stuff know the truck's coming?"

Bishop laughed, "I don't know about moose, I've not seen any around these parts for a while. I don't think bears aren't nocturnal, and deer see well at night. I think the lack of headlights probably lets them get out of the way without being a 'deer caught in the headlights.'"

Despite having Terri's night vision pressed against his eye, Nick wasn't convinced. "Bishop, this just seems like a bad idea. You're going what, 50 miles per hour and using that little scope? How will other cars see you?"

"What other cars? Jeez, Nick, we're out in the middle of the desert after the shit has hit the fan. I've not seen a car on these roads since those Colombians. They would use their headlights."

"Well. . . . Okay. . . . If you say so."

"You'll get used to it, or end up with a black eye. You shouldn't press that thing so hard against your skull, buddy. If you break it, Terri's going to kick your ass."

"What are you doing looking at me? Keep your eyes on the road, damnit!"

Bishop couldn't resist, and pushed down on the gas pedal, the truck accelerating to almost 70.

"Okay, okay, okay. I'll shut up - just slow down, please."

A few hours later, Bishop pulled the pickup to the side of I-10. This part of West Texas was sparsely populated, and while rare, abandoned cars did exist along the interstate. Bishop declared, "According to this map, the exit is about two miles ahead, just around that next bend. I wanted to stay back because I'm pretty sure these guys will have night vision and possibly thermal imaging. It would suck to announce ourselves by driving too close."

Nick agreed, "Given what you've told me about their equipment and tactics, I would say it's almost certain."

"This is going to be very tricky. Thermal is next to impossible to defeat. We have to find a place to observe the building without being detected."

The two men exited the truck and made for the open desert that surrounded the big road. The curve in I-10 had been constructed to bypass a small outcropping of foothills. The elevated, rocky terrain signaled the northern most edge of the Glass Mountains.

As they approached the rise, Nick stopped and whispered to Bishop, "Don't go for the highest point on that ridge. If I were them, that's where I would put a trip line or two. Pick a spot that's high enough, but not the obvious choice."

Bishop voiced his agreement, "'Bout time you started earning your pay."

Caution was more important than speed when going up the hillside. The terrain was littered with small gullies, clusters of scrub oak, and knee-high cactus beds. The duo's progress slowed even more as they approached the summit, taking every precaution not to expose the thermal signatures of any part of their bodies.

Nick whispered, "At this time of night, with the cool air, our body heat will look like a Vegas neon sign if anyone's watching. We've got to find somewhere that will allow for maximum visibility with minimal exposure. Vegetation does a good job of blocking radiant heat, but I don't see much around."

Bishop continued to move along the backside of the ridge, looking for a good spot. The two stalkers had traveled almost 50 yards before Bishop waved Nick down and pointed. A slab of sandstone the size of a pool table had split away from its mother formation, probably before humans had inhabited this section of North America. The "V" shaped opening had been the perfect place for a larger-than-normal cluster of oak to take root and make a stand against the harsh desert terrain.

The trees had littered the area, with a significant amount of fallen limbs, dried leaves, and other dead vegetation. The rock formation had acted like a dam on the river of air that constantly swept over the hill—the narrow gap blocking the wind from naturally scattering the debris.

"Perfect," Nick whispered, "Now if we can just see the building from there."

Bishop pulled his baklava mask out of his back and pulled it over his head. "Until my body heats this up, it should work for a few minutes."

Crawling up behind the formation, Bishop slowly peaked through the brush. Raising his night vision, he scanned the area below and could clearly make out the shape of a small metal building and gravel parking lot.

Backing away, he motioned for Nick to see for himself. "I think this vantage is perfect, but take a look."

A few moments later, the big man crawled back, nodding his head. "I don't think we're going to do any better. Did you notice the trash?"

"No, what trash?"

"There's a barrel full of trash to the south of the building. I don't think it's left over from the original occupants. Someone's staying in that structure."

"I can't believe the guys we're after would make a mistake like that. That's Basic Concealment 101."

Nick thought about Bishop's remark for a moment, and then replied, "They're probably bored or cocky. Either one can make you sloppy. Besides, put yourself in their shoes, would you expect anyone to discover this hideout?"

Bishop wasn't convinced. "I don't know, Nick. I've never seen anybody execute small unit tactics like they did. Their weapons and equipment were top shelf. If it was the same guys, they infiltrated an Army base that was locked down pretty tight. I can't believe an organization like that would screw up with waste discipline."

"Nobody is perfect, my friend. Let's take turns keeping a watch on the place. It could be interstate refugees and not some super bad-ass team, too."

Bishop and Nick decided the best way to remain undetected from below was to push Bishop's rifle through the brush pile, and use the long range 24-x scope. Unless fired, the rifle would remain the same ambient temperature as the surrounding rocks and shouldn't be detectable from below.

Nick suggested, "Let's take turns scouting the place.

The guy that's off duty can watch our six and make sure no one sneaks up on us."

Bishop agreed and took the first shift.

It took a while to find a position that was both comfortable and concealed. Nature's random compilation of the dead refuse didn't naturally provide a good spot for a man with a rifle. Taking his time with slow, deliberate movements, Bishop eventually managed a good line and proper brace for the weapon.

The moon was about half full, and the sky above was absolutely clear. It was one of those crisp winter nights where there was plenty of light to see the surrounding terrain without using night vision. *We caught a break there*, Bishop thought. Getting the night vision monocle to cooperate with a high-powered scope was always a difficult task of focusing two different devices while obtaining the perfect eye relief.

The building was less than 200 meters away, too close for the optic to be used at full power. Scaling down the magnification to 8-x provided the best all-around view of detail and width of field. A quick scan revealed what one would expect from a deserted business on the outskirts of civilization. The windows appeared to be completely dark, either covered to hide internal lights or displaying the natural blackness of an unoccupied space. There was no way to be sure.

The parking lot of the former garage was pea gravel and mixed stone, tough desert plants having taken root in several spots. The paint on what would have been the public door was faded and chipped, the visible windowsills matching in both color and disrepair. The raw wood exposed by the lack of protective pigment sported a bleached color of gray; evidence that the sun had ruthlessly attacked the surface for some time.

Nick was correct. There was a trash barrel some distance south of the building. The 50-gallon drum was a common receptacle in this part of the world where many people still burned their household refuse. Bishop could make out the random assortment of lumpy looking contents, but even the highest zoom couldn't discern enough detail to identify specific items. Still, the barrel was over three-quarters full.

Unlike grass lawns back east, the hard packed gravel and sand surrounding the place didn't leave any evidence of foot traffic. Bishop studied each individual patch of weeds between the building and the trash barrel, looking for a sign of a beaten path. He just couldn't be sure.

Bishop had been scouting the building for almost 20 minutes when he pulled his eye away from the optic and checked his watch. It was just after 3 a.m., and the desert was completely at rest. Many people referred to midnight as the witching hour, but men who spend significant time in the field know it's 3 o'clock in the morning when the world begins turning at a slower speed. The rhythms of life's activity seem to be at their low tide during those wee hours. Tonight, his wife in peril, Bishop didn't have any problem concentrating or staying awake.

What did begin to trouble him was concern for his wife and child. Waiting on the trackers at The Manor had given him plenty of time to worry, sort, and fret over what was happening to Terri. His emotions had ebbed and flowed, ranging from boiling, sulfuric rage to debilitating sorrow. Throughout the process, one thought kept forcing itself into his mind - old advice given long ago by the colonel during one of the countless hours of training conducted at HBR.

"When you're the only salvation … when you're the only option, the difference between winners and losers is focus. Athletes call it 'closing out the victory,' boxers call it 'killer instinct,' and warriors call it 'becoming cold-blooded.' You have to develop the mental discipline to push fear, anger, stress, and insecurity aside and perform. In this line of work, lives will depend on it. Success or failure is at stake."

Bishop fully realized he'd never been tested like this. Visions of Terri being tortured and abused tried to assault his thinking. Images of a dead newborn and a murdered wife made desperate attempts to dominate his mind. It was mentally exhausting to push them aside—to deny access to his consciousness by those debilitating images.

"She needs me now more than ever," he thought. *"She's probably down there, cold, lonely, and frightened. She's wondering if help will come. I'm here, Terri. I love you more than anything, and I'm here. Hang in there, baby. I'm coming."*

More than once during his shift, Bishop thought about charging into the building below, guns blazing. The colonel's advice from so long ago helped to push the urge aside. He knew the men who held Terri were professionals, and in a way, that helped ease his apprehension. While it wasn't a certainty, Bishop believed these men had some logical reason for taking his wife. They weren't a random bunch of criminals who happened upon a pretty, helpless woman. They weren't extortionists, wanting something in exchange for her return. It wasn't a vendetta, a cruel attempt at extracting revenge on Bishop for some past deed.

They wanted something from Terri—something that they considered important enough to waste extremely valuable resources and lives to obtain. Just because Bishop didn't know what they sought didn't mean it wasn't important to whoever was driving their operation.

Bishop's analysis was interrupted when movement from below caught his eye. There it was again! It wasn't the building itself, but a strand of vegetation some 50 meters away. His first thought was a jackrabbit. The movement had been low to the ground at the edge of the brush. The second occurrence made it clear—that wasn't any rabbit.

Now focused on the spot, Bishop zoomed in the optic and studied the area carefully. He detected movement again at the edge of his scope. Looking at every weed, branch, and rock, Bishop couldn't quite make it out, but something was out of place.

Three minutes later, it all became clear. A man rose from the brush and walked to the edge of the building, where he was met by another. Bishop could make out body armor, load vests, and assault rifles. These were no random interstate-refugees. The new man made for the brush pile and Bishop watched, fascinated as he cut behind the foliage and then just disappeared. The men below had done an expert job of constructing a camouflaged hide, not dissimilar from what an experienced deer hunter would build at the start of a new season.

Bishop had gotten lucky catching the shift change. The hide also made sense, as it would afford an all-around view of their hideout without exposing any sentries to an observer. Slowly, Bishop pulled away from the riflescope and returned where Nick was sitting on a rock.

"It's them. I caught the sentries during a shift change. I'm sure it's them."

In the yellow light of the moon, Nick's expression took Bishop aback for a moment. The big man's eyes flashed cold, his mouth forming what could only be described as an evil grimace.

"Good. I'll leave the planning up to you—just make sure I get my payback. Nobody shoots my son and walks away if I can help it."

Bishop realized Nick, like himself, had been analyzing recent events in the cold solitude of the early morning hour. Bishop's news had clearly arrived during a bout of internalized anger.

"Nick, I'll be blunt, that's not my highest priority right now. If it comes to that, you'll get your chance, my friend. I wouldn't even think of denying you that. As far as the planning goes, let's work it out together."

"I'm cool with that, brother. I figured if it were my wife down there, I'd want to control the op. What do you have in mind?"

Bishop paused for a moment, picking his words carefully. "I think it's quite simple really. I'll stay here and make sure they don't go anywhere. You head back to Meraton and gather up every man you can. If we have enough forces to surround the place, I think we can force their hand."

Nick thought about Bishop's concept. "You really think that will make them release Terri?"

"I can't imagine these guys are on a suicide mission. I don't believe they're military or even mainstream government. I think if we give them the option of giving up their hostage or dying, I believe they'll release her."

Nick grunted. "If you negotiate a deal that swaps Terri for their freedom, then I don't get my payback."

Bishop nodded, "I suppose that's right. Do you have an alternative?"

It was Nick's turn to do some rationalization, his response reaffirming Bishop's trust in the man. "My revenge isn't worth risking Terri's life. We'll do it your way. Can I have the truck keys, Dad? Please?"

Bishop tossed his friend the keys. "I expect you home by 11, young man, and fill up the tank before you bring it home."

Nick laughed, adding, "I'm going to take the route back through Alpha. I only counted about 15 volunteers in Meraton, and I bet we'll need double that."

Bishop watched his friend trot down the hill and disappear around the bend before returning to watch Robinson's garage.

Chapter 14

Fort Bliss
January 6, 2016

Senator Moreland was slightly embarrassed at the reception that awaited his arrival at Fort Bliss. The honor guard, reception line of officers in full dress uniforms, impressive row of armored vehicles, and hustling Secret Service detail all seemed a bit overwhelming.

One of his primary concerns had been the transfer of security, a fear that Wayne wouldn't trust the government specialists lead by Special Agent Powell. Moreland had been a little surprised by how effortlessly the private security had faded to the background and been replaced by the men in dark suits.

Moreland's other fears were quickly dissolved by the reception. His reservations about landing square in the middle of what Wayne had termed "the enemy camp," weighing on his mind. Being the leader of the Independents one minute and the Commander in Chief of the opposing force the next was an unusual situation to say the least. His aide's reassurances seemed to be spot-on, as always.

The five-hour flight from West Virginia had passed quickly, but after the festivities on the tarmac and a tour of Air Force One, Moreland was exhausted. After informing Wayne that he'd like to rest for a bit before proceeding with any other activities, Agent Powell had pointed toward the huge aircraft and said, "You'll be staying aboard your plane, sir. I feel it's the safest place while we're here at Bliss." Given the attempt on his predecessor's life, it made sense.

There were a million things to do, including the swearing in ceremony, burial of the former president, and countless affairs of state.

~  ~

Agent Powell arose early, unable to sleep with all of the anticipated activities planned for the new president. As usual, his first thought was to inspect the area around Air Force One where the president-to-be was sleeping.

Making the rounds and chatting with the various agents on duty went smoothly—all of the Secret Service and military personnel were alert and at their posts.

Powell craved a cup of coffee and was sure the Air Force steward would have the galley in full operation by now. As he made for the ladder to board the giant aircraft, activity at the nearby hangar drew his attention. Powell could see his man talking with someone at the opening to the enormous building. In addition to the oddity of such an early morning visitor, the location was where the service stored its equipment. Oddities couldn't be ignored in Powell's line of work. After all, Bishop and Terri's attackers were still at large, and many unanswered questions about the assassination of the previous president still remained.

The service always brought its own vehicles wherever the president traveled. On this specific trip, the two armored limousines had been left at Andrews, the transport aircraft delivering only the four up-armored SUVs and two additional escort vehicles.

Delivering an armored motorcade to every location visited by the Commander in Chief was an expensive, time-consuming endeavor. It was also the only way the service could guarantee someone didn't plant explosives or electronic devices in the various transports required for a presidential road show.

As Powell made his way closer to the hangar, he noticed Wayne talking with the agent guarding the facility. The president's future chief of staff was holding a piece of paper and appeared agitated.

"Good morning, sir," Powell said as he approached Moreland's aide.

Wayne looked over, nodding with a curt, "Agent Powell."

"How can we help you this morning, sir?"

"I need transportation. My sister lives in this area and is very ill. I would like to see her before the end, and it appears as though today is going to be the best opportunity given the president's schedule."

Wayne handed Powell the paperwork, a quick glance verifying it was a note from the president, authorizing Wayne to requisition government transportation for himself and a modest security force.

After giving Powell a moment to read the documentation, Wayne continued. "I'm not sure who to ask or where to go. I need two large SUVs, or trucks, or Hummers, or something. I'll have myself and seven security men."

"Seven?" Powell was skeptical.

"Yes, since the Secret Service is now officially responsible for the president's well-being, I'm going to utilize the private security for this trip. After I return, their contact will be terminated. The world is a dangerous place, I hear."

Powell was in a bit of a quandary. Officially, the man standing next to him wasn't a member of the executive branch, at least not yet. Unofficially, Powell knew that he would be working with the man for many years. The new boss had made it clear that Wayne was to be his next Chief of Staff.

The agent's initial thought was to call General Westfield and try to arrange military Humvees, but the base commander was a stickler for going by the book. Wayne's civilian status would cause the general a mild coronary, delay the trip, and probably not endear Powell with his future co-worker.

"We can take care of your needs, sir. Would two of our units provide sufficient space for your team?"

Powell pointed into the hangar at two large, black SUVs.

Wayne smiled and replied, "Why, yes. Those would do nicely. Thank you, Agent Powell."

Robinson's Garage
January 6, 2016

Bishop watched the false dawn illuminate the eastern sky and checked his watch again. Nick had been gone a little over an hour, and he estimated it would take at least four, maybe five before his friend returned with the cavalry.

Being alone on the hillside didn't help Bishop's outlook on the near future. To guard his thoughts from wandering to the melancholy, he attempted to keep his mind occupied with pre-planning the next steps once help arrived.

The noise of an engine interrupted his plotting, the sound causing a double take at his watch. There was no way Nick could be back already, and Bishop began to fret that something had gone wrong with his friend's mission. Crawling back from his observation point, Bishop moved quickly to a position where he could see the lanes of the interstate below. The first indication that it wasn't Nick was the small white dot of headlights in the distance. The single point of light quickly showed a twin, and soon there were four individual headlamps approaching from the west.

Less than a minute later, the two vehicles passed by Bishop's observation point, and he hustled back to watch in complete puzzlement as the two large SUVs pulled into Robinson's Garage. Before the first unit had come to a complete stop, three men jumped out, immediately forming a perimeter around the second. Were it not for the load vests, visible assault rifles, and military style fatigues, Bishop would have thought the security detail was from the Secret Service.

One of the bodyguards opened a door on the rear SUV, and a single man stepped out into the light. Bishop zoomed his optic as the fellow looked around and then apparently cut a joke with the members of his entourage. The closest guards laughed while the VIP stretched his arms and then began walking toward the entrance of the garage.

~  ~

Terri was experiencing a whirling carousel of emotions that alternated between fear and rage. As if the isolation hadn't been bad enough, her cell was cold and completely lacked anywhere to sit other than the toilet bucket. It was impossible to sleep sitting on the uncomfortable device, and she was sure that was by design. The single meal she had been served wasn't nearly enough to replace the calories her body was burning trying to keep her and the fetus warm. Her shivering was soon accompanied by leg cramps, numb fingers, and sniffles. The cramping interrupted her pacing, the only way she could generate body heat.

When the sun peeked over the horizon, her room instantly began to warm, but it wasn't nearly enough. She had toured the small room with her arms wrapped tightly around her torso numerous times. But after an hour, the effort had become exhausting, and the muscle cramps returned shortly after discontinuing her trek.

The lack of sleep played into her state as well. She was growing another person inside of her, and that required a lot of rest. Several times during the long night, she had secretly wished her kidnappers would torture or beat her instead of letting her freeze to death.

The sound of the vehicles outside had multiple effects. The interruption of the silence was welcome, as was the distraction of new activity. For a moment, she thought of rescue, but that idea passed quickly. Instead, a feeling of dread welled up, fueled by the realization that something was likely to happen soon, and she couldn't imagine any scenario that had a happy ending.

Terri couldn't be sure how much time had passed since the sound of the engines outside. It seemed to her like it was over an hour, but time was playing tricks on her mind. She even began to wonder if her captors had forgotten about her. The sun's slight warming of the air helped eliminate some of her discomfort, but she still was suffering badly. Her renewed pacing was interrupted by the guard's voice sounding from behind the door, the sound making Terri jump in surprise. The identical command was issued, "Move to the far side of the room away from the door."

Well, she thought, *as least they're going to feed me again.*

The grinding noise of the bolt was immediately followed by the opening of the door. Rather than throwing in a meal, three large men stepped inside of the room. "Come with me," one of them commanded.

The expression of hatred on Terri's face was ignored by the trio, the talkative one stepping out into the hall ahead of her while the others followed behind. She was led to another empty room that contained two plastic chairs and a small table. Two clear bottles of water sat on the table. "Take a seat right there," commanded her jailer.

Terri sat where ordered while the three guards stood by different walls, their positions forming a triangle around the prisoner. A few minutes later, the door opened again and an unarmed, older looking man strode into the room, his intense scrutiny focused on Terri.

Circling the captive once, the man settled, choosing to stand behind the opposite chair. "I'm very short on time young lady, so I'll be direct."

The man pulled back the chair and sat down. Reaching for the bottle of water, he unscrewed the cap and took a sip. "Let's begin. When did you first meet the former president?"

Terri tilted her head, surprised at the query. "Is that what this is all about? Is that why you risked the life of my child?"

The man's voice became cold and low. "I'll repeat this first question only once. When did you first meet the president?"

"I don't know the date. I found him hiding in the bushes next to a home in Alpha a few days ago."

The interrogator smiled, "Very good. Who was with you when you discovered him?"

"Some men from Alpha and our friend Nick. He was the one who recognized the man we found hiding as the president."

His eyes never leaving Terri's face, the man across from her paused for a moment. With a completely different tone of voice, he asked, "Are you cold?"

"Yes."

Turning to one of the guards, the questioner said, "This young lady is cooperating so far. Please provide her with a blanket."

Without acknowledging the command, the man left immediately and returned a short time later with a plain wool

233

blanket. The guard unceremoniously handed over the cover and returned to his position beside the wall. Terri wasted no time draping the wool cloth around her shoulders. She looked at her interrogator and said, "Thank you."

"Don't thank me just yet, young woman. We have a lot to talk about, and I can just as easily have that luxury taken away. Now, back to our business. How long before he was killed did you find our cowering chief executive?"

"It was approximately 30 minutes . . . maybe a few more . . . maybe a few less."

"And was the Commander in Chief in your presence the entire time between his discovery and eventual death?"

"Yes . . . as far as I can remember. I've already answered all these questions for the Army and Agent Powell. Why don't you just. . . ."

"Guard! Remove the blanket and this woman's blouse."

In a flash, the blanket was ripped away, and then Terri's shirt was literally torn from her body. She sat breathing heavily, her arms crossing in modesty to cover her underwear. Terri's fright was soon replaced with anger, the pressure building in her throat. The man across from her seemed to sense her reaction and spoke before Terri could erupt.

"We can do this the easy way, or the hard way. I can have you bound naked on the cold floor and use any number of pain inducing devices on your body. We can play with extreme heat, electrical shock, and simple blunt-force trauma—the options are practically endless. I'd prefer not to invest the time, but I will utilize those measures if you don't cooperate."

Terri nodded, icy fingers of fear spreading through her chest.

"Besides you, did anyone else speak with the president before his was shot?"

Terri replayed that fateful afternoon in her mind. After a bit, she responded, "No, not that I can recall. He spoke with my husband and Powell after he fell, but before that I think I was the only one."

"If I asked you to repeat your entire conversation with the president, would you be able to do so?"

It took some effort for Terri to focus. The room was very cold, and she hadn't eaten since the night before. The potential violence in the man across from her had filled her mind, and it was difficult to concentrate.

"I think I could . . . at least most of it."

Her captor must have noticed Terri shivering. He motioned for the guard to return the blanket.

Waiting while Terri adorned herself in the cover, the man rubbed his chin.

"This is a very common interrogation technique called positive reinforcement. Rewards are easy when you do as instructed. Punishment will be harsh when you don't. Now, tell me everything you can remember about the time you spent with the president. Start at the beginning and leave out no details—no matter how small or insignificant."

It suddenly dawned on Terri that she wasn't going to survive. The man across from her was well dressed and powerful. Obviously, he was either wealthy or influential. There was no other explanation for his command of the men around him, regardless if they were sworn or hired. Given his line of questioning, his genre was most likely political and that meant one thing—he wouldn't leave any witness to his crime alive. Dead pregnant women tell no tales.

Given the realization of eventual death, her panicking mind could form only one strategy—stall for time. She had to drag this out in hope that Bishop or someone would locate her. Time was her only weapon. The man wanted to know details. He wanted her to talk, so talk she would. Conversation ate time.

"Before I begin, I need to tell you what was going on that day; otherwise my conversation with the president won't be clear."

The interrogator smiled, "Providing a context makes sense, please proceed."

"The town of Alpha was divided into two camps. A group of escaped criminals controlled most of the town and a church congregation trying to hold out. The leader of the church was. . ."

The gentle knock on the door had the desired effect, bringing Moreland out of his deep sleep. The shades had been drawn over the row of windows lining the executive cabin aboard Air Force One, denying the sleepy man any reference to the time of day. Despite a moment of not knowing where he was, Moreland answered, "Yes?"

"Mr. President, good morning, sir. This is your wake up call," sounded Agent Powell's voice through the thin door.

"Thank you, Special Agent. I'm awake."

The door opened and a young Air Force steward pushed past the Secret Service man, opening two of the shades,

235

while Moreland rubbed his eyes. "Would coffee, eggs, and toast be agreeable this morning, sir?"

Moreland took a moment to sort out the question. "Well, thank you for the offer young man, but I typically like fruit in the morning. Where's Wayne? He should fill you in on all of my odd personal habits."

The steward looked at Powell, expressing perplexity over the question. Powell scowled, his brow knotting tightly. "Mr. President, Wayne left the base early this morning. He said you had given him the day off to visit his sister. He had an authorization bearing your signature to requisition two vehicles."

Moreland's head came up, a questioning look on his face. "That doesn't make any sense. Wayne's sister died almost a week ago. It was the first vacation he'd taken in years. I wonder if he means to visit her grave."

Powell didn't like what he was hearing. When a new administration came to Washington, it wasn't uncommon for friends, family, and political allies to abuse the power of the office and their relationship to it. Most of these instances were minor infringements, such as inviting friends to the White House without informing the Secret Service, or showing up at Andrews and demanding a tour of Air Force One. Powell had learned a long time ago to gently but firmly squash any such activity or it would get completely out of hand. Signing the president's name, however, was a serious breach.

"Mr. President, did you sign an authorization for Wayne to use those assets?"

Moreland waved off the question. "No, I didn't. Wayne can sign my name so well that I can't even tell the difference. He's been with me a long, long time, Agent Powell. I'll remind him my John Henry is a more sensitive matter from now on."

The soon-to-be chief executive seemed to be pondering his conversation with his aide when he stopped and looked at Agent Powell, "Did you say he requisitioned two cars?"

"Yes, sir. He stated that he needed two because he was taking half of your former security force with him in case there was trouble while he visited his sister."

Moreland chuckled, "Well that's odd. We only brought two of those large young men with us on the flight. Why would he need two vehicles?"

Powell suddenly found himself on the balls of his feet, his instincts sounding an alarm. "Sir, I was there. He had seven heavily armed men with him. Are you sure you only brought two security men with you?"

Moreland frowned, "I know I'm old, Agent Powell, but I'm not senile. Besides, the plane we flew only holds six passengers.

236

How could Wayne, seven others, and me all fit?"

Powell had to admit the senator had a good point. His mind started replaying the encounter this morning, trying to piece together the puzzle. *Was Wayne being kidnapped?* Clearly, the man had been nervous, but Powell had written that off to concern over leaving the confines of the base. The agent then remembered the equipment the security force was carrying. Thermal imagers, night vision, Infrared lasers, and weapons even he couldn't identify. *I need to brush up on my hardware,* he thought. *I'm supposed to know what's available. This is the second time in the last five days I've seen something new out here in the middle of nowhere.*

A streak of understanding flashed through the agent's mind as he connected the dots. He engaged the radio on his wrist, "This is one. Condition Yellow ... I repeat ... Condition Yellow. I need General Westfield to immediately lock down the base. No one in or out. Secondly, I need the general to meet me at Air Force One as soon as possible. Out."

Moreland gave Powell an expression of concern. "What's going on, Agent Powell?"

"I believe your Chief of Staff has been kidnapped, sir. I think there is a strong possibility it was the same people who attempted to assassinate your predecessor."

~  ~

Terri did her best to ramble about every detail she could recall from the president's last day. The weather, the battle for Alpha, and the military clothing the man had been wearing were all verbalized in gory detail. Whenever possible, she would divert to a background story and then pretend to lose her place.

The man across from her sat quietly, absorbing every detail and occasionally interrupting with a question. As time went on, she could tell he was becoming more and more impatient. Twice in the last 20 minutes, he stood to stretch and strode around the room while she continued with the narrative.

After over an hour of describing what was less than 30 minutes with the now-dead Commander in Chief, Terri rubbed her stomach and said, "I'm hungry," which was absolutely true. Her captor looked at one of the guards and nodded, the man leaving the room immediately.

Eating the MRE wasted another 20 minutes, Terri chewing each bite like it was her last. More than once, the thought occurred to her that this might indeed be her final meal.

237

She wasn't going to be able to continue this stall tactic much longer.

When she had finished every last crumb of the food, Terri pushed at the empty container on the floor next to her chair. "I would like to stand for a little bit, please."

"As long as you keep talking, I have no issue with it. But that does bring me to a point. I know you're stalling, young lady, and it's not going to do you a bit of good. There are 10 professional security men here. Even if your husband did find us, a rescue would be out of the question."

The man's statement struck a nerve with Terri. The energy being digested by her body was emboldening her spirit, and a little bit of sassy crept into her voice. "Why don't you tell me what it is you want to know? Why are we playing this game?"

The interrogator spun on his heels, a look of disdain glowing in his eyes. "Okay, maybe your method will expedite my goals. I want to know anything the president said about his assassins. Any detail at all."

The question seemed odd to Terri. She had been trying to figure this all out since the beginning, her theories floating between another coup attempt and some deep-seated hatred of Bishop for spoiling the first one. Now that she faced the person who was clearly driving all this craziness, she didn't think either was his motivation.

"Let me see," she began. "As he and I walked back to the church compound, he mentioned how frightened he had been during the shootout. He talked about being embarrassed over begging for his life when it looked like it was all over."

The man crossed his arms and took a menacing step closer to Terri. His voice was practically a hiss, "Did he say anything about who the assassins were?"

Strain wrinkled Terri's brow as she desperately tried to remember the president's words. "Yes, as a matter of fact he did say something right before he was shot … I'm trying to remember his exact phrasing . . . but. . . ."

The man sprung, unleashing a violent shove that slammed Terri against the wall. He was on her before she could even protest the attack, drawing back his hand and slapping her face.

"This is important! Stop delaying!" he screamed.

The impact against the wall had pushed the air out of Terri's lungs. She couldn't have answered to save her life. Again and again and again, the man slapped her, the blows stinging unlike anything she had ever felt before. She tried to move away, but he had her pinned. The open-handed strikes stopped for a moment, and she thought the attack was over. The next impact wasn't a slap. A tight-fisted full punch jarred Terri's head, her vision darkening to blackness, and sounds of bells rung in the recesses of her mind.

The interrogator stepped away, watching Terri slide down the wall, her body crumpling on the floor. The woman's face was bright red and blood dribbled from her nose and lip.

Straightening his jacket, the man looked at the nearest guard and ordered, "Come get me after she wakes up," and then promptly left the room.

After he was gone, the guard looked at his two comrades and whispered, "What the hell is this all about? This is off-the-fucking scale insane, man. This woman isn't any threat to anybody. What are we doing here?"

One of his peers agreed. "I'm with him, Deke . . . this isn't what I signed up for. Who tortures a pregnant woman who hasn't done shit? I was told this whole setup was a matter of national security. This woman is as much a threat to national security as my 90-year-old Aunt Helen. Why is he asking her about all this crap? Who gives a rat's ass what the dead prez said?"

Both men looked at Deke, who was clearly as confused as they were. "I don't know either, guys. Let's get her a blanket and do what we're told until I can figure this all out."

~  ~

The sound of pounding boots, warming turbines, and shouted orders filled the tarmac at Briggs Field. Agent Powell watched the Army troopers board the three Blackhawk helicopters, the scene reminding him of a similar event just a few days prior—that episode in preparation to rescue a missing president.

Powell turned to Moreland, yelling over the rising cascade of men and machines preparing to launch. "Sir, again, I must protest your coming along. You are the next President of the United States and far too valuable to our country to risk going on a mission like this."

Moreland smiled at his protector, "I'm going, Special Agent Powell. That is my best friend and most loyal supporter who has gone missing under some very dubious circumstances. I'm going to see with my own eyes exactly what's going on. I don't think the nation would be in the same place right now, if more of my predecessors had gotten their hands dirty. Besides, there seems to be more than enough men to protect me on this little jaunt."

Powell gave up the argument, mumbling to himself that the man was stubborn and secretly praying he wouldn't be so rash once he was sworn in.

Looking around at the men comprising his security detail, Powell did have to agree that Moreland would be well protected. In addition to the Army assault teams, he had five fully fortified agents to keep the next president safe.

The co-pilot waved through the bubble shaped glass, indicating their aircraft was ready to be designated Army One, pro tem. Patting Moreland on the shoulder and motioning toward the bird, the executive detail all ducked their heads and jogged toward the aircraft.

Two minutes later all four Blackhawks lifted off, the formation heading east into the bright sun.

Bishop's radio crackled before he heard the distant hum of car engines. "Bishop, we're here."

Keying the push-to-talk button, Bishop acknowledged he was listening.

"I've got over 20 men with me, and we are about 10 minutes out. Everything still status quo?"

"No, two SUVs, full of armed men, arrived a few hours ago. Since then, everything's been quiet. There are at least 10 shooters inside that building now."

Nick seemed unconcerned, "We'll be there shortly."

Just as the engine noise reached Bishop's ear, it stopped. Fifteen minutes later, he could observe the large group of rescuers gathering at the base of the knoll.

Bishop joined Nick's posse and found a flat area of soft sand. Using his finger, Bishop drew a map in the earth while onlookers gathered around.

"We'll split into four teams. Nick will take out the sentry . . . here. Once he does that, I'll approach from here and disable the two SUVs. After that, each team will take a corner of the building and form a skirmish line behind the best cover available. I want our numbers to be visible, but not easy targets. I don't think they'll shoot, but I can't be 100% certain. Once all four sides of the building are covered, I'll approach and call them out."

Bishop looked around the group, noting that all heads were nodding. Focusing back on the map, he continued. "The ATVs are most likely stored in this bay behind the closed overhead door. Some of them might make a run for it on those units. Job one, and this is incredibly important, job one is to not allow anyone out of that building. If they try to use Terri as a shield, leave it up to me. I'm the one that has to live with the results—good or bad."

No one had any questions, and within a few minutes, Nick moved off into the desert, his critical phase of the plan dominating his thoughts.

Nick's mission required approaching the guard's hide from the rear. Looping wide through the desert, he made good progress through the open terrain using distance rather than cover to conceal his approach. Bishop watched his friend from the hilltop using his rifle optic, and after 30 minutes he could see Nick was ready to spring on the guard's hide.

Zooming his optic slightly, Bishop watched Nick stalk the hidden sentry, each step carefully placed and measured. When the big man was within a few feet of the hide, he lunged. Bishop shivered—a passing sympathy for the poor soul who had just been surprised by the ex-Green Beret. Within seconds a single arm appeared out of the brush pile and waved toward the hill—the signal that Nick now held the sentry's post.

Bishop was next, taking a route down the hillside he had studied during the wait for reinforcements. Taking his time to detect any tripwires, Bishop eventually ran across the open parking lot and to the first SUV. His thought on the hill had been to use his knife on the tires, but as he approached closer to the vehicles, he noted the front plates said "POTUS." *Shit*, he thought. *These are Secret Service units. They'll have run-flat tires.*

Keeping an eye on the nearby door, Bishop made his way around to the driver's side and checked the door. It was unlocked. *No*, he thought. *I wouldn't be that lucky.* Reaching in, he found the keys still in the ignition. In a few moments, both sets of keys were in Bishop's pocket.

"That's two mistakes you've made," he whispered. "Maybe you guys aren't so hot after all." Reaching up to touch his head wound reminded Bishop that he'd better not get cocky.

Staying low beside the SUVs, Bishop watched the four teams spreading out across the desert. Choosing to conceal the inside of the hideout had resulted in a double-edged sword for the kidnappers. While it was impossible to see inside the building, it was also impossible to see out. They had put all of their security eggs in the sentry basket, and Nick had taken care of that.

Fifteen minutes later, the radio sounded with two clicks, followed a few minutes later by two more. The teams were in position.

Bishop walked to the corner where he could see both the side entrance and the overhead garage door.

~  ~

Terri's face felt puffy and swollen, and it hurt to breathe through her nose. One of the armed guards had checked her pupils, looked at her face, and announced she would be fine in a few weeks.

More important was the damage done to her ego. She had never had anyone lay a hand on her before, at least not since childhood spankings that she couldn't remember. While watching television shows and movies, Terri had always believed she would react with anger toward any attacker. She would observe the female actors cower after being struck; always thinking *I'd fight back like a lioness if some jerk laid a hand on me. Kick him in the nuts!*

Now, sitting alone and very uncertain about her future, she wasn't feeling any aggression. It wasn't the pain or any petty vanity about her bruised appearance—that meant nothing right now. It was the terrible anguish of being helpless that dominated her thoughts. She had never experienced such a sensation. Having zero control of her well-being seemed to hollow out her soul and drain the energy from her body. Any will to fight had been literally beaten out of her.

When the interrogator stepped back into the room, it felt like the walls moved several feet closer, and the air became difficult to breathe.

There weren't any apologies, not that Terri expected any. "I need to know what the president told you about his assassins, and I need to know now. Time is up—no more games."

Terri had anticipated the question. Since the guards had helped her into her chair, she had been thinking of nothing but answering this lunatic and getting it over with.

"I asked him if he planned on escalating the war in Louisiana. He replied that he was going to pursue a peaceful solution. I then commented how that showed more forgiveness than I, personally, was capable of. I told him that he was doing the right thing, putting the country before any revenge against those that had tried to kill him."

Her captor leaned forward, the corners of his mouth twisted in a grimace. "And . . . and . . . did he say any more?"

242

Terri sighed, "He said the Independents hadn't tried to kill him. He said he knew who it was, that there was an . . . uhh . . . an ulterior motive."

The man leaned back in the chair and stared at the ceiling. Terri watched, fascinated, the transition in his demeanor unlike anything she'd ever witnessed. His reaction reminded her of someone who had just been told he carried some horrible, deadly disease, and had a short time to live.

Her abductor exhaled deeply, his eyes showing nothing. "No, he didn't." It hadn't been a question, but a very clear statement.

"What?"

"The president didn't say that, and you are going to testify to that fact."

Terri was very confused. "But . . . but he did say that. I remember it clearly."

Again, he became agitated, leaning forward in the chair with eyes full of hatred. "No he didn't say any such thing," he hissed. "In three days, there is going to be a group of senators at Fort Bliss. They are going to hold a hearing. You are going to testify that the president believed the attack against him was perpetrated by the Independents. There will be none of the ulterior motive nonsense or anything said about pursuing peace."

Terri shook her head, "I don't understand. You want me to lie? You want me to fabricate a story?"

Her captor bolted upright, grabbed the chair, and threw it against the wall. He turned and began screaming at Terri. "You will repeat exactly what I tell you to say, or we will come. We will come in the middle of the night and we will kill you, and your child, and your husband."

Terri forgot about the beating. Thoughts of the cold cell, hunger, and the endangered child growing inside her were pushed aside by the realization of what this was all about. She had been pulled into some sort of political power struggle by the mere act of listening to a distressed man—a man who just happened to be the president. A compassionate conversation was to blame for all of this suffering—a simple talk with another human being who wanted to share his inner thoughts.

Terri couldn't help herself and snorted, the outburst becoming a giggle of sorts. "I'll be happy to lie, but I need to know why I'm committing perjury."

Wayne smirked, "I am with the Independents, and our leader is the next in line to become president of the United States. I can't let that happen."

Terri was trying to think it through, "So you want me to let everyone think the Independents actually did try and execute the president? That doesn't make any sense. Why don't you want me to witness your innocence? Why. . . ."

Recognition crossed Terri's face. With a look of horror, her eyes met the interrogator's scowl. "You want the war to continue. You don't want your leader to become president and make peace."

Terri stood again, turning to face the wall. She took a deep breath and pivoted to face her imprisoner. "No, I won't do it. I won't be responsible for the deaths of thousands of people. No deal."

The veins bulged on the interrogator's neck, his face flushed red. Pointing a shaking finger at Terri, his voice boomed through the room. "You simple-minded little harlot! You're nothing more than a marriage-whore, selling your body to a man you pretend to love in exchange for security and necessities. How dare you insult the leaders of our species—the people who try and guide our race forward? How dare you belittle those who sacrificed everything for a cause, a cause to improve our very existence? You have no concept. You are unqualified to comprehend, let alone judge such men."

Terri thought for a moment. She pointed at her bruised face. "*This* is a cause?" She rubbed the raw skin on her wrists where the nylon ties had eaten into her skin. "*This* is building something better?"

He waved her off. "Sacrifices must be made. Collateral damage and suffering are the unfortunate byproduct of any revolution."

It was Terri's turn to explode in anger. "Ego is affecting your reasoning. You and the leaders of our country have lost touch with reality, sir. I give a shit less about the president or the government as a whole. They're not great men to be worshiped, let alone respected. They are nothing to me. That respect was lost years ago . . . by me, and by most of the people I know. The only ones who care about that drama anymore are the actors onstage—the audience left the theatre a long time ago and asked for a refund on its way out."

It was her captor's turn to do the unexpected. Rather than launch into a tirade of angry insults, he laughed, shook his head and looked down. After a few deep breaths, he grinned at Terri and said, "I apologize, young lady. I wasted my time. I shouldn't have expected someone like you to understand."

Terri tilted her head, "Please, sir. Don't confuse a lack of understanding with a complete lack of interest. You and our previously elected officials are irrelevant. There's no country, no society, no taxes, and except for a rapidly decaying military, no authority. The power that you and your kind do wield is becoming extraneous—more so every day. I hate to be the one to break the news to you, but there's not much future in political power. Perhaps you should think of other work. Farmers are in short supply, I hear."

The man paced a few steps and then spun around and spread his arms wide. "Those with me have sacrificed so much. We are on the brink of pulling this nation from the ashes—of building something better for all. Yet, you dismiss our cause with impunity. Before we end this conversation, I'd like to know why. Please indulge me with that final transfer of logic."

Terri did the unexpected—she shrugged. Her captor wanted a debate. He seemed to desire an intellectual dual of some sort. Terri wanted to sleep and, adding insult to injury, yawned. After looking around at the guards, she finally focused back on the furious maniac standing in front of her and said, "I'm finished. Your game doesn't interest me. I think watching paint dry would be more important. Shoot me if you're going to. Let me go if you're not. I'm not going to be the cause of more suffering and death. I won't be the cause of a civil war."

Wayne paced a few steps before he came to a conclusion. "I do have some small regret that you've reached this decision. The best case would be for you to testify. Since that's not going to happen, the next best scenario is for you to never testify." Without further thought, the man pointed to a nearby guard, and ordered, "Execute her," and proceeded for the door.

Despite anticipating those words for hours, Terri's heart froze. A human voice commanding her death impacted her far differently than she had imagined.

The guard glared at his master and responded, "No."

The interrogator stopped mid-stride, acting as if he hadn't heard the guard's response. "What did you say?"

The large sentry loomed above his master, his voice steady and sure. "I said 'No.' You heard me loud and clear."

"You are denying a direct command?" Turning to another of the guards, he commanded again. "You shoot her then. This one doesn't have the guts."

The answer from the second man was the same. "No."

The boss' eyes flashed anger, his head snapping from one jailer to the other. "What is the problem here, gentlemen?"

It was the first sentry who responded. "We are under contract to protect you and the senator. That's it. We all signed up to conduct legal operations and preventative actions. Executing someone isn't legal—I don't give a rat's ass what excuse you dream up. This woman didn't do shit to anyone. I heard it with my own ears. Even if she had, we don't execute anybody."

The interrogator's voice grew low and harsh. "You signed up to do as ordered. I was very clear in my agreement with Mr. King. I needed a team of his absolute best who could handle anything."

The expression on the large sentry's face stopped the speech. Realizing he wasn't going to get anywhere with the hired help, the interrogator reached for the small of his back and produced a pistol. "Fine," he said, "I'll do it myself."

Before he could take a single step, a shot rang out.

Terri jumped as the sound reverberated through the metal walls of the building. Her heart sang with joy when she heard Bishop's voice ring out. "You inside the building – I only want the woman. Send her out, and I'll be on my way."

The three guards exchanged glances, and then moved with unbelievable speed. The interrogator was bracketed by two of the men before he could react, the bookends of muscle and weapons hustling him toward the door. Terri was just as harshly lifted from her chair and moved to the hall where she was shoved to the ground and ordered, "Stay prone and don't move."

Chapter 15

Bishop stood fifty feet from the garage with his rifle pointed into the air. For a brief time he thought his challenge wasn't going to be answered as there wasn't any visible or audible reaction from inside the building. Less than a minute passed before the overhead garage door opened and a single figure appeared. The man carried a SCAR rifle across his chest, casually strolling a few steps in Bishop's direction.

"I gotta hand it to ya, slick. I sure didn't peg you as being so tenacious."

Bishop didn't care about the man's opinion. "Hand over my wife, and we'll all go away."

"And who might 'we' be? I only see one lone ranger who's missing part of his ear."

"I've got 20 men with me, and your little hacienda is completely surrounded. Give us the woman, and we'll be on our way."

The man opposing Bishop snorted, shaking his head in disbelief. "You don't really expect me to take your word for it, do you? How foolish would I feel if I found out later you had bluffed me?"

Bishop moved his hand slowly and deliberately, careful not to project any offensive movement. He waved in the air. "Look over my shoulder," he challenged. "I think you'll see that I'm not in a bluffing mood. I want my wife back."

At Bishop's signal, several men rose from behind rocks and bushes. Most of them brandishing their weapons and making sure there was no doubt about their intent.

"Where's my sentry? I assume you didn't just kill him for sport."

Bishop nodded in the direction of the hide. Nick lifted a large branch of foliage, exposing a man on his knees with hands behind his back. The rather pitiful looking ex-sentry was bleeding from the nose. Bishop repeated, "I want my wife back. I don't give one shit about what you guys are doing or why. It's none of my business. Give me the woman and leave us alone."

The guy with the SCAR looked around and nodded back at Bishop. "To be blunt here, slick, I'm not in charge of this party—not exactly, anyway. Let me go inside and convince the boss you mean business, and perhaps we can strike a deal."

"You have three minutes," Bishop warned. "The longer

this drags on, the more chance someone will try and do something stupid. Stupid is going to equal death today—there's no getting around it."

Bishop's comment earned him a slight grin and then a nod of understanding. Pivoting, the man returned briskly to the garage. Bishop held tight, hoping this would end quietly, hoping Terri was unharmed. Just as the man disappeared into the dark shadows of the former business, Bishop's earpiece sounded with the voice of a frightened man. "Bishop, we've got more company. I can see four helicopters headed right toward us from the west. They'll be here in less than a minute."

"Roger that," he responded into his microphone. Looking at Nick, Bishop shrugged. "What do we do now?"

Nick waved another man up to watch his prisoner. As soon as he was free of guard duty, the ex-Special Forces operator headed off at a full run, clearly having the intent to investigate what had just been broadcasted. Bishop had no choice but to wait and see what his friend reported.

There were only two options as far as Bishop could determine. Either the copters were bringing the bad guys' reinforcements, or not. If the aircraft were armed in any way, the whole thing was over. His group didn't have the firepower or skills to ward off an assault from the air. If the transports contained more armed men, then it was still over. Despite the bravery and local knowledge of the men Nick had gathered, they wouldn't stand a chance against superior numbers of the type of operators Bishop believed they faced. The four approaching birds could hold 20 to 25 men and that would simply tilt the odds too much in the opposing side's favor.

Terri. Bishop's mind started rolling though any option to get Terri out before they had to retreat. He decided to press his opponent before the copters landed.

"Hey inside! We're running out of time. Let's get this over with. Stop being clever, and send out the girl."

Nick's voice sounded in Bishop's ear. "They're military birds, Bishop. I don't think they're gunships. They'll be here is a few seconds."

Bishop glanced to the western sky but couldn't see anything. He took two steps toward the garage and then instinctively ducked as one of the helicopters zoomed over the hill and flew past very low. Glancing up, he could see Agent Powell looking down as the bird flew past.

~ ~

248

"What the hell," mumbled Powell under his breath. His two missing vehicles were down there along with several men scattered around the building—and then there was Bishop. *What is Bishop doing here? What's he got to do with kidnapping Wayne? Was I wrong about him, was he really involved in all of this?*

Powell quickly determined there was only one way he was going to find out. Turning to the pilot, he shouted orders. "Have the troops land to the north and form up. We'll join them."

"Roger that."

Nick's voice sounded again. "Bishop, they're landing about 400 meters north of us. What do you think?"

Bishop could see the entire situation was getting completely out of control. Too many armed men and no one knew who was on which side. "Pull pack," he barked at Nick. "Bring those teams back behind me. Don't engage or give the Army units any excuse."

"Sounds good to me. We're on our way."

~  ~

Terri was lying prone on the cold concrete floor, her emotions fighting between absolute joy and dread that something terrible was going to happen to Bishop. Since the leader of the armed guards had returned from talking with Bishop, he and his men had been discussing the situation among themselves. The interrogator appeared in shock, sitting with his back to a wall and his head between his knees. Terri hadn't seen him stir since being forced to the spot by his bodyguards.

It appeared to Terri that the crowd of armed men was near reaching a decision when the helicopter passed overhead. The leader of the guards had sprinted to the open doorway and glanced up, shaking his head and then returning to his comrades. While Terri couldn't hear the conversation, the new arrival clearly wasn't good news for the guards. The interrogator didn't seem to notice.

Nick seemed winded when he transmitted again. "Bishop, we're falling back to your six. We'll be passing behind you and on the western side in a minute. The birds dumped over 20 men, and they've formed up into a skirmish line. They're heading this way in a hurry. I expect them to arrive at your location in less than four minutes."

Bishop forgot radio protocol and replied with a heartfelt, "Shit."

He took two more steps toward the garage when the negotiator appeared at the edge of the shadow. "You've got a deal, slick. My men and I want to head east and take our equipment with us. You can have the woman as soon as my guys are clear. We no longer have a dog in this fight."

"Send out Terri, now. We'll honor our word. Send her out, and we'll just melt away."

"No can do, slick. She's our shield right now. If I send her your way, there's nothing to stop you guys from turning this building into Swiss cheese with all those deer rifles pointed this way."

"I'll tell you what—I'll trade places with her. My men won't shoot while I'm inside."

The man didn't answer, instead he disappeared for a moment, and when he returned, Terri was standing beside him. Bishop's feelings soared when he saw his wife. He looked her in the eye and winked—trying to let her know she was going to be okay.

Without another word, the armed men from inside began pushing out the ATVs, each having a strapped pack of supplies tied to its cargo area. Bishop counted three machines in total. Next, two men ventured out, pushing out off-road motorcycles. No one started any engines.

Bishop approached Terri and her jailer. He made it to within 10 feet when the guy held up his hand and said, "That's close enough, slick. We'll be out in a minute."

A man in civilian clothes walked into Bishop's view. He was clearly very angry, and his gaze was focused on Terri. The guard walked over to the civilian and tried to take him by the arm, but the guy would have none of it and shook him off. Whispered words were exchanged, the civilian's eyes never leaving Terri. Given her expression, it was clear to Bishop that his wife recoiled from the man, taking a half step away from him. Bishop managed another sliding step closer to Terri.

The exchange between the guard and the older man went back and forth, gestures from each becoming more and more animated. Bishop crept another step closer to his wife, his instincts telling him something was wrong.

Bishop was close enough now to pick up some words of the heated exchange going on next to his beloved. He heard the guard protest, "Up to you. I'm done with this," and then wave his arm through the air in a motion of dismissal. Spinning away abruptly, the guard motioned his men to continue and walked away from the civilian.

The now isolated man never let his eyes leave Terri, pure hatred pouring out of the guy's face. Bishop wanted Terri to

250

move toward him, hoping to meet her in the middle, but his wife kept staring back at her antagonist and wouldn't make eye contact with her rescuer.

It's now or never, he thought, and took another step toward his wife. The motion distracted the civilian and he sprung, wrapping his arm around Terri's throat and producing a pistol, which he pointed at her head.

"Stay back," he announced. "I've got nothing to lose anymore."

Bishop abruptly halted his forward motion. The hostage taker looked over Terri's shoulder and demanded, "Lay down that rifle. The pistol, too."

"Come on, friend," Bishop said. "This is over. You're surrounded by 20 good shots who happen to adore the woman you're threatening to kill. Give it up, and walk out of here alive."

The man pulled the hammer back, the blue barrel tight against Terri's temple. "Put them down or you see her die right here."

Bishop nodded, and pulled the rifle's sling over his shoulder, moving slowly so as not to startle the man holding his wife at gunpoint. Bishop set the rifle on the desert floor; the pistol soon followed. When he stood, Bishop managed another half step closer to his adversary. With both hands in the "Don't shoot" position, he prompted his aggressor, "What now?"

Before the gunman could answer, movement over his shoulder drew Bishop's attention. Two soldiers appeared around the corner, their weapons up and ready. When they saw Terri with a gun to her head, a clear hostage situation, they retreated immediately. With his attention focused on Bishop, Terri's abductor didn't see them.

While he couldn't hear their radio transmissions, it wasn't difficult for Bishop to imagine what was being said. Normal infantry isn't trained to deal with scenarios like this. It's not something the big Army teaches their men how to handle, especially with civilians involved.

Bishop decided to distract his opponent. "You realize you're not going to get out of this alive if you harm my wife."

"Save your breath, young man. I'm going to keep this young lady between you and me. She and I are going to walk out to those Secret Service cars sitting outside. We're going to take one of them and leave. I'm assuming you didn't disable our transport in any way?"

"As a matter of fact, I took the keys." Bishop patted his pants pocket. "I've got both sets, right here."

"Well, at least you're honest. I'll need those keys, of course."

"Friend, I'll be happy to hand over both sets. I'll even open the door for you and load up your bags. Please just let Terri go, and I'll escort you to your ride."

Bishop detected more movement over the man's shoulder. He couldn't be positive, but he thought it was Agent Powell glancing around the doorframe.

Without warning, a new voice sounded out from the hallway, "Wayne? Wayne, what are you doing?"

Moreland pushed his way between his Secret Service escorts and out into the open floor of the garage. "Lord in Heaven Wayne, what are you doing? Put that gun down. I don't know what's happened, but we can fix this."

Bishop noticed Powell holding back the two startled agents, both of whom wanted desperately to retrieve their charge.

Wayne spun to face the new presence, pulling Terri with him, maintaining her as his shield. He began backing away, head snapping back and forth. Bishop thought the guy was going to panic at any minute, his erratic body language indicating he was spiraling out of control.

"Senator," Wayne said, "I'm sorry, sir, but this has gone beyond anything you can fix. Leave, sir. Get out of here. Let me do my duty."

Taking another step forward with his arms spread wide, Moreland spoke with a calming voice. "Wayne, I'll be sworn in as president in the next few days. There's very little I can't fix after that. Now tell me what's going on, my old friend. Let's work this out together, without any bloodshed."

"No, Senator, you're not going to be sworn in as president. I've found evidence you ordered the assassination . . . that you ordered the Independents to kill the president so you could take over. Senator, you should fly back to West Virginia and rally the council. You should take your rightful place and lead the Independents to victory."

Moreland was clearly puzzled by the babbling of his assistant. "Wayne, what are you talking about? You know I didn't order any such action. Why are you saying this?"

Subconsciously, Moreland took a step toward Wayne and his captive. Bishop saw the pistol move from Terri's temple, the barrel making a slow arch toward the advancing politician.

"This young woman will set the record straight!" spouted Wayne. "Tell them . . . tell them what you told me."

Terri took a deep breath and closed her eyes. The emotional elevator ride from certain death to rescue and now back to believing she was going die had an impact on her thinking. She looked Moreland in the eye and said, "The president told me the Independents didn't have anything to do with the attempt on his life."

"No! That's not what we agreed!" Wayne shouted, and spun Terri around. Bishop saw the pistol being pulled back like Wayne was going to use it as a club.

He rushed at Wayne.

The three steps to the man threatening his wife's life seemed like a mile. The fractions of measured time didn't register in Bishop's mind. There was no sound, as if a stifling cloud of noise-muffling air had descended on the scene.

Simultaneous with the first step toward his target, Bishop's hand reached for the knife on his vest. As his foot pushed with every sinew and muscle in his body, the blade began to clear its scabbard. Terri was being pushed away as Bishop's boot landed, the muzzle of the pistol reversing course and seeking the new threat. As Bishop leaped into the air, the black hole at the end of the weapon aligned. To Bishop's eye, the business end of the barrel looked large enough to swallow a man. Gravity ceased to be a factor and time slowed—his body seemingly suspended in mid-air.

As Bishop slammed into the pistol, his right arm thrust with every ounce of power his body could muster. He felt little initial resistance from the collision, the impact resulting in a brief slowing of his momentum and then a sensation of falling. An enormous blast filled his ears, immediately followed by a crushing, hammer-like blow to his chest. A sensation of burning fire spread across his ribs as he landed on top of his target, the impact so violent Bishop bounced off the body beneath him, finally rolling to a stop on the hard concrete floor.

A brief moment passed while Bishop gathered his wits. He rolled to his left and immediately saw his knife sticking out of the gunman's chest, the pistol lying harmlessly a few feet away. His next thought was for Terri. His vision was becoming milky around the edges, but he managed to find his wife crouching nearby—a look of horror on her face. Bishop smiled and tried to rise up onto his elbow, but his arm wouldn't cooperate. Puzzled, he looked down at his numb limb, surprised by the sight of a growing pool of red liquid spreading across the cold, gray concrete background.

Bishop was suddenly very tired. He didn't have the energy to sit up or speak; even breathing seemed to be an exhausting effort. Letting his body relax and resting on his back, Bishop thought he'd never felt such a lack of strength or energy. *I should be happy*, he thought. *Terri is safe, but I'm too weak to even smile at her.*

His wife's beautiful face appeared in his vision, an

angelic glow surrounding her eyes that reminded him of the warmth of her love. Bishop didn't see her stringy hair or bruised face. In his mind, Terri was an image of perfection, her presence projecting a sense of harmony and tranquility that filled his mind. Terri's lips were moving, but Bishop couldn't hear any words. He wanted to reassure her, to let her know what he was feeling. "I love you," he managed, but the words sounded distant and weak. Bishop saw the light around Terri's face change colors. It was a curious effect, almost dreamy and perfect for such a beautiful woman. He felt sad when Terri's image became smaller. More emptiness, as her loving face finally faded to a pinpoint of bright light. And then there was total blackness.

~  ~

Moreland knelt beside Wayne, both men's faces ashen. Wayne's eyes were open, but unfocused, his chest rising and falling with uneven cycles, struggling to supply his body with oxygen. Moreland was in shock as well, still unable to comprehend the violence he'd just witnessed.

Taking the dying man's hand, Moreland's gentle grip caused Wayne to turn slightly and smile at his old friend. "I'm sorry, Senator . . . I didn't have any choice."

"Why, Wayne? Please tell me . . . why?"

Wayne's eyes scanned the area, apparently checking for someone within earshot. In a low voice he responded, "Senator, I pledged to a cause I believe in . . . the Independents. I gave my word of honor. I couldn't let you become the enemy— the president of the United States. There is no hope for the existing hierarchy, sir. There was only one way I could stop you—to make the world believe you had ordered the assassination. That would have forced you to continue the cause of the Independents, more motivated than ever."

An Army medic knelt beside Wayne and began to cut away at his shirt. The man was a veteran of two recent wars and knew immediately there was no hope. Looking up at Moreland, the corpsman simply shook his head and mouthed the words, "I'm sorry, sir."

Bishop was also receiving medical attention, and the prognosis wasn't much better. Nick pulled Terri away, comforting her in his arms while the sobs racked her body. Terri kept peering around Nick's shoulder, trying to watch what was being done to her husband. She really couldn't see Bishop's face anymore, his mouth and nose covered with an Ambu bag.

Another man was working on Bishop's chest, and Terri cringed when she heard the man comment that the bullet had "hit his shoulder right above the armor." Bishop had always told Terri body armor left exposed areas – that it wasn't the perfect shield.

Two men appeared with stretchers right as Moreland reached up and gently closed Wayne's lifeless eyes. As Bishop was being lifted, Terri moved to go with her husband. A man wearing the rank of sergeant stepped in front of her, but Agent Powell overrode the gatekeeper, and Terri was escorted to the helicopter.

Little of the trip back registered with Terri. The medics had hooked an IV into Bishop's arm while another man took his vitals. "It's up to God and the surgeons at Bliss," one of the medics had said.

"He's strong, but that's a nasty hit," commented the other.

Terri sat in silence on the floor of the helicopter and held Bishop's hand. *Don't leave me, Bishop. God, please don't take him from me. Fight Bishop! You fight harder than you've ever battled anything before.*

The men from Darkwater moved off into the desert, but couldn't go far in any direction without running into either the Army or Nick's posse. Deke didn't want an encounter with either side.

His men formed up the ATVs and checked on their wounded comrade. Moving an injured man always held the possibility of reopening a wound and the increased risk of hemorrhaging.

"Where are we going to go?" asked one of the team.

Deke responded, aware that everyone was intent on his answer. "We'll hang out here until things clear out back at that building and then move back in. It ain't the Four Seasons, but it will keep the sun off our head until we can arrange transport."

"And who is going to arrange transport? We all flew out here on the client's private jet."

Deke reached into his pocket and produced the modified cell phone. "I can call the home office on this. Mr. King will figure out a way to get us home. He's managed to pull our asses out of worse situations."

Grim spoke up from his stretcher, "That may take a while. It's not as if he can charter a plane or rent a chopper to come get us. I hope we've got plenty of supplies."

"We're counting on you to shoot wild game, Grim. You're going to be responsible for feeding us," remarked one of the men.

Moses noticed movement and called Deke over. The big dude who had disabled their sentry was walking toward the gathering. "What the fuck does he want?" someone asked.

"I don't know," responded Deke, "but it can't be good."

Nick approached within 50 feet of the contractors and stopped. His rifle was slung across his back, barrel down.

"I got no issue with any of you except the man who shot my son in Alpha. I've got a score to settle with him."

The challenge caused several members of the team to chuckle and a few whispered comments about how outnumbered this crazy guy was. Deke started to respond when Moses motioned he'd take care of it.

Moses walked a few steps closer to Nick and said, "Now don't you just have the biggest pair of nads on the block? Just casually strolling up to nine guys and calling somebody out. I think you've seen too many movies, big man."

Nick smiled at the response. "Do you have any children, operator?"

The question took Moses by surprise. He couldn't think of any clever answer, so he simply told the truth. "Yeah, I've got two daughters. I ain't seen them in a while though."

Nick's smile disappeared. "And what would your reaction be if someone put a 5.56 NATO round into one of their chests?"

Moses didn't hesitate. "I'd kill the fucker . . . slow like . . . he wouldn't die well."

Nick nodded, "Well, I think one of you esteemed gentlemen put a round into my 15-year-old son's chest, and I want justice . . . right fucking now."

Deke couldn't hold back any longer, the day's events shortening his temper. "I'm so sick of this shit. Every fucking swinging dick thinks we are some gawd awful lawless killers or some shit. I've gotten used to being called a gun for hire or a mercenary or even a bounty hunter, but a baby killer is just too fucking much. Nobody here shot your kid, dude. We don't operate that way."

Nick grunted, "So none of you elite operators were in the Alpha courthouse at about 0500 hours a few days ago? None of you brave fighting men got caught looking through records and charged up the stairs where you shot a 15-year-old boy?"

Deke looked back at Grim, the two men's mouths opening in surprise.

It all became clear to Deke. "That was you? That was your son at the top of the stairs?" Deke took a step closer to Nick, the anger in his voice sharp and hostile. "What kind of fucking father are you? Are you dense of something?"

The response initially surprised Nick, but the big man recovered quickly. "Oh nooooo, you don't. You ain't putting it back on me, shitbird . . . send the fucker out that. . . ."

Deke interrupted Nick's rebuttal, cupping his mouth and yelling, "I've got men at the top of the stairs!"

Deke stared at Nick, "Isn't that what you yelled at us? Isn't that exactly what you said, right after firing shots in our direction?"

Nick couldn't respond, his mind spinning. *Yes*, he thought, *that is exactly what I said*.

Deke continued, "So I've got some cowboy shooting up the basement and rather than drop the hammer on your ass, we go charging up the stairs to get out. You yell out that warning right before we hit the bottom step, I look up, and there's a guy pointing an AR15 at my head. I shot your son, dude. I put the round into his chest, but I swear I didn't know it was a kid. There was no way to tell in the dark and with the speed of the moment."

Nick met Deke's stare and took a step toward the confessor. The last thing any man in West Texas wanted was to go hand-to-hand with Nick. On top of his size, training and experience, he was a parent whose offspring had been harmed by another. It was a combination of skills, capabilities and motivation that would render the ex-Special Forces sergeant practically invincible.

Deke seemed to sense this, but held his ground, readying for the bull's charge. Deke was building up his own storm of rage, and it wasn't defensive. Throwing his rifle to the ground and making ready with his fists, he challenged Nick. "Come on in, big man, if that's what it's going to take. You clearly suck as a father, and the boy will be better off with his mother after I take care of you. My old man was just as stupid as you are. This is going to feel good."

Something registered in the man's words and Nick pulled up short. "I did say that . . .you wouldn't have known. . . . He's a big kid. . . . It was dark."

"Look, pal, I don't know what you guys were doing there. I don't know why anyone puts a rifle in a 15- year-old kid's hands. I'm not walking in your shoes, and I'm not anybody's judge. The fucking world has gone crazy, and people are doing all kinds of weird shit. But I'm also not a guy who shoots a kid on purpose. I thought your son was a man trying to kill me, and I defended myself. I bet you would have done the same thing in my shoes."

A change came over Nick. His shoulders slumped and his frame relaxed, a look of understanding crossing his face. Without a word, he walked to Deke's rifle and picked it up. The action caused several Darkwater weapons to point at Nick, but he ignored them. Brushing off the sand, he handed the weapon to Deke butt first and looked his former adversary in the eye. "I got no quarrel with you. You're right – I would've done the same."

Everyone relaxed, especially Deke. Nick turned to walk away when one of the Darkwater operators said, "Hey! I know you. Didn't you serve with the teams down at Bragg?"

Nick stopped and turned around, looking at the speaker. "I spent half my life sweating in those gawd forsaken Carolina pines. Yeah, I've worked at Bragg more than I care to remember."

"You were our night ops instructor - Class 309. I hated your sadistic ass." The guy turned and looked at his co-workers and continued. "This guy was pure fucking evil. I wanted to kill *him* more than any terrorist."

Nick grinned, "Good. That means I did my job."

The Darkwater operator stepped forward and offered his hand. "I changed my mind the first time I got separated from my team in the sandbox. I thought Haji was going to skin my sorry ass alive. I made it back thanks to what you taught us."

Nick shook the man's hand. He started to turn away again but stopped and pivoted back to face the group. "Where are you guys going?"

Deke responded, "We are going to hang out here until I can get some transport out of this shithole. We're just waiting on the Army and your guys to clear out."

Nick looked over his shoulder at Robinson's garage and then back. "There's no water around here, and I'm guessing you don't have that much food. Besides, you've got a wounded man. What are the chances your ride will show up before you start eating cockroaches?"

Deke smiled, "No clue. This whole gig kind of blew up in our face. We had no idea that Wayne dude was a nut case. I've got to get in touch with the home office and see."

Nick thought for a moment and made up his mind. "Why don't you guys come back to Alpha with us? You can stay in town at one of the hotels. There's no room service, but we have electricity, running water and food. Stay as long as you need to. Sleep in a bed."

Moses spoke up over Deke's shoulder, "A bed? Did he say we could sleep in a bed *and* take a shower?"

Deke wasn't sure. "I don't know. A lot of people don't like our kind around. Word will spread quickly who we are and that generally leads to trouble."

Nick shook his head. "I wouldn't worry too much about that. The town's just getting on its feet, and people have enough to worry about. I know the mayor, and I'll put in a good word for you."

The Darkwater team talked it over for a few minutes before Deke looked up and nodded. "If you're sure it's okay, a bed and running water does sound nice."

~  ~

The mirror reflected the image of a tired man. Dark circles accented the crow's feet surrounding Moreland's eyes, his skin pale and expression hollow. He had imagined this moment before, part of numerous fleeting fantasies during his budding political career. This single day had been a focus of the past—the day he would be sworn in as the president of the United States.

Those daydreams of fancy first occurred when he was a younger man, a freshman senator, full of the future and of himself. Another bout of glory-induced fantasy had been whipped up when the first bill bearing his name had passed into law. The mind-movie had been replayed several times since, prompted by a landslide reelection, a well-received speech at the national convention, and a phone call from a leading contender discussing a vice president position on the ticket.

Moreland sighed, absentmindedly adjusting the knot in his necktie while he inventoried the differences between those fictional portrayals and the hard, cold facts of today's ceremony. He wasn't feeling any of the emotions he had once imagined. There was no joy or atmosphere of celebration. Lacking was the crowd of encouraging supporters spouting slogans of a better future or renewed hope for country.

In fact, the few aides present aboard Air Force One were sullen and quiet as they went about their duties. It wasn't a time of glory, honor, or achievement. Dark clouds loomed on the nation's horizon, and anyone who knew what was happening at the highest levels of government could see them. Not only was the US in shambles, her political leadership had been decapitated.

Wayne's actions only added to the self-doubt and insecurity. Never had his trusted aide given the slightest indication of his zealous beliefs. There hadn't been a single hint of treachery or misconduct. Beyond the death of his friend, misgivings filled Moreland's conscious, negative thoughts centering on trust and motivation. How many more of Wayne's ilk stalked in the political bushes surrounding the presidency? Could he ever trust anyone again?

Moreland finished his face-to-face meeting with the mirror and turned to exit the executive suite. Opening the narrow aircraft door, he was greeted by Agent Powell and a few others waiting outside. Moreland nodded silently, his attention finally focusing on the Secret Service man.

"Agent Powell, we have a stop to make before the ceremony. I assume there wasn't any issue making the necessary arrangements?"

"No, sir, General Westfield, four senators and I will all be witnesses."

"Very good. Let's get this over with."

Moreland and his security detail proceeded down the steps of Air Force One, immediately entering an armored SUV. Presidential limousines weren't necessary here; there wasn't any public to impress with pomp and circumstance.

The passage of the four-car procession through the streets of Fort Bliss was most likely the least celebrated presidential drive-by in modern history. The occasional soldier who noticed the flags brandishing the seal of the executive branch would stop and salute, but other than a few circumstantial onlookers, no one seemed to notice or care.

The emergency room entrance had been chosen for Moreland's visit to the base hospital. Powell had wanted the meeting to take place aboard Air Force One, but the man about to take the oath of office had refused. "We've put these people through enough already—we can make the trip," he had firmly stated.

In a bustle of activity, Moreland's door was opened, and then he was escorted through the double wide automatic entrance to the medical facility. Two empty corridors and another set of fire doors later, Moreland saw General Westfield at the head of a group waiting in the hall. The general saluted. Moreland shook hands as introductions were made. As soon as the preliminaries were completed, Powell looked at the nearby closed door and nodded. "If you're ready, sir."

"Yes, I'm ready."

Powell opened the door, the sound of a heart monitor and other medical equipment filling the air. As Moreland entered, the young woman lifted her head and stared at the visitors. The man everyone referred to as Bishop was beside her, unconscious in the bed. A forest of tubes, hoses, and poles surrounded the couple.

Moreland focused on the young woman. Clearly exhausted and probably worthy of being in a hospital bed as well, she gazed at him with a blank expression, almost as if he wasn't there. Her face was bruised and welted, her wrists completely wrapped in bandages.

"I'm sorry to disturb you, young lady. I wish this could be left for another time, but unfortunately, it cannot."

Terri shrugged her shoulders, her projection of disdain clear. With a voice scratchy from crying, she answered, "Whatever. What do you need me to do?"

One of the senators stepped forward and unfolded a sheet of paper while another produced a video camera. "Ma'am, we only have a few questions, and then we'll be out of your hair."

Again, Terri shrugged.

After being asked to state her name, Terri took an oath that her statements were truthful. Two of the senators then began quizzing her about the brief time she had spent with the former president. The preliminary questions were soon followed by the heart of the matter.

"Did the former president make any statements to you regarding his assassins?"

Terri nodded and then responded, "Yes, he did. He stated that he knew it wasn't the Independents that had tried to kill him. He stated that the attempt on his life was staged so the Independents would be blamed, but he knew there were ulterior motives."

The lawyer-turned-politician continued, "You were recently abducted, held hostage, and interrogated. Could you expand on what your interrogator wanted to know or what you learned during that time?"

Terri stated what she remembered of the ordeal, her voice weak and monotone. After finishing, the men thanked her and left, leaving her alone with Westfield and Moreland in the room.

"How's your husband doing, Terri?" Moreland asked.

Terri's expression became dark, her voice low. "Just leave. Please, just leave us alone. That man lying there is a better human being than all of you combined. Go back to Washington and play your little power games . . . just leave us alone."

Westfield tried to help. "Terri, we had to do this today. This man is going to take the oath of office in a few hours, and we had to clear his name before the ceremony. You were the only person who could do that. You have to understand how critical this is—how important your testimony is."

261

Terri looked at the general, venom filling her throat. "I understand, all right. I comprehend more than you give me credit for. You've all forgotten what this country is about. You've all lost sight of the purpose of the whole thing—the people. Individuals like my husband, a man who probably isn't going to live through this. The father of my unborn child. Go on back to Washington, sir. Do your best. But I want to warn you, it won't do a bit of good. It's too late."

Terri's words didn't seem to affect Moreland. He appeared to shrug them off as the ranting vent of someone who had been through too much. After an awkward period of silence, he looked at Bishop. "Godspeed to your husband, ma'am," and then left the room.

Westfield hung back for a moment and smiled at Terri. "If you need anything, anything at all, my door is always open." Without waiting on a response, the base commander pivoted and exited the room.

Terri was alone again with Bishop, and that was just fine with her.

For a while, she rested her head on the bed at Bishop's side. Nurses came and went, trying their best not to disturb her, a few suggesting she rest on the couch nearby. But Terri knew her place was next to Bishop's side, and she never left him.

A few hours later, the room was filled with a distant roar. Terri stood and moved to the window, curious about the source of the sound. In the distance, she saw Air Force One rise into the air, the giant aircraft's engines causing the window to vibrate. "Good riddance," she said and returned to her vigil beside her beloved.

(THE END)

Dear Reader,

I hope you have enjoyed *Holding Their Own IV*.
I'm looking forward to sharing two more volumes of this saga, with the next, *Holding Their Own V: The Alpha Chronicles* to be released around May of 2013.

Regards,
Joe Nobody

Made in the USA
Lexington, KY
14 September 2015